What Love Looks Like

stories

Pamela Hull

PAGE PUBLISHING, INC.
Conneaut Lake, PA

First originally published by Page Publishing 2021

ISBN 978-1-6624-5972-6 (pbk)
ISBN 978-1-6624-5973-3 (digital)

Printed in the United States of America

Other Books by Pamela Hull

Where's My Bride?
SAY YES! Flying Solo After Sixty
Moments that Mattered

As always, for

Paul
Geri and Bobby
Neal and Jennifer
Josie, Peter, Evan
Burt

May it ever be so.

Thank You

Joelle Sander
Teacher, painter, writer, editor
This is our fourth project together. I write;
she reads and edits in her tiny hand.
In the end, there is a book.
No writer ever had a more honest friend or critic.

Not for a moment, beautiful aged Walt Whitman,
have I failed to see your beard full of butterflies.

-Garcia Lorca

Contents

Tossed from the Sea

Composed and serene, she sat in the same spot almost every day, from late afternoon until the first stars appeared in the darkening sky. Gazing straight out at the ocean, even when a light mist rolled in, her hands remained clasped on her lap, as though she were awaiting an important personage.

Or perhaps she wasn't waiting for anyone. Perhaps there just wasn't anything or anyone in that house that made her want to go back inside.

Set apart from its closest neighbor, her cottage of white clapboard was cozy, charming in its tidy snugness. Two rocking chairs rested on the porch four steps from the small path leading to the sandy beach. Roses wrapped around corner posts, and baskets of purple lobelia hung from the eaves. Luxurious red geraniums in white lattice boxes graced the front windows. Oddly, however, the woman was never seen watering or trimming this bountiful garden of planters and baskets.

Every day, a young boy named Joseph, about twelve years old would be a good guess, wandered the beach down by the water where the waves broke and collected around his feet. In no hurry to get home, his meanderings were wedged into the few hours between school and supper. He would do anything to escape the fighting that went on between his folks, paining his soul and scrambling his mind. Always his house was filled with the aura of struggle and strife. When Joseph sensed his father coming for him, he buried his face in his hands, red and furrowed from the whacks and punches. His two sisters, Darlene and Lila, were mercifully ignored as they shielded each other in corners and closets. Joseph felt guilty at running away and leaving them, but there was little he could do to protect the three women, his mother most of all, huddled within those pitiful rooms.

By the time Joseph appeared on the sand, most beachgoers had packed up and gone home. Almost no one was around but him and the woman. It was obvious he would notice her sitting there - that queenlike pose, that timeless sense of calm as she stared out at the water, taking the measure of those tides, in and out, or waiting for a fisherman to haul his catch up to the dock or, better yet, dreaming of exotic ports as a glamorous cruise ship passed on the horizon.

He thought she must be about seventy, though how could a kid really know somebody's age unless it was another kid's, and especially someone that old? She was much older than his mother but not as old as his grandmother, who wore loose house dresses and filled bird feeders all day. Sure, the lady had wrinkles on her face, but anyone living at the beach had those eye creases from squinting into the sun. Her thick dark hair showed flecks of gray and was fixed in a long braid that fell down her back. She was small-boned with a gymnast's body, neat and trim. His mother was only thirty-seven but looked tired and older than her real age. His father was three years her senior but looked surprisingly younger. Maybe it had something to do with who gave the beating and who took the beating.

Had the woman on the porch ever had bad times in her life? he wondered. He hoped not. Those thrashings his father handed out were *bad* - bruises all over his young body, a broken rib or two occasionally that he taped under his sweatshirt, welts on his back, the red blood drying brown.

Down here in the Carolinas, the weather was mild most of the year. Thankfully, Joseph was able to escape to its tranquil beauty almost every day. He was mighty grateful to live near this particular beach with the dramatic, seaward face of the barrier islands just offshore. In the balmy air and the precious solitude of those vast spaces, he could almost imagine that everything in life was possible. But in reality, it was just the opposite. *Nothing* was possible; so filled was he with helpless despair.

Day after day, as he strolled along the water in front of her cottage, he was drawn to the woman sitting so still. Although neither was particularly looking for company, it seemed inevitable that these two would become curious about each other. But did she notice him like he did her? *Naw*, he thought. An adult woman wouldn't notice a twelve-year-old kid in shorts and T-shirt unless he belonged to her. Anyway, she never looked directly at him, and he never turned his head toward her, though he did peek at her from the corner of his eye.

Why did he even care?

One evening, helping his mother with the supper dishes, he asked, "Mama, do you know the lady in that white house who sits on her porch all afternoon?"

"I don't know much about her," she replied, "but it seems she has sat on her porch like that forever. I think her name is Ena."

"Ena?" he repeated.

"Ena," he said again to himself.

On his walks, he picked up odd-looking sticks and shells. He'd turn them around for inspection - looking for what? - then fling them out to sea. He wished he had his own dog that would chase after them, a dog he would call King. But Joseph knew he'd never own a dog. That animal would get marked up black and blue by his father's boot for sure.

While he was thinking this, he kicked up some sand, suddenly noticing a shiny object. He brought it up close. A broken shard of colored glass. Turquoise so clear it was like holding a raindrop that reflected the sky, right in the palm of his hand. Walking along, he wanted to find more. And yes, there was another - a small piece the size of a quarter, the pale rose of an egret's wing!

His pace was earnest now. Something had stirred in him - the beauty of this tiny object thrown up by the sea. Why had he gathered only sticks and shells before? Wasn't he looking carefully enough? See there! This time, a pale yellow, the color of the roses climbing the posts of Miss Ena's porch.

As the sun sank closer to the horizon and the sandpipers raced along the shore on their skinny legs, Joseph thrilled to his unexpected awakening. He was simply stunned. For the first time in his young life, his chest felt strong and expansive, his heart fluttering like a wild bird. This unexpected surge of power, strange yet enticing.

He hunted and scrambled for more fragments, diligently parting the grains of sand wherever he saw a glint of color or a small crevice that might afford a hiding place. Various blues and purples appeared like ice, like iris. Pink, frosted like cotton candy. Then on a particularly heartsick Sunday when his father liquored up and chased his mother clear out of the house and he, covering his ears against her cries, sprinted to the beach, there, at his feet, without any digging, he bent down and picked up a spectacular deep-red shard. The color of blood.

Joseph's mind now opened to a world beyond home and school, distracting him from his abiding inner turmoil, directing his mind to a new devotion. He marveled that the discovery of a few pieces of glass could be so life-altering. He was giddy with appreciation for this gift but anxious about its fragility. Could he allow himself to believe it was real and true? What if his father read his mind, reached into his pocket, and flung his newly-prized objects into the trash? Longing to share these ideas, he somehow believed the mysterious woman on the porch would understand. Yet he kept his secret close and stayed away. Never in his life had he allowed himself to talk to a stranger. Even the *idea* of trying to explain what he felt about those glass pieces when he didn't fully understand it himself would surely shut down his tongue.

What if the lady laughed at his notions?

Joseph quickly turned his mind to what it *could* absorb, to gathering information.

What were these small treasures? Where did they come from? What were they made of?

In the library, he discovered they had a name.

Sea glass.

These shards were actually broken pieces of ordinary glass refined over hundreds, even thousands, of years by ocean currents. The violence of their turnings in the waters was so severe that the edges had been worn smooth enough for a baby's touch. Sea glass, yes, he was sure that's what they were. The pictures in the library books looked just like his samples.

Joseph's imagination quickened. Even the name *sea glass* drew his fantasy. Not a harsh, stolid word like *stone* or *rock* but almost musical and poetic like *sea urchin* or *mermaid*. He began to make up stories about the origins and adventures of each piece - an amber one from beer bottles on dueling pirate ships, the pale pink from a lady's perfume bottle thrown as a toy to a pair of playful dolphins - all to emerge as found treasures tossed up on the beach.

He had eight pieces so far, enough for the beginning of a collection. Obviously not rare, scattered along the beach as they were; still, Joseph considered them precious in their beauty. And dazzled he was at their resilience from a long and turbulent ocean voyage, objects burnished and polished, their luster like jewels. *Brave little creatures,* he thought.

His mind, once opened with this curiosity, now quickly moved on. After discovery, there was research and learning, then something new - definition and discrimination, honing his eye. Which pieces would he keep? Which would he discard? He wanted to save only the ones that seemed special in a particular way, those that showed unusual markings or unique characteristics like a rare color or shape.

After his walk, pleased with his newly acquired pieces of the day, he would sit on a rock wall and pull them out of his pocket.

Then he would talk to them. "Forgive me," he apologized softly as he made his decisions. He turned them over, held them up to the light where he could see through them to the wavy ocean beyond. Some offered a warm glow in his hand. Others were cool. After he made his choices, he would say goodbye to one piece or another as if to a good friend, setting it carefully down in the sand, putting the rest back in his pocket.

Saturday afternoon was his father's day off. It was only noon, and already he was sitting at the kitchen table holding a bottle of bourbon in one hand, a glass in the other. The bottle was still almost full, but Joseph sensed a spiraling rant, and off he ran from the house. He knew that running was a despicable, cowardly thing to do, but he was just a boy, so he ran. When he got to the beach, breathless, he stopped abruptly. As his feet sank into the welcome warmth, he saw that Miss Ena had not yet taken her chair.

Hey, wait! His head snapped awake. He had a preposterous idea. Could he do it? What would she think? Would she say anything? He thought of the woman he knew in the next town who had never spoken in her entire life.

But Joseph's thought emboldened him, so he walked quickly to her porch. There he left the emerald-green glass piece at the foot of her chair. Would the bright color catch her eye?

Then he ran off, afraid to look back.

When one does something that takes courage, that courage grows bigger and bolder. Joseph began to arrive at the beach earlier every day before Miss Ena appeared, leaving a glass fragment in the same place near her chair. First, the blue piece, like hyacinth, like larkspur. Then the romantic pale mauve one. Each time, he noticed that his find from the previous day had been picked up. This both pleased and frightened him. Pleased that she had received it but frightened for his audaciousness, that he dare trespass on her property. And worst of all, that Miss Ena might consider him merely a silly kid picking up scraps like kids do who run to their mamas with hands outstretched shouting, "Look what I've found!"

But all these weeks, he had been reading about sea glass in the library; and with what he now knew about this worldwide phenomenon, he was no silly kid.

He hadn't yet seriously considered *why* he left his precious sea glass on the porch of this unknown woman; but he guessed it was because she, like he, was a lover of sand and sea. And perhaps like Joseph himself, she had a terrible sadness inside her.

*****

Joseph never forgot "that first time" when, after two more weeks of his walks on the beach and more of her silent sitting, Miss Ena appeared on the porch first. On a little wooden table, she had set down a pitcher of lemonade and two glasses with daisy designs she had chilled in the freezer. Just like the piece of frosted white glass he was saving for a future visit! But now he would bring it for her tomorrow. Would she make the connection between the two - her drinking glasses and his offering?

She made a small gesture toward him, a few fingers moving from her wrist. Was she beckoning to him? He looked around, then up again. She repeated the gesture. Yes, it was for him. He came cautiously, as nervous as a cat walking on hot cinders, the way he approached his own home, wary of what awaited. The lemonade was reassuring, a gesture of kindness.

The moment of approach felt supremely important. He felt he should stand before her with his hat in his hands, as his mother taught him to do when he was in church, except he didn't have his cap. He dug his toes into the sand and curled them under as if the familiar warmth would keep him steady.

Suddenly he was standing at the lowest step of her porch.

Gradually, he looked up.

Now he saw up close the lines on her face, her thick hair in a single braid, her tight, small frame. As she held up the pitcher, she extended a small smile, shy and sweet. She wasn't scary at all. In fact, Joseph couldn't imagine why he'd ever thought she might be.

"My name is Ena," she said. "You must be thirsty after your long walk.'"

"I'm Joseph, ma'am," he managed. "Yes, I'm thirsty. The sun is hot today, and I forgot my cap. But don't get me wrong. I love to be in the sun. I hope you like the bits of glass I left," he blurted out. Embarrassed by his enthusiasm, he attempted a cover-up with more talk, chatty and fast. "I read all about them in the school library, how they're formed and everything. Imagine finding them buried in ordinary sand right here."

"Oh, sand isn't ordinary, Joseph, not by a long shot," Miss Ena replied. "Sand is the end product of many elements, like decomposed rocks that erode over thousands and tens of millions of years, and composed of all sorts of organic products made from iron oxide or volcanic material. And do you know that sand is found all over the world in dozens of colors? Some famous lady writer once said, 'In every curving beach, in every grain of sand, there is a story of the Earth.' No, sand is never ordinary. In fact, sand is a miracle."

Joseph listened closely to Ena's words. She spoke like a teacher, but what he loved most about her talk was the poetry she found in things like sand and water that he had taken for granted all his life.

This is a heap of talking for two strangers meeting for the first time, he thought. After they finished, each suddenly felt awkward, and so they sat silently, stars popping out all around a crescent moon. Both had more to say, they surely did, but for now, they needed some time to think about what was happening.

Joseph stood up. *My father is going to wallop me good for staying away so long*, he reminded himself, but what he said was "Night, Miss Ena," and he walked quickly along the sand. Not looking back, he didn't see her raised hand, waving at his departure.

Miss Ena thought, *What a lovely boy. How his eyes shone when I spoke of the sand.*

And Joseph thought, *Thank goodness she's not scary. She must have really liked my special green piece. I'm glad I took a chance and left it.*

The next day, Joseph again shuffled shyly along the beach toward her cottage. Miss Ena was waiting with her pitcher of lemonade and two glasses. This time, there was also a plate of cookies. *Ginger*, he thought, by the sharp smell and still warm.

"Good afternoon, Miss Ena," he said.

"Joseph," she answered kindly.

As she poured the lemonade, he laid a pale-gray frosted sea glass fragment on the table. She picked it up, let it lay in her open hand. "This one reminds me of a day at the beach just before a storm. Not a dreary day but, rather, a melancholy one."

They sat companionably, not talking, enjoying the cool drink and the cookies. But how to begin?

"Sure is kicking up a frenzy out there," Ena suddenly said.

"Maybe a heavy rain tomorrow," Joseph answered.

After an hour of weather talk, Joseph said, "Have to be getting home now, Miss Ena. My father doesn't want me out late. I've lots of chores to do at home."

"Then why don't you come a little earlier tomorrow, Joseph? We can start our visit a bit sooner so you don't get in any trouble."

And with that special invitation, their meetings took a critical turn toward ease and welcome.

Each time Joseph arrived at her porch, he laid down another piece of sea glass. A beautiful amber fragment that reminded him of Carolina sunsets. Then a pale green one, lovely as jade. Miss Ena had brought out a pretty white dish and arranged them in a grouping that Joseph thought looked like something someone ought to paint. The sun blinked onto the porch, setting the stones afire. It was a sharing of profound intimacy, she in her chair a few feet from the step on which he sat. The cookies, the sea glass, a kind of giving of themselves, one to the other.

As they began to talk, Ena was impressed by Joseph's knowledge of marine life and taken by his imaginary stories about the origins of his glass pieces. And Joseph was thrilled by Ena's special interest in the sponges of the Carolina coral reefs and her current knowledge of sea life, she being so isolated and all.

After a few days of ordinary talk about respective interests and consumption of cookies, shortbread on this day, suddenly, Ena opened up.

"When I was young, my mother died of cancer," she told him. "Living near these reefs and becoming aware of their possible contributions to cancer remedies, it was a natural choice to make their study my work."

This confidence led them into speaking intimately but cautiously. It was clear Ena held in secrets and Joseph, his shame.

Ena then proceeded, quite casually, to shock Joseph utterly. He had speculated, of course, that she might be a retired teacher or nurse, her children far away, or a spinster. But she was none of those things.

"He died on a diving expedition," she began. "My young husband, Connor. We were divers together, well-known as explorers of the coral reefs. Then one day, there was a horrifying accident. Something was faulty with his oxygen. From a distance, we saw bubbles on the surface as he tried to find air. But we couldn't reach him in time. When we were finally at his side, he was drifting on the gentle waves, like a sleeping prince, his blond hair tousled, falling over his cheek."

Miss Ena stopped, distracted as she stared out at the ocean. Joseph wondered if she thought maybe today would be the day her Connor would float back to find her waiting for him on their porch. She continued.

"After he died, I carried on our work for a couple of years, but my heart wasn't in it. We had been a team. The joy was gone."

Joseph wiped his eyes. He thought his mother had a sad story with her mean and brutal husband who drank his paycheck as soon as he got hold of it. But Ena's story was different. Hers was a story of love and unbearable loss. Not like his mother, whom he knew would be better off without her husband.

Joseph's heart was so tight he couldn't turn toward her. She was sitting still as the sand. He was ashamed at having so much feeling. What should he do with this much feeling?

After some quiet, he looked at Ena and started slowly describing his two sisters - Darlene, fourteen, the one who wanted to get far from home so badly that she looked for any guy to take her away; and Lila, two years older than Darlene, relieved to have secured a job as a nanny on a nearby island. From there, Lila had told Joseph that she would figure out what to do next; though in truth, Joseph doubted that would amount to much. He knew too many young girls like his sisters who never got more than an island or a job away from their home their whole lives.

That's enough, Joseph then thought, *telling these stories about my sisters. I can't share about my parents right now. Not with Miss Ena, such a fine, welcoming woman. Not after learning about her sweet prince who died. She might think I'm cruel like my father. Unworthy to sit on her porch.*

After a few days, Joseph thoughtfully laid the gorgeous purple glass piece, his best, in her dish. Watching it flicker and shine, Joseph thought that if he could present Miss Ena with something especially beautiful, then surely she would see something good in him.

Finally, gathering his courage to be honest about the hardest thing, he impulsively cried, "My father's very mean to us. He hits us hard and a lot. I hate him."

The plaintive yet enraged voice of a child, Ena thought.

As sympathy spread across her face, his heart fell open; and there it was, all of it - the confessions, the sadness, his powerlessness and the entire family drama. And most heavy of all, the guilt at his rage toward his father. Painful sobs devoured his whole being.

Ena sat down on the step beside him. Tenderly, she took him in her arms and let him cry until the stars came out. She held him close as she had never held a child of her own. *The pity of it*, she thought. *My darling Connor and I never had a child. Our child. We had always thought we'd have time.*

When the tears slowed, they remained together, Ena's arms still around him. And as they watched the North Star grow bright in the sky, an idea unfolded in her mind, like the morning glory vine growing on her back fence, its petals tight in the dark but unfurling slowly as the daylight appeared. A big, bold, beautiful plan, each detail slowly and fully becoming sharp and clear. Possibilities exploded in her head.

I will groom this boy as if he were my own, she decided. *Joseph is only twelve but already possesses a deep knowledge of oceanography and sea life. And especially of his dear sea glass. But so, too, is he informed about the endless varieties found on beaches around the world.* Ena marveled. It was as if Joseph had already spent many adult years studying, exploring.

"Joseph," she said, pulling back, turning to face him directly.

"I have a plan. We are going to work together. You will learn everything about marine life that I can teach you, and then you will go on to an oceanographic institute. If you work hard, I will see to it. I still know people who will take you on if I present you as the able student you are. Go home now, but come back tomorrow right after school, and we'll get started.

"What do you say?" she asked, peering into his face.

Stunned, Joseph had no words, only the sure nod of his head. Yes yes yes! He stumbled on the step, unable to conceal the tears still streaking his cheeks. His head full of dreams, he ran home, his heart pinned with possibility and a future life of which he had never dared dream but which he would now trust in Miss Ena's hands. For all that to become reality would require intense, unrelenting study; but if Miss Ena thought to give him her time and effort, he would do whatever it took.

And so they spent four years together, in the spare hours he could steal from home and after his regular school classes. Miss Ena brought out her old workbooks and acquired many new ones. They studied long and earnestly, day after day, summer, winter, textbooks and papers, quizzes, reviews. Under Ena's keen direction, Joseph learned to write scientific proposals, summaries, and "plans of intent" as she called them.

And as Ena promised, when Joseph was sixteen, she called two of her old professional colleagues from the oceanographic institute who appeared on her porch to talk with Joseph and sip her home-made lemonade. The three men took a long walk along the beach way beyond the dunes until she lost sight of them. When they gathered on her steps again, finishing off the plate of cookies, they said, "Ena, this boy is a gem, just like those beauties filling up your bowl of sea glass. You taught him well. He has a real love for learning with a full heart that few people possess."

"What say you we start this boy at the institute come fall? We'll deal with his folks. If anyone has any objections, we'll take care of them."

Joseph fell to his knees. He took Ena's hands in his and laid them against his cheek. He looked into her face and could not say it directly, but she knew what he was thinking and he knew she knew - no real mother could have done more. And no son could love more.

Everyone present was proud of this extraordinary young man, even Joseph himself. And as the stars came out and they finished discussing plans and arrangements, all four sat in silence listening to the sounds of the surf, the waves cresting, crashing, curling their way to shore. Eventually, one by one, each of the men stood up and walked quietly away.

As head of his class, Joseph was to give the graduation speech. He had wanted to surprise Ena with its themes and theories, but a few days earlier, she had teased the information out of him. With a grin, he told her, as he would later tell the others, what the honorarium consisted of that was accorded him for outstanding academic work - his participation in an upcoming expedition to the West Coast, in California, Oregon, and Washington, one of the largest but least known aquatic environments on earth. "And guess what we are to research, dear Ena?" Joseph playfully asked. "Ocean mapping of deep-sea coral sites and sponge habitats!"

Now at last, on this special graduation day, they were both ready. Ena adjusted the blue velvet hat she was wearing to the ceremony.

"Connor, my dearest, such a marvelous young man," she murmured, carefully stepping off the porch in her new shoes. "Two grand degrees and deep-sea coral sites! What do you think of that!"

Later, after the excitement and the speeches, the smiles and the tears, Ena joyfully reached for her Joseph. As he swept her up in his arms, she whispered a small prayer for their towering victory, "*Dear God, bless our boy. Keep him safe.*"

Now she was home, gratefully resting her feet and rocking on her porch - their porch - reviewing precious moments of the day.

The pride she felt in his respectful manhood made her knees tremble, her heart sing. Sometimes when these happy tears caught her throat in public places, she felt like a silly girl, but she was too old to worry about making a spectacle of herself. Yes, she helped shape his brilliant mind, but never for a second did she think she had anything to do with forming his noble character and, of all things, studying deep-sea coral sites! Perhaps he would take long strolls along those shores and find rare examples of sea glass for their collections, hers now filling an enormous bowl by her bedside.

She looked around at her blooming garden and thought, *Ah, perhaps one the color of dusk, or perhaps one the color of dawn. Or perhaps one the color of Joseph's eyes, shiny seal brown with golden specks deep in their centers.*

Lotsa Lovin'

There was lotsa lovin' back then.
Nothin' but lovin' all the time.
Yelp'n' and hoot'n' with lovin'.
All these twenty years.
And then we had to stay in the same five rooms for twenty-one days, and it was all over.

I'm supposin' most folks look back on their early days of court'n' with fondness, but mine offered up a little more - a special prayer of grace that maybe God was goin' to give me more'n my share.

Young Jake with his blue eyes and strong arms and always lookin' at me with that special "You're my gal" kind of thing that just melted my heart.

And this despite lotsa worryin'. His daddy dyin' in that bad fall and he called back home from agricultural school and thrown right into the farm'n' so young. But he never raised a whimper, just jumped right in takin' care of his mom and two sisters. And no problem it was, just the workin' from dawn to dusk. And the farm in just a few years, when he married me, prosperin' and goin' from being a decent farm to bein' a flourishin' farm. Seven new workers added, farmin' and milkin.'

Those were real good days.

Most of the time those years, we had plenty of rain and plenty of sun in decent amounts of each, even with drought now and ag'in and that beetle thing that just ate up all the corn. Oh, and that tornado that came down ten miles east and just missed us. But mostly, the corn was so high we couldn' see to the end of the fields when we were sittin' on the porch, those silks flyin' in the breeze, happy as corn can be. The cows were birthin' those calves and milkin' steady, and oh, our farm was a pretty sight. Sometimes Jake took a few extra minutes at midday with lunch gettin' cold on the table for a bit of lovin' and my quickly puttin' the three babies in the back room.

That's how it was back then. And yet, tired as we were, the dishes done and the last cow milked, we sat on the swing outside on the porch, holdin' hands and watch'n' the moon and the stars shinin' down on our faces.

Our kids began to walk, then run. Then they rode ponies, then horses. We hired five more workers. The guys built another couple dozen feet onto the bunkhouse, then another two bedrooms onto the house. We all worked sunup to sundown, and I managed to have a girl in twice a week help'n' with the chores. Jake and I still had a sit on the porch in early evenin' though now he fell asleep more often than not with all the rockin' back and forth. Still, a great comfort, my Jake rockin' away, the moon lightin' up the yard, the bales of hay, the corral. So bright was the moon some nights I could make out every last blade of grass in those stacks all piled high, perfect and sweet. It was a good life, and don't think I didn't say a prayer for that when we went to church on Sundays, givin' thanks for all of us sittin' round the supper table.

And then, before I knew it, the kids were grown. One by one, they took off to agricultural college down by Clayton Township, haulin' their duffels and spreadin' aroun' lots of goodbye huggin'.

The first time it happened, I paid it no mind. By then, we were married maybe a dozen years, more or less.

Jake comin' home extra late from that yearly grain market, farmers from all over the county meetin' up and havin' a good time after the hard tradin' was done. But long after midnight, where was Jake? Bars were closed. Grain market or not, farmers had to get up early the next day. I sent Tom, the head hand, out to find him. A couple of hours later, the two of them came in singin' "Who's Gonna Feed Them Hogs" - not drunk, just happy. I put Jake to bed and my heart to rest. My man was home, safe.

Six months later, the corn was cleaned out of the cribs, loaded onto trucks, and hauled into town for the corn auction. Again, farmers came from near and far, catch'n' up on the news and gossip. Who was plant'n' what? A good year, this one; but next year, who knows? Any new tips for puttin' in the lettuce?

And for a second time, it was past midnight, and Jake wasn't home.

This time, I saddled up Beulah before callin' Tom.

"Hey, Sadie, no need," Tom said. "I can get old Jake myself. Get yourself off to sleep. It's been a long day."

"Forget it, Tom. I'm a-comin'."

The town was dark 'cept for a light behind the blacksmith's shop.

"Let's take a look," I said. "I'm gettin' worried." So I kicked old Beulah girl to pick up the pace.

And I swear, enterin' the shed there, so help me God, I found Jake sprawled naked on a dirty mat between two plum-tuckered-out women - prostitutes.

Well, everythin' changed that night. No more happy yelpin' in our rooms. No more midday lovin'. Jake tried everythin' he could to show me he felt bad. But I was real angry, real hurt. Not even a dozen bunches of those wildflower lilies that I love could turn me 'round. I was a-hurt'n', a farmer's wife all by herself miles from the nearest friend or farm for visit'n' and sharin.' And that was a fearful thing. So I buried it all inside, one big iron ball of hurt.

As often happens in life, time either softens a bad thin' or sets it in stone. Jake brought home lots of them lilies, built a new swing for the porch, the kind with the soft seat that I always wanted. He even ordered me a couple of new dresses from that Sears Roebuck catalog. But he never really said out loud, "Dang, Sadie, I'm real sorry." Not once. So don't think that didn't stay hard with me. But round about then, the boys began returnin' home to work the farm. So after maybe a year of plantin' and milkin,' I softened just a bit and let those pitchers of yellow lilies stay put on the kitchen table. God's work, those flowers, and tossin' 'em in the trash seemed like a sin. But that iron ball in me remained, rollin' around, shiftin' back and forth.

It was one of those long days of cleanup after the harvest. The workers were finishin' their chores - chattin', tellin' jokes. Everyone was worn out, and the guys were lookin' forward to a few weeks off, headin' into town or off to their families. After cookin' two shifts of meals for weeks on end and helpin' with the harvest, all I wanted was to lie down on my soft quilt and sleep for two days. Do a real wash, rub some salve into my chapped hands.

After dinner, Jake and I were slowly rockin' on the porch when Pete Turner rode his sweaty horse right up to the first step, raisin' a heckuva lotta dust and yellin', "Sadie! Jake! The fever. It's done come. Started right at farmer Jim's place, and it's movin' up here at lightn'n' speed. This one hittin' both the animals and the folks. Stay inside, Doc Mercer says. Sheriff puttin' notices up all over the county. Feed your stock then straight back into the house."

We did as we were told. A fever in these parts can get downright nasty, kill everythin' in its way.

Jake went to the barn to see the animals, give the guys their pay, and send them off. I went inside, swept the floor, closed the winduhs, and stuffed rags into any holes in the floorboards.

All of a sudden, Jake and I now had a surprisin' patch of free time. Somethin' farmers almost never get, maybe once over a lifetime. What would we do with it, with little effort due? There was little cookin' what with the boys on a roundup way up in the hills where they would stay for a few weeks at least. Jake had to set aside most of the chores 'cept for feedin' the animals. And in the long nights of last winter, I had caught up on all my sewin', and Jake had mended the ragged saddles. Empty time sat bitterly silent in our house.

I was fear'n' a little, more 'n a little. There was still that big thin' between us, that thin' with those whores. We didn't so much as give it a nod, but it was there between us anyway. And if Jake couldn' tell during the lovin' now and ag'in, he must have been blind as a bat.

Well, sure as those cows needed milkin', their udders full to bustin', in the quiet of the evenun', it all came back to me like a wallop to the head. Suddenly I looked at Jake and saw him in the shed with those scabby women, the shockin' sight just poppin' up again whole and ugly. Him lyin' on that grubby mat, legs and arms of those two whores shamelessly draped over his naked body. The old hurt just swelled up, and I began to hate him.

And every day that I sat in that rocker, watch'n' him smoke his pipe, I hated him more.

Nineteen days we spent rockin' but for the times when Jake fed the horses, milked the cows, and I cooked the supper. It was a rough go. When we sat in our chairs after supper, we hardly said a word, though Jake tried a few times to break the quiet.

"Sadie, honey, are you feelin' well?"

"Sadie, honey, I know this is hard on you."

"Sadie, honey, remember that ride we had out to the north pasture the first week we were married? Spread out on the blanket with that crazy beautiful purple sky? We hadn' ever seen a sky that purple before. Made just for us, you said."

I turned my head away. When he said that, about the purple sky, that ole iron ball rolled on into my gut like a horse had kicked me in the stomach.

And so the days passed. Hay for the horses, flapjacks for supper, the smell of Jake's pipe. The clackin' of my knittin' needles. The squeak of the chairs, back and forth. Rockin', rockin'.

It was on one of those sorrowful evenin's that the iron ball just plum fell out on the floor between us as if I had dropped out a baby, and I opened my mouth. I thought the sounds would come out roaring, but I only sent out a whisper. Did he hear me?

"Jake, why did you do it?" I asked.

"That's a mighty small voice, Sadie. Do what?" he asked, his fingers twitchin'.

"Mess around," I managed.

The curtains quivered; a water beetle scuttled across the floor.

Jake was workin' his brain to remember. *Mess around? I wouldn't do that to my Sadie*, I thought he murmured, or maybe I was just wishin' he had.

Jake got quiet tryin' to work this out, just look'n' down. *This have to do with our lovin' stuff? Bein' so closed now, so unfeelin', maybe?*

"Sadie, aw, we were just foolin' around after the corn was shipped off. Yuh know, too many drinks at Sam's place, those gals buzzin' around like flies. Didn't mean nothin'. Not a single thing."

"I didn't see other farmers lyin' on the mat. Only you," I answered.

"Maybe they didn't get so liquored up, a bad thin' to do, I know. Should've come right home. But we had all worked so hard, so long, from sunup to sundown, day after day. And all that worry about how the crop would turn out. Remember? We wanted a little fun."

"Do yuh think *I* was sleepin' all day? Do yuh think *I* wasn't workin' just as hard, year after year? And all that work takin' the youth right outta me. When I look at the moon now, I wanna take out the rifle and shoot it up. That's what you did to me. Make me wanna shoot the moon right outta the purple sky. Jake, did I ever say no to you? Your own Sadie wasn't enough for yuh?"

In my heart, I wondered about them yearly grain and corn sales goin' on, dozens and dozens of 'em. I never went into town lookin' for 'em after that second time. What the heck did he do all those other sellin' days he drove that wagon into town? Shoot, when did it start? Is it still goin' on? And here he sits makin' excuses, not a word sayin' "I'm sorry."

If he does that, say "I'm sorry" and mean it, I might give in, Sadie thought. *Not all the way but just to make the sight of him okay for us to go on. Sayin' sorry means somethin'.*

Well, I had my say, at last, but it didn't give me ease or set the subject to end. No, sirree. Oh, he had picked me some flowers from the fields and bought me those two new dresses though they wore out soon enough. But he never said he was sorry to me, his lovin' wife, all those years.

I had kept that pain deep down inside. I thought if I didn't bring it up, it wouldn't bother me. Boy, was I wrong. As wrong as I could be. I almost felt worse for speakin' up 'cause now it's out there and nothin's different.

And that was the end of our talkin'.

It felt real bad, this hardness in my heart. But I had had a lotta years to let it grow.

On an afternoon when there were still a few days of late sunsets left, mornin' snow startin' to show some frost, Pete Turner rode up, his horse's hooves beatin' on the ground.

"It's over. It's over. Open your doors!" he shouted.

"Let out the animals! Run in the fields. See you at church on Sundee!"

Slowly, I got up from my chair and gave the floor a good sweep. Tied back the curtains. Then I walked outside, sat in the swing for a little push back and forth, glanc'n' over the yard. Just a few twigs and dried leaves from fall, the garden finished for now. Then back into the house where I pulled out a small bag from under the bed, folded in my three dresses, my good shoes, and a couple of aprons. And while Jake was in the barn, I saddled up old Beulah, directed her to the gate, and rode off without a word.

After I left, sure as anythin', Jake just rocked out on that porch many a night, thinkin', *Sure, it was a real bad thing I did, those whores and all, but the drink made me pay my brain no mind.*

I knew that man so well. I know just how it must'a went. The stars shone down on his face just like when I sat rockin' with him, and he felt the deep loneliness. Jake did lots of thinkin' on those nights after I left. He didn't realize I had carried that hurt with me so long. He thought that maybe me being a bit touchy in the bedroom was 'cause of all the women stuff that happens at my age, that change in moods and feelin's.

After a while, the rockin' made him feel bad. He didn't like rockin' all alone.

Where'd she go to?

It was real tough without me, the harvest'n' and the men needin' to eat. The woman who used to help me now only came in once a week, her granddaughter want'n' some babysitt'n'.

But they managed, and here he was off to the corn auction again. And for sure I knew what happened next.

As usual, the farmers gathered from all over. Jake was watchin' the auctioneer yellin' out the prices, and not such good ones this year, the darn July without enough rain when old rancher Higgins moved in alongside.

"Hey, Jake," he said, "Good to see yuh, boy!"

"Hey, Higgins," Jake said, "how yuh doin'?

"Yuh know how it is, some days are better than others. Say… I caught sight of that sweet Sadie of yours all the way up in the corner of the state over near Beaver Creek. She was walkin' into a dry goods with a basket over her arm. Looked rather fetchin', I might add, and wearin' a pretty pinafore kind of thing. What was she doin' way up there anyway?"

After he paid his hands for a week off, Jake saddled right up and rode straight north to Beaver Creek. Just hung out on the street in front of the dry goods store for a coupla' days, and sure enough, there she was. Prettier 'n' ever. Wearin' that pinafore thing old Higgins had touched on. She sure didn't have that dress when she was home with me.

Sorry was growin' like a tree inside me. Sorry was the sorriest I'd ever been.

Just then, she looked my way. And suddenly, I started cryin' just like a dumb kid who fell off his horse. Cryin' hard. Lord, I felt shamed.

She took a step toward me, reached out her hand, then stopped. I looked up and cried out, "Sadie. I'm sorry. I'm real sorry."

My heart gave in just a touch, Sadie thought. Sure, I felt a tug for the old days and a heap of sorrow. Who could forget lookin' at a purple sky when you're young and in love? And birthin' three kids and workin' the farm? But that hurt had started a long time ago, and it just kept build'n' and build'n' all those years, and now I just couldn't pull those early feelin's back. Not the way I wanted.

Lookin' at Jake, I thought, *He never tried to find out what was goin' on with me, and he musta' felt somethin' was wrong. And now, this. But it's just too late. That iron ball is never goin' to go away. It's still here now, and if he's cryin' and sorry and it's still in my gut, well, what then?*

And besides, I thought, *I'm doin' okay up here in Beaver Creek. I really am.*

Only forty-three, I was still full of strong feelin's. And besides, I liked workin' at the dress shop, chattin' with all the ladies and not doin' that hard farm work for the first time ever. And Lord, earnin' some steady money that didn't wait for the grain or corn to come in.

Last Sunday, I had sat with a nice fella at the church supper. We were just chattin' about this and that when he said somethin' about his daughter and young folks not knowin' about real lovin' till they were hard in the fields together for many a year. Right away, I had teared up.

When he put his hand on mine and said, "Gee, Sadie, I'm real sorry. Did I say somethin' wrong?" I realized that a man could make a mistake and maybe heal a woman's heart right then and there by sayin' "I'm sorry" and meanin' it.

But it hasta be then and there. Later, anytime later, a year, ten years, is too late. Stewin' with a wrong never makes anythin' right.

The Vacation

As Zoe put down the phone, she thought, *What could I have possibly been thinking? I'll have to call them back in the morning and see if I can get out of it.* She thrust her hand into the bag of Oreos, rummaging around. Finding only two, she popped them both in her mouth. Not worth the effort of folding the bag and putting it back in the cupboard.

She then pulled out the exercise video she had ordered three weeks ago, clicked on the television, and positioned herself in front of the sofa. But when the Pilates teacher Stella appeared in her size 2 leotard and the thighs of a beauty queen, she felt a pain in her stomach - Oreo reflux? Perky Stella cheerfully greeted her audience. "Welcome, all of you exercisers out there! Are you ready? Let's get started!" and put one dainty toe in front of the other. Zoe turned off the set, and Stella's diminutive figure disappeared into blackness. *Tomorrow*, she thought, *tomorrow, I'll try tuning in again. Maybe.*

She took the stairs two at a time. Halfway up, she paused to catch her breath and reached the top at a more sedate pace. In her bedroom, she slipped off her clothes, thankful for the hundredth time that she had finally stored the full-length mirror in the back of her closet. She wondered if she could squeeze into a size 12 dress if she didn't eat a single Oreo for a whole week.

As she turned on the hot water, she was filled with the usual self-loathing she always felt whenever she ran her hands down her ample hips.

Zoe Sumner had been second in her law school class. She had missed out on being first by a tiny margin, a situation that irked her no end. But in her late twenties, she had already achieved substantial academic acclaim. In addition, people liked her. Always smiling, she was reliably generous in taking on an extra burden at work or covering for others. She would drive a friend to the doctor even at the last minute or babysit for a desperate pal on the weekend. A giving nature, everyone said. Her weekends were mostly spent in the company of legal papers, so she often welcomed a brief interruption. You could call her a "people pleaser," someone who never said no. Maybe there was some deep psychological reason for this attitude, but helping others gave her genuine pleasure, the feeling of doing the right thing. Why else would she have become a public defender? Unlike her classmates who had scooted off to corporate law firms, their starting salaries likely double anything she could hope to make even twenty years from now.

Zoe never saw in herself what others did - a personable young woman, gracious and spirited with a pert nose and keen gray eyes. They loved her curly hair that bounced when she turned her head though she hated it. Practically from the day she could walk, she envied her mother's straight black hair as straight as poured ink, no curls, and edges blunt cut. In her head, she fought the idea of herself as "full-figured" although others might describe her as voluptuous. She never considered the possibility that she had any quality others would admire or desire. A situation made worse by having a mother whose size 6 wardrobe never wavered.

Others also envied her quick and irreverent brain, her astute resourcefulness in handling the guilty *and* the innocent. She had an enviable gift for compassion but also for toughness when required that any of her female colleagues would have eagerly exchanged for their straight hair and size 10 wardrobe. If she only knew. But she didn't.

Considering her physical virtues as defects created an air of inaccessibility that put men off from approaching her romantically.

Or perhaps her fear of rejection sent off an aura that discouraged their advances. She also wondered if her independent personality was intimidating. Zoe's only rendezvous in ages was a blind date set up by her mother last year with someone named Devin, an encounter hardly worth remembering. A brief coffee then nothing further. Dinners and movies with fellow law students or colleagues didn't count as dates. In any case, she maintained a heavy workload, in part to avoid thinking too often about her personal situation.

In the morning, as she packed her leather briefcase with papers from her two cases, *Gibbons v. Littlehorn School District* and *Jones v. Hanover*, her cell phone beeped. Hurrying out the door, she put it on speaker as it went to voicemail.

"So happy for our talk yesterday, Ms. Sumner. Thank you for the deposit on a weeklong getaway at our Club Med in beautiful Martinique. We look forward to meeting you. The brochure and forms are in the mail."

Oh shoot! Right! I remember now, she thought, scrambling for her car keys. *I actually gave the woman a deposit. It was that glass of wine I drank!* Zoe never used up her vacation days, just kept turning them over year after year. She hardly ever considered the possibility of days off. With her desperate clients and desk perpetually stacked with cases, it seemed an indulgence. *But hey, a few days in Martinique? Why not?* she wondered as she started the car. *Their late-spring deal is an alluring bargain.* But then she was overwhelmed with remorse and regret, anger, and blame. Club Med was a famous getaway destination, and this one in particular was for singles. The women she knew who had taken such a trip were thin as noodles, the guys trim as models. No, this would never do. She hadn't even owned a bathing suit in several years. Not since she snagged hers on the locker door at that Monday night swim class at the local Y. "Weight Loss for Young Adults," they had called it. Who at Club Med would wear a one-piece suit with a skirt like their grandmother's? Oh, no, at Club Med, it would be all-in for bikinis.

She put the whole issue aside as she organized her desk for the morning's work. It was a long day of writing briefs and reviewing legal arguments. There were constant interruptions by her secretary, calls from opposing counsel, and a quick stop in the judge's chambers to settle procedural issues for an upcoming trial. When she arrived home, exhausted and feeling fat and annoyed because she had eaten a supersized lunchtime sandwich - rare roast beef with mayo on a baguette - set before her by her paralegal Thea, and she not taking twenty steps of exercise the whole day, she had forgotten about the Club Med business. Looking forward to a dinner of pasta while she watched *Jeopardy* followed by a hot bath, she was bothered to find the answering machine lit up. Darn, and after business hours too. Landlines are so archaic, she mumbled. No one uses them anymore. Who could this be? She pressed *Play* and once again heard the chipper "Hello, this is Club Med calling." Zoe hung up. She'd call back tomorrow and request a refund of her deposit, opening up the package of shortbread cookies she had promised herself she would not touch until she had lost two pounds.

In truth, Zoe had never taken a "vacation" as an adult except for legal conferences - *The Rights of Abused Women* or *Adoption for Singles*, meetings like that. But the woman's calls were a tease. She started to have second thoughts. *Perhaps I* should *look further into it*, she told herself. *After all, I will have cleared my desk of my two big cases by then. My colleague Ned could take charge of whatever new work comes in.*

Zoe *was* in desperate need of a few days off. And more than entitled to take them.

Was this phone call *fortuitous*?

She vacillated between her personal desire and her daily work habits, an indecisive spot in which she almost never found herself.

But then her heart's rhythm sputtered once again. Bikinis. Bodies thin as straws.

So she started to strategize. In law school, Zoe got sterling marks for strategizing. *I can buy a whole slew of bathing suit cover-ups, long ones to my ankles to wear as beach attire. Bring along a heap of books. Why must I swim at all? I'll find a shady spot and stretch out on a lounge chair. Let others frolic in the pool. Singles pool parties are always raucous anyway, the worst kind of superficial and exhibitionist behavior, everyone flirting and preening. The club sits at the ocean's edge. A nighttime swim in those inky waters would obscure details and definitions, hands down better than any pool.*

And the evenings? Likely the same posing and strutting all through the comedians and the singers, the dancers and buffets. *Why not do similar cover-ups with an added sparkle on my sleeve - a few sequins or beads? Maybe even a short slit up the side. No need to wear miniskirts or those strapless things that could hardly be called a dress. Besides, I won't know anyone,* Zoe thought. *Who must I please but myself? Isn't this what a vacation* should *be? A time to do whatever you like and no one to tell you what to do or how to do it?*

The reality of a brief vacation grew more alluring. Oh, the pleasure of leaving behind an office of folders and lawyers, grim faces, and testy judges. Off to sunshine and palm trees with sumptuous meals, a bed with crisp linens.

Zoe chose not to cancel, and in a timely manner, the booking form and glossy foldout arrived at her door, dense with photos of coconut trees, golden beaches, starry skies. And a request for the balance due.

Over a dinner of grilled salmon and broccoli - one small serving each - her mother neat and prim with her straight hair, slim skirt, and high heels on an ordinary Tuesday night. Zoe told her parents of her plans. "How lovely," they said, but Zoe had caught her mother's first reaction before the enthusiasm appeared - grave, wide-eyed doubt. Surely she had the same thought as her daughter - bikinis.

Zoe sent in a check to secure her place. Then she spent two weekends traipsing through department stores shopping for cover-ups, deliberately passing the cruise wear department, bikinis clipped on hangers like birds on a wire. Reluctantly, she purchased a one-piece suit in the marked-down section, holding it against her fully clothed body. Trying it on in front of a three-way mirror in a well-lit dressing room was simply unacceptable.

On a hot spring day, Zoe found herself on a jet flying to Martinique in the French West Indies. Feeling almost no guilt and surprisingly giddy, she looked out the plane's window as the tall buildings of New York gave way to the peaceful, endless ocean. Didn't she deserve an occasional week of rest and play in the sun? Denial of pleasure was not a deliberate choice she ever consciously made, but one that nevertheless had moved forward on its own, as if on autopilot. From the brochure, she knew the resort was set on a small, semiprivate peninsula at the mouth of a beautiful inlet that leads to the Caribbean Sea. As a lawyer, she always read through every document requiring her signature, including the small print, so she was now familiar with the area's unique marine life, the culture of its native peoples.

In her luggage were eight cover-ups, a single bathing suit, and a half-dozen books. Two bottles of sunscreen, Safari perfume by Ralph Lauren. Although her personal challenge would be about bodies, hers and theirs, she told herself that a 14 was not a disreputable size, so why not think differently about it and make it entirely acceptable in her mind? Everyone knows that women's clothes today fit one size smaller than they are labeled. So there! If she could only believe that.

A trim, dark-skinned man wearing a crisp white tunic met her at baggage claim. He gently walked up to her and placed a necklace of orchids around her neck. She hadn't yet seen the sign "Ms. Sumner," so how did he recognize her? She shivered to think she was that obvious a tourist. Did he see her as a *needy* one? And isn't this custom of wearing leis a Hawaiian tradition? She felt silly wearing this showy necklace of braided flowers. Besides, it made her look even bigger than she was.

Zoe sat quietly in the back seat of the silver limousine. Neither driver nor passenger spoke, but when she occasionally met his smiling eyes in the front mirror, it was an uneasy glance. His look seemed brazen, impertinent somehow. Was he guessing how long it would take her to hook up with someone? Assessing her character as he had the hundreds of others he had driven in this manner, making outrageous presumptions? Perhaps it was just an innocent smile, a friendly "Welcome to Martinique" smile. The luxurious car glided along wide boulevards lined with coconut palms and quaint hotels. White stucco houses perched on hillsides looked down on the blue ocean and soft white sand that ran alongside. *This must be what the French Riviera looks like*, Zoe thought. *Or maybe the Greek islands.*

The car turned into a circular drive and stopped before a long, low structure crowned with a straw roof in the style of a wealthy Caribbean plantation. The driver opened the car door, offered his hand, a slight bow. Her luggage was whisked off to the front desk, though she hardly noticed, so taken was she with the casual chic of the building's architecture.

Thank goodness, she reassured herself, *this isn't one of those fancy hotels of marble and glitz where one dresses up for breakfast.*

As Zoe signed her name on the ledger, she looked around at the magnificent open-air facilities. A bar made of seashells glittering with a thousand bottles wound through the lobby and out to a sweeping stone patio. The open dining room with round tables covered in starched white cloths waited patiently beneath a blue sky and, just beyond, a turquoise pool as large as a lagoon in which couples sat on bar stools sipping drinks. And everywhere, talking, laughing, padding softly on cushioned feet, were slender men and women. *No*, Zoe thought, *skinny, not slender.* The women's cover-ups were skimpy things, a piece of lace, a scrap of batik, a drape of sheer organza tied low on the hips.

The bellman, in his white T-shirt stamped with Club Med across his chest, deposited her and her suitcase in the high-ceilinged room, decorated all in white with touches of natural straw. Fans rotated leisurely from the ceiling. Tropical scents of oils and creams, strawberries and salt, filled the airy, sumptuous space. With a lilting *"Bon séjour, madame.* Enjoy your stay, madame," he bowed and withdrew, his shiny eyes mischievous, sparkling. The driver, the bellman - would there always be an insinuation or expectation of something provocative from members of the staff? Or was her imagination wandering again? When the door clicked shut, she threw herself on the bed in front of the tall French doors he had thrown open to the glorious outside scene and sobbed her heart out.

Eventually, when she sat up to wash her face, she wondered, could her sadness really be all about dress sizes? It seemed a trifling concern here in this beautiful place, especially when she considered her many clients' dire troubles. No, Zoe knew it was more, going way back to when she was a little girl, never feeling as pretty or slim as the next one. Her mother always reassured her, "We all have different strengths, Zoe. You are the smartest one in the class." But what good was being smart then, when pretty was everything? Her girlfriends took photos with their arms around boys at New Year's Eve celebrations, and she had snapshots of herself with her parents and Aunt Sadie and Uncle Harry.

And here, now, her loneliness was amplified with floor-to-ceiling, wall-to-wall mirrored tiles in the bathroom. The mirrors had a wavy texture, so she was not only compelled to see her body from all sides, but it seemed they were mocking her as if she were in a carnival fun house.

As she furiously rubbed sunscreen into her cheeks, she decided, *Oh hell, I've paid for this vacation. I'll make the most of it.*

Her suitcase held books on the magical Creole spirit of Martinique that she expected would permeate the place. On the plane, she had skimmed the first chapter, which described remnants of the non-Anglo-Saxon culture that once dominated southern Louisiana and had been transported here to flower once again as well as a discussion of the exotic fusion of spectacular cuisines - West African, French, Spanish, Haitian, American.

As her thoughts turned to the possibility of a superb meal, she suddenly got hungry.

So she plucked the volume on the history of Buccaneer Creek, the complete name of the facility being *Club Med Les Bouceniers*, shoved it in her purse, and found the stairs.

The bar was outrageously social, laughing young folks standing three deep, flirting, chatting, arms draped over the shoulders of strangers. Everyone within her view held a frosted drink topped with a slice of orange or lemon peel, a tiny paper umbrella. Wisps of cloth thrown over their skin hardly covered their nakedness. She wasn't surprised, but still, she was momentarily stunned or, rather, dazzled, by hordes of beautiful single people all gathered in one place, eager to party. She instantly knew she had already lost on two counts. No one would ever approach her. And if anyone dared, she would withdraw, not knowing how to engage in this casual behavior which, from the looks of things, led to casual sex. Even worse, it was apparent that having two or three, maybe more, partners was not inconceivable. Zoe's head spun with her old concerns that if naked, her tummy roll and that bit of cellulite on her outer thighs would be visible.

Threading her way through the bar, she ordered a diet Coke with a twist of lime. When the bartender - were all the staff hired for their youth and good looks? - in his blindingly white Club Med T-shirt, held up one of those paper umbrellas, she shook her head. "No, thank you." Faintly humiliated by ordering a soda like a dork - her mother hated that word; "Use *socially inept*, please" - and not a sweet liquory drink, she edged away, feeling increasingly out of place, the way she felt in most rooms outside the courtroom.

Far off, she noticed the exotic *palapas* placed at intervals along the sand, open-sided dwellings, or huts with thatched roofs made of dried palm leaves. Charming and discreet, they were prized for providing a modicum of privacy for a day at the beach. As Zoe edged around the pool, she was splashed by glamorous divers, cheered on by glamorous viewers. That was the only word that came to mind - glamorous this, glamorous that. She eventually found a shady spot under an awning and settled down as gracefully as possible on a chaise longue, tucking her cover-up around her legs and pulling out her book on Buccaneer Creek. But reading was not in the cards for her this day. She kept peering over its cover at the spectacle before her. Would she have had more success with her book if she had chosen the romantic poems by Pablo Neruda or Grace Paley?

Another young man in the ubiquitous white shirt suddenly appeared at her feet. *"Puis-je vous apporter quelque chose, madame?* May I get you something? A bite to eat? Some fruit?"

"Non merci," she answered, wondering if it was their job to speak to guests in both French and English just for additional flavor.

And then she fell asleep.

When she awoke, her mouth was dry and bitter. The crowd looked different. A few lingered in swimsuits, but the rest were now arrayed in elegant evening wear. Men in tailored summer jackets and linen pants, no ties. Emerging from starched shirts, their strong throats looked manly, sexy. Women drifted about wearing filmy garments that swirled at the hips as their strappy sandals clicked across the patio. Some dresses fell to shapely ankles, slit long and deep up the sides. Many of these were backless and the fronts indescribable, little as there was to describe. Most wore dresses so short that in her wardrobe, they would have been called a tunic worn over pants or a long blouse. Guests leaned against walls and trees and chairs like so many sinuously clinging caterpillars.

The waiter who approached her earlier - she must ask his name, and did she tip him now or at the end of her stay? - had left a plate of dark purple grapes and pineapple kebabs on the table at her elbow.

The next day, she again found the same place, and again the scene was too tantalizing for even Neruda's poems. Instead, she focused on quelling her envy, her mind pulling apart and putting back together issues of self-realization. She heard her mother's voice, "Sometimes a smart girl like you doesn't know what is best for herself." Growing up, she never knew what that meant. And she didn't know now. She followed how the guests moved effortlessly from one person to the next like a game of chess - bodies making their plays, scoring points, switching off, and going on to the next challenge.

This is not the place where she would realize her true self.

On the third day, as Zoe sat down on the chaise longue, something unexpected happened. Just when she had closed her eyes, a deep voice asked, "Excuse me, what are you reading?" Zoe was startled awake, thinking, *What a silly question! For heaven's sake, he can see what I'm reading.* The *Buccaneer Creek* cover was facing up, Neruda tucked underneath lest anyone think her weird for reading poetry.

Zoe was surprised, shocked. No one had yet talked to her. No one had even looked her way. And certainly no man this decent looking even though he wore ridiculous red-and-yellow flower print shorts that reached his knees, unlike the Speedo bikinis all the other men wore. His shirt was white cotton and covered his bare chest, again, not like the other studs parading around shirtless. Decent looking but not handsome. Stocky, solid, but not heavy.

So how do you answer an absurd question like that? Zoe thought, desperate for a flirty throwaway.

"Oh, my version of Erica Jong," she answered. He didn't laugh at her reference, which he clearly didn't understand. *Stop trying to be funny*, she scolded herself.

"May I sit?" he asked, looking around for another chair. "My name is Blake."

Zoe immediately crossed and recrossed her ankles, tucking in her cover-up, seeking a good position where her best side showed - the left, she just decided - and otherwise fidgeting herself into her most attractive pose. Blake just sat one leg across the other thigh, watching her. She noticed then that he had curly hair like hers. His eyes were very blue, but that may have been a reflection of the sky or the pool.

Why me? she thought.

Then Blake spoke, "I'm not into these casual pickups. I feel pretty awkward around here."

Zoe instantly relaxed. There was something tender about him, open. *But be careful,* she also thought. Was there something wrong with him? It didn't appear so. There he was sitting comfortably, looking untroubled and mellow. When did *normal* become refreshing? she wondered.

"Would you like a drink?" he asked.

"Did you come down with friends?" she asked.

"That guy in the blue suit lounging over there was in the Olympics two years ago," he pointed out. "Diving."

"Aah, of course," she said. "Diving."

"And that girl," he added, pointing to a sunbathing beauty, "won the Olympic swimsuit competition."

They both laughed, finding it easy to now move on to personal information.

"I'm a veterinarian. Just finishing my training and taking a week off before my first professional job."

Oops, she thought, *I hate animals. All that dog and cat hair, and what use is a goldfish swimming around in a bowl of water that needed to be changed all the time?*

But Zoe acted interested, asking if he had any special animal stories. And indeed, Blake had plenty. The one about the time he was on safari and a wolf had come into the tent and he was the only one who would dare try to coax him out. She shuddered and turned the conversation to safe subjects, such as, "Have you ever been on a

Club Med vacation before?" And "Do you have any domestic pets that are happy in small spaces?" Blake inquired about her work. She answered briefly, in no mood to discuss subjects that brought her mind back home.

Chatting amiably until the sun set, Blake asked, "Will you join me for dinner?" And her instant recall - *I only have those long cover-ups. But maybe I can put up my hair with an antique clip, use roll-on mascara, and clip on the gold-link necklace.*

"I'd like that," she answered.

As she changed for dinner, Zoe thought, *The thing about these vacations is that there is never enough time. Time to really get to know each other, time to ease into a relationship. But then again, isn't that the whole purpose? Not to know each other that well but just to have fun, whatever that consists of?* Still, she thought, in their long afternoon exchange, they had made a good, if not substantial, start of becoming acquainted.

Their meal was lovely, the conversation warm and easy. Candlelight by the pool, steamed sea bass with olives and tomatoes, each course served carefully and thoughtfully on large white platters held by discreet waiters who hovered as you made your selection. After dessert, Blake asked if she would like to swim in the ocean. Her heart butterflied, but she thought, *I can do this. It's dark out there.*

She met him on the sand where he was waiting in his red-and-yellow flowered trunks. Letting her cover-up slide down, she ran into the water before he could take a good look and think, *Oh no, chubby.* The night was warm, and the moon cast silvery threads over the dark water. Immediately, she was totally engulfed, lost to everything but the starry sky and the vast, deep spaces. She had forgotten this sensual pleasure of total immersion, not having swum in the ocean since she was a little girl when her parents had rented a house at the south shore of Massachusetts for the month of August. And never had she been in the ocean at night.

It was when Zoe and Blake sprinted squealing out of the water and he placed a towel over her shoulders that it really all started. As Blake rubbed her back, thrilling vibrations aroused nerves that woke up and became painfully intense as his fingers slipped off the towel and made soft circles on her arm. Turning her slowly around to face him, he lifted her chin and kissed her gently, their lips salty and delicious, each of their tongues licking the brine off the other. And she thought, *I didn't need a bikini after all. This is the experience everyone here has come for, the experience some enjoy for the moment but others hope will turn into the tale of a lifetime.*

The problem was that Zoe was a serious, not a frivolous, person. That precise, legal head of hers was always in session. Whatever this turned out to be might mean everything to her. But who exactly was Blake? *What do I know about him besides his animal tales? There hasn't been enough time. Does it matter? Yes*, she thought. *Of course, it does, unless I want to turn into something I've always despised, one of these party girls who look no further than the moment.* But as he kissed her again and his big hand slowly moved up her spine then down, over and over, making excruciatingly exciting small motions at the small of her back, her mind lost control.

Just let yourself go, she decided in a fog of desire. For tonight, just tonight, she didn't have to dream she was a size 6 in a two-piece bathing suit. It didn't matter one bit.

Of course, the trouble with such an evening is that you want more of it.

Only four days remained, four days of swimming in that abiding, mysterious ocean at night - she had not gone so far as to swim in an open pool in full daylight - and delectable dinners, then dancing in Blake's arms. On the dance floor, their bodies fit where they felt right to fit. Silently, she thanked her mother for all those dancing lessons she was forced to take as a kid - ballet, hip-hop, the waltzes where another girl was forced to be her partner. Well, here she was!

For a large man, Blake was graceful, nimble. They twirled and swayed to the Caribbean sounds of reggae, salsa, calypso. Her confidence aflame after their previous evening together, she raised her arms and moved her hips and didn't give a damn about whether or not she was doing the correct steps or had the right rhythm. The bongos, a trumpet, Spanish guitar, and those steel drums echoed off the walls and sent the birds a-twitter. The guitar player even handed her the maracas and let her have a go at leading a conga line. The happy room was open to the evening air, to the black of night. Against the darkness, flaming torchères stuck in the sand blinked like fireflies on the faces of the guests, on the roofs of the *palapas.*

Blake didn't seem to think a long cover-up meant to wear over a bathing suit was an inappropriate evening dress. Hadn't he said twice, "You look fetching tonight, dear Zoe"? *Dear Zoe*, she thought. *No one but my father has ever said that to me.*

On the sixth day, Zoe was absolutely sure. She was in love completely. And it seemed Blake as well, though neither actually said the words "I love you." Naive and inexperienced in these intimate matters, she worried, *How does one really* know *what a man in love acts like? How do I act myself?*

Surprise! They lived only fifty miles apart. So naturally, plans for their future together started forming in her head. So far, everything had been assumed. It was assumed they would dine together and swim together. It was assumed they would spend heavenly nights together either in her room or his. She assumed their relationship would grow. She still marveled at how she, a "fuller" woman, an outsider in her own mind all her life, could have fallen in love so deeply. And with a man who sought her out without any guile or scheming.

But inevitably and too soon, it was time to leave. She folded her cover-ups, packed her bag. Beneath the bed, she spotted a sock of Blake's. As she fondled it lovingly, a sudden pain tore through her chest that was so sharp she thought it might be an attack of her heart, her lungs, her gut. But no, it was only the reality of farewell, of separation. Is this how a kid feels on a carousel? Begging the ride master, "Please, please make it last just a little longer, please, just one more turn before the music stops"? She repeated and repeated, almost moaning, *It won't be long now, not long at all.* He would speak shortly. Likely he hadn't wanted to spoil their last evening together with practical talk of parting.

Anyway, there was an urgent message from Ned at the office that needed her attention. And another crop of vacationers was on its way.

As she left the room key on the dressing table, she wondered how soon it would be appropriate to invite Blake and her parents for dinner together at her apartment. Luxuriating in possible ways to tell them the good news, she thought rather smugly, what would her mother say now?

Jean-André waited at the door to the limousine. Did every guest have his or her own personal staff member for the entire stay? She gave him a wide smile and a strong hug, which didn't seem to sur-prise him, as she and Blake swept inside.

She refused to cry.

Blake was so quiet, holding her hand, looking out at the clouds. Was something wrong? Was he also unhappy at their imminent sepa-ration? The flight was halfway home, and he still hadn't spoken. She sat mute, refusing to speak first. Not until they were circling around getting ready to land, not until after the two cocktails, and only when Blake started to get light-headed did he put her hand to his lips (a proposal!) and say, looking directly at her, "Zoe, when we land, don't be surprised if a woman comes running to me. My wife plans to meet the plane."

Zoe's throat shut down. *I should have known. A seven-day whore. A fancy unpaid Club Med whore. That's all I was. One of those promis-cuous party girls.* Her silent screams roiled with rage. Could outsiders hear the wailing of a stupid, foolish heart? She longed to tear at the seatbelt and run down the aisle, but the landing sign was blinking. Never would she be weak in front of this deceiver, this poseur. This hypocritical liar. Could someone be so careless with another person's feelings? With another's *life*? *Her* life? This was not just a week of carefree vacation to her, a sexual romp making one's daily reality after returning home more palatable. This week meant shedding her past, finding a future.

Perhaps it was her fault, so obviously vulnerable and trusting. She had taken him at his word, those loving whispers in the night. If she were one of those other girls, she would not have made this mistake. Her eyes would have seen clearer. Maybe she *wasn't* thin enough. She hadn't worn a bikini and swum in the pool. Is that what he wanted?

When was he planning to tell her?

And why did his wife let him go off like that? Did they have some accommodating marital arrangement?

She couldn't bear his elbow touching hers. Her thoughts turned feral. *I could kill this despicable man.* A user. Was he even a veterinarian? Did he make up everything about himself? *Dear Lord, who the hell* is *this guy?* she thought bitterly. *And I gave him everything of myself so easily.*

He had seemed so sincere.

"Zoe, c'mon, I never made promises. Why does anyone go to Club Med?" Blake tried, leaning in toward her. "Wasn't it special for a few days? You're a great gal."

She pushed him away, refusing to talk for fear her words would pour out uncontrollably venomous, accusatory. - an endless rant. *Had he done this before? Does he do this regularly?*

She was in the aisle and out the door before he even unhitched his seatbelt. When they walked separately into the terminal, she saw a woman fly by, waving and calling, "Blake, Blake!" But she refused to lift her head or look back.

Outside was sunlight and taxis. When she was settled in a cab and gave the driver her address, he turned with a wink and a smile and asked, "Lady, did you have a good vacation?"

She would never, ever, tell her mother or any of her friends about Blake. Never. But if she did, she knew what they would say. "Oh, we're so sorry, Zoe, but you'll get over it. Now you'll recognize the right man when he comes along."

She wondered how a nice girl like herself would react to such advice, petty and insensitive as she thought those words were. She wondered how she would answer. And then she knew what she would say.

That she was grateful to her body for the first time in her life that she now knew its pleasures, both receiving and bestowing, that although she could now begin to feel secure enough in herself to resist her mother's comments, it might take some work to achieve the whole of her confidence after Blake gave it then took it away.

And although he was the first, no one in the world could reassure her that he wouldn't be the last.

Where's Molly?

My name is Lucas, and this is our story, Molly's and mine. I'm an old man now, almost eighty-five. Although I can't make any sense of it, and I've tried for years, I remember everything as if it happened yesterday. Maybe in the telling, I'll find some clue that I've overlooked.

Molly and I thought our father was the most glamorous man on earth who worked in the most exciting place in the world. In fact, the way he talked about it, and the way we saw it, sometimes we thought he *owned* his world.

Our dad, Sam Thurman, was a national park ranger in Everglades National Park in southern Florida.

"It's the largest tropical wilderness in the United States," he told us.

And we told our friends exactly what he told us: "The park is full of leatherback turtles and Florida panthers and West Indian manatees and alligators and dolphins and hundreds of mammals and different kinds of animal species. And pine flatwoods and seagrass marshes and coastal mangroves and the most gigantic cypress stands on the planet! One hundred forty feet high and thirty-five feet wide, some of them. Do you know how thick thirty-five feet is? Bigger than most of your living rooms, maybe even twice as big!"

In fact, we'd get out of breath talking about it and would have gone on if our friends hadn't stopped us. "Hey guys, we live here too, remember? We know all about those gators and turtles. Nothing new to us."

But my sister Molly and I knew our dad's work was something very big.

Being a ranger wasn't any old job. It was special. The Everglades was a historically significant place. Everything about it was exotic. People called it the Legendary River of Grass. Molly and I knew it was home to some of the rarest wildlife in the entire country. Dad even wore an official uniform - gray shirt and green pants, on his sleeve the National Park Service's symbol of an arrowhead, and the famous broad-brimmed felt hat with a crease on either side of the crown. A gold badge was pinned to his chest and a gun fit snug on his hip. Cruising around all day in his own assigned airboat, he whizzed through marshes that actually *were* a grassy slow-moving river. That airboat was quite something, Made especially for navigating shallow waters, it had a flat bottom and was powered at the back by giant fans, or propellers, rather than a motor. It glided over the sawgrass and cattails like a dream, reptiles and mammals of all kinds keeping a lazy eye on it from the shore. Creatures in the swampy water quickly paddled out of its path as if giving deference to our dad's rule.

I loved the names of every living thing. Take the snakes: yellow rat snake, corn snake, southern ring-necked snake, striped crayfish snake. All those names fired me up as a young boy and still do as a matter of fact. I learned way more about life from one day on the boat with my dad than I did in a whole year of school. Because of dad being some sort of boss, Molly and I got to go to places forbidden to everyone else.

We knew that being a law enforcement officer inside a national park preserve was one of the most dangerous places to be an officer. The rangers had very little backup, always being short-handed, always recruiting. The territories they covered were remote and vast, and there were many dangers involving both humans and animals on land and on water, though danger from humans was often the least of their worries.

Our friends' dads were plumbers and shop owners, bus drivers, and bank tellers. Molly's friend Maisie Sue's dad was our doctor. And my friend Jess's father ran a tram bus that traveled along the Tamiami Trail, where the alligators and crocodiles hung out along the river banks. The scaly, slithering gators with their long pointy snouts, the crocs with theirs, flat and broad, both of them giant lizards, just like in the movies. A couple of dozen tourists would shout from inside the tram, pointing and taking pictures. Maybe they were trying to scare off the poor creatures, though believe me, *nothing* scares those critters. I thought the opposite. Those listless lizards were just plain indifferent to sightseers.

None of my friends had a dad who edged their kids in real close to the black bear and the Atlantic bottlenose dolphins, who drove that airboat real close to the gators, or took them to special fishing places hidden in the cypress groves. There was this place called Sawgrass Recreation Area, the official fishing spot for visitors. But Molly and I went to our "Thurman Family's special place" where no visitors were allowed. We sat quietly with our lines dangling in the water until we caught a few bluegill and black crappie and chain pickerel. Now and then, even peacock bass to bring home and grill for supper. Lord, I love the sound of those names. Sometimes I whispered to the water, "Hey, bluie. Hey, pickie. C'mon, take a nibble." I'd say the joke starting its way up from my chest, "Hey, crappie, what the heck are you doing?" Then Molly and I would laugh so hard we'd chase the fish away for a good ten minutes.

My mom, Linn, was a weaver. But she was no ordinary weaver, the kind who uses a huge loom and a foot pedal and weaves the yarn in and out with a shed stick to make fabric. Rather, she had made her own small loom, a rough kind of thing, a wood frame nailed together, some yarn or string strung between. Then she'd gather twigs and stones and dried leaves, all kinds of things that she found on the ground. She'd permanently fix them into clever arrangements stuck between those threads and yarns and turn it into something special you could hang on your wall. Picture a spider's web and its lacy filaments spun to trap bugs for food. And then imagine the nature's leavings and cast-off stuff she collected somehow fixed to those filament threads. It made no sense if you watched her work, just looked kind of junky in the beginning, but in the end, that thing she took off her loom had become a fascinating work of art.

We were all so proud of her when she sold a piece at Smallwood's Store, this famous place on the mosquito-infested mangrove island of Chokoloskee. To celebrate, Dad and the two of us went on a special hunt in the woods, searching for unusual items for her supply like the feathers from a roseate spoonbill or dried cattails, for example.

Smallwood's was a rust-colored wooden building on pilings at the river, first built in 1906 as a true frontier outpost. Long before a small road was built, you could only get there by boat. It was a trading post for all kinds of adventurers who didn't want to be found, the reason why they lived in the swamp and hiked and fished and lived in the wild. In the wet season, the swamp angels, we called them, those fierce mosquitoes, made life hell. Ate you alive. And there were mosquito-borne illnesses, West Nile virus and dengue fever, from some of those insects though I was interested to learn that only female mosquitoes bite. They need blood to reproduce. Molly sure didn't believe me when I told her that.

Today, Smallwoods remains pretty much the same, sitting with its dignity intact on its great wooden posts that rise from the bank of the river except, of course, they no longer stocked the salted mullet and basic supplies needed for survival by the men of those earlier days. The old goods have long been replaced by hundreds of historical artifacts, making it a prized museum so filled with intriguing displays that you could spend a year in there looking around without seeing it all by a long shot. There is always an old-timer like me hanging around who can tell you a thousand stories about the place and all its characters, then and now.

Ninety percent of the artifacts are original to the store; it looks as though nothing has changed in over ten dozen years. Prominently displayed is the history of Southwest Florida's pioneers who had tamed this vast and wild wilderness known as Florida's Last Frontier - the Calusa Indians, the first, followed by the Seminole and Miccosukee Tribes that traded here. On walls and shelves are authentic Seminole crafts and carvings along with alligator heads, animal hides, books of legendary characters such as Edgar "Ed" Watson, who was shot by a group of locals right on this site and whose ghost is said to inhabit the premises at night. Totem poles, knickknacks, and products from way back like Target Hawk-Eye cameras were crammed into the corners. And at the back of the store, the porch hovers over the tumbling waves where the Ten Thousand Islands silently reside, a magnificent, mysterious labyrinth of water and mangroves. Many a day did I spend imagining what life must have been like in those *really* old days.

Mom was so proud and excited when a stranger bought one of her works. She'd daydream of it hanging in a home or business in North Dakota or Texas or even up in Canada, someplace far away. "Wonder what it's like in some of those places," she'd say as we sat around the supper table. "Texas with its ranches and huge open spaces, or North Dakota with those gorgeous mountains and forests. And snow! Imagine snow." So filled with wonder was she that I'd dream about those places too.

"Living in a swamp wears you down, day after day, this humidity all the time," she continued, "and always worrying about the kids taking chances near those gators or running into a pygmy rattlesnake hiding under the leaves."

Mom didn't exactly complain, just talked kind of wistfully. As a kid, it bothered me. We loved the Glades so much, and here she was, kind of tuckered out and worn down except for the excitement she got up for her weavings and thinking up stories about those faraway places.

On my twelfth birthday, when Molly was ten, our parents planned a special celebration. Dad put us both in a canoe and paddled us into Hell's Bay, the site of the Everglades chickee huts. These were traditional Seminole structures smack dab in the middle of the bay. Huts that were open on all sides. Really, crude camping platforms set in the water with an elevated floor and greenish-yellow palmetto leaf thatching for the roof. Those leaves were star-shaped and up to twelve feet long so they spanned the entire top of the hut. I looked up at them and thought, Gosh, nature sure was amazing. The design of the thing was kind of having your own man-made miniature island in the open water of a mangrove swamp. Dad settled us down, told us he would be back in the morning, then left us overnight with sandwiches and blankets.

At first, it was really exciting when Molly and I watched the wildlife onshore and played games with birds sitting on the rails. But when it got dark, we huddled real close together under our blankets. Spooked by the weird grunts and splashes of marine life and animals growling and snarling on land, all of it friendly by day but frightening by night, we didn't get much sleep, that's for sure. This was the first time we were ever out alone in the swamps at night. It's supposed to be a "birthday treat," my folks said. The next morning, we were darn happy to see Mom rowing toward us, shouting, "Hey, you two explorers! Did you have an exciting adventure?" And darn glad we were to be in that canoe going home, I can tell you.

Skimming over the boggy waters, I realized that once I had been out overnight like that, it kind of did take the scare out of the thing. So when Dad asked me, "Do you want to go camping again on the platforms with your friend Jess when it's *his* birthday?" I said, "Sure." Maybe that's what my dad figured. It was time for me to be a man. And to see if I could take care of Molly. I wondered if he was worried when he left us that night. But then, he knew he had taught me about the swamps since I was a little kid, so maybe he just wanted me to learn what I should and shouldn't be scared of.

So this was our life.

Molly and I were tight little critters together, barely able to wait every day till school was out and whooping with joy when summer was on. The start of our adventuring through the Glades. Molly herself was tough. She'd climb any tree right after me, even got more bites on her fishing line than I did. And she never showed she was scared of any old croc even when one sneaked up on her and she raced into that canoe like lightning, beating that paddle to death to get the heck out of there. We were real close, each other's best friend all through those early years.

Then one day, with no warning at all, our lives changed. So quietly that for the rest of my days, I couldn't figure it out.

Jess and I were chasing possums and rabbits in his backyard, When Jess and I chased small animals, I was always late for dinner. Finally, I came home dirty and hungry to find Dad sitting in the kitchen, his big head in his hands. The belt with his gun was on the table, his hat on top. He looked so sad. I had never seen him like that, a man who loved his job and his family.

"Lucas," he said, and I knew by his sorry eyes and the way he said my name - all serious - that something terrible had happened. "Can't dress this up in any way, Lucas. Your mom's gone, and she took Molly with her."

If you had told me that a monster gator just gave birth to a passel of possums, it would've seemed more real to me.

"Well, you know your mom has been spending a lot of time over at Smallwood's with that part-time job she took up. Seems she met a fellow there from Colorado, come down sightseeing for a couple of weeks. Seems like he was taken with your mom and she with him.

"This is all pretty new to me, buddy. I had no idea. But she left a note. Are you ready to read it?"

Ready? I thought. *I'm sixteen. I can chase crocs and shoot a gun, thanks to you. What do you mean 'ready'? But not for this.*

"Here's her note." Dad handed it over.

Sam, honey, it's not your fault. I do care for you. But living in this swamp for twenty years has plum worn me out. I can't stand it anymore. The swamp angels, the animals, everything so hot and humid and isolated. Yes, isolated my whole life. I've never even seen a big city. And along comes this customer, Ned, and he asks me, "Who did these beautiful weavings?" And we got to talking and he told me stories of Colorado, where he's from. The mountains and snow and wide-open spaces with horses and cattle. Snakes too and some bobcats but no panthers. And for sure no gators. And I just wanted a change really bad. While I'm still young. We talked a few times, him always stopping by the store and telling me some about himself. So when he asked, I decided to go back to Colorado with him.

I didn't know what to do about the kids. That part broke my heart. I know they're so close, but I decided to take Molly and leave Lucas with you so you won't be lonely. It seems fair that way. May the kids forgive me for splitting them up, but they would be all grown up in a few years anyway, and who knows if they would even stay around then. Please show this to Lucas. Tell him I love him and how much I loved their growing up. But honest, Sam, I had to go. This swamp, it was wearing me down.

Love,
Linn, Mom

Dad and I couldn't speak. We must have sat there silently for hours till he finally got up and started scrambling some eggs. *Darn it*, I thought. *Molly is just a fourteen-year-old kid. What's she going to think about this? I'm two years older, but even so, my life is pretty much ruined.* There was nothing for me without Molly. And my dad? His life was over. How will he come home to this house every night? And what about the days he loved so much with Molly and me when he could sneak us out for our adventures? I stayed in my room and cried for a whole week. And then, when I changed those sheets wet from my tears, I found Molly's note sticking out of the corner of my bedroom rug.

> Lucas, no time. Have to leave in half hour and get all my stuff together first. No idea about this crazy idea of Mom's, but I'll sneak you letters somehow, from wherever we're going. Lucas, my dear brother. What's happening? Don't forget me, and someday…gotta go.
>
> Love you,
> M

Molly needed me, and I couldn't help her.

Well, I did stay around, but it was lonely the whole time. We did our best, Dad and I, but two guys together aren't always the best communicators. I became a park ranger too, with a gun, a badge, and the arrowhead symbol on my sleeve. What else did I know? But ten years later, when Dad got mauled and died in a surprise tangle with a black panther, I had no reason to stick around.

I sold our house to Jess's sister, who had just gotten married. Then I packed my things and set off to my new job at Zion National Park in Utah, a neighbor state to Colorado. As far away from Florida as I could get but as near to Colorado as I could manage. Maybe I could somehow track down Molly without even knowing anything about Mom's husband, his name, or whereabouts. Maybe I would someday see Molly walking into a store, and I would be right there.

Gone were the marshes, swamps, gators, and cypresses. Here were canyons, mesas, rivers, forests, natural stone arches, buttes, breathtaking mountain panoramas, canyons reddish in color, and tan-colored Navajo Sandstone eroded by the North Fork of the Virgin River. Zion was a totally different world. There were nineteen species of bats in that park. The only thing remotely in common with the Glades was the abundance of reptiles. In spring, everything the eye can see was covered with flowers - prickly pear cactus, sego lily, Indian paintbrush, showy stone seed. I was still fiercely taken with the names of things and rolled these new ones off my tongue as if I'd known them my whole life.

And another kind of nice thing happened. Always thinking of myself as a loner in the wilderness, now I became interested in the towns just outside the park. They were filled with lovely inns, western-style decor, art galleries, farmers markets, and nearby hiking and bike trails. I could've lived a cheaper way out in the country, but I have to admit, I liked being in town with all those small-town charms. Plus, maybe it'd be easier to spot Molly there. Nothing was so big that I didn't know everyone around. And the gorgeous sunrises and sunsets almost made me cry with their beauty every morning and every evening. Nothing like them, such broad streaks of brilliant reds and oranges that sometimes I couldn't believe they were real. And when those rays of color set on the red walls of the canyons, well, it felt as if the whole valley was on fire.

In all the years since Molly and Mom left, neither my dad nor I had ever heard from either of them. Way back when they first left, Dad tried to track them. Park rangers are good at that stuff with all their government connections, but he never knew Ned's last name, and he never found out anything about them. I guess Mom must have married Ned, but how do you track a man named Ned in Colorado? Smallwoods didn't even have a trace of him, so maybe his name wasn't even Ned.

This is how I figure it. Maybe our mother told Molly some bull story like it was better to cut off all communication for some dumb reason. And by the time she was old enough to think it all out, I had probably moved three or four times. No way would mail get to me with one address after the other like that, or maybe she had been forbidden to write, or maybe they lived in the mountains so Ned had to come into town to get the mail and Molly couldn't get her letters out. All I know is that she probably wouldn't believe a thing without talking to me. And that she thought about me as much as I thought about her, that we both had aches in our hearts for losing each other. It makes me so sad to think of her writing a letter to me then being unable to post it. I try not to think about that too much. Instead, I put my mind to this possibility. Molly married, probably at a young age, and had a really nice husband and many kids who loved her and whom she loved back and that there was lots of hugging in her life. I sure hope so. And despite the anger I still feel at my mom, thinking all this time it was a terrible thing that she did, I also hope she had gotten to visit a big city. Maybe Denver.

Maybe she actually lived in Denver.

I'm in this nursing home now, and I guess I should feel lucky. I know there aren't many places like this around this part of the state and none at all where southeastern Utah joins Colorado. With all my aches and pains, it's good to have someone take care of me, my wife gone so many years now.

My life is now almost at an end.

It was a life, like so many lives. Some years were good, some not so good, but when you have such a strong familial bond when you're young and it's ripped away without even a goodbye, you never get over it. At least I haven't. I always had the sense that my wife June thought there was an old flame in my heart that hadn't been put out yet, but in truth, it was only Molly.

I read a lot of books these days. And I play cards with other guys on my floor, especially my pal Gerry, who reminds me a lot of Jess, always telling stories of the skunks and rabbits around his old house. I guess this is what you do when you are getting ready to die - tell stories so maybe someone will remember something about you. My own kids are far away, so I can't tell them stories anymore. My girl, Molly, named after her aunt, is somewhere in Maine, as far as you can get from Utah - an outdoorsy kid like her dad and grandfather. And my boy, Sam, named after my dad, is somewhere over in the Philippines, in the army. I pray the two of them don't lose touch with each other. I tried to raise them close, but you never know how life will treat you. I can only hope they end up living near each other. They write and call me regularly, but nothing can take the place of seeing each other for real.

So now I have to write down this last important part because this is the part that God has sent down.

One day, I was playing cards with Gerry and beating him good when Jeannie the nurse came over with my pills - three each time, four times a day. And she said, almost by accident, "Lucas, do you have any relatives around here?"

"None that I know of, young lady. Why do you ask?"

"We have a new patient on the third floor, someone named Molly Thurman. I thought maybe you were related. Not many Thurmans in these parts."

As tears sprung up and my nose started to run, I had no words, only a throbbing in my chest. Could it be possible?

I wheeled myself down to room 332 and peeked in the door. A white-haired woman was lying in the bed. I knocked lightly. A weak hand lifted and waved me in, and in a few turns of the wheelchair, I was at Molly's side.

Slowly, with great effort, she looked my way. Right away, I could tell she knew who I was. She did that thing with two fingers we always did when we caught a fish and had to be quiet—just splayed them over the sheet. I took her hand, and we sat quietly like that for an eternity of time and distance, mistakes and regrets. Tears of love and sorrow ran down our cheeks like rivers. As I bent over to wipe hers away, her hand grew cold in mine. And I just sat that way for a long time until a nurse came in, covered Molly with a sheet, and wheeled her away. But I knew for sure it was my Molly. She had held on for as long as it took to find me again, and then she let go.

Alice in the admitting office told me, "When her husband brought her in, he was pretty sick himself. Said he was checking himself into a hospital in Denver. He told us the only name she wanted on her forms was Molly Thurman."

But at least she had a husband, I thought. She hadn't been alone. I sure hoped he was good to her. At first, I thought about hiring a detective. Maybe there were children, cousins for my own children. But I gave it up. I was tired and old and plain sick at heart. It was almost time for me to die too.

Did Molly have a contented life?

Had my mother been happy with Ned?

Did they live in or ever visit Denver?

Had the breakup of our close family actually been worth it to our mother?

Magnificent Irony

S he was as lovely in grace as she was beautiful of face.
Folks everywhere turned to look as she walked by, whispering, "Wow, did you see that?" Blond, blue-eyed, and slender like a Dane but actually Irish with a natural blush on her cheeks like a pretty doll all grown up. When she spoke, her brogue sang and danced like the Irish valleys rise and fall. But unlike many foreigners, she had no shyness in her. She went happily about her duties as a nurse at the assisted living facility, humming to herself, greeting others with her sprightly "Good mornin', darlin'. How are we feelin' today?"

Beloved by her patients, she always took time for a chat, sitting by their bed as if she had nothing else to do. Enthralled, they remained still as statues when she told stories of her ancestors and Ireland's legendary kings. Everyone thought her life was full of delicious adventures. With her charming and generous nature, how could there be sadness in her? But the patients only knew the apparencies of her surface pleasures, not the depth of her personal woes. The private life of this Irish beauty was as dramatic and mysterious as the emerald hills of Ireland. No one knew that this lovely gal, or "lassie," as the associate director Carl called her when they were alone, carried with her real heartache.

Her name was Rose, and when the patients saw her coming, they would sing or whistle (in reality, it was more like warbling) "My Wild Irish Rose." Over the years, she had heard that so many times it no longer annoyed her. If the patients found pleasure singing to her, listening was the least she could offer those in their beds and wheelchairs.

But really, what was her mother thinking when she named her that?

Rose was unmarried. She had one biracial child, Andy, four years old. His father was a suave, seductive black man, the only man she had ever found irresistible. Now Rose was desperate for another child, but there were problems. Thomas was married. He had a wife, three children, a Tudor mansion, and a prominent role in the community. When Rose and Thomas had had their lusty, adulterous affair, she had believed in happy endings. Young and innocent, she was a mere twenty-three and he an elegant thirty-two. Of course, he would leave his present life to begin anew with her. Were they not enchanted with each other?

And eventually, there was little Andy, their son, who looked so much like his father - the long nose, dark eyes set far apart, the narrow face.

It was only after Andy began crawling around their small apartment and Thomas did no more than rush in and out that Rose began to realize he would never forsake his lawful family. She went into a period of mourning, enduring nights of tears, and remorse until she decided, *If I cannot shake him from his wife, I'll settle. As long as Andy will be nurtured and loved, I'll accept Thomas's sporadic appearances. At least the child, however meagerly, will know his father.*

But on an afternoon that gave no indication of being extraordinary, their lives were abruptly, and unexpectedly, upended. An upheaval that set in motion a lifelong vendetta between the two.

It happened on Andy's fourth birthday. Thomas had promised an extra hour or two longer for his visit. Determined to make it memorable for the three of them, Rose floated balloons from the ceiling, hung streamers from lamps and railings. Tucked into a straw basket in the kitchen, a sweet caramel-colored kitten awaited. Thomas arrived with a flourish, bearing a chocolate cake and a wooden train set.

When he saw his father, Andy laughed and squealed, rushed over to him, shouting, "Daddy, Daddy, Annie burfday!" In his little fist, he clutched the string of a red balloon. But Thomas could only stare blankly at his son. Unresponsive, his arms hung awkwardly at his sides. Rose stared. Was he ill?

Thomas had just had a vision that felt like a punch in his gut. But his trouble was not physical. It was in his head but a punch no less real. An absolute certainty popping up and looming large that before today was just a vague, harmless notion he had banished from his thoughts. But at this moment, here it was, the simple truth - he could no longer deny or avoid paternity. Andy now required more adult attention. He was asking for commitments. A trip to the movies. A day at the zoo. Playing with a toddler in his room was one thing, but taking on the obligation of this child forever was another. Not with a wife and three children and a successful law practice elsewhere. Andy clearly endangered everything in Thomas's meticulously arranged life. In that moment of joyful celebration, as the boy with his own features ran eagerly toward him, Thomas recognized the true potential danger his own child presented. So he silently turned and walked away.

Rose didn't grasp Thomas's startling epiphany. What had happened? She called him a few times, but her messages went to voicemail. A week later, Thomas picked up and whispered into the phone, "It's over. The boy is your problem, not mine. Don't ask me for anything. You chose to have him."

She shouted "Bastard, bastard, bastard!" over and over as she paced the rooms in her small apartment, furious but helpless, the air oozing from her lungs.

When Thomas didn't show up for two weeks, Rose read Andy a story about a man who looked like Thomas and was taking a long trip around the moon. "He's going into space," she said, "and we may have to wait a long time till he comes back. But when he does, I bet he will bring you some rocks from the very surface of the moon itself. See?" She pointed out, as they ran to the window. "That moon right up there."

Rose figured she bought herself some time with that story. When he asked, she would tell her son that someone taking a trip into space could also visit the moon, the sun, and all kinds of places and be away a good long time.

For a few months after she told him the story, Andy asked, "When is Daddy coming back? I really want to see the moon rocks."

"He's busy teaching other space daddies how to steer the rocket," she answered.

What will I do now? she fretted, preoccupied with her wretched dilemma. Along with Thomas's absence was the end of the few paltry bills, twenties, occasionally a few fifties, that he had slipped her now and again when it suited him. But it wasn't the end of the emotions she felt, cheap and used when she saw him lay down those bills on the hall table. Days of rage and fury left her exhausted with Andy, testy at work. Another year went by, then another, her despair increasing. As he grew older, Rose's answers about Thomas became weaker and more ridiculous. Besides, her son had studied about astronauts in school and how long they could stay up in space. One day, when she attempted a feeble explanation, he had said, quietly and simply, a precocious seven, "Mom, forget the excuses. If he wanted to see me, he would." And with that, Andy stopped asking about his father. Meanwhile, Rose's heart, powerless to remedy, wept and bled.

Andy now began asking for things she couldn't afford - a bike, some video games, a basketball. So eventually, despite her moods and pouts, she finally decided to fight back, the Irish in her rising up in full measure. If she could no longer command Thomas's personal attention for Andy, she would compel substantial legal payment from him for the boy's needs, a computer, a week at camp. Besides food and clothing, what about his sports equipment? A move to a better school district?

These were modern times, Rose thought. Women had legal rights, tenuous though they may be. And men had obligations. If Thomas refused to claim or even visit his son, at least he should pay for his absence with decent support. But she wouldn't fool herself. Thomas was not a doctor or a bricklayer. Nor a teacher or banker but a successful attorney, a criminal defense attorney. It was in the courtroom, making arguments, that he garnered his fame. And suddenly Rose, a working woman, never before engaged with the legal world, not even having a single friend so attached with sources and advice, now had to confront a powerful and vindictive opponent.

A nurse on the floor offered Rose the name of a legal aid society that would take her child support case for free if she qualified economically. Rose was skeptical. What kind of professional would work for nothing with low-income people? Who paid their salaries?

But this Irish lass smoldered at seeing Thomas in the newspapers with his gussied-up wife at a gala for underprivileged kids or for inner-city education programs, their arms around each other. Always charities for the poor, the deprived, yet he gave nothing to Andy, his own child. So she made an appointment with Legal Aid and showed up at the address clutched in her hand, a run-down building in a poor part of town. Instinctively, she held her purse close. The discreet, weary *L* and *A* of the sign out front were peeling around the edges. With a gloved hand, Rose pushed open the dented door and stepped inside.

With her legal aid attorney, Giles, looking and acting like a law student, she went to court month after month fighting for Andy's support payments. This "pro bono" lawyer, ineffectual each time, enraged her. But what had she expected?

Thomas, of course, never bothered to appear. His masterful legal team represented him with briefs and papers, managing to have the records sealed. It was a ridiculously unfair contest, but there was just enough leeway from a sympathetic judge now and then to keep the case moving along. Sometimes one responded sympathetically to her situation, the helpless mother of a young boy whose father had abandoned him, grasping the emotional cruelty the father inflicted. Those judges knew what men like Thomas were up to with their phalanx of attorneys, entitlement apparent in their spiffy suits and Rolex watches.

The time she took from work had dire repercussions. Every hour gone, she was docked salary from her meager check. Still, she was forced to return to court time and again, handing over rent and grocery receipts, trying to gain whatever monetary increases she could. The judge granted just enough allowance for Andy's food and clothing but not enough for his math tutoring or for a bike, a computer, or hockey skates. And even with those paltry sums Rose was granted, she was forced to get a second or third court order to compel payment while Thomas continued to live lavishly on his two-acre estate. When her child lawyer cleared his throat one day and brought this discrepancy to the judge's attention, the man seated high on a platform behind a broad desk peered down at him over his glasses, banged his gavel, and declared, "Out of order."

Out of order?

Aghast, her fist raised, Rose shouted, "Is this legal?"

And the judge found her in contempt of court.

All this time, she desperately wanted another child for Andy's sake to not be an only child, to not be alone should something happen to her. And she had more love to give. Andy had already begun to show fears and anxieties - his dependence on her, worrying over every little thing she did. "Mommy, should you be out in the dark? What if you don't come home? Mommy, can I sleep with you? Mommy, all my friends have brothers and sisters."

On her part, she had become a hoverer, a worrier, like her own mother whose smothering had hampered the joy and freedom of her own childhood. She had always chafed against it, and here she was, raising her own child the same way. In the few years since Thomas left, Andy's every move caused her alarm - fear of him falling off his bike, walking alone to his friend a block away, a bite from a neighbor's dog. Danger lay everywhere.

Yes, Andy must have a sibling.

While Rose plotted and schemed, friends arranged blind dates. She conceded that a simple, decent man would do as a suitable father, even if not an appropriate life partner for her. Rose was looking for acceptable genes. So she dressed up and went out - first with a professional tennis player, skinny like she liked; then an accountant with a steady job; and even a doctor. But the tennis player turned out to be an alcoholic. The accountant was indifferent when they made love. And the physician? Short and fat, and the idea of those genes scared her off. Each experience was a dispiriting encounter, depressing, demeaning.

Yet she persisted. She was promoted to head nurse on her floor. Two of her favorite patients died. She continued to fight in court. Her lawyer Giles was now engaged. Andy became a teenager and grew a short beard. And still, she had not found a fitting partner to parent another baby. Rose had the sense no man wanted to take on a relationship that included a biracial child.

She signed up with online dating services. Her posted picture showed a young woman wearing a black dress with low cleavage and mascaraed eyes, soft hair in a loose upsweep revealing her graceful neck. She wanted to look glamorous but worried that she looked like a whore. Still, she accepted dates from strangers every weekend. Often, they were twenty years older in person than in their photo. Some made aggressive moves toward her. Soon enough, she took down her posting.

Rose turned forty. At work, the staff and patients gave her a birthday party. She ate chocolate cake with mocha frosting and salted caramel ice cream. Later, Andy treated her to a double whopper at McDonald's and handed over two goldfish in a big glass bowl. When he fell asleep, she looked the truth straight on. Her hopes for another child were over. She spent the whole long evening crying into her pillow.

Slowly, Rose felt herself assuming a new persona. She became a Rose that no one, including herself, recognized. Her bubbly core hardened, formed a shell around her emotions, responsive only to the nub of pain she bore. Resentment curled inside her like a parasitic worm, unable to live on its own but thriving in her gut. Her patients didn't sing to see her come. Rather, they greeted her solicitously.

"Are you feeling well this morning, Rose?"

"Are things okay at home, Rose?"

"Maybe a few days off would be good for you, dear."

She interacted less with her patients, even the ones she had lovingly attended over many years. Refusing to look at Thomas's picture on the society pages, she canceled her newspaper subscriptions. One of his fancy suits alone would pay three months' rent on an apartment in a neighborhood with a respectable school.

Bitterness continued to fester. Her lovely features, once fragile and delicate, disappeared beneath a furrowed brow. Tiny lines formed at her lips and forehead, feathering her eyes. A random date or two turned up, but sensing her disdain, the men never returned. She thought about her mother, Moira, naming her Rose. Surely she expected her daughter's life to unfurl like a wonder of nature, one glorious pink petal at a time. *Hah, what irony*, Rose thought.

Joyless, Rose did her job and returned home to Andy, now taller than she. He was in his teens, starting to date. She poked and prodded at his social activities, creating unnecessary ill will between them but unable to help herself.

One day on her way to work, she glanced at the headlines in the newspaper on a sidewalk stand. There it was, big and bold on the front page.

Famous Attorney Thomas Carnes Shot by
His Wife at Their Lakeside Vacation Home.

What? Thomas shot? *Her* Thomas?

Shocked, she walked back to take another look, put a few coins in the slot, and pulled out a paper, scanning the article as she walked. *Murder. Unexplained. Gun. Police. Lake. Point-blank.*

I wish I had done it myself was her first thought. Her second was *Why did his wife murder him with such evident advantages in her life?*

After work, Rose rushed home, turned on the television, and remained fixed on the screen hour after hour. She thirsted for details, for photos. And there they were. Thomas's family and professional life unraveled right in front of her, while she sat on her old blue sofa watching endless replays.

Thomas's crimes were astounding, confounding. He was handsome, smart, and successful - the first African American to make full partner in his prestigious firm. But it turned out that he was also a criminal, embezzling large sums of money from his clients' accounts, sleeping with women to seduce them into hiring him, betraying their trust, and selling information from their estates to interested parties - a moral reprobate, a thief, a perjurer. Why?

The police had a long list of women named. Everyone, client and colleague, had once admired him - everyone but the women he betrayed, Rose thought bitterly. His partners claimed innocence. What did his wife know? Yet despite the extensive media coverage, Rose had an uneasy sense that all, in fact, was not known.

Sitting on her sofa, Rose was aggrieved over possibly serious repercussions. She had just last year given up her court pleas and prayed that no information about her would turn up. But would the police come questioning, causing trouble at work? They would surely be searching through relevant records, especially those involving connections with women.

And Thomas's children!

So far, she only saw photos of his three young girls being dropped off at school, hurried into and out of cars. There were a few photographs when the children were toddlers and the family a few years later, playing tennis at the lake. No word about Andy. Would he be spared the public humiliation of having been born of *that* father and of her own shameful involvement?

"Why are you watching this same news every night?" Andy asked, plopping down with a box of pizza. Rose turned to him, her eyes, soulful. When she started with "Honey, I'm sorry," Andy was startled. He looked from his mother's obvious distress to the handsome, middle-aged black man on the screen with Andy's very own smile, his own eyes. The room grew still as Andy pulled up his own vague memories of a man with a toy train and balloons hanging from the ceiling. He paired them with a few remarks his mother tossed off here and there over the years. Finally, Rose said, "Yes, honey, I'm afraid so."

Finally, Andy broke into the quiet. "Mom," he said, "he was never a nice man. He left us, remember?"

Did she remember? She remembered nothing else.

Rose replied, "But I *thought* he was nice a long time ago. I wouldn't have become involved with him otherwise. And despite everything, look what a fine young man you turned out to be even with that father. Andy, to me, his worst crime was that he was a missing person. Someone who went missing in our lives."

"What about his three young daughters?" Andy asked.

She couldn't believe that his first thought was for others, not himself.

"Whoa, Mom, easy does it," he said as she hugged him. "I didn't even know the man. I haven't seen him since I was…four, was it? The birthday in which he brought me a train then left my life forever, and you started telling me that story of the guy traveling to the moon. Why the hell should I give two cents for him? But he should be in jail, not dead.

"You know, Mom, I never knew him to really miss him. Heck, you played ball with me and went to all my games and did a thousand things some fathers never do."

Rose had been prepared for a terrible scene - bitterness, recriminations. Andy might have stalked out. Instead, he said gently, "He must have been some dude early on, though," as photos of the young and handsome Thomas appeared on the screen. "I can see why you were attracted to him."

Still, Rose held back, thinking, after all, *Andy doesn't need to know everything. My endless court appearances and Thomas's repeated rejections of him, his unwillingness to provide support, now even worse in light of the fortune he had amassed.*

As her son put his arms around his mother, she thought, *Well, saints be praised. My boy is comforting* me *rather than the other way around.*

"Andy, honey, you are my life, always have been. But you are, above all and despite everything, so very special to yourself."

Somehow, I did an extraordinary thing, Rose thought. *I raised an honorable, loving man.*

Yet Rose's anger about Thomas did not abate. Why would it disappear, even dwindle, because Thomas was dead or because her son had such an impressive reaction? Rose wanted revenge. She wanted justice. She was a frustrated woman filled with the sense of being on a mission. But how would she bring that determined self to fruition? And what would her mission be?

At the assisted living facility, she gave notice for fewer hours.

Thanks to television reporters, Rose now had Thomas's address. She saw photos of the street he lived on - the bastard, his wife, and three kids in that gorgeous Tudor mansion with its many gables and its half-timbering design. Desperately eager to drive by his property, she waited two months until the photographers had dispersed. She also held back until Andy had left the house for a summer job, but those weeks of waiting turned out to be precious indeed. She and Andy had continued to talk about the mysteries surrounding Thomas's murder and their own confusing emotions of many years past. For mother and son, it was a good period. So when she eventually drove her old Ford out of the city, onto the highway, and then into the luxurious enclave of the wealthy, her anger had just settled on simmer, not boil.

Just in case there was a lone reporter still lurking, she put on her oversized sunglasses, lifted her shirt collar up to her chin, and slunk low on the car seat. Thomas's wife, whom the public called "the murdering bitch," had been released on bail and was now living at home. Who was with her? Guards, family, friends?

As she turned onto the leafy street, Rose recognized landmarks from the television coverage - the stately white Colonial residence on the corner, then a Country French stone behemoth with a slate roof. And suddenly, there it was. The expansive frontage of Thomas's property, the home to which he returned after spending glorious nights with "his Rosie girl." Surrounded by a high iron fence, a surveillance camera was mounted on the gate, a security company placard stuck in the ground.

Rose sat for a few minutes, her heart thrumming, expecting a barking dog to pounce on the car window or a guard to tap on the glass with his knuckles. Someone would surely take notice. Her humble car was obviously out of place on this distinguished street of foreign cars and sport utility vehicles. She had no direction, no plan, only a ravenous curiosity about Thomas's wife. His widow.

Hesitantly, Rose opened the car door, walked slowly back and forth. She was alone on this picturesque road. *Is a camera recording me?* she wondered. *If so, why doesn't someone appear to check me out?*

The gates were locked. All was quiet. There was nothing to see, so she got back in the car and drove home.

Every day after work, she followed this same routine. On those days when she was not working, she spent long hours at the site. When Andy received a college scholarship, he moved out of the house and into a dorm. Departing with three duffel bags, a camera, and a computer slung over his back, this gave her more free time. So she took to bringing her lunch, parking under a willow tree, its droopy branches concealing the Ford. Occasionally, a black limousine would emerge from the woody grounds. Darkened windows shielded the occupant. The gates would part, and the sumptuous vehicle would glide past. Then the gates would close, and the splendid automobile would drive past the white colonial mansion, then the one of stone, then turn the corner.

A hush settled again over the scene, and Rose would be alone once more. Would Thomas's wife ever emerge from those gates? She couldn't stay in her house forever. Was there a back entrance somewhere? She slowly walked around the block, looking, and discovered that she couldn't penetrate the perimeter. Massive trees were thickly clustered, like a forest, and a formidable high wall of iron posts topped with barbed wire surrounded the luxurious estate.

Good, Rose thought, *it seems there is only one way in and out. I can't be in the front, back, and sides all at once.*

But then Rose almost missed her!

One day while dozing off, she sensed a small movement rather than actually witness a specific action. Startled, she sat up and wiped the spittle from her mouth just as Thomas's widow came out through a small door beside the gates, so well-conceived that Rose hadn't noticed it. A paisley scarf was wrapped around the woman's head. Concealing most of her body was a dark green parka like a man's hunting jacket. Two handsome but rowdy German shepherds strained at the leash, pulling at her as she turned to latch the gate. She seemed diminutive as a sparrow. *How remarkable*, Rose thought. *She is walking right here before me. How easily I can approach her! Unless those dogs attack me.*

Rose trembled. She felt as unprepared, as scared as when she had gone into labor with Andy.

But now, as then, she had little choice but to go ahead.

"Excuse me," Rose ventured.

Startled, the woman turned. The first thing Rose noticed was that the roots of her hair were gray while her shoulder-length tresses were dark brown. Instantly, Rose felt pity.

"I thought everyone had left," the woman said wearily. "If you're a reporter, I have nothing to say."

How would Rose identify herself? It hadn't occurred to her to lie.

Before she could find the words, any words, the woman whispered, "Wait. I know who you are. You are one of my husband's old lovers. The mother of his son."

Rose was aghast. Had she heard correctly? For once, Rose's chatty tongue was mute. Thomas *told* her about Andy? About *me*?

"How do you know?" Rose sputtered.

"Because I know the type of woman my husband was attracted to," the woman answered, her tone harsh, sardonic. "Pretty, very pretty, blond, slim, often foreign."

Rose thought, *Yes, a harsh tone, but also one of shame.*

"You can see I'm not his type. Short, dark, and not so slim, having borne three children. And he always told me he had one special one. And you are here. So you must be the one."

Her voice sounded tired and faintly bitter, though she was not disinclined to talk.

"May I walk with you?" Rose asked, trying desperately to grasp what the woman had just told her.

The woman nodded, and they strolled quietly along, each of them struggling to make sense of this unexpected encounter and Rose this shocking revelation. Out of the silence, the woman suddenly burst out with, "Thomas and I had three girls. He always wanted a son, but after those three, he stopped sleeping with me. He had other women, but I looked the other way for the sake of the girls."

Everything for our children, Rose thought sadly as she bobbed her head in agreement.

"It's a big house. We lived separate lives," Nina added, a small dip of her shoulders down the road. "But during one of our ghastly fights, he threw this at me, 'You're too weak to have sons, but I don't care. I already have a son.'

"After all he had put me through, I couldn't take those words, that degrading insult. That's when I shot him."

So she murdered Thomas because of me? Rose was stunned.

Wasn't his murder about embezzlement, fraud, and other criminal dealings? Rose had so many questions. If Thomas was so desperate for a son, why did he deny Andy's existence? *Maybe he wanted Andy to be legitimate*, Rose speculated. *Part of his family*. And black, not biracial, so there would be no scandal.

They continued walking along the leafy road, the dogs snooping, tugging, and whining. When they arrived at an old stone wall, the woman tied them to a tree, and the two women sat.

"My name is Nina," the woman offered. "But you must already know that."

Rose stammered, "Yes, of course. Your name was all over the news for weeks."

"Right," said Nina, "the murdering bitch."

"I never believed that," Rose said, "because I knew Thomas. I knew the cruelty he was capable of and how years of muffled anger and abuse could make someone do unimaginable things."

Rose, the hardworking, dedicated nurse, pretty, Irish, still charming in her forties; and Nina, the wealthy, attractive black wife living in the gorgeous home, with an extravagant lifestyle. They had both given their hearts to the same obscene man, a criminal. And each of them was now grieving over the misery he had caused them and their children.

As Rose looked into the face of the woman before her, she knew that although they had both suffered anguish and despair, Nina's pain was worse. She had three children; an unfaithful, thieving, and abusive husband; and had made a vow to keep the family intact at an appalling cost. And all those public events at which she had appeared on his arm, knowing their marriage was a fraud. How could she, Rose, be equally indignant before someone who had endured more humiliating betrayals than she?

They began to speak hesitantly then more assuredly.

"How are your daughters managing?" Rose ventured.

"Well, you know, it's a process. Therapists come to the house. At first, they wouldn't speak to me. Then they realized I'm their only parent. And they started to take a good look at their father. How old is your son? What is his name?" Nina asked.

Questions flew from her lips as if she had been waiting forever for the other's answers.

"Did Thomas visit you and Andy all these years? Did he acknowledge Andy? Does the boy look like my husband? Did Andy want to know his father?"

Then Rose.

"Did you ask if he ever contributed to Andy's support?"

"Did he tell you about me as well as about our son?"

Their mutual curiosity was relentless, insatiable.

With every word, every confidence, the women grew bolder.

"Way back, I didn't know about your son," Nina said. "But I knew there had been someone special who meant more to him than just the women he routinely played around with. He'd never give me a divorce. Too much bad publicity for his firm."

Rose and Nina had walked the road back and forth several times. The dogs were impatient, pulling on their leashes, howling for food. At the gate, Nina took Rose's hand. "Will you return?" Nina asked. "I'm now starting to take the dogs out for walks every day at this time."

Rose nodded. "Yes, yes, I will."

And so she did.

And as they talked and their stories unfolded, the two women became friends.

Thomas's colleagues provided Nina with superb legal defense. Most of them felt pity for Nina and were grateful the law had not also implicated them. Rose, her staunchest supporter and, by the look of the courtroom, her only friend, the others having deserted "the murdering bitch," sat quietly in the back whenever Nina's presence was required. A little under two years passed this way with many motions and appeals. Nina was at home on bail all that time, and the two women maintained their routine - walking the dogs, chatting, sharing.

The verdict was read on an ordinary October morning - innocent by reason of extreme mental cruelty. Nina was released for good. The case was no longer closely followed, and only a handful of reporters had been sitting on the back benches. Now they were sent off to pursue other assignments, and life was calm on Fairhaven Road. Nina's children were on their own now, married, working. At the time of the murder, there had been hysteria, rebellion, and a kind of madness in the house. But the therapists had done their work well, and now all three girls felt they were allowed to love their mother but also feel fondly toward their father if they chose although conditionally, considering the reality of the bad things he had done.

On one of their walks, the dogs especially rambunctious, their leashes tangled and caught around Nina's legs. The ground was slippery from heavy rains; and she fell hard, a nasty collapse, causing fractures in both ankles. Requiring ongoing medical care, Rose offered to move into the big Tudor house and take care of her. When

Nina politely demurred, "Oh, no, it's far too extravagant a favor," Rose insisted.

"I won't take no for an answer," she said and gave final notice to her job. After decades of diligent service, her leaving was sorrowful for all at the facility. The staff showed up with tears and flowers, speeches, and chocolates. Marion and Theresa in their wheelchairs and a dozen others in theirs planned a little skit of farewell in her honor. Rose, wearing a wreath of artificial flowers the women had woven in crafts class, sat in the center of the group. And of course, they ended their modest tribute with a chorus of "My Wild Irish Rose," setting an extravagant bouquet of deep red Crimson Glory roses in her lap.

That evening, Rose had qualms about her decision, unsure how she would feel living in Thomas's house. But when Rose wheeled Nina around in her wheelchair for a tour, Nina pointed out that Thomas's leather furniture and dark wood cabinets were gone. Even the books in the library and the shelves themselves had been dismantled. In their place, the bright flowery chintzes that Nina loved. So Rose easily buried her concerns, and their situation turned into a perfect arrangement.

Nina's healing took several months, and by the time she was strong on her own legs, the two women were inseparable.

"Rose, you simply must move permanently into one of the empty rooms here," Nina insisted. "Let's just keep on together. Housemates forever!"

And so it was decided.

Andy now lived in California but kept in close touch with his mother in New York and visited her often. A congenial young man, he was graciously accepting of their unique arrangement, gratified that his mother was living comfortably and not by herself. Nina's girls were also agreeable, relieved their mother would not be their responsibility. Since their geographical differences were significant, the adult children hardly ever met; but when they did, it was harmonious, even lively. Rose and Nina shared the hope that perhaps, eventually, they might all become good friends.

When they were finally up to it, Nina and Rose set off on various tours to foreign destinations. They enjoyed their lives as neither ever had before. Nightly, they reviewed with delight and a touch of relief that a woman doesn't need a man to have a good life.

"Hasn't ours been the most magnificently ironic story ever?" Nina asked. "Two strangers who formed an abiding friendship from lives of torment and struggle." And they clicked their glasses, sipped their champagne.

Yes, they had splendid times with their unexpected good fortune, and often on the streets of Paris or Rome, they felt they had attained an acceptable happiness.

But it was also true that Rose and Nina were haunted by regrets and lamented the barren, wasted middle years when a woman comes into her own fullness. Not knowing the kindness and thrill of a man's welcoming arms was an incalculable loss. And when those painful emotions arose in the midst of the luster and glory, the two women could easily turn brittle and pitiable, fearful as angels whose wings had been clipped on their journey down to earth, trusting some higher power would carry them down to a soft landing.

The Lost Child

I sat helplessly beside the bed of a woman who might or might not be my mother.

Unable to bear the silence and the specter of imminent endings, I held her wasted hand and asked, "Are you ready?"

"Are you?" she whispered.

But in truth, I couldn't be sure she had even spoken.

When I had entered her room, her eyes fluttered and looked directly at me. I assumed she smiled, but did she really? That faint quiver was likely only imagined, my longing so great for even the slightest reaction. But if she *had* indeed murmured those words, "Are you?" then at this time, in this place, this much I would now have - the long-awaited, coveted motherly concern for me.

It was not an easy sitting, this death vigil, as others called it. The turmoil of a lifetime's hopeless searching was squeezing my chest. I had never been so distressed, not even when I had faced down that man about to kill me with a cleaver.

I prayed for a personal reckoning with my mother. If this opportunity passed, my regret would be unbearable. Yet as urgent as was my need to speak, my enthusiasm was tamped down. Anger and disappointment rendered me almost incapable of reasonably confronting this challenge.

Talk to her, I thought. *Say it. Say "I love you" even if you have doubt. Say "I know you suffered." Say "You did a noble thing." Say it or you will spend the rest of your life as a useless drunk.*

Tell her that I now *know*. Ask for forgiveness for not knowing sooner.

Sorrowful, crucial minutes passed. I watched the clock's second hand go round and round until, at last, I managed a throaty, mangled gasp, a stricken "I'm sorry, Mother." But why was I sorry? Was I alone to atone for the way our lives took shape and finally turned out?

To my shame, I burst into tears, bawled like a baby, whimpering and hiccuping. Oh, the humiliation. My shirt was stained with tears.

Then as I sat there, wretched and confused, the veined and gnarled hand I was holding grew still.

Had she heard me? I looked into her face. Was it peaceful or sad, remorseful? Did she understand what it took for me to spit out even that meager "I'm sorry"? It wasn't "I love you," but it *was* something. It was now too late to know if she had been aware. From now on, I could only surmise, as I'd done my whole life.

As the afternoon sun grew weak in the sky, patients napped while nurses worked quietly at their desks. I quivered by her bedside, a sorry specimen of a man. I had botched it, my one last chance to straighten things out.

So with the day's last rays of sun dappling the tile floor and the city outside dim and low, I laid my head down on the bed next to her quiet body, my hand still in hers, taking time to remember.

First, I remembered yesterday. The train trip up from Philadelphia to Boston. It was during that ride when I considered yet again, in my middle age, that universal brotherhood was merely an illusion. Oh, sure, we're all flesh and blood. We all cry, hurt, know joy. But that's where we part ways. We don't all have the same opinions, not even remotely similar ones in many cases. And we certainly don't all have the same values. Not all of us cherish life nor honor death in a similar manner, for example. Some of us could point a gun at an innocent stranger and shoot. Others would step in front of that gun for the same stranger.

My train car was half full that weekday morning. Some passengers worked at laptops. Many played games on their phones. Some read newspapers or dozed. Within view were a dozen people, but not one glanced out the window. Not even for a moment. Several were children, irrevocably bound to their mechanical devices. Perhaps the landscape did not draw their interest on this dark day that could be depressing if one thinks of landscape only in terms of color.

Stop judging, I scolded myself. *Isn't it enough that I'm looking out the window? Well, no, it's not. With whom will I share this beauty if no one else sees it?* How odd that no one, no one at all other than me, was drawn to the melancholy landscape of the Connecticut coast, this sweet scene with its irresistible charm of inlets and coves, snug harbors and neat white fisherman's houses, and the train rumbling on. I was reminded of my journalism days in England when I rode the trains to and from meetings of Parliament, to villages in the Cotswolds, the Scottish Highlands, and along Ireland's rugged coastline, always looking out the window, trying to imagine how people lived, guessing their needs. And when returning home from a bloody war, how I wallowed in my sadness at knowing that these same unassuming, peaceful folks from these lovely places were likely both the soldiers and the victims in my stories.

As the train roared on, faster now - we were ten minutes behind schedule - my sight barely latched onto bits of roofs, steeples, porches, yards. There was a dog, then a man. Just as I conjured one narrative at a station stop, the train started up again, and the image disappeared.

Ah, now New Haven station. Young people departed; others boarded. I knew for a fact that the gothic gray stone spires and turrets and steeples of Yale University lay just beyond the immediate buildings. Not that I could see the actual structures, only the sharp thrust of intricate masonry into the sky. Yet they were certainly there.

Would I feel the same about my mother? Must I have evidence in hand to understand her experience, or would my knowledge of the war and its damaging consequences sufficiently fill in the blank spaces?

The scene outside changed. Houses and harbors were momentarily gone. Now I saw lonely fields waiting for spring. What I learned on this ride sounded so ordinary when I wrote it down, but here it was.

"One blink and the world turns." That was what I learned on this ride.

And this: "Know what is special when you are in it. Be aware that though the gift is merely bestowed, you are with blessings." "Remember this," I told myself when I arrived at the hospital with remorse at my elbow, self-pity in my heart. "The trick is that I must look up. I won't realize anything if I don't."

And with that thought, the train pulled into Back Bay station in Boston.

My earliest memory of my mother was her handing me over to a friendly neighbor woman who lived downstairs. And that hardly a memory, more of an impression. Later, in fact, I was told I cried mercilessly. She also handed over a bag of diapers and my favorite blanket with the dancing bears. Then she left me, never to return. It was in the aftermath of the Second Great War, and the world was heading toward the 1950s.

The neighbor's name was Mila, a good woman. She did the best she could for me. And told me later, "Yes, your mother cried as piteously as you at her leaving. And no, I had no idea of her plans. I don't even think Hannah was her real name. She just asked me to take care of you without another word. People did strange things in those years, for all kinds of reasons."

Mila's husband had been recently killed in a motorcycle accident, leaving her with two young ones to raise, Edith and Karl. We were never hungry although an occasional meal was leaner than we would have liked, but I remember always having a safe bed with her own kids close by. It wasn't a bad way to become an adult, but at age eighteen, I took off, determined to become an investigative reporter, someone with access to government files, to find out what happened to my mother.

It was an uneasy quest, with my constant doubts, my outrageous arrogance. I began to compare my life to others and found mine wanting, never knowing either my mother or father. I thought I understood others' joys and pain, but really I had no idea what their personal journeys involved. I continued to litter my life with misconceptions and mistakes, refusing to accept that nothing was ever as it appeared. But it was a time like all those after any war. My search would be arduous, with the likely result of failure. People changed their names. Families were separated, lost, or resettled. Their homes and towns were destroyed. I was just one of many casualties of war. But it was my great misfortune to think that I was unique.

Neither drink nor work nor women could make up for not having parents. I kept returning to Mila, my sole connection to my mother, who lived in the same flat her whole life. Once again, that patient woman and I reviewed our information. We both assumed the name Hannah, by which Mila knew her, was invented. She hadn't given me up for adoption or left me at the door of a church. She hadn't sold me. No. She handed me over to Mila wrapped in my favorite blanket. She had made a choice, conceived a plan, and followed through.

Why?

"Your mother never told me anything," Mila repeated for the thousandth time. "The war was over, but maybe she was doing some dangerous work. Maybe your knowing about her would endanger you. What if she were working for the resistance, still active, or doing secret work for the Allies? So much was still going on in those days with the Russians and the Brits and the camps and the trials. Who knew? It broke her heart to leave you, I can tell you that. I only knew she was alive by envelopes that would occasionally appear with money for your care. Always from a different city. And always tucked inside was a brief note, 'Give my beloved Max a kiss from his mother,' year after year, the same words. The envelopes stopped coming after you left, indicating clearly that she must have kept track of you. But that's all I know."

After I searched for years and the name Hannah from a certain town in Germany didn't reveal itself in any way, I realized that tracking her would be impossible. Like so many others, she was a missing person, vanished, erased. And I was a lost child.

To whom did I belong? It was unacceptable to consider myself an anonymous soul walking the earth with no attachments or loyalties except to Mila.

When my two marriages failed, I wasn't surprised. I had never given either woman her fair share. I didn't understand a woman's needs nor they mine.

"You have no emotions inside that body of yours," Gerda, my first wife hurled as she slammed the door behind her.

"You live in your shell, like a big turtle. Your head sticks out, but no one can get past your hard casing," Elsa, my second wife, hurled as she zipped shut her suitcase. I was loath to take on a third, both these women with the same complaint. Why would another feel differently? Besides, I had professional assignments all over Europe and the United States. Better not to be married with the itinerant life of a roving journalist. Moreover, neither wife liked it much when I spent evenings after work in bars, where my mates called me "the friendly alcoholic," the guy who could hold his liquor when he was working, the guy who took the most dangerous assignments. The men I met there and the women too provided good enough attachments to satisfy my meager emotional needs.

On a muggy Philadelphia afternoon in summer, it happened. I found a clue. Had I been less vigilant, it would have sailed right by me. Of all places, this remarkable moment occurred almost incidentally, in the records department of city hall. I was researching local anti-Semitic crimes and how they were spreading throughout major US cities. I had developed a nose for sniffing out vague possibilities, for successfully chasing markers and signals others ignored. I had a hunch about this particular story, and since I always follow my hunches, I found a desk, spread out the material, and began to take notes.

After the war, select groups or persons were formed undercover to ferret out German war criminals and bring them to trial either in Israel or before the World Court. These were unknown to the public and operated in a dark web of secret linkages. I now read about an important case that had been settled recently. A war criminal captured in Paraguay was tried and sentenced to death in Israel. Although mentioned somewhat mysteriously in only the vaguest terms, it seemed that three women were responsible for the man's capture. All the women were over seventy, an unusual age for this task. The writer of the article surmised that all must have come from small towns in Germany because the man on trial had been tracked to an obscure village. Those three must have been purposely assigned, being especially knowledgeable about rural life, local geography, and certain tactical methods known to dwellers of those locales - hiding places, farm life, and such.

That last piece fit the meager facts I possessed. My mother had lived in a small village in western Germany, outside of Koblenz. She would have been over seventy. Yet why tie my mother to such an undertaking? Such a life? Still, my journalistic instincts flared. The odds were long and shaky, but if the leads were strong, the rewards could be stunning.

Huddled into myself, I clung to the table as if I were facing imminent peril. The very notion of my mother as a freedom fighter, a spy, was absurd. Or was it? But I was desperate. Any nugget that fit the demographics on hand set me on fire, though I knew my mother could have been anywhere in the world. She could even be dead. Nevertheless, I homed in on this small scrap of information.

Immediately, I flew to Vienna, then Rome, then Paris, hunting down these hidden enclaves and organizations that engaged in tracking down the war's evil criminals. Some were known to the UN, others only to Israeli Intelligence where I had a contact or two. I climbed countless stairs to the top floors of drab apartment buildings, knocked on grimy doors in office basements, a mere number half-scratched on a glass door. After two full years of searching, I was still stymied. Frustration slipped into despair. In all my encounters, I was given only blank stares, a handshake, and led politely to the door. No one anywhere knew anything. I couldn't pry loose the slightest opening.

By now, I had given up drinking and the low nightlife found in bars. If my mother were alive, I would not face her as a wastrel. I tried to imagine what in my mind constituted the perfect child, the dutiful child, the good son. But what did that consist of? What kind of son would my mother have wanted to raise?

It also occurred to me that no one trusted me or ever would. I didn't look like a Jew, with my fair hair and soft gray eyes and height, very tall, towering over my dark-haired Jewish friends.

It was time to give up, to quit my wandering, to settle down in a cozy town somewhere and get a simple job.

Then, in a totally unexpected manner, an acquaintance gave me renewed hope. He didn't realize this, of course, unaware as he was of my grievous past. Exhausted from a long day, this fellow journalist and I schmoozed together in a deserted newsroom. With the blue neon lights blinking and the hour late, I had offered some homespun philosophy as his head collapsed onto the desk, his scrawny arms making a pillow. Was he listening or sleeping?

I crossed my ankles on top of the table and fiddled with a toy kaleidoscope left by one of the reporter's children. As I twirled the cylinder in my fingers, I mused out loud. "Retrieving memory is like squinting through this kaleidoscope," I said. "Give the tube a shake, and an infinite number of patterns are formed. A mosaic of perfect symmetry. But give it another shake, and a new design appears. None is ever duplicated as with memory."

My pal hadn't moved. I continued, talking to myself out loud.

"We recall moments of memory differently at different times," I said, shaking the kaleidoscope. "Nothing is predictable, but alluring possibilities exist."

As I stood and readied to leave, I heard a very tired but clearly audible "Bullshit." Maybe my pal was listening after all, or maybe he was just being a wise guy. It didn't matter. Just saying the words aloud - "Possibilities exist" - gave me the renewed vigor I needed to continue my search.

I returned to Vienna and told my story about looking for my mother to anyone who would listen.

Then one day, in still another drab, monotonous office, a dignified, gray-haired older man received me from behind his desk. An Israeli flag stood in the corner behind him.

"Make yourself comfortable," he said. "Now tell me from the beginning."

As I leaned forward into my words, earnest and tearful, the man sat back and listened carefully. Brows furrowed, lips pursed, hands folded on the desk, he looked just like what he was. A tired, sad fighter for Jewish justice. He asked no questions. But when I was done and wrung out and the man had taken my measure, his brows relaxed, his hands unclasped.

"I know a woman like this. She may well be your mother," the man told me. "But she's old and left our service a few years ago."

What is he saying? Here, now, these words? My nails dug into my flesh. I tried to keep my breathing even.

"She came to us as a young woman. Her eyes were soft, like yours - I remember that. She told us her story. After the war, a half-dozen Germans were testing their revolvers in a field, just fooling around. Her husband was walking by on his way home. They asked,

'Are you a Jew?' To which ridiculously, naively, he admitted 'Yes,' thinking, Why not? The war was over. What harm now is there to the truth? Well, he found out. They stood him in front of a tree, trying to shoot off his hat. One of them was drunk and missed and shot him in the head, leaving him to die there in the field. Later, in the village, these louts laughed about it over their beer and schnitzel.

"A friend of your mother's overheard and told her what had happened. It was soon after that night that she came to work for us. She wanted revenge. But she also sought justice. There was some vague mention of a baby, but it was so long ago I don't recall the details. Everyone who works with us tells a monstrous story of some kind.

"She stayed with us her whole life, unearthing evil men, the ones who escaped, working with lawyers who fought for decency and virtue." Sweating, I sobbed openly before this kind man who reached out and placed his hand on mine. "Don't be ashamed to weep," he said tenderly. "We Jews do nothing but shed tears. The oceans are full of them."

"Give me a day and let me see what I can find out," he added, gently resting his arm on my shoulder.

A week later, I was on the train to Boston.

The name given to me by the old man was Sophie Schroeder, likely the last one she had used. He also gave me the name of the Boston hospital in which she lay dying. So now I found myself passing charming towns and villages, the waters and boats of Long Island Sound, the coves and the houses with front porches, and those spires of Yale University. Fidgeting and restless, I arrived at Back Bay Station where I got off and walked to the hospital.

A formidable, sprawling brick complex loomed before me. Somewhere in there, in a cubicle of a room, a tiny woman with a magnificent heart was about to die. Was there time enough left for us?

I made my way up in the elevator and stood outside her door, number 45, shifting back and forth, smoothing my hair back like a kid. What would I find after more than fifty years?

A slight push opened the door. There was a table holding liquids and lotions, a water jug, a pair of glasses. A sheet was pulled up to the woman's chin. A pair of closed eyes and fluffy white hair were visible. I had no photos, no letters of corroboration as to her identity, only the words of that old man from Vienna. As I stepped inside, a ghastly thought suddenly ripped through my brain.

Was this really my mother? Out of misplaced kindness, had the old man sought to appease my aching soul with a lie, thinking it the moral, right thing to do, putting at last another suffering Jewish heart to rest?

I sat now in a chair beside the bed. Gently, I took her hand, and that is how we lingered until the sun set. I could see immediately that any words concerning the past would have to remain in the past. There was no more talk left in her. And what was left in me? Loss, and regret. And the death of hope for finding redemption. And yet, I said it, "I'm sorry, Mother," for a thousand reasons I would never understand and just as many that I did.

I picked up her glasses and held them to my heart, whispering the words I feared most but could no longer hold back.

"Are you ready?" I asked.

"Are you?" I thought she murmured.

But in truth, I wasn't sure if she had actually said those words or I had only fancied she had.

"Doctor, You're Joking"

"Oh, go ahead, Emma, do it," my best friend Anna urged over our arugula salads. We had just started our third diet of the month.

These past two years, I had stood before the mirror playing with my face, pulling cheeks this way and that, pinning up my hair, then letting it down, lowering eyelids, then opening wide, all to create a face without pouches under my eyes, a face ten years younger.

Despite many positive boosters lifted from books, slogans, friends, billboards - "Your face reflects your life. Celebrate every line," "Your face reflects your worldly wisdom. Show it off" - such words did not move me.

Was this issue about self-love? Or should I think of it this way - facial improvement as a step toward a more positive attitude for myself and my life?

By the time we finished lunch, Anna had grown weary of my complaints, and I had agreed to make an appointment with a plastic surgeon.

I was full on into thinking about this adventure as I crossed Park Avenue at Seventy-First Street, searching for the numbers on these elegant buildings, mindful that alert doormen might think me an unwelcome intruder, poking around. Ah, there! The shiny brass plaque with his name inscribed in elegant cursive and underneath, in bold, "Plastic and Reconstructive Surgery."

As I gripped the hand-carved mahogany door handle in the shape of a ram's horn, I thought, *This pull is acceptable on a private bank*. But in this venue, my dollars would have paid for such a feature. Smooth as a violin casing, it was set into a stainless-steel door with beveled glass inserts, the work of a talented craftsman hired by an expensive designer. All for a doctor catering to a select clientele.

"No charge cards," I had been told.

Carefully, I pulled. Then I was in.

Oh, the absurd attention I had given to choosing a blouse, the length of my skirt, even a trip to the hairdresser for a quick blow-dry.

But then I was going to meet a man who would change my life.

I must remember to call my sister and apologize for criticizing her last year when she told me she had undergone a Botox treatment. "Ridiculous, inauthentic, be who you are. Age gracefully, naturally," I had argued. "No aids or supports." But Anna had changed my mind. And here I was, overpaying but willing. After all, it was only this one time, this $400 in cash for an initial consult, just to see what he said.

Admit it, Emma. Admit why you were so easily convinced.

Your new pen pal from the West Coast was coming for a visit. He wanted to meet you after all the "remarkable, stupendous" work you did drawing those cartoons for his latest book. And all was done long distance, by computer. He called you "keenly talented," and after you sent him the photo that Anna took, the one you forwarded after two hours spent on twenty others - and the final choice a three-quarter view in partial shadow - he added, "Beautiful." Although he admitted to looking me up before offering me the contract and knows how old I am. He being seven years my senior, cheek pouches might be something that wouldn't surprise him. *Ridiculous*, I scolded myself, *wanting to offer this man you have never met the suggestion of what you looked like ten years ago. What if after your meeting, you find him patronizing, self-serving? Or, horrors, what if he has a wrinkled neck or a floppy tummy, being seven years older?*

"Hi there," Perky Tara chirped.

I looked for a receptionist's desk but saw only a single slab of highly polished black marble shaped like the prow of a ship. Was she even twenty-four? Hair swept up with the figure of a model about to take her turn on a fashion runway.

"Hi yourself," I replied in my most perky voice.

The three others seated and waiting looked up, startled. Was I too perky?

Here, I was soon told, we who sit reverently are called "clients," not patients. An ether of hallowed deference surrounded us, so unlike the mood of other doctors' offices, the distant memories of my obstetrician's waiting room filled with wailing infants, mothers shushing, big-bellied gals complaining to the office staff about sore backs and swollen ankles. Not perky Tara but reliably fiftyish Helen who would not commit the unforgivable sin of being more beautiful than the patients.

"May I use the bathroom?" I requested after I filled out the forms with the Mont Blanc fountain pen and leather clipboard, not the usual Bic attached by a string to a battered wood board. In this office you asked for permission - not just "Where is it?" but "May I *use* it?"

Aromatic with potpourri, I thought the choice of scent, Cedar Shavings in a Rainforest, was a bit suffocating. The sink was hand-painted with pink peonies and shiny green leaves, the same design on the back of the toilet. I gently flushed the real gold handle, with the same scrolled design as the matching gold faucets. I expected Porthault linen towels but was surprised to find paper ones that I had seen in Gracious Home - white camellias winding around silver latticework.

When I emerged, two new "clients" beyond the original three, who were nowhere in sight, were focused on their paperwork. I started adding and multiplying. Cash only, $400 per consultation, ten minutes each, patients seen all day on Tuesdays and Thursdays.

My pen pal had called last night.

He had asked, "Are you a sissy on the open road?"

Why did he ask? Did he have plans?

So I surrendered to the lure of Narcissus, vainglorious images, and false gods of beauty.

A reward for living a mindful life. Or a frivolous whim? Think what you will. But a choice for self-love.

A pair of camelback sofas in deep rose velvet faced each other on opposite walls, and between them was a round brass drum table trimmed with the same black marble as Tara's counter. Splayed open was a copy of *New York Magazine*, noting "Best Doctors in New York 2012," revealing the page of the doctor right now listening to a patient's woes behind exam room 3. Line drawings of the Greek architectural orders hung on dove gray walls. A pair of black mahogany Regency armchairs with seats of mauve damask, gold gilt on tips of arms and feet.

One was occupied by the lone man among us. Handsome, elegant, sixtyish, expensive suit, silver hair, jowls in place, smooth forehead, I guessed. Some problem under his clothes or facial maintenance, those mandatory touch-ups now and then?

A young Manhattan society matron in the other chair, tan in her white lace sleeveless dress, looked like she hadn't eaten yet this year.

"Ms. Ransoff," Tara whispered.

I was surprised they used last names, such clients desirous of anonymity. Also, I was accustomed to nurses wearing scrub suits and bellowing out your name and glad you were to hear it after an hour of waiting. But not here. I smiled at perky Tara as she passed me into the hands of Lovely Lisa, a young belle of about thirty wearing a straight skirt with a flared hemline, tight tank top, and backless mules that slapped against her heels as she led the way for the final trek down the hall, both sides wallpapered in the famous Angelo Donghia pattern of small circles and squares.

The decorator had also been busy in the doctor's personal office.

Slate blue suede walls, matching blue suede on sofas, detailed mahogany cabinetry with volumes bought by the foot and interspersed with the requisite brass obelisks and ivory carvings. On the antique desk were three worn leather books stacked at just the correctly casual angle - *Ancient Greek Government, The Clavichord in Shakespeare's Times, Epicurus* - the magnificence of an exalted eminence.

His chair was a high-backed piece of furniture, a throne of hand-stitched leather. A big man, this surgeon. Lovely Lisa dared to sit there asking me medical questions I had already answered on those five pages I had filled out with the gold pen.

Lovely Lisa then led me into an exam room as large as my own bedroom in which I have a desk, an armoire, a chest, a computer center, twelve feet of bookcases, and a king-sized bed. I waited, expecting a tall, handsome fellow who read *Epicurus* dressed in surgical scrubs, starched white coat thrown over, a harried demeanor, so many patients outside his door.

Footsteps, a flurry, and the knob turned. In a heartbeat, a short, tiny man was seated on a stool ten inches from my face. So fast did he show up that I instinctively pulled back. Did he think me rude?

What did I see?

I saw a dark-blue suit with cream pinstripes, wide lapels; one of Armani's subtly flamboyant styles - gold cuff links with his initials in block letters and a red-striped silk tie knotted at the throat so beautifully it seemed the designer himself had attended to it; gorgeously streaked gray hair (*Who does his hair?*); and glasses that must have cost as much as a dermabrasion.

A weak handshake.

"So, my dear, are we here for a little freshening up?"

I looked at Lovely Lisa. Did he even glance at those five pages? "No, not a freshening up. I'm fresh enough. Crows' feet at the eyes and laugh lines at the mouth don't bother me. Just these small pouches on the cheeks, Doctor. A small needle injection, please, to deflate their power. Simple, easy, and I will be gone. See, like this," I said as I made a slight pull left and right. "Not a facelift, just this very small pull left and right."

"Sorry, can't do that," he said. "Fat over the bone, nothing to do for that."

"What?" I said. "Doctor, you're joking. You're board-certified in two surgical specialties! You transform bodies, a sorcerer who mends and repairs!"

So straightforward to reduce those pouches - a half-hour's work. I was sure of it. Perhaps he misunderstood.

"Just the cheeks, please."

"Sorry," he answered, rising, hand on the doorknob. "Come back when you want to freshen up a bit."

Lovely Lisa turned and followed him out, Manolo Blahniks flapping.

Did the boss pay for her clothes? Were they a legitimate office expense?

I turned over my $400 to Perky Tara. Yes, I was defeated, dismayed, yet more grateful than despairing, relieved as I was not to go under the knife of a short man in a fancy suit who had books on his desk with fake fronts that a stranger had bought for him.

There was other business to attend to before meeting my pen pal. First, to the ophthalmic surgeon for the tightening of a tendon on a weakened eye muscle. Then the colonoscopy, and finally, the abdominal hernia repair. Four months' worth of attention before he arrived.

The eye surgeon's office door was one of many down a long hallway of a standard, gray concrete medical office building. Its glass window was stamped with his name in printed capital letters, like that of a private detective or a dentist.

A sheetrock partition with a hole cut out for the receptionist held a shelf containing business cards and pamphlets on eye care. Also on the Formica counter were two wooden clipboards with Bic pens dangling by a string.

Aurora shouted, "I'll be right with you. Four phones going here."

I sat comfortably on one of a dozen chairs, all surely from Office Depot and upholstered in dark brown Naugahyde. On the walls, two prints. One of the Eiffel Tower at night, one of the Empire State Building at dawn.

Eventually, I was put in a small exam room by Aurora herself - table, chair, cabinet, computer on a swivel table. And on the wall was a giant poster of an eye, arrows and lines pointing to its various components - cornea, lens, pupil, and so on, each part in a different color. It was a frightening thing to think of knives making incisions in those delicate structures. As I turned my back to it, realizing I was wearing my usual black pants and black turtleneck, not a skirt with a sexy swirl, there was a discreet knock. The doctor appeared - short, pepper-and-salt beard, and twinkling eyes. Some mischief there. A firm handshake. He wore rumpled khakis, a plaid tie, no jacket. Examining my eyes, he turned my head this way and that. Then he asked, "As long as we are correcting your eye muscle, did you ever think about taking care of that puffy part over your cheeks? I can do that for you at the same time. You'll look much better."

"You can do that?" I shouted joyfully. "Reduce the pouches? Isn't that fat over the bone? I was told it couldn't be done."

"Of course, it can be done," he said, chuckling. "Who told you it couldn't? Some fancy doc over on Park Avenue?"

"Deal," I said. "Go for it."

Yes.

The eager face of my new friend popped up, fantasies churning. So *this* is Emma, he would think. He might even say it out loud.

So now, after all the feverish doubts and grumbling, I was huddled in the back seat of a taxi at five in the morning. The skies were gloomy with rain. Fog obscured the road, dimming the trees. The driver was a Pakistani learning English. He asked, "Miss, do you think I said 'Good morning' and 'How are you doing today?' in an acceptable manner?"

And I thought, *I hope the doctor had a good night's sleep and nothing to drink but coffee.*

We were driving to my appointment with the surgeon. Anna would pick me up later. But now I reviewed the plan, reexamined my doubts. What if I found fault with my new, irreversible look? Who was the French poet who first said, "The eyes are the windows to your soul?" Wouldn't smoothing out cheekbones affect the eyes, altering who I am? When painting a portrait, even a tiny brushstroke is transformative.

I thought of my surgeon, who was even now grabbing some breakfast and driving out into the stormy morning. I thought of the words of the small man in the fancy Armani suit - "Can't do it" - with not a word of explanation from Lovely Lisa as we walked back down the hallway, her shoes padding along. Perhaps a procedure that every so often produced an unsuccessful result or something to do with fees? Ah, well. I looked out the rainy window, conjuring up my reliable bravado. While I knew full well that the character of the tormented Narcissus is the bread and butter of every plastic surgeon's practice.

This venture, I decided, was the ultimate act of self-love.

Was that a good thing or a bad thing?

As the driver approached the hospital, looming out of the ghostly fog two lights ahead, I pictured my doctor in his unpressed khakis, by now at the hospital, changing into surgical scrubs and waiting for me.

I can't do this, I thought. *It's too indulgent. I'm too nervous, fearful. I'm not beautiful enough, not rich or thin or good enough. I don't* deserve this luxury. *This kind of thing is for others, not for me. Hush.* I admonished myself. *You are now only one light away from the out-patient surgery entrance. Why devise scenarios that obstruct? You made a mindful decision. You chose a fine doctor. This choice will be to your benefit. Do not think of it as a selfish act. Think of it as something that will enhance your life, your attitude. And you can then give that gift of yourself more joyfully to others.*

Slivers of dawn were just now emerging between the murky, wet trees. I began rummaging in my purse for the fare when we arrived at my destination, brightly lit up in huge red neon letters.

I was ready, but as to how this day would turn out and whether or not I would be a different person after, I had no idea.

Coming Home

"I'm bringing a special date home for the weekend," I told my mother, calling her from my college dorm room.

A feathery gasp. Silence. Clearly, she was unprepared.

I knew her sharp mind was bleeding for a reason, any reason, racing along like a river undammed.

But not fast enough.

"Why don't you both come just for the day?" she asked.

My old ambivalence erupted. I was young, crazy mad in love. Resentment settled like bilge, and my toes curled under. It was a comment I had heard before, always that same directive - "Meet a nice man, and bring him home for dinner, but don't stay overnight. Later, maybe, after you're married." Never in my life did my mother ever say why, though I made plenty of guesses.

Brian was eager.

"Julie, honey, it's time to meet your parents," he said with a sly look and a mischievous tap on my knee. "And besides, we're going right by your house driving up from Baltimore, a perfect overnight stop. Gives us a good chance to get to know each other. Don't you want that too?" He was puzzled, concerned.

Could I say no? Like my mother, excuses ran wildly through my brain but none rose to my lips. And not a one that would make any sense and not cause me shame.

"Just around that corner," I pointed. "Take a left."

Brian would see for himself. He's smart. He noticed the details.

The driveway of my childhood home came into view. I'm not sure why, but now that I'm an adult, every time I came home, my heart fluttering like a trapped butterfly, I feared that the house would look different. Maybe the beautiful pink roses were torn out, or the shutters painted yellow without anyone asking me, or maybe an entirely different family would live inside. But there, in front of us, was the familiar gray clapboard, the white shutters, and black doors. The widow's walk around the third floor was freshly painted, and the scarlet rhododendrons along the wall were blooming their heads off. I could see into the corner of the backyard where the gray Adirondack chairs - to match the siding - with their slatted backs and wide armrests, had been put out.

Stepping out of the car, Brian stretched his long legs and took my hand. "I can smell dinner from here," he said. "Lucky me. Maybe it's Eileen's fricassee and noodles that you're always talking about."

"Be sure to come through the front door," my mother had warned as we hung up the phone. "I'll be waiting for you there. Don't go through the kitchen."

I knew that order would be issued. I had expected it. Meet her before we met the housekeeper and in the living room, most impressive. I also knew that she had shut down the spontaneity of a first meeting.

So of course I did the opposite. Brian and I ran through the side door into the kitchen - right into Eileen's loving arms where she was waiting, working over the stove, looking for us.

Dear Eileen, almost an older sister, came to live with us from Ireland when she was seventeen. Even after twenty years, she looked the same in her pale-blue house dress and ruffled apron. Her raven hair had been teased into a short bouffant. Touching the corners of her wide smile were tiny creases of concern. After all, her favorite child was bringing home a serious boyfriend.

Nothing had changed in our kitchen, so obviously dated from the fifties - an off-white polka-dotted linoleum floor, white metal cabinets. Next to the fridge was a black-and-white speckled top on the Formica table, banded around the edges with aluminum trim like in those old television shows *I Love Lucy* and *The Golden Girls*.

"Eileen," I said. "Here he is." I smiled, urging Brian forward.

She was shy in his company, six feet one, handsome, and spirited. His presence filled the kitchen with the energy of a young racehorse.

"Julie has told me how special you are," Brian said as he lifted Eileen off the floor in a hearty hug.

"I didn't know you would be so tall," she said, blushing, her wooden spoon waving above her head.

Brian and I dashed over to the stove, lifting pot covers, inhaling garlic and onions as the white wine gently disappeared into the creamy sauce. Eileen had quietly stepped back, watching Brian, taking his measure. When we were done fussing, I snatched a Coke and sat at the table, beaming as Eileen laughed at something Brian had whispered. Something about "Did you make your special fricassee just for me?"

"You should go see your mother," Eileen prompted, just as my mother walked into the kitchen.

"I heard the commotion," my mother snapped. "I was waiting for you in the living room."

Had Brian noticed her tone?

My mind was conjuring up possible excuses. It hadn't happened yet, but it would, later.

We walked down the hall, passing the dining room table set for dinner. My father wasn't home at this early afternoon hour. *Thank you, Eileen*, I whispered to myself, *for taking the plastic covers off the sofas*.

The questions began. It was not a conversation but an inquisition. Yes, my mother was concerned with my well-being, but still…

"What year are you in law school? Where do your parents live? What does your father do? Does your mother work?"

Oh, for heaven's sake, I thought. *She appears to be such a snob.* "*What does your father do?*" *Is she serious? He has only been in her company for five minutes. Either he'll survive the grilling or not,* I told myself. *I can't do a thing about her.*

"Second year, Philadelphia, an accountant. And no, she's a painter. Her workshop is at home," he offered.

Brian winked at me. He nodded in the direction of the stiff rose- and ivory-silk-striped Napoleonic sofa on which no one ever sat and which an antique dealer called "rare," and smiled again. I calmed down. Poised and sophisticated, he would not be unnerved by her interrogation.

As they continued the conversation, my mother suddenly appeared to be flirting! Laughing timorously and putting forth a facade of class and motherhood. Men found that demeanor attractive; women found it wanting. What did Brian think?

"Oh, we know people in Philadelphia. Do you know the Silvas, the Jeremy Silvas?" she asked.

Unable to handle these pretentious questions, I left them together and went into the kitchen to keep Eileen company as her hands performed three tasks at once.

"He's quite dashing, isn't he?" she ventured.

"Sure is," I began as the door flew open, letting in both the wind and my father, flushed and earnest, stumbling over the threshold in his haste. As I hugged him fiercely, I knew that the mood in the living room would soon shift dramatically.

"An old client just as I was leaving," he offered. "Where's this special Brian fellow you've been talking about?"

He rushed ahead of me, so keen was he to meet this "special fellow" of mine.

"Brian, welcome," he said as Brian stood up. "Can I get you something to drink? You've had a long drive. Sit, sit." The air in the room relaxed. My father crossed his legs. Brian sat back in his chair. They grinned at each other. And as they chatted easily back and forth,

I abruptly became aware of the gorgeous purple and white lilacs in a crystal vase that Eileen had placed on a side table.

During dinner, did Brian notice when my mother said to my father, "Dan, you have some sauce on your shirt?"

Did he see my mother's glacial expression when my father asked, "How long will you be staying?"

After a friendly evening of social exchanges, my mother said, "Brian, let me show you where you are sleeping." She led him to one of the four bedrooms on the second floor, the one between mine and hers, at the end of the short hall from my father's.

As they toured the bathroom and found the towels, the small comforts, that place in my heart that was agitated and worried began to expand. *Maybe this time they will be careful*, I prayed. *Maybe this time they will be extra quiet.*

After my mother sorted us out and after the house was peaceful and calm, I fell asleep in my childhood bed.

And woke at four. Startled, waiting. An hour later, the familiar sounds began…feet running along the hallway, a toilet flushing, a door closing. I lay dead as a stone, straining to listen. A scurrying? A rustling? Did Brian hear? Was he opening his door, peeking out to see if the household was in need or waking up early?

But I knew, in fact, it was my father scampering into my mother's room so that when we awoke, it would look as if he had been there all night. Since this only happened when my sister or I brought home a date, my father had forgotten previous admonitions from my mother about discretion. He also forgot to close his own bedroom door so anyone using the bathroom could see his bed had been slept in.

The next morning, there were chatty farewells.

"Drive safely. Call when you get there. Goodbye, goodbye" as my parents escorted us out the front door. When we were on our way, Brian remarked, "Well, that went well, don't you think?" Since he didn't ask any personal questions, I decided he hadn't noticed, or was he being prudent?

With my parents having separate bedrooms, would he think they didn't love each other or were not romantically inclined to be together? Or worse, was he fearful that we would have a similar arrangement, the two of us in a marriage without physical affection?

It isn't my fault, I wanted to tell him. *Don't ask me. I don't know.* I could not remember their ever sharing a bed. Even on vacation in a hotel, they reserved twin beds. No, I never asked them about it. How could I? Would you ask if they were your parents?

I could only pray that if he was thinking about this, he would also know that it would never happen to us.

Brian and I did marry, sleeping in the same bed our entire marriage. We never spoke about my parents' arrangement; but many years later, while visiting my brother Ryan, watching our children dive into his swimming pool, I brought up the subject.

"Did you ever think about Mom and Dad and their separate bedrooms?" I began.

Ryan looked over, shifting in his chair, dubious at discussing such private issues with his sister. He was particularly unhelpful with subjects of a personal nature.

"Maybe he snored," I began. "Maybe he was a restless sleeper."

"Maybe she snored," he countered. "Maybe she was the one who was restless."

"Maybe one of them didn't like sex," I pushed. "Or there could have been some physical issue?"

"Maybe, maybe, maybe," Ryan answered. "We'll never know."

"Well, think some more, and we'll talk again." He frowned and threw a ball to his little girl.

But I never stopped speculating. Sometimes my sympathies were with my father, other times, my mother. Who was deprived? Who was inflicting the emotional damage? The sadness of it, the pity of it, haunted me all my adulthood. Was it mine and Ryan's fault? Was this mystery destined to remain forever clouded in conjecture?

More than once, I was on the verge of talking about it with Brian; but my unease, deep and profound, held me back. Surely he would have gentle words but likely no answers, so I chose to bury this issue somewhere dark and hidden.

As I passed from young adulthood to middle age, my thoughts became more, not less, despairing. In this center of my life, when my folks were old, my mother's sister-in-law visited. The two women sat on the porch while I lay in the hammock, a distance apart. If I hadn't been nearby, if I hadn't been casually dozing, my parents would have remained an enigma to me forever. In any case, it seemed, entirely by chance, I overheard this:

"Look, Angie, how beautifully Julie and Ryan have grown up," my mother began.

She then took a deep sigh, paused, started up again. "I did the right thing. Remember when the doctor told me I shouldn't have other children after that disastrous C-section with Julie? Well, I couldn't let her be an only child, could I? So now I have my Ryan and they have each other."

She rested her head, sipped her tea.

"But after that, the doctor laid down the law," she recalled, her voice edged with sadness rather than grievance.

"This is your life," he said. "You were plain lucky. Don't have any more children."

Sudden tears soaked my cheeks. The dispiritedness I had harbored for so many years fell into a deep crevasse. Now what rose up teetering on its dangerous edge was the dreadful horror of insight.

The pathos of the physical aspects was apparent, but how had they coped emotionally? In this small town where they were known by everyone. My mother's character tinged with bitterness; my father working fourteen hours a day? I thought of the photos when they were young and beautiful. I thought of my husband from whom I could hardly be separated a single night.

Finally, I shared with Brian my confusion and regret at not understanding the simmering thread of connection between my mother and father. His kind expressions of understanding were consoling, but I was still at a loss regarding my parents' choices. The sorrow hung firm, failing to dissolve or even subside.

Miss Charlotte's Garden

The property extended beyond our sight, but if you measured it by the spot where neighbor Munson's property began, it consisted of about a dozen acres. The small part we *could* see, the part we *came* to see, were the gardens surrounding the snug old farmhouse on a hill. Folks said the house dated from about 1750, one of the oldest around here. Some say it once sat on Mohegan or Pequot Indian land.

Surrounding the white colonial homestead, spreading far off to a grassy knoll, were gardens and meadows of riotous, savage beauty. Picture the color red. What is red? Cerise, mauve, scarlet, claret, carnelian, burgundy, crimson, pink. Then imagine the variations of whites and blues and greens. Now you know what we saw looking into Miss Charlotte's garden, an acre of splendor, farther even with a pair of binoculars.

All planted and cared for by Miss Charlotte's hand.

In early April, when the winter freeze had begun its thaw and the sun stayed longer in the sky, folks all around called out to each other - on the phone, at the diner, in the post office, the shops.

"It's time! Charlotte's garden! Let's go!"

Spring had arrived after the long, harsh winter. The tiny yellowish-green shoots were appearing on the trees, eagerly hatching along their branches. Everyone piled into their cars, their pickups, revved up their cycles. Even old man Granger sat high on the creaky tractor he called Maude. They came from up and down the valley in this fertile Connecticut farm country, even from two hours west into neighboring New York - all ages, city folks, country folks. Two buses were taken up by the ladies' garden club in town. In fact, anyone who had ever heard about Miss Charlotte and her garden came to look, to be astonished.

Viewing was most crowded on Sunday afternoons. Church in the morning then over to Miss Charlotte's garden before the family dinner. Many came regularly every Sunday, knowing how a garden changes and not wanting to miss anything new.

First to unfurl were the flowering trees. Ornamental pear and Chinese magnolia, pure white. Weeping cherry and spreading dogwood, vibrant in pink.

Off to the side, the orchard began right at the road then marched clear out of sight into the woods. Petals fluttered in the breeze like bridal veils at a wedding procession.

Beneath the trees were swaths of lilac tulips and yellow daffodils.

Wisteria, like purple plums, was strung on wires between the house and shed. Pendulous masses but feathery like elaborate necklaces, draped over the roof, hanging from the eaves. Their thick gnarled trunks coiled tightly together, determined to wrap around the house, pillar, and post.

Fragrances from the orchard rose like a mist and overcame the senses with their sweet, heady breath. Butterflies were frantic with delight, swooping and perching, especially the monarchs, black and orange with black-veined markings. "Whoosh, whoosh, butterflies!" children cried, sending them aloft in great swarms, like bits of colored glass falling from heaven. The quivering hummingbirds too danced around the scented verbena, milkweed, jasmine. The freesia. There were plenty of bees, a dream site for one of the smallest of earth's creatures. The children especially loved the exotic black-and-white swallowtail with its long, forked tail, particularly enamored of Miss Charlotte's Queen Anne's Lace. "Look, see that! That bird looks just like a kite!" they shouted. Pointing to its tail.

Year after year. This same grand opening up. When winter's gloomy darks lifted, spring's promise welcomed us to Miss Charlotte's ravishing garden.

"How does she do it?" people asked.

What would appear next? They inquired of each other every Sunday, making guesses. Accurate timing of her planting was essential to ensure the peonies blossomed just as the white snowdrops, like milk's droplets, faded. There was never an empty spot as one plant dwindled and another arose, never a wayward weed or droopy bloom. And every shrub, every plant made demands according to its own particular habits - seeking more sun or less, some rain but not too much. Various heights and shapes blended happily so we could enjoy how the groupings lived congenially together.

Parked cars stretched way down to the highway, a good fifty lengths. Children plucked wildflowers, sticking them in their hair while their parents swapped stories of last year's showing: "Those elegant dogwoods, do they seem just a bit more exuberant this year?" Strangers pointed out to strangers, "Would you look at that, those sunflowers, sunny faces broad as dinner plates, all the way up to the second story!" And this: "Whoever saw a pink lilac? Aren't lilacs purple or white?"

Folks in these parts owned some land beyond their front and back yards, some more, some less. Many allotted a meager space for a patch of marigolds or mums, a few rose bushes, to provide a small bouquet for the kitchen table. But most grew beans, tomatoes, corn, something useful, to help with the owner's purse. "Much as we'd like to plant petunias like Miss Charlotte, we can't eat petunias for supper!' they'd say.

"So who *was* Miss Charlotte?" people asked each other.

Almost everyone knew of each other's families from generations back, yet they didn't even know Miss Charlotte's last name. Or even if she was a "Miss," though that's what everyone called her. No one ever asked her directly. Perhaps it was mystery enough to be intrigued by the veiled shapes and contours with which she passed among them. Not stand-offish, just set apart in the way a queen is admired but removed from her subjects. There was an ineffable quality about her, yet she was not unfriendly. Her aura ran still, though there *was* often a small exchange - a nod, a simple "Good day," a touch to the brim of one's hat.

Folks guessed Miss Charlotte was in her late forties. She walked straight and tall despite the years spent hunched over her flowers. Her hair was bleached in sunny streaks, pulled loosely back at her neck. It was apparent she had been pretty once, but now her strong face had weathered from the sun. Very slight wrinkles tugged at the corner of her eyes, but God's hand had put them there, and the neighbors, diligent churchgoers, honored that.

Miss Charlotte usually wore a long denim skirt and a light-blue work shirt with the sleeves rolled up. Unless it was her khaki pants with the deep pockets on the sides for a pair of garden gloves. People followed her comings and goings, marveling at how one woman created a living, wondrous sight for them all to enjoy. A mighty dollop of respect trailed her steps as she strode from Pete's Hardware to Sam's Seed and Grain and, finally, to Tom's Market, before heading home.

How did Miss Charlotte spend her time during the long winter months? we wondered. Surely she had all the colors of African violets - pink, purple, white - blooming on the kitchen windowsill. Perhaps falling from the ceiling in macramé netting, lacy asparagus, and Boston fern. A tall fiddle leaf fig tree spreading its leaves in the living room window?

Was she lonely? The romantic in us said yes. But who could know for sure? The only Miss Charlotte we knew, the shadowy public presence, was the lady with the wide straw hat and white gloves wrapped around her sturdy trowel, head bent, knees to the ground. Working the soil.

Another year, another spring.

Phones started ringing; a buzz was heard in the streets. Folks reminded each other in the shops, the diner. The postmistress Miss Annie told anyone who bought a stamp or retrieved a letter that it was time to visit Miss Charlotte's garden!

After church, the cars and jeeps, bikes and tractors, rolled slowly up to Miss Charlotte's old farmhouse on the hill. From afar, we could see her beautiful trees beginning to show off their emerging colors. As we approached, we sat up straighter, tidied our hair, tucked in our shirts, readied our cameras.

But what was this?

Miss Charlotte's lawns were untended, gone to seed. The detritus of winter lay forlorn, unraked. Nothing was readied for planting. The trees were covered in blossoms, but they dropped their blooms on forsaken, desolate land. Even the few purple crocuses valiantly trying to push through the earth did so halfheartedly.

Cries arose from every quarter.

"Where is she?" everyone muttered to each other. "Miss Charlotte should be in her garden by now!"

"Look!" a child called out. "Look there!"

"For Sale," the sign said, stuck in the hard ground beside the rusty mailbox, so reluctant to show its face hidden by the viburnum bush that we almost missed it.

Underneath was a name.

Ms. Jane Hobbes, Realtor, 74 River St., 553-7934

Quickly, everyone got back in their cars. A long line of vehicles slowly made its way to the River Street office of Ms. Hobbes. Had something terrible happened to Miss Charlotte? How could we live without Miss Charlotte's garden?

Folks waited anxiously in Ms. Hobbes's office. Men leaned against the fireplace, squatted by the window. Children sat cross-legged on the floor, fidgeting. Women propped wherever they could against the desk, the cabinets. Molly Jenkins, significantly pregnant and a bit wobbly, sat in the brown armchair, everyone keeping a close eye. Molly had particularly loved the black raspberry bushes tucked around the front porch - would she be all right?

And so Ms. Jane Hobbes began.

"I'm so sorry to say this, but Miss Charlotte died a few weeks ago."

The listeners gasped, put hands to their chests. "Just as the magnolias were about to make their grand entrance," Ms. Hobbes sighed. "Not from a terminal illness or some runaway virus. Not from an accident, a plow out of control, or a tree branch falling. In fact, the medical examiner couldn't quite figure it out until I went over there and had a good look around.

"And then I realized how she died. No doubt about it.

"A broken heart, it was."

A broken heart? Miss Charlotte with a broken heart? People didn't understand.

"I will tell you how I made sense of it," said Ms. Hobbes as we all sat like stone carvings. Even the children thought, *The butterflies!*

"There was a big chunk of land behind the big red barn that you couldn't see from the road. It was in that space that Miss Charlotte planted her finest garden."

We waited silently until she was ready.

"Let me describe that garden," Ms. Hobbes began.

"There were four sections. Each told a different story.

"Flagstone pavings formed a path connecting all four areas together. Loosely placed, the stones gave a sense of enclosure, but only a sense. They didn't actually enclose anything. Along the path, there was an informal hedge of elderberry and nearby her cherished camellias, the luscious lilacs bushes.

"The first section opened up in a rather rough but simple way. Two thick upright pine posts with a third one nailed across the top provided an entrance of sorts. One step in, and the change was upon you, a transition from the ordinary to a space in which a noble spirit seemed to reside. That's what it felt like, like a spirit hovered there.

"A manly garden.

"Hardy perennials, severe and precise, stood in line, like a headstone. Then a grouping of dwarf evergreens in stone containers, dense like a small forest. On a splintered wood table, a leftover bonsai, now grown wild, in a black pot. Bare stalks of hydrangea in a corner that would never see another spring. To the side, a toothless rake and a wheelbarrow. I lingered for a few minutes, picturing how flourishing a space it must have been.

"There was a sturdy stake about five feet high, thrust snug in the ground, with another horizontal board across the top.

"*Todd*."

"His name had been written on the board in beautiful script with dark-green lettering. On the bottom, four pine trees, their sharp needles meticulously painted. There were even a few tiny pinecones on the ground! And above, the sun's bright rays cast dappled light onto the branches."

Ms. Hobbes paused. We sensed a terrible tragedy about to unfold.

"The next section just beyond was larger than the first and divided in two. A peeling white wooden gate three feet wide directed me in. Both sides were planted with the same clues of boyish adventure, rotting tomato vines and dead ears of corn. There were the remains of a rabbit cage, its door flapping back and forth. Birdseed scattered from an overturned dish. A swing hung from a sugar maple tree. It was a bit eerie, a sad scene reminding me of an old black-and-white photograph portraying a scene once joyful, now abandoned.

"*Ethan*."

"A separate post, with another board across the top.

"His name, *Ethan*, was boldly stenciled in red and yellow. A collie puppy was exquisitely painted on the white background, the leash from the dog flung around the *n* in his owner's name. Its furry hairs, each one separately rendered so carefully, had started to fade but still looked so real I felt I could just pick up a brush and wipe down his coat. At his feet, a gnarled play toy, an old rag doll.

"And then...*Sam*."

"On the horizontal board, the name *Sam* was printed in shades of blue. The *s* was in navy, the *a* sky blue, the *m* a deep royal. Below *Sam* was a rowboat with oars, oarlocks, two slabs for seats, and the edge of a life jacket. Across its prow, *Sam* was written in navy script."

Ms. Hobbes stopped talking. We wiped our cheeks.

"And the last," she started again.

"More?" we cried - a mourners' chorus. Hadn't she said enough?

"A gateway of white lattice," Ms. Hobbes continued, "covered with the bare stems of climbing roses. Dead petals with curly brown edges, scattered on the ground. A doll's wooden cradle, bleached and worn from the weather, lightly rocking like a ghost."

Ms. Hobbes stopped. Old Granger brought her some water, a chair.

"Thanks, I just have to get through this," she said.

"*Emma*."

"Emma's sign was exquisitely painted with yellow daisies and white roses. Oh, Miss Charlotte had spent a lot of time writing this name, I thought. In fact, she wrote it three times. *Emma, Emma, Emma*. Like a plea, begging, 'Come home, come home, my dearest daughter.'"

When she finished, no one dared to speak.

We now understood what Miss Charlotte had done with her days during this long, cold winter past, the one she knew was her last.

When she could not bear it anymore, she painted memories.

Then she gave up.

Ms. Hobbes, though her eyes were sad and her throat raspy, managed. "And beyond Emma's arbor, one last grave. Mr. Holmes, the funeral director, followed her written wishes. A simple white board is marked in plain letters.

"'Charlotte, inconsolable wife and mother.
A garden for my loved ones. This is what love
looks like.'"

Molly bent over, sobbing and rubbing her stomach. The men
looked out the window. Women reached for tissues. Children were
wide-eyed as Ms. Hobbes continued.

"I searched through the archives at the library and found out
what happened. A fire in which her husband, Todd, and the three
children perished. Ten hours' drive east of here. Only Miss Charlotte
had survived, out shopping for children's clothes, the new school year
coming up."

Eventually, into the silence, a small voice murmured, "Why
didn't we know?"

"We could have offered friendship," said Pete's wife, Dana.

"We should have suspected something, a woman alone," said
Miss Annie.

Molly looked up and whispered, "Did she think we knew and
stayed away on purpose out of respect or not knowing what to say?"

"What kind of people are we?" old Granger asked.

"A solitary soul, she lived as she wished," Ms. Hobbes answered.
"And decided to make a shrine to those she loved in the only way she
knew how."

Who would ever buy Miss Charlotte's house? Who could live
there knowing her story - the barn, the woods, the petaled remains
of roses and hollyhocks - imagining three young children swinging in
the shade of the sugar maple, their collie puppy playing at their feet?

"Perhaps someone could write a short story about Miss
Charlotte," Tom from Tom's Market suggested. "The library in town
could place it on their shelves under 'Of Local Interest.'"

"Would it be better to plow it all under and let someone build
a new house?" asked Pete from Pete's Hardware.

"Or maybe keep it as a farm? Plant some corn or wheat, maybe stable a few horses?" added Sam from Sam's Seed and Grain.

"How about celebrating her life and honoring her family by selling the property to a family with lots of children," Ms. Jane Hobbes suggested. "Miss Charlotte's place is meant for children. Knowing her story, they might even maintain a small flower garden. Then when it's time, pass that effort on to the next family."

"But what if, after maybe two generations, a family forgets or neglects to talk about Miss Charlotte's garden?" Tom's teenage daughter, Jackie, asked. "What if someone doesn't remember it as it really was? The memorial gardens behind the barn, the wisteria on the roof, the tulips spreading out under the dogwood trees. What then?"

"Oh no," Molly cried, "we can't let that happen. Miss Charlotte's garden spread magic over all our lives. It's *our duty* to keep that memory alive. Future generations up and down our lovely valley simply *must* know about her roses, her lilacs. The butterflies swarming around the verbena, the jasmine! Oh, wasn't it all so marvelous?"

"No, no! We mustn't ever forget," Molly cried, weeping and distraught, her hand massaging her considerable belly round and round to protect and keep it.

Once Was Enough

For a man only in his late forties, in fine health, Andrew Garvey was a lonely soul. He was also charming, handsome, and thoughtful.

However, he wasn't sure how much longer he wanted to live despite the fact that he was a beloved figure who had achieved worldwide acclaim.

The Pedersen Museum - everyone called it the Peds - was a diminutive gem of an art venue, and Andrew Garvey was its new director. This small but exceptional museum was located in northern Pennsylvania in an abandoned mill town that had been deserted for twenty-five years by the time Andrew Garvey arrived. A ghostly composite of forlorn stone structures, it offered the well-traveled the sensation of being at Stonehenge in England. Formerly a prosperous area known for its production of textile products powered by the river running through its center, the town was no different from others in the area. All the mills in this part of the state had suffered a similar fate, long ago closing shop and moving down-country to the warm Carolinas.

The mill buildings that remained were a marvelous spectacle of old brick, elaborate stonework, arches, arcades, tunnels. When the architect for the new museum laid eyes on these buildings, he rethought his previous design concept. The museum would no longer be a free-standing entity some blocks away. Spectacular brickwork such as this, the architect decided, was far too special and rare not to be repurposed. *Who builds like this anymore?* He thought of Mill City Museum in Minneapolis, but unlike the Peds, Mill City was a Minnesota Historical Society building. *His* structure would be far more provocative and modern.

And so it was. The completed museum's angles and planes jutted out in various configurations from parts of the mill itself. As visitors meandered through, every view offered unexpected high drama - gigantic artworks, interactive sculptural pieces, brilliant colors against a background of brick and stone. A flamboyant marriage of yesterday and tomorrow. Genius, they said. Spectacular, dazzling.

Previously, Andrew Garvey had held the esteemed position of Chairman of the Fine Arts Department at nearby Herald College. Yet after many years, he had grown tired of its rural setting and the meager resources of the modest village down the road. Yes, there was a dynamic college life that beat strong. And after you turned off the highway and drove beyond the gates, the presentation was idyllic - a lovely array of gray stone buildings, some with turrets, all with leaded windows, green playing fields popping up between them. Dormitories were more than a century old with the same architectural charm and the formidable Gothic library roosted grandly at the end of Herald Walk. But outside those gates, there were cows everywhere.

Andrew coveted an appointment in a large city - any city, but a city in which he could walk far and wide where great cultural events were happening night and day. But then the Pedersen opportunity arose, and unfortunately, the location was even less active than the Herald campus.

However, in its favor, the Pedersen was an entirely new venture. Whatever mark Andrew Garvey stamped on its face would be his sole imprint. "A seductive allure," he told himself. Was it his fault that a rich woman wanted to build the museum in that particular area to honor her Scandinavian parents who had owned a dairy farm close by? That she remembered her childhood with the greatest joy and a generous purse?

When the board of trustees was searching for its first director, they had considered candidates from all over the country, but Andrew's name kept reappearing as the most viable choice. He personally knew everyone of importance for three hundred miles, within which area lived an abundance of wealthy patrons. Such a benefit could not be underestimated.

Still, his widower situation was on the minds of the Pedersen board. A wife would be desirable when Professor Garvey attended museum functions. When he hosted literary soirées in the spectacular director's residence atop the museum. The men in the elegant conference room debated and pondered, even extended the interview period. A coveted position, the competition was fierce. Finally, they decided, yes, Professor Garvey would indeed be their new director. Besides, such a brilliant, attractive man would undoubtedly find a wife in the near future. The spouses of the board members had an abundance of single female friends. They would see to it.

So Andrew made an auspicious lateral move rather than a glorious leap upward. He was relieved and grateful, anxious to be gone from Herald, where bitter memories were scattered everywhere.

Sometimes one takes a chance, throws his hat in an unknown direction, and comes up with unexpected splendor. And so it was with the board's hiring of its new director. Pleased with their choice from his very first days, they watched with wonder at the schemes Andrew laid out for their approval. He resolved that his exhibits would be so compelling that critics from all over would visit. *To this old mill, this obscure spot on the map,* he told himself, *I'll bring the world to honor an architectural masterpiece.*

From the beginning, he planned his course in minute detail. Even the extravagant opening was arranged to occur in the fall against a backdrop of spectacular red and yellow foliage, the surrounding colors of the oaks and elms complementing the Peds's brick and stone. In the late afternoon, the sun lit up the entire complex, reflecting nature's brilliance, creating an aura of a unique, almost hallowed environment.

Andrew usually staged live performances along with the display of avant-garde works - massive sculptures one could walk through, sit on, each position eliciting different responses according to what one viewed or heard at the moment. Daily, he blessed the Peds's architect for creating unusual spaces to accommodate his creative efforts.

For example, there was an exhibit to convey the moods and mysteries of color. One entered a long tunnel made of Styrofoam tubes. All sides of the tube were painted black so you had no sense of in and out or up and down. There was no sound, emphasizing the full impact of black's finality. But near the end, the tube took a sudden sharp right turn so that as you exited, the tunnel's sides, top, and bottom were painted the pale blue of clouds and sky. As were the walls and floor of the museum when the tube opened to daylight. Here at last, to the visitor's relief, there was faint music, something lovely like Brahms or Beethoven. And there you had it, Andrew's way of conveying how blue and black altered your emotions, your perceptions, the very beat of your heart.

His shows indeed drew applause and more, veneration tinged with awe. Folks who lived two thousand miles away and planned to vacation in this part of the country included the Peds as a must-see feature of their trip.

Occasionally, directors at other museums tried to copy elements of Andrew's presentations, but they were less inclined to take risks than he. They lacked the ingenuity of approach that was his alone and failed to pull off something equally spectacular. None ever got the simulation just right. They were imitators. Some said, "Impostors." An attempt to duplicate might elicit this remark from viewer and critic alike: "Acceptable but certainly not in the same league as Garvey at the Peds."

Although Andrew's artistic results were often shocking in their originality, none ever veered into the weird or obscure. Rather, viewers could always relate intimately to what they were seeing. To welcome the coming spring, he planned an interactive show including all the main downstairs rooms. Visitors would wind in and out of the indoor artworks then proceed through the arches to the outdoor sculptures and plantings. Each participant would be given a map offering clues to the next item, while actors dressed like figures in the Peds's paintings were stationed along the way. Somehow, indoors and outdoors were both tied in with a scavenger hunt, the prize being a gift certificate to any of the shops in the village. Particulars would not be disclosed until close to the opening date. Andrew purposely kept the details a mystery to create the excitement of live theatre - a dark stage, then suddenly, the lights go on and the curtain rises.

As the museum garnered fame for its own successes, so too did its arrival awaken the derelict town. Such deserted properties often offer remarkable facilities with unlimited potential. Empty buildings with structural integrity. Rock-bottom rents. Abundant space. The comeback began slowly with the opening of a tiny shop next door to the museum that sold Peds-related goods - postcards, photographs, souvenirs. A slew of crafts shops then quickly popped up on adjacent streets, offering everything homemade: honeycomb candles; exotic papers turned into note cards, stationery; purses, wallets, folio covers of colored leather. Jewelry for all ages, woven items inviting to the touch - afghans, place mats, sofa throws, and handblown glassware. A few cafés with funky decor provided unusual coffees and muffins stuffed with cashew pomegranate and almond orange chunks. Most of the craftsmen worked on premises. Visitors meandered in and out of the odd streets, speaking to the artists and buying little treasures to bring back home.

In the center of the mill's main building was a soaring, massive space. From its four sides, the architect had built galleries with glass walls that thrust forth like the prow of a ship and looked out to the building's noble arches and intricately patterned walkways. Director Garvey decided to turn this open area into a permanent bazaar. Dozens of artisans and antique dealers rented partitioned spaces and set up shop. At the far end, the solid wall was replaced with glass so that the massive wooden water wheel, a nostalgic relic from the old days, was visible. Nose to the glass and the viewer could watch the powerful waterway splashing and gurgling over the rocks on its way downstream.

And so a small community of talented folks began to thrive, supporting the museum in ways befitting their unique skills. Often, they were called upon to assist or participate in Director Garvey's exhibitions. Many became good friends with the director himself.

But despite his work being effusively praised, what he longed for most still eluded him - the erasure of memory and the arrival of serenity.

No one at Herald College spoke about it anymore. It was really only the old-timers who occasionally brought it up. However, many years ago, the college had been overtaken with memorials, programs, tributes.

"An unspeakable tragedy," everyone had said. "Poor Professor Garvey."

Their admired chairman of the Fine Arts Department had originally arrived at Herald with his wife, Jocelyn, the perfect complement to his illustrious stature. A svelte honey blonde, Jocelyn was immensely likable. She loved having teas for the faculty and the nervous, admiring students. All who entered her rooms were immediately at ease. Even when she was pregnant, she continued to entertain. When she and Andrew welcomed a daughter, she was back pouring tea and uncorking the wine in no time. They named their child Emma, but only until the toddler was introduced to Ms. Bonet, the fetching French teacher who thought Emma too serious a name for such an endearing little thing. "Emmie, I think it must be," she said. And so it was from then on. Mr. Thurmond from the history department, a native of Dublin, called her "Emmie, me darlin'."

As soon as she was walking steadily enough, Emmie was seen everywhere on campus with her father, hopping along stone paths, swinging her legs from a wooden bench, hiding behind trees. No one ever heard her whimper or moan or stamp her feet. The students adopted her like a pet, often vying for babysitting privileges. Sometimes Andrew would sit Emmie on his desk and spread out crayons and paper so she could copy figures at her whim from his library of beautiful art books. "The eye," Andrew told her, told his students, his colleagues, "we must cultivate the eye."

He adored their child and strove to make her comfortable with the world. Soon enough, it became clear that Emmie was developing "an eye" as she skipped along, commenting on colors, sizes, textures, and their specific features while her father walked proudly alongside her.

"Daddy, the library's my favorite place. Oh, look at that painting over the doorway! Is that a mooral?"

"Mural, darling," Andrew replied. "Yes, it is."

"See that bench with designs on the arms that look like roses! Isn't that pretty? Who would think of making a bench with roses on the arms? And, Daddy, there! That tall post looks just like the painting I made last week with my feather brush. Does that post have a name?"

"Yes, sweetheart. It's a type of stone called marble."

Northern Pennsylvania had long, snowy winters. It was on such a night, snowy, dark, and cold, that Jocelyn and Emmie were driving along the poorly lit highway that led home. Two more miles. What would she make for dinner on short notice? Jocelyn wondered. On both sides of the road were vast expanses of empty fields and farmland. No houses or shops that might offer the barest flash of light. Jocelyn drove slowly, fearing this ride in the dark, but they had been unwittingly detained. After Emmie's piano lesson, Mrs. Howe had offered freshly made oatmeal cookies and tea. Could she refuse Emmie's plaintive plea, "Mommy, please?" Still, now that she was finally on the road, Jocelyn was annoyed that her visit had taken longer than she expected. Coming from Texas, she was always surprised how fast the dark seemed to descend this far north.

Later, everyone said the same thing. Likely Jocelyn was singing to second-grade Emmie her beloved "Eensy Weensy Spider," Emmie's favorite childhood song long after she had learned to read and write. They were almost at Judd's Corners when out of the thick black night, two large deer leaped from the woods onto the road. Paralyzed by the car's headlights, they stood fast. Jocelyn crashed directly into them. All the highway patrol found was a smoldering heap of mangled steel and bodies, human and animal.

After a couple of weeks' mourning at home, Professor Garvey returned to the classroom, but now he walked alone from one building to another. There was no child bouncing by his side, no small voice calling a greeting to his colleagues, "Good morning, Mr. Thurmond," "Bonjour, Ms. Bonet," offering her sweet smile, accepting Mr. Thurmond's wink, throwing back Ms. Bonet's kiss. He avoided the conviviality of the faculty dining room, took his lunch at the desk in his office, hardly lifted his head striding across campus. His usual cheerful greetings, "Morning, Dave. Morning, Stuart, Hello there, Jeanine," were weary and sad. Everyone understood he was carrying a heavy hurt in his heart. Courtly and poised, with sea-green eyes and dark hair stippled with gray, Andrew was quite attractive to women. But no longer did he tease or playfully engage with them as he previously had, and only occasionally, for the sake of his position, did he attend a dinner party. When his hostess would seat an attractive single woman next to him, he found it an easy, even pleasurable task to engage in ordinary conversation, but in the end, he said his good-nights and went home alone.

Now, after almost six years at Pedersen, Andrew Garvey remained unwed. No one talked about it anymore. Apparently, none of the blind dates set up by the board members' wives had moved forward. "When it happens, it happens," the friendly tongues murmured. But as it turned out, on a late fall afternoon, a former student at Herald stopped in at the Peds's office. He was on his way from Boston to Chicago to check out this remarkable new museum and look up his old teacher.

"The director is in the park taking a rare afternoon off," his secretary said, pointing east.

The student made his way down the winding streets, charmed by the homemade wares. At the end of the shops was a perfect pocket park - small and tidy and happily cared for with its prim iron benches set aside beds of red and pink poppies. He found his old mentor at the bottom of a slide in the children's playground, arms wide open, poised to catch a little girl with blond curls screaming with pleasure. As he caught her with a smile and a hug, he swung her around, and together, they ran to the swings. The student stood a way off and watched the activities of this little girl and a dignified man acting like a child himself. Seated nearby on a bench, clapping her hands with delight, was a lovely woman with long dark hair and flashing eyes black as night. The two on the swings kissed the palms of their hands then blew the kiss to the woman waiting on the bench, who reached out and caught it. An interruption would be intrusive, the young man thought, backing off. He would see Professor Garvey that evening at the opening of the *Crafts from Indigenous Tribes* show.

Director Garvey entered the evening festivities with this graceful woman on his arm. *Ah,* the student thought, *the lady in the park.* Surprised and pleased, the guests in tuxedos and long gowns turned toward the attractive couple, whispering to each other, "Who is she?"

"Did you ever see such a gown?" "Is she a colleague? A girlfriend?" She was both, they were to find out.

"Ms. Olivia James, my partner," so Andrew introduced her. "Ms. James is a curator at the Shanomah Museum in Chesterport."

"Aah," the crowd crooned. To the chairman of the board, Andrew added, "Ms. James and I met when I was planning this show. Quite a remarkable expert on Indian tribes of the Midwest, this young lady."

Andrew took Olivia's arm and led her around the room, making introductions.

"Olivia James, Dave Carson, Olivia James, Ed Folsom, Olivia James, Tom Benedict." She *was* quite something, they thought, not conventionally pretty but exotic, ravishing, actually. And look at her gown! Made of velvet and linen and burlap remnants cleverly sewn together into a beautiful garment. When asked, Ms. James twirled around to show off the meticulous tailoring: "It was made specially for me by the women of a small tribe in North Dakota. They live in clay huts built into the side of a mountain, and yet they managed to turn out this wonderful dress."

Well, I did it, Andrew said to himself. *I made my statement. Now they all know.* And Olivia won the room.

The following week, at the Peds's annual staff picnic, Olivia and Andrew and five-year-old Jenny, with her bouncy curls and blue gingham pinafore, walked together into the park. Everyone murmured, "This is it! Director Garvey has now been seen twice with the same woman!" Little Jenny's appearance sealed that certainty. The delightful child was entirely comfortable with adult strangers, trotting from one to another. "Look at my shiny new bracelet with the red sparkly stones," she said to anyone nearby, holding up her arm, giving it a shake.

Andrew thought, *Bringing Jenny was a good thing. Olivia always has the right sense about these things. What a relief. It's done.*

Or almost done.

For all his stepping into a new love, Andrew was, in fact, reluctant to marry. Ever since Jocelyn and Emmie died, he had the dark feeling that their deaths were his fault. He should have been driving, although Jocelyn always took Emmie to her piano lesson by herself. They shouldn't have been on a highway at night. Emmie should have been in bed. He hadn't shaken the notion that he himself might bring bad luck. Better not to marry Olivia. Divorced, she agreed to go along with this arrangement. He would make it right with the board. There would be little objection - after all, he knew at least two members who had girlfriends as well as wives. *On second thought, maybe I won't bring it up*, he decided. *My personal life is none of their business as long as I am bringing renown and revenue to the Peds.*

Like Emmie, Jenny accompanied Andrew on his rounds. With his frequent riddle and joke-telling, he exuded a sense of mischief, of playfulness, which she loved. But Andrew also possessed another irresistible quality - he could think like a child. He understood Jenny's mind.

Andrew set up a small desk in the corner of his office and gave Jenny postcards of the paintings owned by the Peds. She kept busy copying them into her sketch pad. When folks came in and out to see Andrew, she remained sitting quietly in a corner, head bent, happy in her work.

Living high above the museum in that marvelous space overlooking the churning stream that emptied into the Allegheny River, provided a delightful nest for the loving threesome. When Andrew walked across the room to the windows opposite, he was pleased to look down on some of the shops with their clever signage. Most were handmade by Noland the wood-carver, whose shop was tucked snugly between the watercolorist Gina and the herbalist Colette.

Olivia kept her old job, and the museum retained modest quarters for her should she find the drive back to the Peds too onerous. Northern Pennsylvania could have severe winter blizzards. But after two years, she quit her position as curator and took on the mantle of consultant. It wasn't the hands-on, decision-making position she had before, nor did she any longer enjoy its public perks, but she was ready for a change. When she told Andrew, he whooped and hollered, took his two gals right over to the ice cream shop, gesturing to the tubs of frozen treats - chocolate, strawberry, pistachio: "Ladies, whatever you want."

It was only when Olivia became pregnant and Jenny was seven that Olivia's attitude toward marriage slowly began to change. Was it the pregnancy? she wondered. This sudden discontent? Was it Jenny's question: "Mommy, why don't you marry Andrew so he can be my real daddy? If you're not married, you're just friends. Jimmy in the row behind me at school says so."

So she made Andrew's favorite dinner, a fish platter of shrimp, crab, oysters. Homemade brown bread, tubs of her special coleslaw. In her first trimester of pregnancy, the mere sight of it made her nauseated. Turning from it, she nibbled dry crackers to calm her stomach.

"Andrew, darling," she started.

"Yes, sweet girl, what is it?" he answered, looking up.

"Our life together has been lovely, don't you think?"

"Even this very moment!" Andrew replied enthusiastically. But he lay down his fork with trepidation in his heart. Did she have bad news? A difficult request? He waited for her to continue with *but* or *if only*.

"A baby is coming. The older Jenny gets, the harder it is to explain why we're not married. If we lived in a big city with a cosmopolitan mix of parents, it might not be a problem, but out here, all her friends' parents are married. Only one is divorced."

As Andrew heard Olivia's words, right then, it erupted, that terrible memory of a dark and snowy night and his feelings of helplessness to protect his family. The pain still simmered. The dread still boiled. Andrew knew he could only be happy if he were free of inflicting his curse on others. Gently, he took Olivia's hand. Softly, he said, "Liv, you knew from the start how I felt about this."

"Yes, but things change. Life changes. Children get born, children get older, and sometimes that means doing things differently."

"Liv, let me try to explain once again. What if something happened to any of you? No matter the circumstances, no matter if you are a thousand miles away, I would feel it was my fault. You just can't know how things like this will turn out until after we live together for a hundred years," Andrew teased, trying to smile. "Please understand my concern. As a husband, I may be plain bad luck."

Abruptly, they came back, the superstitions of his Russian grandmother, even though he had worked hard to root them out. Fanciful, crazy stories she had told him at bedtime when he was a child. Always, there was a devil and an angel. A devil ready to pounce and punish, who followed your every deed and watched you in the night. Who exacted retribution for a lie or a misdeed with deprivation or death, snatching from your embrace something you cherished. Remembering his grandmother's finger, pointing, shaking at him, Andrew shuddered.

"Of course you're right, Liv. I'll try to think further on it, but I simply can't say yes right now."

With that, they got up from the table and did the dishes together. Jenny came out from her bedroom in her pajamas, asking for another hug and drink of water. And then they all went to bed.

These concerns began to create shifts and fissures in Olivia's heart. *If he loves me, why not marry me?* she asked herself. What was the difference, really, between living with or without a ring? Wouldn't he marry for Jenny's sake? Olivia tried to think clearly, knowing her body's hormones were racing around and settling down in all the wrong places. Yet despite the effort to keep a level head, she felt hurt and resentful and began to fear a slow turning away from Andrew. "It's time for him to get over those feelings from so long ago," she muttered. If we all carried around old hurts, we would all live only tentative lives. No one would ever take any forward step. Determined not to beg or issue an ultimatum, lash out in anger, or hurl harsh words, Olivia kept returning to this same thought: *If he loved me, he would.*

Sitting in the obstetrician's waiting room, Olivia thumbed idly through a design magazine. As an art connoisseur, she loved to look at photos of outrageously beautiful homes and glamorous destinations. Now, in her hands was a special issue on the famous historical center city area of Philadelphia, the dozen museums, the plethora of antique shops, the glorious old apartments with high ceilings, ornate woodwork, fireplaces. She tore out the page of realty listings and stashed it in her purse. She couldn't stop thinking about it even when her feet were in the stirrups of the examining table, even when she lumbered over to the shop that sold maternity bras. Not even when Andrew walked in the door, smiling to see her and Jenny.

Olivia and Andrew had their baby. Another girl, Tessa, thrilling her older sister who vowed to take care of her all by herself. Andrew, of course, adored the charms of his little girls. Another beauty now trailing at his heels. Yet he still said nothing about marriage.

When Tessa was six months old and Olivia felt strong once again, she retrieved the page of Philadelphia realtors and made two telephone calls. Both agents sent pictures to her cell phone with reassurances that an appropriate job would be easy to find. So many museums in the area, after all. Were these actions part of her post-birth adjustment? she wondered. Everyone knows that women exhibit all kinds of moods and strange behaviors after giving birth. Whenever she thought of leaving Andrew, she would put her hands to her face and weep. *But isn't it my obligation to give my girls the finest life possible?* she pondered. *To not have them stigmatized forever because of me?*

Yes, Andrew was the best of fathers. He and Emma were magical together, as Olivia was certain he would be with Tessa. But her daughters would be illegitimate. Bastards. It was odd how the brain worked, Olivia observed. Once her mind opened to the slightest tug in another direction, the hardest thing in the world was to bring it around again to where it was before. She had already begun to anticipate the possibilities of living in a diverse, exhilarating city. To leave this place where for years she had existed within two square miles.

But first, she would try again.

"Andrew," she pleaded, "I don't want Jen and Tess to be different in that way. Please."

"Liv, honey…" he started, but when he saw her face - disappointment or fury? - he bit off his words. "Livvie, as I said before, I need more time to think about it."

Fed up, Olivia said to herself, "I'll be damned if he thinks marrying me means nothing more than granting a *favor*."

Three weeks after her final plea, it happened on a sunny spring morning when Andrew was holding his weekly staff meeting.

"Liv, Tessa, Jenny! Hey, my ladies, where are you? Everyone ready for the park?" Andrew shouted as he sprinted eagerly into the apartment. There were no replies. No toys, no noises. Then he saw the note. Falling into a chair, he held his head and sobbed. He didn't have to read it. He knew. He knew that gone is gone whether by two deer in the road, a blue automobile, or a curse for which he felt responsible.

Andrew washed his face then sat again. The man who, to the outside world lacked nothing, now felt the loneliest man on earth. He walked to the window and looked down on the piney woods, the lively stream. The scene had always soothed him but not today. Now he was acutely conscious of nature's intent - a landscape eternally present - yet in the moment of glancing away then turning back, everything changes. The trees lose their leaves, the sky darkens, the stream dries up.

The note explained Olivia's concerns about the children, her regret that he was unwilling to marry her. That she had too much pride to force herself on him.

"Andrew, dear, you had said you would think about it, but you never brought it up," she reminded him. "I love you, but I won't come back."

I did my best, Andrew told himself, pacing, weeping, cursing. *I'm a good man. I was a good husband and father to Jocelyn and Emmie and tried to be the same kind of man to Olivia and the two girls.*

Andrew drew the window shutters against the bright sunshine, against the view, and collapsed in the chair like a wounded beast, defeated, dying. It was ironic, he thought. *My profession places me smack in the center of crowds all the time. People like me, and I enjoy the sociability. In the rarefied sphere of museum directors, I've been able to sail through without any serious grievances or conflicts. And yet I'm a personal failure. My second love, my second chance, the children, gone.*

Jocelyn, Emmie, Olivia, Jenny, and Tessa - five women he adored were absent, missing. Surely Olivia would find someone to marry. Jenny would no longer have any use for him. Tessa would never know him, and she was his *real* child.

He sat in his chair until the sun set and the stars came out. Then he moved to his desk that faced Noland's little shop and wrote a resignation letter to the board. He had fame. He had money. It was love he didn't have.

When that was done, he went back to the chair. He would have to leave this apartment from whose windows he had watched the world turn, fall to winter, winter to spring, to summer, to fall, and back again. Should he follow Olivia to Philadelphia and beg her to marry him? Likely not. She had made it clear she wouldn't marry someone grudgingly doing her a service. Nor would any woman. What a fool he had been. And yet, what if he *was* bad luck?

Andrew settled the afghan over his knees. Like a small child, like an old man. He had no plan, no possibilities, no hope. Adrift and untethered, Andrew fell asleep where he sat.

When he awoke, light was blinking through the slats of the shutters.

Evelyn and Annette

Everyone called them the Golden Girls of the Roseland Ballroom. Glossy and glittery as the sun and stars, they never appeared one without the other.

Evelyn was tall and willowy, a gorgeous blonde, wavy platinum hair piled atop her head in swirls and pinned with an antique gold clasp.

Annette was also tall and slim, but she a gorgeous brunette, her hair long and glossy, spilling elegantly over her shoulders like a mink cape.

Young and feisty and first cousins, they were as close as sisters. Standing at the threshold of the throbbing ballroom, watching thousands of dancers twirling under the lights, at first glance they could be mistaken for Betty Grable and Katharine Hepburn. When they appeared, everyone gasped, and there was a sudden parting of the crowd. Several men made their way over, extending their arms to escort the lovely young women into the room, abandoning for the moment - and in the middle of a Viennese waltz or a lively foxtrot - two women awkwardly waiting for their return.

When the Roseland Ballroom opened in midtown Manhattan in the 1920s, it immediately exploded upon the spectacular city with its extravagant, glamorous ballroom café. No one had ever seen anything like it - a glitzy showplace in which to see and be seen by other New Yorkers. Opening a few weeks before the start of Prohibition only added a delicious sense of mischief to its cachet. The Great Depression had fallen upon the country, but that didn't stop those lucky enough to scrape a few nickels together to share in the reveling.

The "poor man's nightclub" it was called - the packed crowds, low entry fee, and the choice of ordinary dress, men in working suits and ties, women in their day dresses. Almost every night, three thousand men and women showed up for dancing to the sounds of renowned society orchestras. Just like a movie set, every evening was a Ginger Rogers/Fred Astaire happening.

The ballroom's vast ceiling was covered in dark-blue muslin studded with tiny twinkling lights. Lit by neon lamps in graduating shades of color from daffodil yellow to rose pink, the room cast an ethereal glow over the dancers who seemed to float in the shifting light like mysterious shadows. The newspapers of the day described the atmosphere as "phantasmal."

In the early days, the Roseland was known as a spot for "whites only." But since those who paid their admission were crazy for dancing of any kind, the rise of the great black jazz musicians, Louis Armstrong and Count Basie and their orchestras was inevitable, bringing down the house every night.

And Evelyn and Annette were there. They came to dance, but they also came to find husbands.

Yet fun ranked topmost on their minds. Handsome men bowed before them and led them out to twirl and swing to the romantic music of Tommy Dorsey and Benny Goodman or to shimmy and shake to Fletcher Henderson's jazzy rhythms. Even the chandeliers quivered and shook.

Despite all this glamour, Evelyn and Annette were practical women. During the day, both were schoolteachers in the New York City schools, helping support their poor families on the Lower East Side. They lived in the same worn building, Evelyn's family on the third floor, Annette's on the second. Overcrowded tenements lined the street. Vendors with carts pulled by feeble horses sold every type of merchandise just outside their door. From morning to night, they touted their wares, shouting, bellowing. It was a noisy neighborhood, the horses adding to the pandemonium, snorting and stomping.

Both parents of Evelyn and Annette had emigrated from Russia. Both their fathers were disabled, unable to work, their mothers weary from bearing children and living in poverty. Both girls shared a bedroom with siblings.

No wonder they dreamed of an exciting life. And why not have it at the Roseland? On some unexpected night, those dreams might be realized. So young, only in their twenties, anything was possible. Even the appearance of a wealthy husband to take care of their families.

The girls had something else in common. They loved to shop.

Each hoarded a dollar from their weekly paychecks to set aside for buying pretty dresses. Afternoons they eagerly met and scavenged the used clothing stores on the Lower East Side for unique cast-offs from wealthy matrons. Dresses with flair - a pleated skirt, a touch of chiffon, something coquettish, something affording a sight of their long legs. They were lucky, often finding treasures marked down several times. With $3, you could buy yourself a beautiful garment. Nothing fancy, just simple, but elegant. And certainly, the clerks in those days were grateful for even a paltry profit.

Their mothers scolded them as they showed off their frocks, "Better to buy a chicken for the pot."

But when the mothers thought further, they decided that perhaps the clothes would contribute to their girls making a good marriage. So despite their ambivalence, they both wielded magic with needle and thread, mending a seam or repairing a hem. In the end, when their daughters looked like beauty queens, ready for an evening out, the two mothers leaned back on tired sofas, their own clothes threadbare and dowdy. Overwhelmed at producing such beautiful daughters, they murmured softly, "Only in America."

And Evelyn and Annette sailed forth with hope and pluck, the lovely curve of their lips enhanced with free lipstick samples from the cosmetic counters at Gimbel's and S. Klein's.

Into this grand social American phenomenon, however, reality tested Annette's mettle.

She was myopic. Hopelessly, irretrievably myopic.

Unable to focus more than five feet away without unattractive glasses, Annette's world was a haze of cloudy mists.

"I refuse to wear these things when I go out," she cried to her mother, flinging the tortoise-shell glasses with the thick lenses across the table. "Why me?" she moaned, her mother helplessly twisting her apron. Unwilling to limit her marital chances but helpless to see without them, Annette made her choice. Leave the glasses home.

So when Evelyn and Annette entered Roseland and the men came strutting over, Annette couldn't tell if an approaching escort was someone she welcomed until he was almost upon her. Flustered and uneasy, she was often confused by a last-minute choice, while at the same time she was forced to maintain her congenial demeanor. As she fumbled her way through, Evelyn strode forth with great confidence, sending flirtatious motions to lucky possibilities across the room. Annette asked herself, did Evelyn have her choice of the room's most eligible men while she was tossed the odd sorts, Evelyn's leftover pickings?

My eyes, my eyes, a schoolteacher's eyes, she cursed. Brought low by such a ridiculous but serious limitation. There was no remedy, no surgery, no alternative devices. Not even pretty frames. Only those bulky, awkward lenses over her lovely face, hiding whatever free samples of mascara Gimbel's put out on their counter. One night, she brushed on Gimbel's latest, the exotic "Rising Moon," dark gray with a silver sheen running through; but behind her glasses, her eyes looked smudged.

Yet hadn't there been Albert who had told her just last Tuesday evening as he dipped her low in an intricate tango plunge, their noses almost touching, "What splendid, limpid eyes you have!"

Returning home, tucked into bed, she had wondered, *Could he be the one?*

Evelyn was found first.

As the two women hesitated on the threshold of the ballroom, a man named Henry maneuvered himself to the head of the line. He took Evelyn's hand and for the rest of the evening managed to keep other suitors from cutting in and whisking her off.

"Masterful," Evelyn later said to Annette, "a take-charge kind of guy. Not bad-looking either, rather cherubic with that round face. Starting to go bald, but we can't have everything, right?"

Evelyn plopped down on Annette's bed and continued.

"He owns a dry goods store with his brother, Sam, three streets away from this very spot, and they have plans to open more someday. Best of all, he owns a Model T Ford! Can you imagine? Oh, bliss! Out of the city, into the fresh air!"

"Annie," she asked, "what do you think? He's a nice enough man even though he also has to support his mother and two sisters. I *do* like him, even though I'm not over the moon. Does that matter? Mama says you get to love your husband after you're married for a while."

Annette, her glasses now firmly fixed, faced Evelyn from the other bed, and replied, "Oh, Ev, are you sure he is *the one*? Are you sure you're not *rushing*? A mother and *two* sisters? Weren't you looking for the moon? Have you tried long enough? You're only twenty-two!"

And yet Annette knew that if she had been asked that question by Evelyn when her world was insecure, unclear, and blurry, glasses in her pocket, Evelyn might well have answered, "Take him, he can provide a good living."

So despite the fact that Henry didn't send Evelyn over the moon, despite the fact that he was losing his hair, Evelyn married Henry, and they settled into a large apartment with his elderly mother and two sisters in the back rooms.

Evelyn, of course, stopped going to the Roseland. As did Annette, her heart no longer up for the adventure with her dreadful myopia and lacking the support of Evelyn by her side. But how she longed for the old days, when the two of them, arm and arm, shopped after work and gossiped about the exploits that might lie ahead. Annette felt a profound nostalgia and was just a bit remorseful. She kept wondering, *Why did Evelyn choose so quickly?*

But again, their families were poor. The Depression was raging, and Evelyn's parents thought Henry a suitable provider. And everyone felt the deprivation of hard times.

After work, Annette began taking long walks in a nearby park filled with fountains and playgrounds. On a warm May day, she was sitting on a bench reading *Jane Eyre*. The spray from the dolphin's brass mouth - her favorite fountain beside her favorite bench - left droplets of tiny diamonds on her silky hair. Loathe to return to the crowded apartment with the smells of onions and chicken fat, she put her head back, her face to the sun, and thought, *It's a lovely day.*

Just when her mind was on that last thought, a man with a dog stopped directly in front of her, blocking the sun.

"Excuse me," he said. "I see you're reading Charlotte Brontë."

So close he was practically standing on her toes, this nice-looking man with dark-brown hair, wearing a suit, his shoes polished. And something else she noticed. The dog, a spaniel of some kind, waited patiently on his hind legs, not yelping or nipping or causing trouble.

She had to squint directly up, hand shielding her eyes from the bright light, to find his eyes.

"May I join you?" he asked.

And so Morty found Annette.

"This is my favorite fountain," Morty said. "I come here often, but I haven't seen you before."

"I've only started coming," Annette answered. "I used to spend the afternoons with my cousin, but she just got married."

"*Jane Eyre*, I see," he continued. "The bittersweet and the tragic. Best of all, redemption, all there right in your own two hands. And do you believe, Miss Annette, that love always brings happiness?" he asked, leaning toward her, his eyes direct but tender and soft too, like the color gray. His closeness did not alarm her. Rather, she was intrigued - had this man, this stranger, actually *read Jane Eyre*?

"So you're a teacher, and I'm a dentist, or rather, an orthodontist. Sounds dreadfully boring, I know, but it's rather interesting overall."

Although his prospects appeared sound, most of all she liked when he listened closely to the stories she told about her students. And asked her questions, such as, what did her favorite student Joey want to know about math when he was cleaning the blackboards after school? When she paused after answering, he added, "A teacher who molds minds is the physician of the young." She felt proud, and he smiled sweetly - a sturdy, manly smile.

Later, Evelyn asked, "Annette, are you *sure*? Are you settling? Nothing is worse than settling."

Three years later, the two cousins gathered in Annette's spacious apartment, watching their toddlers, Ari and Chani, scramble around the floor tossing stuffed animals at each other.

"Annette, I'm at my wit's end. I can't stand my husband," Evelyn said. "He always puts his family first. We don't have a minute alone, the three of them still living with us. The other day I was arguing with his mother about new curtains. She didn't like the ones I had picked with geraniums and daisies. When I told her to mind her own business, this was my apartment first, Henry actually lifted his hand to me. Lifted his hand! Though he brought it down right away. And that wasn't the first time. There have been small jabs and smacks. What's next?

"Well, I almost picked up Ari and ran out of the house. But where would I go?"

Evelyn's meticulously coiffed hair that was her joy when the two of them had sashayed into the Roseland in the old days was now loose and lank, pulled off her neck with an awkward bow. Her soft, flirty lips were bare of luster.

Annette grew thoughtful. She said a silent prayer of thanks that her Morty loved to brush her hair, help her with her coat, rub her feet after a hard day. She took off her glasses, wiped them carefully, put them back on.

What did Evelyn expect her to say? What *could* she say, their two marriages so different? She wanted to say, "Evelyn, you chose too soon. You knew Henry came with problems, that large family of his, a sick mother, two sisters, and you taking it all on as a newlywed."

Here before Annette sat her best friend in the world, dear Evelyn, her own cousin, like a sister; and she could not speak even a meager truth. How could she tell her that she and Morty made love several times a week? That when she took off her glasses, those once-hated spectacles, he asked her to put them back on.

"You were wearing them when we first met when I thought you were so smart," he said. "When I fell in love with you."

His mother took little Chani once a week so the two of them could go out to dinner to a restaurant with roses on the table. She wore her pretty green dress, and over the soup, he told her that "taking a walk in the park that day was the luckiest day of my life."

After the story Evelyn had just told her about Henry lifting his hand to her, Annette knew she would comfort, support, and encourage. But she certainly wouldn't share about those personal things between her and Morty.

How could she?

A Walk in the Woods

H elen and her women friends in this Philadelphia nursing home were all aflutter.

It was Friday, the day the hairdresser, Mona, was on premises. She had a full day of silver-haired wash and blow dries. Wheelchairs were lined up in the hall outside her salon on the seventh floor. The ladies gossiped and complained as they waited their turn to be gussied up then to be sent out renewed and gorgeous into the world for another round of bingo.

The great buzz today was whether or not the manicurist, Yvonne, would also show up. In that case, they would have pretty hands as well as hair when they placed their numbers on the bingo boards.

Helen wheeled herself out the door. *All done*, she thought tenderly. *Now I will look my best for my Alfred when he comes for his weekly visit at 2:00 p.m., right after lunch but just before my nap. He shows such consideration for me, respecting my desire for a nap, timing his visit perfectly for my needs.*

Helen kept wheeling until she arrived at the social hall where her dear friend, Sarah, was waiting. These two could not have been more unalike. Helen loved to talk, and Sarah, shy and reserved, never tired of listening to her friend's stories, hideous though some of them were. Although Helen had three wonderful adult children and five grandchildren, she was German, Jewish, and a Holocaust survivor. Sarah was American and had never married, nor had she ever had children. And she had never lived more than a hundred miles from this nursing home. Every word Helen uttered captivated her, or so

Helen thought. Sarah's faded blue eyes, cataracts in both and glaucoma in the left, seemed to focus intently on Helen's lips when she spoke. In truth, however, there were times when her seemingly rapt attention might have been due to her failing eyesight.

Among Jewish Holocaust survivors, Helen belonged to a small group of those who were willing to speak publicly about their experiences during the war, to share the grave importance of that brutal era. Helen spoke particularly about Dachau, the concentration camp to which she was sent while millions of her fellow Jews were likewise rounded up and dispersed to other camps in Germany, Austria, and German-occupied Poland. She often addressed schoolchildren, church and synagogue gatherings, and any other organization that asked. It wasn't easy for her. Every time she talked, it brought to life the terrible tragedy of so many. Not that she didn't have nightmares still about it, but she was adamant others should *know* and learn and never forget this monstrous regime of evil that sprung from an educated people. And now, she would speak here, whenever it was requested. Helen had survivor friends who never said a word about this barbaric time in their lives, either in public or in private, withholding from their entire families the stinging emotions of their intensely personal trauma. Others fought to forget, if that was even possible, the inhumane treatment to which they had been subjected. Many simply did not have the words to describe the damage buried in their souls. Still, others looked only to the future, where they might find some good.

Helen and Sarah settled down in their wheelchairs near the window, looking out on the pond. "How lucky our spot is free today or we would have had to face the parking lot again," Helen said, laughing. Sarah could hardly wait. "Helen, tell me that part again, the part where you met Alfred."

Helen sighed. "Again? You have heard that story half a dozen times."

"Yes," Sarah said, "again." She snuggled into her chair, spreading the lap robe over her knees.

And so Helen began.

"I'll start after the liberation," Helen said, "when the brave American soldiers in their jeeps flooded the camp. There were hundreds of them, waving American flags and tossing out candy bars. Horns blaring, voices shouting, 'We're here, we're here, you're safe!'" Helen then paused, took out her tissues, and wiped her eyes as Sarah patted her hand. "All of us on the brink of death, so weak and sick," she managed, her throat whispery, breathy when she told her story, even after all these years. "And so many dying right then, right as those jeeps rolled in, even before the soldiers could put us on stretchers to carry us out away from all that filth, that stench.

"But those of us who were saved by those smiling boys, well, a blessing on their American heads. Our saviors, really. Unable to even extend a hand or manage a smile, we were mute with gratitude. And who would even have wanted to shake our hand, skeletons covered in rags, oozing with disease?"

An aide came over bearing a tray of cookies. Annoyed at the interruption, Helen nevertheless looked them over for her favorite, almond with sesame seeds. "Aha! Here it is," she exclaimed as she plucked a stray from the pile of oatmeal raisin. The women nibbled and sipped. When they shifted in their chairs and Sarah gave a tiny burp, Helen was ready to continue.

"Where was I?" she asked, momentarily confused.

"When the American soldiers came into the camp in their jeeps," Sarah urged.

"Oh yes. Well, I'll skip over the next part, where we were taken to various hospitals for medical examinations, given new clothes and real food for the first time in years. Can you believe many of us got sick eating real food? Our stomachs couldn't take it. Then we were sent to displaced persons camps where the Jewish agencies composed lists of survivors and decided what to do with us."

"Yes, yes," Sarah said. "Hurry, get to the Alfred part."

"Don't rush me! I'm getting there!

"Six months after I had settled into the DP camp, there came a day when I was strong enough and willing to take a walk outside the grounds. They allowed it as long as we stayed close by. The camp was surrounded by lovely woods, and it was spring. The grass smelled delicious and fresh. Sarah, the beauty of the woods and forests in Germany. If you only knew! I cannot describe the feeling of freedom. Imagine being kept like an animal for years and then walking out by myself. Looking at ordinary things with new eyes, birds hopping from branch to branch. Clean air and sunlight! Not dark and hazy from the burning of human flesh.

"All of a sudden, as I was enjoying my little stroll, out of nowhere, a young man appeared and walked toward me. I was frightened out of my wits and ran behind a tree. Could he be a Nazi? He might assume I was an escaped prisoner. Were there Jew haters still lurking in these woods? I wondered." Sarah sat still, held her breath.

"Softly, the man said, 'Don't be afraid. I won't hurt you.'

"He had an American, not a German, accent. A great relief, I can tell you. Even so, who could believe him? This blond fellow with brown eyes, a crooked smile with a deep cleft in his chin. And tall. So tall that he cast a shadow from the sun. He had a small scar on the side of his face, near his right ear. No one coming from a camp trusted anyone no matter what they were told or what kind of accent they had. But then he reached down and plucked a yellow wildflower growing at my feet. With a smile, he held it out. A flower! It was the first one I had seen in four years! Stunned, I backed away, fearful and confused. I was thinking that no Nazi had ever given a Jew a flower before.

"And then I remembered this. Many times, a commandant would visit the camp, always with a snarling, ferocious dog at his side. Often, he would throw scraps to the dog meant for the prisoners' meager meal, and suddenly that animal would become docile, and playful. Like handing me a flower. A treat for an animal to keep him quiet. A bribe. Still, I told myself, we had been liberated. The war was over. And so when he asked me to sit with him a while, I did, though my heart was pounding. Honestly, realistically, how could I escape? In two leaps, he would overtake me. I had no choice. And the gift of the flower *did* show some kindness. Two logs there were, facing each other in a clearing, so we sat. He talked. I listened. What could I say? Describe where I had been for three years?"

Helen paused. The two ladies rearranged themselves. Sarah smoothed out her lap robe, adjusted her collar. Helen sipped her tea.

"As a hundred warnings swirled through my head, I heard only bits of what he was saying. 'American. Left my company. Hated killing. Must not find me, court-martial.'

"Chipmunks dashed by our feet. A deer moved in the distance, a pretty thing, yet all I could think of was there were days in my recent past when I would have killed for some deer meat.

"Suddenly, everything began to feel strangely personal. I began to feel uneasy and rose to leave, backing away, keeping watch in case he made a sudden move toward me.

"'Wait,' he said, 'Will you meet me here again tomorrow?'

"'I don't know,' I answered, frightened of what I was doing, talking to this stranger.

"As I ran away, he shouted, 'Alfred! My name is Alfred!'"

Too soon, the aide was at their side. "Nap time, ladies!"

"Oh darn," Sarah said, "just when you were getting to the good part." The two friends turned their wheelchairs to the door, throwing kisses at each other. "Again tomorrow," Sarah reminded Helen, "right after lunch."

Well, it was a long story, and it took many days, just as Sarah liked. And she constantly pleaded with Helen to repeat certain parts, especially the part where Alfred gave her that yellow flower. Those stories kept them busy many an afternoon.

In fact, Helen had been married to Alfred for fifty-two years now. Her Alfred, right downstairs on the men's floor in room 3H.

They had come to the United States together, and she had studied to become a nurse. The desire to care for the needy and ill was her way of giving back to those soldiers and doctors who had saved her life. Alfred sometimes complained about her long hours at the hospital, and sometimes he made a jarring, inappropriate remark, "My dear Helen, sometimes the weak and the infirm are best left untended." This bothered her, but she figured he too carried his own demons from the war.

Their life had consisted of the usual joys and sorrows - three healthy children, two heartbreaking miscarriages; Alfred's positions as a language teacher (he had picked up German and French in the service); taking them from Rhode Island to Ohio to Connecticut; children's illnesses (measles, pneumonia, scrapes, and falls); and yes, domestic squabbles and moody willfulness. But there were also apologies and amends. Although she had to admit, it was easier for her than for Alfred to say I'm sorry. Sometimes she grew downright impatient coaxing those words out of him. And when she was successful, she often felt he was doing her a favor by saying them.

But most important was Alfred's conversion to Judaism. As they were preparing to come to America, Helen was taken aback by his suggestion of conversion in a time and place of chaos and upheaval. There were endless forms and so much activity at all hours, groups coming and going, that she didn't question him closely. Besides, she remembered thinking it would make things easier when they had children.

The patients were intrigued when Nomi, a patient with Parkinson's disease, showed up. Someone new to shake up their daily routine. Although she needed help walking and dressing, her memory and mind were knife sharp, clear all the way back to her childhood.

On the fifth day after her admission, when Nomi and Helen were having breakfast, Helen discovered that Nomi was also a Holocaust survivor. And further, she too was not reluctant to talk about the unspeakable horrors of those days. Here, at last, was a kindred spirit. All of Helen's other listeners were just that, listeners, as to any dramatic story. Those who didn't know about the concentration camps listened in utter disbelief as if they might not have believed her. However, Nomi would know Helen's heart and she Nomi's.

After they finished their oatmeal and Helen told Nomi that Friday was the day for hairdresser appointments, Nomi started right off - in a meandering way, in the manner of older folks, so many memories from a long life braided together like rope, the good and the evil twisting and turning but inseparable. "Oatmeal and hairdressers," Nomi commented. "Remember when the Germans shaved our heads and we had no hair? And as for oatmeal, oatmeal was only a dream. Any scrap of garbage was prized higher than human life. When the Americans arranged for us to go to those DP camps, I had thought that angels had come down to earth because we were given oatmeal for breakfast. Although, she smiled wryly at Helen, "they could have come down a whole lot sooner."

Both sat thoughtfully.

Helen took Nomi's hand. She felt this woman had been sent from heaven to be her soul's companion even though she did have Alfred and her children and the five grandchildren. Poor Nomi's husband had been ripped from her arms at the Auschwitz train station, along with her infant daughter, Shana. In the office of the DP camp, there were lists of names, miles of names, posted by the Jewish agencies of those who were still alive and where they might be located. Everyone in the camp checked those logs sometimes three times a day. Maybe by some miracle, a family member or a friend or someone from their village might still be alive. This is how she now felt about Nomi, as if she were family. All survivors were really family, weren't they?

A week later, with her hair washed and curled, Nomi continued her story.

"After a few months in the camp," she began, "I was given permission to take a walk in the nearby woods. The shade, a breeze, every small moment and object was a miracle."

Shocked, Helen suddenly sat up straight, her hand to her throat. Nomi too had walked in the woods? Of all things. Were all the displaced persons camps surrounded by woods? She asked Nomi the name of the camp. The same as hers! To be in the same camp and take a similar walk in the woods? What were the chances of that happening? A bizarre coincidence, was it not? The shock of this revelation was so unexpected, so great, it was as if Helen had discovered a relative who she thought had died in the crematoria.

"Tell me," Helen asked, "were those woods right behind the tower in the southeast corner? The tall spruce trees lined up in a row as you entered?"

"Yes," Nomi answered. "How did you know?"

"Because I was at the same camp," Helen cried.

Before they could say another word, the aide came toward them. "Nap time, ladies. You can finish later."

Helen's rest was fitful, confused. She fretted over their encounter. Was their meeting destined for some unknown purpose? It seemed so surprisingly fortuitous.

She could hardly wait until after lunch the next day, though she was a bit uneasy at what she might hear.

Hardly had Nomi swallowed her pills, set down her bag, and braked her wheelchair when Helen burst out, "Did you ever meet anyone on your walk in the woods?"

"Why yes," Nomi answered. "What an odd question."

"Such a strange thing. A few of the other women took walks also, but it wasn't until we got to know each other that we felt safe enough to share. A man had approached each of us. He was very friendly, rather good-looking, quite tall with a small scar down the side of his cheek. An American, we assumed. He offered each of us a flower so we wouldn't be afraid, I guess. But we all ran away. No one trusted anyone in those days, not even this man with his American accent. Many Germans spoke flawless English and vice versa."

What? What is she saying? Helen started to sweat. She called for the aide. "Apple juice, Nadine, please, if you don't mind." The aide looked closely, touched Helen's forehead with the back of her hand, felt her pulse. Helen managed to push out the words, "So tell me about the other women who took walks in the woods."

"Do you want to hear this terrible thing?" Nomi asked. Seeing no one nearby, she leaned over and whispered, "Forget the women. That man was a Nazi. A real Nazi."

Helen's pulse throbbed. Looking down, she saw the veins in her wrist swell. Would she faint? "How do you know that for sure? So many different people were wandering around in those days," she managed.

"Two women who slept in the bunks next to mine told me he was a guard in their previous camp. They are positive it is the same person. He did morning and evening roll calls, and believe me, you never forget a face that might put a bullet in your head. The women wanted to report him but were terrified to do so. They just never walked in the woods again and warned others not to do so, either."

Astounded, Helen had so many questions - ominous, momentous questions. But above all, these for herself - why did she succumb while the others ran away? What did they see that she had not?

She told Nomi she was feeling ill and went back to her room. For now, she dodged Nomi's inevitable next question: "So did *you* also meet that man in the woods?"

Was this man *my* Alfred? Helen wondered. Was he really an American or, God forbid, a German?

Was he a Nazi?

You're being ridiculous, Helen scolded herself. *Stop this absurd thinking. You have lived with this man as his wife all your days. You have birthed his children. Surely you would know if he was German, never mind a Nazi. Surely he would have given himself away with a word or a thought.*

Would he? Alfred was a clever man.

It isn't my fault! she silently screamed. *We were all piteously vulnerable in those days, and he promised to take care of me.* Twisting her hands, tiny trails of moisture ran along her neck, dampened her hair. Did she have a fever?

Eventually, after much review, this thought settled her down. The proffering of a yellow flower to various women in the woods outside of a displaced persons camp in Germany's American zone, was hardly enough cause on which to turn a lifelong partner into a monster. Maybe the woman who thought he was her guard was delusional, sick from hunger.

And yet Helen forced herself to review past events which at the moment had unnerved her but which she had brushed off at the time.

There was an incident when she and Alfred were driving to their son's school and a bus nearly forced them off the road. Alfred swerved, cursing in German. She had thought, *In German?* That seemed strange. Well, he *was* a language teacher, she recalled thinking. But then in imminent danger, wouldn't anyone's instinct be to curse or shout in one's native language? When she asked him why he had spoken in German, he answered, "Nah, it's nothing. When you are in a war, you pick up expressions from your enemies." And he patted her knee, saying, "Think nothing of it, my dear Helen."

It meant little then, but now Helen couldn't stop thinking about it. Her mind wandered. *Had I been duped? Was I Alfred's solution for escaping from Germany, for evading arrest for war crimes? What better way to disguise yourself than as a Jew?*

On Tuesdays, Alfred went bowling. She had never met the fellows from his league. "Just a bunch of guys who throw a few round balls down a lane, my dear. Dreadfully boring, I'm afraid," he told her.

She had never had any interest in these companions, just as Alfred never asked her the names of the gal friends with whom she met up late Thursday afternoon to have their nails done. But why hadn't she? Yet why should she have? And this - why did Alfred every Tuesday on his return from bowling go straight to his study where she heard typewriter keys tapping and tapping? To whom did he write at that late hour? If she were not in this nursing home and were ten years younger, she would get in her car and go round to the few bowling alleys in the area and ask questions. Although she guessed most of them would have probably closed long ago.

Helen, stop it.

Yet she could not. She was taken over with all aspects and implications of Nomi's disclosure. Her entire life with Alfred now seemed suspect. Clues began to pop up, take shape - all of them sinister.

Greta, their daughter. Isn't that a Germanic name? He had said his mother's name was Gretchen. Helen didn't like Gretchen, so she agreed to Greta. And their son, Karl. Oh my heavens! Even the spelling is Germanic. She recalled that Alfred was the one to suggest Karl. "Fine," she had said, "but I want it spelled with a *C*, much more acceptable, especially in light of the war still being so immediate, and the *K* is particularly Germanic."

"But spelling it with a *C* is so ordinary," he had replied, adding that he once knew a Carl with a *C* and he was such a stupid boy. He smiled at her, touching her hand, and won her over.

When he offered the name Ansell for her third child, she finally held her ground. "That is such an odd name. Peculiar, really," she had said.

"He will be named after me," Alfred answered. "Ansell, Alfred, they're close. But if you prefer Albert, that would also do."

So she agreed to Albert. Who could say no to Albert? But all three children had German names, she now realized with horror. And after the war, when she read innumerable recountings, she learned that several of the worst Nazi killers were named Albert.

Oh, the things we overlook in life when we want to or when we are persuaded so and for which we make plausible excuses. But slowly, as her mind sifted through memory, it began to shift away from believing her husband. So far, all was supposition and guesses, but she became mindful and cautious.

Helen went back to Nomi.

They were alone. Sarah was playing bingo.

"Tell me more about the man in the woods," she asked.

"What more is there to tell? He was a Nazi devil. The Nazis were all devils, killers. Those women were lucky to get away as fast as they did and to come to no harm."

It was Saturday afternoon, time for Alfred's visit. Helen heard him open the door, push his walker inside, then hesitate on the threshold. By the halting, tentative sound of the wheels, she could tell that his balance was still a bit off from his minor fall last Thursday. But today, he had plucked a red carnation from a bouquet at the nurse's station, tucked it into his shirt pocket, its red crown rather rakish. Still, he was an old man. As she, despite her perm, was an old woman.

"Ah, my dear Helen. And how are we doing this very fine day?"

Suddenly, she was afraid. Who was this man? *Oh, Nomi, why did you tell me that story of the man in the woods? It has changed my life and revived the old fears and despair all these years after we left the camps. I have not yet told her that I met the same man in the same woods. And even more, I had married him. Of all the women, I alone accepted the flower and sat with him on the fallen logs.*

And oh my, Nomi, if you only knew. How can I tell you, my new friend, that the same man, a possible Nazi, a likely Nazi, is right here in this building, a mere three floors below?

Alfred and Helen chatted about their children. Greta had changed jobs; Albert had bought a second car. They favorably critiqued the improved meals of the new chef. They spoke of the woman, Nomi, and how pleased Helen was to have another friend. They talked of the change Dr. Linn made to Alfred's medicines, his blood pressure steady now for two weeks.

But then Helen blurted out, "Alfred, I'm talking with my friends about when we were young. You know how old people reminisce. We're sharing how we met our husbands." Helen sighed wistfully, staring at Alfred.

"Why are you going back so far, my dear?" Alfred asked.

"Why not?" Helen answered. "Why shouldn't we talk about it, about how we met? You never really explained what you were doing in those woods, and Nomi asked me about it."

Alfred stared out the window. The first thing that struck her like an electric prod was that he didn't look directly at her. He was silent, not turning back for almost five minutes. Why would a man be reflective when his wife asked him about their first meeting? Why did he look out the window before he spoke? Whenever Helen told Sarah the story of her meeting Alfred, she was immediately enthusiastic, plunged right in. When he finally turned toward her, his face was vacant, without affect, his eyes the impenetrable smoky color of fog.

"Well, my dear, let's see what this aging mind remembers. I saw you in the woods and knew instantly you were from the camp. Where else could you be from? So I had to be gentle or surely you would have darted off. I think we spoke of my running away from the army. I said I didn't like fighting. That excuse wouldn't frighten you, I thought, and it would explain my presence in the woods."

What? Did Alfred just give himself away? Did he just admit to making up a false story? Her cunning, shrewd, quick-witted Alfred?

"If you didn't like fighting, why didn't you run away *during* the war? This was just after the liberation. The fighting was over. You didn't need to run away," Helen said desperately.

Alfred's flinty eyes narrowed. His hands clenched the arms of the chair, a slight gesture; but in her extreme vigilance, Helen saw it.

"Why are you bringing this up now, my dear Helen, after so many years? Didn't we put the war behind us?"

"But I want to know. You didn't have to make up stories. If you had just spoken softly and not advanced toward me, I probably wouldn't have been frightened. Were there any others you *did* talk to? Others who *did* run away? Is that why you were careful with me?"

"My dear Helen, I just bent the truth a little. Just for the situation at hand. Surely you are not bothered by that small detail after more than fifty-two years."

"Alfred, you know me. I always have to figure out the details."

"Well," he said, patting my hand, "perhaps your mind is making a big deal out of a few inconsequential words. Our thinking is somewhat unreliable at our age. Would you like me to call one of the aides to bring you a cup of tea?

"I must go now. I'm tired," he said as he held onto the arms of the chair and pushed himself up, unsteady on his feet. After grasping the walker, he bent over to give his wife a kiss on the cheek. "Goodbye, my dear, until next week."

Helen waited for him to make a mistake, to say, "*Auf Wiedersehen.*" Maybe he would slip up. But no, he was still canny, this man with the yellow flower. He said goodbye, turned around, and left.

Only after the click of his walker faded down the hall did she realize he had not answered her question. What was he actually doing in the woods?

Helen could hardly sleep or eat. The doctor checked her pulse, heart, her blood pressure. The doubts she was suffering would not be revealed by placing a stethoscope on her chest.

She now recalled picking up Alfred from a late-night meeting in some unfamiliar office building. It was dark, winter dark, an odd time for a gathering, she had thought. She was waiting there, in front; so of course, Alfred was obliged to introduce her. He was jovial enough, but she noticed that left brow of his lift slightly, a rare sign of unease and with cause. His companions were three Germans, speaking tersely but in English, peppered with a German word or phrase.

"Alfred, who were those people?" she had asked later. "We don't know any Germans in this town."

"My dear, don't worry your head about it. Just some old friends from the war passing through on their way to Canada. Fellows I knew from university when I took language classes there. You can't imagine how much we had to talk about after all these years. The moments just flew by."

"Why, if they were old friends, didn't you meet at the house?" I persisted.

"We didn't want to disturb you," Alfred responded. *Disturb me in our own house?* she thought. But it was the blackest of nights, about to rain, and she was not eager for a confrontation. Sometimes one of Alfred's dark moods would last for days. Besides, she had observed that left brow of his, a sign for her to tread carefully. Alfred was not pleased when she asked the same question more than once. "Badgering," he called it.

Helen bolted straight up in bed, thrashing around in her blankets. Midnight, the clock said. A devastating thought flew across her brain. Dare she even think further about it? This was an appalling notion - Alfred working as an undercover agent for the Nazi party, old-timers till flourishing secretly around the world, meeting in secret. This network that she knew for a fact existed. When they met, they sang Nazi war songs, saluted "Heil Hitler," the room adorned with Nazi paraphernalia. Elderly members of the Third Reich lived all over South America, even here in the United States.

And this! Alfred had made three trips during a fifteen-year period to Germany.

"For language conferences," he had said. She simply couldn't recall now exactly which cities. Munich? Frankfurt? Now that she was giving this some attention, didn't such conferences occur regularly in places like Las Vegas or Miami or New York City? After all, he was only a simple language teacher in high school or community college, not a linguistic expert working for the government or some international company. He never asked her to accompany him, but she had been so busy with the little ones that she couldn't have taken the time for such a long trip anyway, even if he *had* asked her. Which he hadn't.

Now Helen was sure Alfred was indeed a German and a Nazi. Well, yes, every German in the war belonged to the Party. She was shocked at the ease with which she swung over to this thinking, yet all the facts appeared true. Who could prove her wrong? She woke screaming in her bed. The nurse came running. "A sedative, Helen, that's what this pill is," she was told. "It will help you sleep. You had a bad dream." She wept until she was utterly exhausted. When the nurse arrived with her morning medicine, she had to change the pillowcase, wet from tears, and collect the sheets that had been thrown to the floor. *Oh, the torment of insight*, Helen cursed. But how could she have possibly known, early on in the woods or even ever after?

As soon as the door closed, Helen sobbed again in her bed, for this was the thought that stopped her heart. She, a Jew, whose entire family and village and six million of her people were intentionally, methodically murdered by the Nazis, had conceived children with a man who was one of those murderers.

Her self-loathing ran like a mad river through her blood.

When she didn't appear in the dining room for two days, Sarah and Nomi asked after her. "Migraine, resting in bed," the nurse had told them.

There was no one in whom she could confide. A friend might believe her or else might think she was crazy. The doctor would put her on the dementia floor. The authorities would investigate, and her children would find out. She could share with Nomi, but her shame was too great at being the fool who had fallen for Alfred's charms.

Thinking of all this, Helen realized what a devastating outcome this would be for her children should they be apprised of these facts. For her beloved grandchildren, whom she dreamed of having long before she ever took that walk in the woods. Her love for them was so overwhelming that she shouted out their names - Hana, Fredrich, Gunnar - one after the other, willing them to be safe.

She *had to* act. She could not live this way, as if she were condemned to wear her guilt like a mantle of sorrow.

Turning over ideas and schemes, Helen lay shivering until her fevered thinking came to a halt. At last, through the scrim of despair, she devised a plan. The event would take place just before Yom Kippur, the holiday on which Jews must repent their bad deeds and ask forgiveness from God and from those they have wronged. The holiest day of the entire Jewish year. Among many customs, one wears white clothing or a robed covering called a *kittel* to achieve purity like the angels. But the simple white garment is also used as a burial shroud, reminding us of our mortality and our need for repentance.

Quite fitting, Helen thought. Like so much wisdom in Jewish thought - life and death together.

All this, she knew well, but once her course was decided, she thought no more of it. Courage was what she needed, and acting in the most ordinary, everyday manner would give her this.

On the designated day, the doctors, nurses, and aides were busy with their usual tasks, preoccupied, distracted. After lunch, she and Alfred were to have their weekly visit, but first, she had her morning oatmeal with Nomi and Sarah.

In her room, she changed into a pretty flowered dress embroidered with roses, fussed over the furniture, and waited for her husband.

Soon she heard the wheels of his walker coming down the hall, squeaky, deliberate, one step at a time. Then all was silent at her door as if he were reluctant to enter. But at last, there was a slight whoosh, and she heard a lively "Helen, honey, it's me!" As he approached her chair, she felt only revulsion, hatred. Several motives held her steady - to avenge her people and to exact retribution for his betrayal of her. And to keep the truth from her children.

She smiled sweetly.

"Alfred, dear. Have a seat," she said, pointing to the chair with the metal arms. As he turned himself around, the walker wobbly and he unsteady on his feet, Helen gathered her strength and kicked the walker from his grasp. Awkwardly but surely, he fell hard. His head smashed into the chair's sharp metal arm. He went down heavily, like a drunk. She had calculated exactly right. He would never get up. Not by the looks of that deep gash in his brain that was bleeding all over the tile floor.

Helen sat a while. When there was no movement of any kind, not a whimper, not a twitch, she waited ten more minutes; and only then did she press the call button. How in control she felt at that moment! How was that possible? She had just murdered her husband! Retribution was sweet. Retribution was fair. Justice deserved to live. But she well knew she had stepped over a critical precipice.

As Helen waited for the aide to arrive, she looked at the old man on the floor. Her mind was focused on her three dear children, on her five precious grandchildren, all living lives according to Jewish tradition. If there truly was a God, she prayed, let there be no Nazi blood in their veins that would ever rise up to cause harm.

I did this for love of them, she told herself. *I did this because of all the forces on earth, other than the will to live, a mother's love for her children stands sure and true above everything else.* How many countless mothers had stood between their child and the gun of a Nazi murderer? How many mothers had held their sons and daughters close as together they fell into the pits or walked into the death showers, the mothers whispering "*Shlof mayn kind*. Sleep, my child," bestowing sweet comfort until their voices were shut down?

Helen looked out the window at the rain softly falling. Soon it would be time for Yom Kippur services. But when she reflected on it, the imminent praying and the chanting, the repentance and atonement that would take place all over the world for twenty-five hours, she was not at all sure she would ask for forgiveness from her God.

Blindsided

Just as Kate shoved off with her ski poles, the wind suddenly shifted and snow began to fall with ruthless fury. *Shoot, a snow squall, total whiteout*, she thought.

What now? Can I make it down with a good run?

Hot with effort, she worked her poles hard, arms and legs pumping, but almost immediately the slope became blurred - no markings at all, nothing but a muddle of trees somewhere off to her right.

Quick, hurry, she thought as the world went dark.

The small log cabin was tidy and warm, a fire blazing, the smell of strong coffee. Kate's leg was wrapped in a brace of some kind, a heavy cloth with a flat board underneath. Outside, the snow piled above the windows in great drifts. Her leg pulsated with heat, like a thousand red ants scurrying back and forth under her skin. She lay back, lost to the world beyond her body.

From her mouth poured grunts and moans like an animal caught in a trap. The pain felt like a burning dagger thrust deep into her the muscle of her leg then pulled out slowly, the jagged edges of the blade turning and turning as it eased itself out. And worse, to endure the humiliation that she had no control over her cries. Then, abruptly, there was nothing.

When she awoke, she heard a quiet movement, like a squirrel darting along a windowsill. A small sound, his body as he moved around now that she was awake, but carefully, tending to the stove, the blankets, her skis. A strong man, a tall man's back, was all she could make out from the angle of the bed. He wore a ski mask that covered his face and head entirely, a blue wool shirt, and boots.

Slowly, he turned, as if even his slightest shift might increase her suffering.

His eyes were tender, concerned. Worried.

Probably one of the ski patrol guys, she thought.

"Hello," she said.

"Hello," he answered. "Don't move. You had a bad fall on that leg, but nothing's broken. A bad sprain, I think, maybe a hairline fracture. I've bandaged it up for now. Here, take this pill and have a cup of the best coffee in Vancouver."

Before she could answer, another shattering scream erupted from somewhere inside her as the spasms kept roiling in and over. She bit her lip in frustration as that terrible shame broke out again as if she were splayed naked before this stranger. When she, Kate, had been the tough one all her life, always the first to get up from falling off a horse, picking up the reins and saying, "Let's go."

He started toward her then stepped back, unsure of how to console her.

She took the orange pill, sipped the delicious coffee. *This must be what they mean by "truckers' coffee,"* she thought. *Those diners in the mountains that cater to the loggers and their crews.* Strong, delicious. *Stay still*, she told herself. Maybe the blade won't find her muscle, her bone. But no, there was more. Exhausted, she lay back, fell asleep again. When her eyes next opened, the man was in a corner chair reading a book.

"I'm Doug from ski patrol," he said, smiling. "We're snowed in for a good while up here. This is the farthest cabin from nowhere, but not to worry. Although the radio is out, we have plenty of supplies. I took the week off, so no one is looking for me, but I imagine lots of folks are looking for you. How are you feeling?"

He doesn't know who I am, Kate thought. *Or he's pretending not to. Didn't the whole world hear Tom Hanks' statement at the awards* dinner last week? *"And now, the most beautiful and talented new face of our industry..."*

How she hated that night. *All I want to do is act*, Kate thought. *To be an unforgettable, imaginary new self for a short time. The celebrity stuff is bull. One minute you're in, the next, you're out. And someone always trying to take advantage one way or another.*

Trouble is, she was always pretending. No one knew the real Kate. The world only cared about the part of her they worshipped. That night of the awards dinner, she decided she had to get away. Just get the heck out and go sit on a beach somewhere.

But where? All she knew were glam places. Malibu. Montauk. Until she saw those beautiful snowy mountains in the back of *Architectural Digest* in, of all things, the issue that profiled her Manhattan apartment. Skiing it would be.

"I'll be back when I'm back," she told her friends. "No calls. Not to worry."

So no one knows where *I am*, she thought with relief. *What a rare pleasure. And this man doesn't know* who *I am.*

"My name is Kate," she offered, but then the pain mercifully dropped her into another sleep.

Sleep and wake, that's all she knew.

When she next opened her eyes, she stretched, tried to turn. Was it two days? Three? The leg had now settled into constant, dull throbbing. She prayed that the terrible misery of the thrusting knife was gone for good.

"How long have I been here?" she asked.

"Three days," Doug answered as he closed his book and padded over cautiously. He adjusted her pillows, his large hands gentle under her neck - very gentle, she noticed. He tended to her needs with the softness of a woman, tucking in edges, smoothing out wrinkles, not to intrude, still wearing his mask. Her jacket hung on a wall peg, her scarf and hat now dried by the flames, alongside. Shocked, she was discomfited. Three days? He must have washed her body, tended to her toileting needs. She couldn't look him in the eyes.

Music was playing softly.

Ah, she recognized Mascagni's *Intermezzo,* its glorious swells and dips an invitation to longings hidden, private.

"Are you hungry?" he asked, as she glanced at his book. Poetry, she noticed. Garcia Lorca - a revolutionary Spanish poet in this room? Here in a remote cabin in the cold north woods?

"Yes, hungry, very much," she answered as he readied hot soup and buttered toast.

Hungry but also intrigued.

Garcia Lorca?

And so she ate. Cautiously, like a cat, looking around. And from his chair, he watched her eat.

After another nap, another orange pill, another coffee, she asked, "Don't you take off your mask when you're inside?"

"Rarely," he said, "and especially not when I have guests."

Their laughter was sweet.

"Really? she teased. "Do you often have guests up here in the wilderness?"

"Well, now that you ask…never." Which made them laugh again.

It was an odd pairing and a curious unfolding. Neither felt any need to contact the world outside that room with the homey fire that burned day and night. Kate didn't ask to be taken off the mountain, and Doug didn't offer to have her moved.

Slowly, they began to tell each other about themselves.

"How did you appear from nowhere in the middle of this great blizzard?" he asked. "Where do you come from?"

"I'm from a small town in Montana," Kate said. "My family are third-generation ranchers. As a child, I learned to ride a horse and very soon after, to rope a calf."

Ah," he said, "so that accounts for your being alone up here. An independent gal, I see. A hang tough kind of gal."

"Perhaps," she answered. "I never thought of myself that way. Anyway, the ranch was in a valley surrounded by mountains. We used to ski all winter. When I started my run, the way was clear. And out of nowhere, that whiteout. Where are you from?"

"The Chesapeake Bay area. I spent my days motoring in and out of the marshes and inlets on my boat. I loved being out there with the birds and the water, so you might call me a loner. But my dad was always pushing me to join the high school football team."

"I was a loner on the ranch also, with my horses and dogs, and happy about it," Kate answered. "I loved those empty skies and endless spaces of sky and mountain. When I was a teenager, boys began calling, but I wasn't much interested. I preferred riding horses to parties."

Should she tell him? she wondered. Yes, she would, see how he reacts.

"One day, I drove with my friend Jeannie to a Bette Davis movie in the next town," Kate confided, "and just like that, I decided I wanted to be the next Bette Davis. The day I graduated from Indian Springs High, I was on my way to Hollywood. I was lucky. Doors opened pretty easily."

Doug was puzzled. Was she kidding, telling this fantastic story? Heck, how would I know about actresses? I never go to the movies. His face told her that he didn't know who she was. The revelation had been a risk worth taking, she thought, pleased. She leaned back. Oh yes, for this brief time, she would enjoy these wonderful feelings of safety and privacy. The ability to say whatever she pleased without consequence. The freedom to be authentic.

"I can see why those doors opened easily," Doug said, smiling.

"Did you ever see the Chesapeake Bay area? It's the most beautiful country on earth. Well, maybe along with your Montana ranch land. My dream was to live outdoors, to be a guide or fisherman, and just work enough to have free time left over to read great books. But my dad had other plans. Since his business was supplying the Naval Academy with its uniforms and clothing, it was either the Academy or Yale.

"So I went up to New Haven. After six months, I came back home. I missed the water and the quiet. And I wanted to write my own life exams. Now I'm taking a year off, getting away from my father, who was not pleased with me leaving school, to see what the mountains offer. Isn't it lucky I did? Here you are."

"Here *we* are," he added, correcting himself.

"Why Garcia Lorca?" she suddenly asked.

"Why *not* Garcia Lorca?" he answered.

They laughed again and began to love the sound of each other's voices.

Doug never removed his mask, but it didn't seem to bother either of them. In fact, Kate began to feel it was a part of him, like his nose, his fingers. In her business, folks had all kinds of strange habits. And it added something to their exchange, almost as if she were in a confessional. A place to tell the whole truth but still keep some distance and not feel overpowered by possible expectations within such an intimate space. They were so physically close in this cabin. For now, it was enough. Comforting he was but yet a man with broad shoulders and muscled arms, so she wasn't past wondering, *Does he have a rugged face? A poetic face? What color is his hair?* She only saw his eyes, intense and tender, both at once.

His voice was protective and low. With infinite care, he changed her leg brace to a soft wrapping, dressed her in his shirts, cooked her light meals, simple but fresh offerings, the fire crackling, sparks darting upward, charring the ceiling beams.

Make her smile, Doug told himself. *Make those beautiful eyes light up.*

"How would you like to be a lady snowman with a red flag warning off other skiers?" he suggested. "I can whip up a pretty good likeness outside, right on the spot."

She laughed, and the pleasure of it thrilled his soul. *I did it*, he thought. *Made her smile.*

So this was how the days passed. Stories of her parents, her sister, the land. His of the woods, the rare birds, his beloved books.

"My sister is my best friend, but I don't see her very often," Kate shared. "The land is always in my dreams. My parents taught me the love of the outdoors."

"A man in the woods can get lost in his dreams," Doug shared. "When all is still in the marsh, I whistle to the birds, and they whistle back. Reading and music are as important to me as breathing."

Doug made crutches for her out of two logs reserved for the fire. Whittling, sanding, binding, while Kate watched his skill. Moving close, he lifted her to her feet, then gently slipped them under her arms. Off she went, wobbling and hopping around the small cabin while the music swelled and the snow fell hard and the windows were plastered in white. Only this indoor world existed - Doug clapping at her clumsy steps and her grinning at him, at herself.

Long, hazy days - a week? Bright with companionship and confidences, as was their growing intimacy, both expanding and tightening.

Feeling the closeness of the confessional, she allowed her words to rush out as they wished.

"I'm pretty, so what? Being pretty prevents me from being honest with anyone. Women are covetous, men are bold. I accept it now just as the way of the world, but I've always longed for more."

"More?" he questioned.

"Yes, more. Just like this. Opening our hearts like we're doing and you taking it in, just for the giving."

Abruptly, suddenly shy, she turned aside, not meaning to say so much. Was it too much?

"And you? she asked. "What were you seeking in those marshes of yours?'

"Just this. Same as you. Opening our hearts, as you said, and you taking it in just for the giving."

They both sat quietly, watching the flames dart toward the ceiling like shooting stars, then disappear without a blink.

Is this the moment? he wondered.

Dare I?

"May I read you one of my favorite Lorca poems?" he asked. "Actually, my favorite from when I was a teenager full of dreams." He inserted caveats and disclaimers for fear of the poem being too bold, too intimate, scaring her off. Also, to protect himself from what he knew was surely coming next - the total unmasking of himself. But it was time.

She nodded. *Yes, yes. Please do.*

Opening to a page in his beloved book, he began, almost reciting by heart.

> "For love of you, the air, it hurts,
>   and my heart,
>   and my hat, they hurt me.
>
> Who would buy it from me,
>   this ribbon I am holding,
>   and this sadness of cotton,
>   white, for making handkerchiefs with?
>
>   Ay, the pain it costs me
>   to love you as I love you!"

He feared to look up, as he sat with his heart banging against his chest, screaming, *Let me out.*

Kate asked softly, "May I see your face?"

He knew this would be the moment she would ask.

The fire crackled and spit. The remains of a burning log collapsed with a fury, and the sweet scent of an erotic elixir misted the room.

Gradually, measured, Doug lifted the edges of his cap and pulled it over his head.

Instantly, Kate thought, *Thank you, God, for making me an actress. Thank you for training me on how to control my face. But all is wanting now. Help me. Help me to show only love.*

"From a fire," he said quietly, "a fire on a remote island, a house burning, a woman and child inside. I was paddling nearby and got them."

His skin was wizened and puckered. There were pale half-moons under his eyes. His wealthy father had the finest plastic surgeons do their best, but the damage had been great.

Only his eyes, fiery and sensitive together, remained intact and lovely by some forgiving grace. Eyes that drew like a magnet, him to her. Eyes she had come to adore.

He watched her face and thought, *No, she is not that good an actress. No one is.*

And she thought, *He knows.*

Doug rose, put his cap on the table, adjusted the pillow under her leg. Discovering that chocolate was her irresistible sin, he put out the chocolate muffins he had baked. As he bent over the table, she reached out, her fingers gently tracing the scars on his cheeks, under his eyes.

She thought to offer some appropriate line from one of her plays, but all was inane, ridiculous. No words she had ever uttered or could now find were true enough for what she felt - love, ambivalence, sorrow.

The air enveloping them was now altered.

Not because they loved each other less. Rather, they loved more, for no longer were there any secrets between them.

She thought, *How can I take him back with me? To my working life? He who lives for the open waters? But how can I live in the marshes and forsake my career?*

And he thought, *She is struggling. But she need not worry. I won't encumber her with my permanent presence and my face as it is, though she is the first woman and the last to whom I will ever open my heart.*

Their reflections were the same. Their questions were the same. Both had the same answers. Is this real, our time here and now? Yes. Is this once in a lifetime pairing a gift, not ours to abandon? Yes. Or have our days here together been mere romantic moments out of time, based on hope and need, not truth? No.

Will any decision, either way, cause us regret or heartbreak?

The room was filled with a thousand songs, a thousand arrows.

The only certainty they held in their hands was this, the one they both knew to be real - that now they had a fateful choice to make.

In the Beginning

Every year, our family's first thought as the holiday of Rosh Hashanah, the Jewish New Year, came around, was this. Should we wear cotton or wool to temple services? Living in a small New Hampshire town so far north, you expected it to be chilly in October, but you couldn't be sure. The weather report usually determined our decision but not always. Sometimes my mother decided, she always anxious for fall clothes after spending two months in sandals and light blouses. And this year, she determined it would be wool. The forecast was not too cool, not too warm, somewhere in between. But it turned out to be very warm, and we ended up wiping our sweaty faces, my parents telling each other, "Well, we were wrong again this year."

Let me out, let me out, I cried to myself sitting on the bench in the synagogue during Rosh Hashanah services. I was wedged between my mother and father, who were listening carefully to the rabbi's opening prayers. But I was eight years old, restless as a cat in a cage, already bored and thinking about my dress. I touched the sleeve, so soft, like skin. It was new and blue, with ruffles, and pretty, but even so, I had wanted the yellow one with the pink ribbons around the collar, the one my mother thought too grown-up for me.

My parents told us we are supposed to get new clothes for this special day. The rabbi just said this holiday celebrates the beginning of "humanity's role in God's world," though I had no idea what he meant. I should have gone to the children's service where I could understand the sermon. But oh no, I wanted to be a *big girl* and sit with the grown-ups, show off my blue dress. Maybe next year my mother will buy me the yellow one with the pink ribbons even though I'll only be nine.

I looked around the large room and counted two hundred people. Against the plain white walls were bookcases filled with thick religious books. A tall, fancy wooden cabinet up front called the *aron kodesh* or holy ark held the sacred Torah scrolls. Overhead, a light was fastened, but Daddy said it's a special light "representing God's presence, and it never goes out." I wondered about that, thinking of the lightbulbs in our house that were always being replaced.

Along the fourth wall were these dazzling stained-glass windows that represented popular stories from the Bible. Adam and Eve, Noah, Joseph. It was a sunny morning, and the reds burned through the glass so bright they made my eyes tear. And the blues were as blue as the swimming pool at camp. I remember when the rabbi asked Mommy to raise money to pay for those windows. She held teas and talks and asked all the temple members to chip in to pay for them. I also remember the Stella D'oro cookies with the chocolate swirl on top that she put out on the side table. There were rows of wood benches with curved arms at either end with red velvet seats, right now filled with our friends wearing new outfits. The ladies' hats were something to see, one fancier than the next with their feathers and bows. Most of them had chosen light wool clothes like ours and were fanning themselves with their hands. Only Mr. and Mrs. Rubin, he in a tan summer suit and she in a pale-yellow cotton dress with loose sleeves, seemed comfortable.

After a long period of chanting, the rabbi paused to catch his breath, and we all turned every which way to wave to our friends. When everyone settled down again, he started to discuss the story of Adam and Eve. *Oh, good,* I thought. *I like this story, although it's not as simple as it seems at first.* Adam and Eve eating the apple from the tree of knowledge. The way the rabbi talked, I wasn't sure if he thought the story was true or not. The snake and the people seemed real but not real, so I couldn't tell. Would Adam and Eve be considered bad their whole lives if they ate that apple? What about me? I snitched an extra cupcake from the cupboard three days ago while no one was looking. Did God know I had hidden it under my jacket? Would he punish me? Was that why my brother Michael wouldn't let me use his typewriter? Why I had to go to bed early instead of watching my favorite TV show just because I had a science test the next day and my mother thought I needed rest even though I told her I had already studied heaps for it?

Rabbi continued to talk about Adam and Eve's disobedience. His words began to make me nervous. Did God's laws and judgment for disobeying also include my mother and father, like when they argued? And Billy's Bakery and Jake's Bike Shop, just everyday places and people in our town? And what about my school and Mrs. Kelly's third grade when I did badly on a test or she got mad when I turned to whisper to my friend Nancy. Did God punish that?

We opened our *siddurim*. On the cover, it says *siddur*, the Hebrew word for prayer book; but my father told me to say *siddurim* when you mean more than one.

After the chanting and prayer went on for a bit, I began to fuss. My mother put her hand firmly on my knee. To make the time pass, I decided to count how many stories I knew on those windows. I knew Adam and Eve with their heads down, punished and sent out of the garden; the evil serpent sticking out his tongue just like I did sometimes when I got mad; and the animals marching into Noah's ark - two fluffy rabbits, two crazy tall giraffes, two big fat elephants, and more. The rabbits would be cute pets, though my parents didn't allow pets because they were "too much trouble."

Next was Joseph and his brothers. I know that one because my friend Shana told me about Joseph. "Can you imagine your brothers bowing down before you!" she had exclaimed. Shana had four brothers who always picked on her. Not mean picking, just kind of teasing, but she didn't like either kind. I was glad I wasn't her. I looked at my father's watch. The hands had hardly moved. When was all this sitting going to be over? I was getting hungry.

Prayers were recited in Hebrew, and although I attended Hebrew school twice a week, so far, I only knew a few letters of the alphabet. However, for this day, my father had taught me to say to everyone we met, "*Shanah tovah, um'tukah,*" which meant "Have a good and sweet year." I still remember his wide smile when I looked up at Mrs. Schaeffer wearing her new beaver hat and said straight out, "*Shanah tovah*, Mrs. Schaeffer."

It didn't exactly bother me that I couldn't understand Hebrew. I liked listening to the rhythms of the chants and prayers. It felt kind of mysterious and comforting. It was nice to just *feel* something for a change. We don't always have to understand *everything*, do we? I thought the English translation from the Hebrew was not very interesting, like my *dull* English Composition Reader. When I read the English, God was always punishing or getting angry or forgiving people if he wanted. How was I supposed to know when he was going to do what? I like things clear and understandable, like the Ten Commandments. But to tell the truth, sometimes there are little differences and arguments to each one of those commandments so that when you should say yes, and when no, well, believe me, you can get pretty confused and can't always tell the right thing to do.

Anyway, not knowing the Hebrew, I imagined the words my own way like God didn't really seem to be doing the best for everyone all the time like everyone said. What happened when Shana asked God to have her brothers stop bothering her and they kept on bothering, or what about me when I snitched that cupcake? Was my punishment to feel guilty when I ate it? What if I didn't feel guilty? What if I actually *enjoyed* eating a stolen cupcake? This business of when God is angry or when God forgives or even when he listens can be confusing. Another thing - why doesn't God take kids' sides when we want him to?

Still, I thought it's special to speak and read another language even though it's not anything I could ever do. But my grandfather does. He reads and writes Hebrew better than English. And my father too - he read on the Hebrew side of the prayer book, not the English side. My grandfather was my mother's father, so she should certainly read Hebrew, but I'd never really noticed if she did or not. Mainly, she was busy watching me and my brother Michael, but mostly Michael. Boys sure would get into a lot of mischief. Now that I think of it, Michael will have to learn Hebrew when he'll have his bar mitzvah in two years! Well, if Michael could learn Hebrew, maybe someday I could too, if I wanted.

Today, and always, the cantor - that was the person who leads much of the service and all the singing - was my grandfather. He was specially chosen because he was the holiest man in our community.

When he prayed out loud, his voice kind of sounded as if he's asking for favors like I sounded when I want something special for Chanukah, like saying *please* extra hard. All my family's friends were here to sing and pray with him. Max the pharmacist and Dr. Plotkin the vet with his tall, skinny wife in her new gray suit. Even Herman, the mechanic who fixed our car and, of course, Mrs. Blum, my Hebrew teacher.

Look how close my grandfather feels to God, I thought. *I would like to be that close to God if I only knew who God was or how to get close to him.*

When my grandfather wasn't singing, my mind wandered all over the place. I kept wondering why I should care about the birthday of the world. What I really cared about was my best friend Gina's birthday. She had asked me to sleep over to celebrate, but my mother had said no. "No sleepovers till you are twelve." What? The yellow dress at twelve. A sleepover at twelve. What's so special about being twelve? I thought all those things while I was sitting between my parents on this important day.

Was the real reason I couldn't sleep over at Gina's was that Gina wasn't Jewish? When I was at her house, everything seemed pretty normal. Nothing particularly religious except for her grandmother sitting on the sofa holding her rosary beads. I liked looking at her doing that. Those beads were very important to her. And Gina's mom, who had polio when she was a child and dragged one foot after the other, was cheerful and friendly. She even asked me to bake chocolate chip cookies with her one rainy afternoon.

Was Gina embarrassed by her mother's limp? I wondered. It was so easy to get upset about all kinds of weird things. When we felt we didn't fit in. Like my friend Judy who complained that her mother favored her brother, Tom. He got all the treats, staying up late or going to a movie on a school night. And my friend Susie got mad that her older sister got new clothes from Shaw's, the department store, while her own were made by her mother on the old Singer sewing machine.

I also thought about myself and this "not fitting in" thing but tried not to when my grandfather was chanting the prayers.

But I thought about them anyway. Could thinking be a sin?

For example, those few holidays like Rosh Hashanah and Yom Kippur when my family went to religious services while my friends went to regular school and I had to go to the temple or those Sundays when my friends went to church while I rode my bike to the park. Even the fact that Katie Sullivan had twelve brothers and sisters seemed to have something to do with being Catholic. And when I asked my mother about having a sister, she said, "Another? Two of you is enough." So then I knew that twelve kids in a family probably wasn't a Jewish thing.

And what about Christmas, when our home seemed to be the only house on the block that didn't sparkle the whole long month of December? My mother was okay with my non-Jewish friends, but only barely. She never said anything bad against them; but in our neighborhood, there were few Jewish kids my age, so she didn't want me to be without friends.

I had some kind of funny sense about all this like not being allowed to sleep at Gina's house. It didn't seem very nice to refuse, but I didn't want to start a big discussion with my mother which I would never win anyway. I just bet that when I was twelve years old, she would have another excuse not to let me sleep over. Gina had never eaten a meal with us or slept over in the extra bed next to mine. Why wouldn't Mom allow that in our own house where she could watch over us?

Well, I think something uncomfortable must always come up with everyone. Look at Judy and Susie and Tom. Everyone had *something* that needed acceptance. And everyone should at least have a kind of understanding so we all knew what was going on and could agree - like whether it was okay to find pleasure, not guilt, in eating the cupcake or if we'd become a bad person from such a little thing. Daddy said one of the Ten Commandments was "Thou shalt not steal." That sounded to me like a punishment would be coming regarding the cupcake.

Even my brother had problems. In his soccer league, he was the shortest one on the team. The other kids called him the Runt. They meant it in fun, but he sure didn't take it that way; it made him really sad and really mad. We're so smiley on the outside most of the time. So why not on the inside?

Gina went to mass every Sunday with her grandmother but also on weekdays when there was a school holiday. Was she as fidgety in church as I was in temple? I often passed her Church of the Sacred Heart and was curious to know what it looked like inside. The shiny gold cross on the roof never fell down or got bent, not even in the worst storms. I bet anyone, even if they weren't Catholic, was impressed when they looked up at that. Stone statues were attached to the walls all over the stone front and around the doorways. Hands of saints were raised high over the people kneeling in front of them. I looked at it almost every day, though I didn't know who the figures were or what they were doing.

So one afternoon, I did it. Sneaked off with Gina to see the inside of her church. I didn't tell my mother. She would have scolded me. "Jews don't go into churches," she would have said. But I was glad I did! For sure, I didn't ever tell her *that* either.

Inside felt strange but exciting. The walls and floors and ceilings were all covered with fancy decorations of figures and objects. Hardly an inch was left bare. It was so different from our temple where there was nothing on the walls or ceiling you could point to and say "That is a person, that is a cow, and a house" except, of course, on the wall with the stained-glass windows. But those images were people and animals, not God.

Here in the Church of the Sacred Heart, prophets and saints and other kinds of figures were everywhere, even on the ceiling, floating overhead like people clouds, like people in real paintings who came to life. There were lots of candles on a table up front near the altar, flickering like fireflies. And there was what Gina told me was "burning incense" that gave off a smell like perfume that made me sleepy and think of *The Arabian Nights*. Gold covered everything, but Gina said it was gold leaf, not paint.

"That's Jesus," Gina suddenly said in a hushed voice, pointing to a man far above our heads hanging from a gigantic cross, his head drooping, hands nailed to the horizontal beam. Blood was running down his body. "He's the Son of God."

What? What was she talking about? A man who was the Son of God? Maybe that's why my mother didn't want me inside a church, seeing and learning these foreign ways. What would my grandfather think to hear that? How was that possible when God had no face and wasn't a man or a woman even though most Jews referred to God as *he* except for my girlfriends, who wanted to call God a *she*. But we Jews all knew God wasn't a man or a woman.

There was even a snack - that wafer you got up at the altar, even though I couldn't eat it because it was only for Catholics! Good thing Gina was with me or I would never have gone inside that first day. For sure, the Jewish God who sometimes punished and sometimes forgave saw everything and would have something in store for me. I'd have to watch out.

When we sat down on a bench, Gina didn't fuss. In fact, she sat very still and closed her eyes; and her lips were saying something softly, a special prayer, I guessed. She was really feeling that prayer, so maybe she forgot I was even sitting next to her.

I wondered how close to God Gina felt in there with those sweet smells and human forms that looked important but really bothered me. The Son of God on the cross was suffering a lot, and many of the shapes looked very unhappy. I wondered if Gina talked to God, "I would so love a bike, and can you make it so my mommy doesn't walk with a limp?" She seemed to believe that the man on the cross would make her wishes come true. Would she stop talking to God if her mother never ran or jumped again?

Then Gina pointed out small attached wooden booths along the wall. "Those are confessionals," she told me. "It's where I tell my sins to the priest sitting inside. There's a little seat and a curtain between us so he doesn't know who I am." That seemed so silly. How could the priest not know her voice when he talked to her all the time? "I have to tell him if I was a bad girl that week."

How was an eight-year-old a bad girl? I wondered.

And what exactly *was* a sin? Was it a sin to borrow my brother Michael's tennis racket without asking? Was it a sin when I called him "stupid" as he raced off on *my* bike just as I was getting ready to ride over to Gina's house?

Was I committing a sin thinking that I loved the smells of that church while I was sitting in the synagogue?

My mother suddenly squeezed my hand. Sometimes she did that as if she were reading my thoughts. Images of Gina and the church flew off in a hurry.

Now I was paying attention again. The rabbi sat down. The cantor took his place.

"Stop wiggling," my mother said. "It's almost over. Be a big girl."

Smoothing my dress and twirling my bracelet, I reminded myself it was easier to do almost anything if I only had to do it two or three times a year.

This was the moment everyone had waited for, the main event of the Rosh Hashanah service. The whole room stood up, serious, attentive. The time had come for my own grandfather to blow the *shofar*, a real horn from a real ram. - a bighorn sheep, a male sheep. It was beautiful, this curved and twisted horn. It was hollow inside so the sound could travel through perfectly. I had hoped they took the horn from a ram that had already died, that someone didn't have to kill a beautiful grown sheep just for our holiday. Blowing it at this service was a call to God, my mother had told me.

My grandfather walked slowly to the Holy Ark then stopped and lifted the ram's horn high above his head. Earlier, I had heard people ask, "Would the cantor hold his breath long enough to reach the high notes? Would he do us proud?"

My grandfather covered his head with his *tallis*, or prayer shawl, and put the *shofar* to his lips.

And then wonderful strong blasts rang throughout the room, bouncing off the walls and ceilings. Oh, so exciting at last! A real show!

"*Tekiah, shevarim, t'ruan*" - our Hebrew teacher Mrs. Blum made us say those words over and over until we were one hundred percent perfect. *Tekiah*, one long note, a call to attention, also meaning the glory of God's sovereignty - I guess this was the king part (*sovereignty* was a new word for me). Then *shevarim* was a blast with breaks like sounds of crying although Mrs. Blum had called those sounds weeping, not crying. And finally, *t'ruah*, was many short blasts like the ram's own noisy bleats, an alarm for us to wake up from our spiritual slumber. I guess that meant I should apologize to my brother and not play his drums without his permission and tell God as well as Michael that I was sorry for intentionally doing a mean thing.

In Hebrew school, Mrs. Blum had described the meaning of *shofar*, that blowing the ancient signals on Rosh Hashanah stood for all the important things Jewish people believed in. "God's continuing kingship," she said. But how could God be a king if we couldn't see him? And then she said, "We are to examine our past behavior and return to God's way." This order reminded me of Gina's confession to the priest. I thought that meant feeling sorry for the bad things we've done and not do them again, like when I sat on my brother's bed with his special Red Sox pennant sewn on just to get him mad. And she added, "Study the Torah more and every day." I knew I failed already at that since I only studied the Torah at Hebrew school, and that meant just twice a week. And Mrs. Blum was late so often we didn't get the full time anyway. There was more stuff about the voice, the tears, and the sacrifice. I didn't pay attention. My friend Shana and I sent hand signals to each other during those parts because we were bored and wanted to play.

Suddenly the blasts ended. The blowing of the *shofar* was over. Everyone smiled at each other, relieved.

"Aha, the cantor did a fine job this year," the people said. "Thank God. But of course, he always does."

The morning prayers were finished. We could now go home for lunch.

I turned to my mother and asked, "Was I a good girl in synagogue today?"

I hoped that as we were filing out of the sanctuary, no one would ask me to explain anything. But sometimes an adult did just that, checked on me to see if I had been paying attention. Such as

"Emma, honey, what did you learn this week in Hebrew school?" But I always bent down at those times and pretended to tie my shoelaces.

Thinking more about it now, I'm not sure Mrs. Blum was the right teacher for the little kids, all those big stories and not always taught in ways we could understand. I thought she needed to give examples from our own lives. Stuff about whispering in class and getting our brothers mad. And ask us questions to see what we couldn't understand, like "Emma, do you know how to ask for God's mercy?" Stuff like that. Then I could ask *her* questions and bring up the forgiveness thing and "God doing the best for us" thing though I wasn't sure I was ready to confess the cupcake thing.

Then one day, I got lucky, same as with my piano lessons. Just as my complaints about going to Sunday school really began to annoy my parents, Mrs. Blum declared, "I'm moving to Florida." And so I quit my Judaism instruction, just like that.

But I realized a few things that Rosh Hashanah when I was eight years old. I wasn't Catholic like Gina. I wasn't Protestant like Mr. Walker who owned the First National Bank. I was Jewish like my grandfather, and although I wasn't sure what being Jewish really meant and why it was so important to all those people, I loved him and was proud of him.

Those feelings were my childhood connection to Judaism.

When I was twelve, my mother let me buy the dresses I liked if she liked them too. This was the year that great things were supposed to happen. I was given a diary with a lock and key for my birthday so I'd be ready to write down all those special things waiting for me.

But not much really happened to me until I was sixteen.

And then, in my sixteenth year, I unexpectedly entered a new life phase. Still a big child, adulthood was yet hovering at my door. Although I was eager and curious about almost everything, I didn't have a true sense of how to handle adult situations or make decisions that required mature insight. But one thing that *was* fairly apparent was the differences between Gina's and my religious lives.

We occasionally went to church together, but she never accompanied me to the synagogue. Non-Catholics were welcome in churches. No one asked your name or if you would like a sprinkling of holy water. In synagogues, not so much. Everyone knew whether or not you belonged. Anyway, in those days - everything is so different now - no one of my acquaintances seemed eager to attend a Jewish service, not even Gina. No one I knew even asked me a religiously relevant question. I entered our synagogue as if it were a special place but without Gina's reverence, who, stepping inside her church, uttered a deep sigh then closed her eyes as she dipped her fingers into the blessed waters of Church of the Sacred Heart and touched them to her heart and forehead.

Now I fiercely wanted those same feelings. But I didn't want hers. I wanted my own.

I didn't understand Catholic doctrine. The idea of the Trinity was strange. How could God be a man? And all the rest - the martyrdom, the taking on of all man's sins - none of it made sense as if each person is devoid of personal responsibility for his own choices.

Yet Judaism didn't make it easy. Initially, it didn't cocoon or envelop you. And there is certainly no coddling. "Welcome, come in," it says, beckoning with its challenging, intellectual wiles. "But now that you are here, study and learn."

At seventeen, I began to study Jewish thought, Jewish history. On my desk at college, Jewish-themed books began to displace those of chemistry and French literature. I was invited by fellow Jewish students to trek around Safed in northern Israel for the summer, and during that trip, Hebrew words began to fall naturally from my lips. Sometimes I even had a quick thought or response in Hebrew rather than in English.

My journal grew fat with discovery. Gina's devotion to her own ways and mine for my grandfather's had provided the sweetener for my own journey.

I fell in love with Judaism as Gina had with Catholicism.

As precious and formative as that diary had been, I have no idea where it is now. Often, we pledge to capture our most intense moments by writing them down, pasting a remembrance here and there. And yet we don't keep it up. Beloved belongings disappear. Why? Perhaps we humans just have a limited capacity for emotional storage or for that which we can recall. No matter. As I am now approaching seventy years of age, that day at holiday services so long ago, when I was eight years old, is still clear and sharp - the blue dress; the scratchy wool coat; the brilliance of the sun burning through the colored glass, causing the reds and blues and yellows to skip along the benches and bounce off the ladies' hats; the fiery red in particular, dancing back and forth across the *aron kodesh* while my grandfather swayed in fervent prayer.

I was beginning to understand my grandfather's impassioned devotion and his most exciting premise - that following the laws of the Torah requires a Jew's most strenuous effort. "'To whom much is given, much will be required.' That's from Luke," Gina whispered.

Sadly, I lost touch with Gina when I left home for college in Chicago. She had won a full scholarship to Catholic University, family and friends crying and hugging at this remarkable honor, cheering in the street as the bus took her away.

It has been more than fifty years ago now. Can it be?

Oh, after these many long years, Gina, my cherished friend, to share with you the paths on which our faith has directed us! I often think that if one stays the course and the end leads to doubt rather than faith, the voyage will still have exacted a life lived with high moral purpose.

Have you remained true to your childhood truths? Have you lived the life you hoped for when we were young and so dear, one to the other, and only time without end was before us?

A Most Uncommon Marriage

When Tess and I first married, what did either of us know of limitation or disability, illness or pain? What did we know of *caution*? We never considered those conditions as being likely, certainly not inevitable, as they came to be. In fact, we never thought of such things at all, busy as we were with work, travel, the children. And now here we were, afflicted with those dire conditions.

Hank's strong head nodded as he dozed and picked at fragments of his long life, as old people do, marveling again how he had gotten away with a secret life all these years.

Now white as chalk, Hank's hair was still thick and unruly. His lean frame had grown a smidge paunchy, his posture a bit stooped, but his brown eyes remained alert, watchful. Sitting at Tess's bedside for countless hours, Hank was feeling an obligation to be contemplative. Time to gather up the loose ends, a reckoning, Hank's friends told him. However, analytical thinking was not something Hank did very often or very well. He was more of an instinctual, off-the-cuff kind of guy.

Tess lay comfortably napping, her wan face now relaxed after her recent injection, a temporary reprieve from her dreadful cardiac illness. Still, even at rest, her breath was labored and raspy, as if her heart were pushing against a boot on her chest. Every four hours, she was given a shot for pain. A minute late and Hank was running out to the hall for the nurse.

Her infirmity had crept up with silent stealth, like a panther after prey. Shortness of breath from walking upstairs or doing light housework, phenomena that often occur with normal aging, were her only complaints. But after the doctor was done hooking her up to wires and bleeping machines, he told them it wasn't the stairs at all. Speaking in cryptic medical jargon that was frightening and mysterious, they struggled to make sense of this fearsome diagnosis. Behind her back, her friends whispered "cardiac cripple" with tears in their eyes and a wringing of hands. They thought she didn't hear, but she did. Tess had always been good with murmurs and innuendos.

Although we've lived together for more than fifty years, Tess's life was different from mine, Hank mused. She always conducted herself without moral blemish. The good mother, the dutiful wife. However, I was a callous bastard, cheating on her over and over yet, Lord help me, loving every minute of it. It's funny how fate plays tricks. Tess, the better person, lay suffering, her life close to its end, and I remained, for now, a healthy witness. Not even overcome with guilt as I should be. But then again, I always believed that though one's actions may be reprehensible, they are permissible if they don't hurt others. And Tess had never been hurt, as far as I knew.

Anyway, why bring the past up now? To what end? I've been discreet, keeping my doings close and private. Surely Tess didn't know about my hidden life. She never accused me or confronted me in any way.

Hank looked out the window at the moving clouds, adjusted the blinds to let in the light. *What Tess and I do know now, however,* he thought sadly, *is this. If two people live together long enough, one of them will become afflicted, and the other will be the caregiver.*

Or one of them will die, and the other will be left alone.

This was the tenth day Hank had kept vigil in this room. He no longer spent long hours in the garden tending his lettuce and tomatoes. How he had loved to take hoe and spade in the hot sun and turn over the winter dirt, bringing up a rich soil, shirtless, tanning his back and arms. Now the ground was hard, branches and debris scattered to all corners. Nor did he play golf with his pals, his reliable foursome of many years - Nicholas, Frank, and Ralph or as they called each other Nickie the Putting King, Frankie Boy the Sharpshooter, and Rafe the Nineteenth-Hole Happy Guy. No more friendly wagers, no more beers after a game. Hank even missed the click of his shoe cleats on the tile floor in the pro shop. Who did they get to fill in for him? he wondered. Was it a new regular or a temp? *I'll call Nickie and find out*, he reminded himself.

Sometimes his friends were good at checking in with him, but sometimes they forgot. When you're older, sometimes a day feels like a week.

Hank had loved getting married. Hank loved *being* married, even with all that came after. Tess was so sweet, and she and Hank desperately wanted children. They were from the same town, knew the same people. The trouble was, as he discovered later, and never realized when they were standing before Pastor Michael, you never know what kind of person you'll be in five years, or twenty. Or truth be told, even next week. Certainly not the same as you were when saying "I do" and making all those reckless promises, *till death do us part*.

Honeymooning in Bermuda, Tess had unfortunately enjoyed food she was not used to - codfish for breakfast, black rum cake, shrimp chowder for dinner. On the ship home, she was seasick the entire trip. Cloistered in our cabin, stewards continuously brought her crackers and ginger ale. I clearly remember her telling me to have "a little fun." I was glad about that. I couldn't have stayed in that tiny room for four days. Anyway, she didn't want me around to see how pale and ill she was, a young bride eager to be attractive to her new husband.

After dinner the first evening, as I was bending over the rails watching the moonlight dance off the parting waves, a dark-haired woman maybe ten years older than I glided over to my side. Her black eyes gleamed like roving spotlights. The chiffon skirt of her pale green dress ruffled gently in the breeze then settled seductively around her slender hips. In a low voice, she asked, "What are you looking at?" I turned. My breath caught as the moon shone like silver tears on her long eyelashes. Leaning against a post like Humphrey Bogart, I answered, "Why, at you, pretty lady."

And that was the first time.

After, he thought, *Damn you, Hank, a husband of merely a week with your bride miserable downstairs in your bed. You're in a bad way if this is the defining moment of your manhood, a man of weak conscience whose nature succumbs to impulse and inclination.*

But I also told myself Tess would never find out, not unless some steward dropped a hint after seeing Loretta and me huddled together near the emergency lifeboats. But the staff on these cruise ships were trained to keep their mouths shut, no doubt well-paid for doing so. Later, when Loretta and I were naked in her cabin, I even told myself that this was a good lesson for a new husband. I wasn't that experienced with lovemaking right then, being pretty young and still fairly unschooled. Maybe I could learn something to take to my poor, seasick Tess.

How easily I had rolled over from the fidelity that I had pledged before Pastor Michael! Opportunity arose, and I took it. No one paid a price. Simple as that had I justified my conduct.

When the boat docked in Miami, Hank thought confidently, *I will make my Tess even happier now.*

Holding Tess's hand as she slept, Hank recrossed his legs, shifted his position in the metal hospital chair, and continued to reminisce about their marriage.

A month after we were married, my boss at a medical supplies company sent me out on the road. I was gone for three or four days at a time, but Tess didn't mind. She was busy teaching fifth-graders and fixing up the tidy house we had bought. Friendly neighbors all around were a reassuring presence. The Murphys on one side, the Sloans on the other, and Tom Lindsay, a widower, across the street. I had played golf with Tom a couple of times, and he was a reliable guy.

Kitty Murphy said we looked like brothers, and he was able to help Tess if she needed a small repair. Everyone looked out for each other, stopped in for coffee, babysat each other's kids.

So I left on my frequent trips with an easy heart, not expecting the surprises that awaited and into which I happily tumbled.

In the offices of almost every doctor and hospital were nurses and secretaries offering startling enticements. Married or not, many turned out to be charming flirts. All he had to do was show up, and sweet voices called out, "Hank's here!" The gals he took orders from and, later in the evening, slept with, had no qualms about what they were doing. But then, neither did he, not after that fleeting episode with Loretta on the ship. Like Hank, these women lived what he came to realize were secret lives. Several of them told him their dalliances improved their marriage.

"How?" he asked.

"Marriage is more fun now. After a while, sex with your husband is so predictable," the thoracic surgeon's receptionist said.

"After you and I are together, I'm happy. Later, after my husband's two-minute lovemaking, I tell him he's great, and he 'feels like a king,'" the nurse manager on pediatrics gleefully whispered.

Over the next few years, Hank was enlightened further: "My husband's a chef and smells of garlic and fish." "My husband's a carpenter and his hands are rough and covered with nicks and tears." "My husband plays basketball after work, and he wants sex before he takes a shower."

With hardly a day's notice, most of these women could arrange a meeting, make excuses for an evening out, that kind of thing. He came to believe that somehow he was being a good guy providing a worthwhile service, showing up neat and clean, rubbing hand cream into his palms at night.

Just like her sister Brenda, Tess and Hank had decided to have three kids. During their childhood, she would take time off from teaching. Tess was in control of those pink birth control pills. When she had those babies would be up to her. With him on the road, she would be their primary parent, and he wanted her to feel comfortably ready.

Almost to the day of their second anniversary, Hank came home from a particularly grueling three-state trip and found Tess happily pregnant. Radiant with anticipation, she was busy consulting graphs and ultrasounds; swept up in the details of what occurred in the fourth month, the seventh, etc.; and spending lots of telephone time with her sister, whose youngest was about to start kindergarten.

He was having a good life with Tess and the babies - Luke and Hannah now - and other women, visited discreetly far from home. That is, until he entered a dermatologist's office and called one of the secretaries *hon,* whispering, "Hey, Sally girl, where are we meeting tonight?" not knowing her husband was sitting at her desk. That was the end of his gallivanting around, at least for a while, though he realized soon enough that if someone has a hankering, he doesn't give it up. At best, he takes a brief pause.

Needing a scotch after that experience, he sought out the hotel bar as soon as he stepped into the lobby. A tall, thin man with a goatee sat down on the adjacent stool. "Are you a betting man?" he asked quietly, one hand wrapped around a martini. Within half an hour, Hank found himself upstairs on the twenty-third floor in a hot poker game that went on for three nights. One night, he lost $1,200; the next, he won $1,400, always coming out just about even. If there were small losses, he could write them off his expense account. On his last night in town, he was given an unforeseen win when the man who came up to him at the bar, took him back to his room and personally gave him a night of pleasure he had never dreamed of.

With two little ones under four and the third and final pregnancy underway, Tess was perpetually worn out. Their supportive neighbors rallied around - Kitty Murphy, Susie Sloan, and even Ted, who shoveled out the driveway after snowstorms and fixed loose shingles on the roof. When Hank was home, he played with the babies, put them to sleep, and read them stories; though he admitted at their early age, he wasn't much help with a dirty diaper.

One afternoon, as Tess and her sister relaxed on the porch, Hank overheard fragments of their conversation through the open kitchen widow. "Oh, Bren, Hank's so sweet, but he's like a big baby. He adores the kids, but he likes his meals on time, thinks a night out would be good for me when all I want is sleep. He means well, but right now, he doesn't exactly fit into the routine, crying babies and all. A part of me is glad he's on the road. Whenever he comes back, the children are thrilled and he spoils them outrageously." Hank didn't mind these words so much. It helped lessen any unease he felt when he was away.

After Brenda departed with a wave and a hug, Tess poured herself a cup of tea and moved to the rocker Hank had bought when she was pregnant with Luke. As she rocked, she thought, *Yes, Hank's a good husband and father, an adequate provider. Really, who can ask for more? Sometimes he does seem a bit distracted, but that's to be expected from a man who switches dramatically from one life aspect to another simply by coming home. And Hank and I are lucky, usually able to resolve thorny issues calmly like our decision to remain in this house and not move across town to something bigger. So foolish to leave friends who are basically family! Or that time Luke at age six was caught kissing Julie Sloan behind the garage or that tense occasion when the IRS did an audit and we didn't know what they were looking for. I don't love Hank as I did when we first married. But Kitty feels the same about Dan, married so long, and with the kids and all. She told me as much last week when we were pushing our carts in Nielsen's meat department, "Tess, marriage always changes with time, one way or another." Hank and I are more like old friends, but that's okay. I also love others like Kitty Murphy and Jed Sloan, and Ted, surely. But I don't want any disturbances between Hank and me. My hope is to raise the kids steady, happy, and strong.*

Besides, I have distractions of my own to keep me busy and occupied, Tess reminded herself.

Inevitably, Hank's company changed his route. He was given a new roster of clients.

Now he met other women in new medical offices. On his first day out, opening the glass door and looking into those wide blue eyes of Dr. Osborne's receptionist, Simone, he was back to his old ways. And in addition to the women, Hank now occasionally solicited a male stranger, deciding that if he scored a big sale beyond expectations, he would indulge. If not, he would wait until he did, prolonging with exquisite anticipation the inevitable prize. Thin or stout, tall or short, it didn't matter. He only sought a man with whom to partner, and he didn't have to soften his hands with cream or cut his nails. Or buy a woman dinner. Hank could just simply be an indulgent, mindless animal. How eagerly he pursued those carnal hours, free from self-control or moderation or consideration of others.

All this Hank recalled as he sat at Tess's bedside. His adultery had been with outsiders, casual encounters that involved no ongoing commitment and meant nothing to him emotionally. But Tess and the children? Without them, life would be unimaginable. He was fortunate that there was only that one close call with the gal he called *hon*, which he never repeated in public. The ease of maintaining this double life was so smoothly managed he never considered its immoral aspects.

When Hank looked at Tess, he often tried to imagine her living as he did. Impossible. When he was home, he happily saw to it that he was an attentive husband and loving father. Why would she seek such reckless diversion?

It was his ability to divide his life into segments that enabled him to carry on like this, Hank decided. One portion for his time on the road, another for being fully at home. He thought men were better able to sort and compartmentalize in these ways. Women dedicate themselves to their families, friends, and work. Women can confuse this desire with that need, often left befuddled by such distinctions.

When Hank was with his family, he offered up his whole self. Every so often, when he returned from a trip, he brought them a treat - a camera, a baseball glove, a pretty bauble for Tess. As they got older, he took them to movies, ball games, camping, hiking, whatever they wanted. In the end, other than the usual squabbles and tensions of growing up, everyone thrived and got along, even after Tess had returned to teaching.

The two of them often looked at the children with tears of pride misting their eyes. Did she ever think, Hank wondered, what a wonderful father he was? Was she just anticipating an imminent night out with one of the neighbors? A movie or dinner with the Sloans or the Murphys? Even Tom, who never found a mate all these years, still filled in nicely as a man who would buy the family a pizza while he fixed up things around the house. Once when Tess had the flu, he even took over the kids, getting them to school, picking them up. Every summer, Hank thanked the group by inviting everyone over for barbecues. Drinking beer, the men watched golf on TV, while the women sat in the kitchen talking and picking at the leftover pie. Life was good, and Hank knew it.

In this way, their marriage accumulated years.

When they had both retired, Hank's company gave him a $500 gift certificate to a home store that sold gardening equipment. Tessa's colleagues said goodbye with an outdoor lunch at The Misty Gardener. There was no more teaching, no more traveling, no more golf.

And now Tess's illness. Barely in their seventies, Hank and Tess's plans for sharing the delights of growing grandchildren were now quashed. This would be a bittersweet journey for Hank alone.

On a rainy afternoon, two weeks after Tess was admitted to the hospital, Hank stood from his chair to stretch and do a few hands-to-toes bends. Then he found his way to the coffee machine on the first floor.

When he returned, Tess was gone, her face soft, her struggle over.

Devastated, Hank collapsed in the chair, took his wife's hand in his. Despite his vigilant watch, Tess had died without him.

The usual tasks of the bereaved lay spread out on the coffee table, the desk, the floor. Listless and distracted, Hank sifted idly through mounds of papers, conferred with lawyers and accountants. He worked slowly, setting aside documents that he had to refile. On the day he would never forget, Hank was sitting in his recliner sorting, arranging, discarding.

It was in the third folder that he came upon them. His children's birth certificates. Had he seen them before? Had he been away when Tess filled them out? There they were, formal and pristine with their fine black lettering, state seals stamped and raised, like a college diploma. He pressed them against his heart. His dear children, now married with families of their own. How blessed they were to have had such a wonderful mother. He hoped, assumed, they loved him as well.

Luke, Hannah, and Miranda.

Suddenly he saw it there, at the bottom of all three pages.

Father's name: Thomas Lindsay

Hank leaped from his chair, scattering sheets across the floor. Had he been wrong about Tess all these years? Had he been a poor husband after all? As far as he knew, his own flirtations had caused her no harm. But this? Her deceit against him was unthinkable. He stumbled from room to room as if the explanation for this betrayal lay in their bedroom or in her sewing corner, anywhere but in that incriminating mess on the carpet. Gasping and heaving, he leaned against the wall, trying to calm his pounding heart.

What were the truths of their marriage? Roiling in questions, he was not yet ready to examine possible answers. Weeks would go by until finally, when he could refrain from sobbing and see clearly, he allowed himself to acknowledge and accept that yes, it was true. He and Tess had both lived the lives required to make a loving home, raise a family, and maintain friends as dear as kinfolk.

Still, he was overtaken with inconsolable sorrow.

His beloved children.

Not his! Not his!

Love Was Our Cry

We both faced the same view, although we were not yet aware of each other's presence.

I stood at the end of a long wall of massive boulders that protected the harbor from the ocean's destructive surges. As the mighty waters rolled toward me, they crashed against the stone wall at my feet before their foaming swirls finally settled down. He stood further along the rock wall looking far out to sea. From that perspective, everything crisp and keen up close eventually dissolved into a distant foggy haze.

This was the scene we had come to paint.

I set down my chair, easel, painting supplies, composing my day's work. Would it be the cove, closed in as the waves break, or just the boulders, the light, and shadows - one of my more difficult subjects? The turbulence of the waves? *No*, I thought. *I'm going to go for it all and paint the entire scene. Water, rock, cove.*

I began to unpack.

My particular passion and the test of my true talent, I believed, was painting *en plein air* or outdoors. Inside, I could be lazy, take my time. The still life setup could remain unchanged for days. The light was always consistent - the identical lamp behind, a fixture hanging above. But nature was fickle. It was essential to capture the scene quickly before the light changed and the view shifted.

Already, today, the light had advanced from the sun hanging low on the horizon to rising inch by inch as the hours pushed on into a full day. By noon, the sun would be directly overhead. *Perhaps*

I'll try to capture the feel *of the scene*, I thought, *an abstract, not the* literal *reality*. It was a good choice given the gossamer mist. Perhaps a mood, swaths of color created with a palette knife for volume. I opened my cases, my chair, positioned my canvas on the easel. *From what angle should I work?* I decided to turn to my right, the better to capture the darker shadows on the water.

"*Va bene*," I told myself, "let's get started."

As I bent down for my palette, I noticed that the man along the stone wall was also a painter. Like myself, he was readying his easel. I could see only his back. Had he seen me?

No one else was about, though given the drama and beauty of the scenery, it was inevitable that others would eventually show up. Passersby always stopped, peering over my shoulder with unwelcome comments: "Why did you put red over there?" pointing. "Do you intend for the sky to have that purple streak?" I'd have to turn my head in the middle of working to acknowledge their remarks, likely lose my focus.

But right now, the setting and light were perfect, and the spectacle before me was my sole concern. Only one other person was nearby, and hopefully, he was also seeking solitude.

Painting well and not paying attention, I was startled to suddenly hear, "Excuse me. I forgot paper towels. Would you have any to spare?"

Brush strokes nicely catching the mist, I was annoyed at the interruption. Turning, I immediately thought, *How nice he looks in jeans*. How many older men wear well-fitting jeans? Long legs and slim torso or have the same thick hair as in their youth, for that matter! I glanced down at my own clothes and was glad a smock covered my worn pants, not neat like his. Why would he wear good pants to paint?

And what did *he* see when he looked at me? A slender woman with long brown hair laced with gray. Pinned up today with an old metal clip in the shape of an acorn that I found in a cereal box years ago. Dignified and respectable, yes, with deep blue eyes, despite my face being that of an older woman.

"Thank you," he said as I handed him some tear-offs. He smiled and went back to his easel. I wasn't looking for company, but still, I felt a little put out that he hadn't offered a few more words. Was my hair particularly unruly?

When, a few hours later, I paused to put down my brushes and pull out my sandwich, I noticed that he did so as well.

"May I join you?" he called from his perch along the seawall.

"Yes, of course," I said.

He carried over his chair and his paper bag.

"I'm Justin," he said, extending his hand. "Oops, sorry. Alizarin crimson on my fingers!"

Laughing, I said, "Hello, I'm Rosa, and I won't even bother offering my hand. Not just alizarin crimson but Naples yellow and ultramarine blue! I'm an unusually messy painter."

We opened our sandwiches and smoothed the wax paper. We were two artists with similar intent - the same desire to look, the same need for space, the same attraction to the same view. The mood was safe and easy.

And we looked about the same age.

In her early sixties, I hoped he was thinking, though I had just turned seventy.

In his early seventies, I decided, though I was never good at guessing ages.

"Do you come here often to this gorgeous spot?" he asked. "It's my first time. I live several miles away. There are coves closer to my home, but I was looking for a new site."

"Yes, I do come often, but at varying times of day to paint the same scene in different kinds of light," I answered. "Like Monet and his haystacks. Or his series of Rouen Cathedral. Do you know those paintings?"

"Of course," he smiled. "Is there a painter alive who doesn't?"

Right away, I felt foolish at asking an artist such an absurd question, but he didn't make me feel foolish. In fact, he made it seem as if my asking was charming.

It was a relief to talk with a man of similar age. To have a conversation without effort. To share the same references and not wonder whether my words were appropriate or understood. These days, everyone seemed much younger than me or very much older.

"Have you traveled abroad to the great museums? I asked.

"Several times," he answered. "But also to great cathedrals and to nature's wonders, the forests of Germany, the coast of Italy. Inspiration is wherever your eyes take you."

"True. Look how exciting this view is, right here," I continued.

We poured coffee from thermoses. Justin held out dessert.

"Share?" he asked.

"Fig Newtons!" I cried with delight. "My favorite cookie since early childhood. Or is it a pastry or a fig sandwich?"

"Help yourself," he said, his clean, paintless hand holding out the familiar yellow package.

"I have not seen or heard anyone mention fig Newtons for at least two dozen years," I observed. He looked pleased.

Although we were comfortable in many ways, we were also hesitant and shy, as new meetings often are. We returned to our easels.

Too soon, it was late afternoon. With the waning light, we were finished for the day. Clearly tired, we both put down our brushes at the same time. It was an awkward moment. Both of us seemed inclined to chat. We took a few steps toward each other then retreated, hesitant. We began closing up, yet we kept looking back and forth. Finally, arms laden, we waved goodbye and walked to our cars.

Did we expect to see each other again? Did we *hope* to?

The next few days rained heavily, with a howling wind.

When the weather cleared, I eagerly made my way back to the harbor. So calm was the water that I marveled yet again, as I always do, how the earth's physical elements change so radically and so quickly. The light was lovely, translucent, slightly brighter than three days ago. I realized that the reflections on the water I had already painted would require adjustments. Less ultramarine, more cerulean. Or I would simply start a new canvas. Justin arrived before me and made his way over to help with setting up. "I brought extra paper towels this time, in case you run out," he said with a smile. "Why don't we have coffee before we begin while our hands are still clean!" When he held out the recognizable yellow package, we both laughed. "I guess this is our new special dessert," he said.

A brief respite, then off to work.

But after we sketched our outlines on our canvases, Justin pointed to the gazebo at the end of the path where the splendid view opened up wide to the ocean. A raised eyebrow, a simple nod, and we were settled inside. A gentle scene of sun, warmth, fig Newtons. Were we poised on the prow of a mysterious ship, past lives behind, and everything before us?

"Are you from around here?" I asked. "I mean, your early childhood."

"I grew up in a house on Lake Michigan," Justin began. "Along the shore were deep forests of dark pine. Have you ever been to Michigan, Rosa? The country is so vast, so grand. We didn't have a big house, but we had astonishing vistas of trees, water, and birds of all kinds. Spruce grouse, piping plover, the golden-winged warbler. And the great gray owl. Families of deer came right up on our porch and, of course, gobbled up our daylilies and roses and ate the fruit right off our blueberry and blackberry bushes."

Justin paused, looked over. I sat comfortably, leaning forward to listen. So he continued.

"At age eleven, I got my own little blue motorboat. That's when I first started to sketch, to record those wonderful sights. I tacked my sketches on the walls of my bedroom so I always had pictures I loved to look at."

Justin was a marvelous storyteller, his childhood depicted in splendid color. So I knew his paintings and his heart would be similarly vivid.

Such a different childhood from mine, I thought, with some hesitation and a whopping dollop of fear. Born in southern Italy, I had left my country as a child. Here right now was a stranger looking out at the same view as I, both of us drawn to this specific place for the same reasons, but our pasts were as unalike as could be imagined.

"I was always drawn to paint nature," Justin continued, "rather than figures or still lifes. I often painted outdoor scenes in an abstract way to get the feeling or spirit of the place rather than the exact depiction. That's when I began to paint with a palette knife. I just scooped up thick globs of color and laid them greedily on my canvas.

"But, Rosa, now tell me where *you* are from. Where did you grow up? I assume you too had an early love of nature. Very often, artists start noticing the details and beauty of scenes and objects at a very young age."

I hesitated. *He's in for a big disappointment. He'll find we have little in common other than our love for art. I am a foreigner. He is as American as the Midwest in which he grew up.* His story was simple, unadorned, one of belonging to a place, feeling the entitlement of it. Mine was one of displacement. How would he receive my words?

Well, he asked, I decided, *so I'll tell him. He's almost a stranger.*

"I grew up in a small town in Italy," I began. "In the south, the Puglia area, but inland, nowhere near the sea. We had a very large family and lived in the same village with many cousins, aunts, and uncles. In our town, even neighbors and shopkeepers were considered family. We were not rich but not poor. My father owned a small vineyard, and when I was a child, life was beautiful."

Remembering, Rosa paused.

"Growing up in a vineyard, you especially notice the trees and vines. It was the Aleppo pines with their needle-shaped leaves and orange-red bark, and the olive trees with their silvery colors that started the artist's fire in me. Two kinds of trees so unalike and yet each so alluring. Do you know what they look like, the Aleppo pines?"

He nodded, and I went on.

"Same as you, from early on, I had the desire to draw. I kept a sketchbook and pencil in my bike basket, even when I went on a brief errand. But one day during this idyllic childhood, I overheard my mother and father having a serious discussion. They thought I wasn't listening, but you know small children. Their ears are always open. Whether or not they understand what they hear, ah, that is a different story. Anyway, this was a few years after the war. My father told my mother we had to leave Italy.

"Why now? I wondered, sitting on the floor in the pantry, eavesdropping.

"'I no longer trust the men who run the government,' he told my mother. 'My vineyard might be taken over by the state at any time.' She reluctantly agreed, so they arranged to come to America. My parents were very brave leaving everyone they had known all their lives.

"Anyway, he was right. The government confiscated our property for the state. But when we finally arrived in Minnesota with all those forests, I still had lots of trees to paint!"

I pulled out from my pocket a couple of old dried oil tubes.

"Here are a few I stashed in my coat when we left, all those years ago."

I held them out to Justin.

"I keep them with me when I paint. Somehow, they seem to make my work a little better, reminding me to be sensitive to people and places. And also that everything is constantly changing one way or the other."

Justin took my hand. "I'm so sorry about that, you having to leave Puglia. Minnesota is very pretty, but it sure isn't Italy."

"Yes, everything does change. But sometimes change can be for the good, like here we sit now, talking about our childhoods. And we never knew each other before."

We were quiet for a long time, then returned to our easels. We each needed to think about our sharing, to let my mind imagine a little boy in a small boat on Lake Michigan and his, a little girl from Puglia on a bicycle - "in Italy's heel," as I had described it.

When we were done for the day, Justin made this suggestion. "If it's a pleasant day tomorrow, would you like to take a walk before we begin our work?"

"Yes, that would be lovely," I replied, thinking, *This is a real date.*

"Good, let's meet at the gazebo. After our stroll, we can gather our supplies."

The next day was beautiful, balmy, and clear. Dare it be otherwise? So we continued talking as if there had been no interruption of a long, solitary night.

Out of the peaceful calm, Justin said, "My wife died five years ago. She lived for three years while dying of cancer. A terrible ordeal, poor thing."

"My husband died two years ago of a heart attack," I answered.

"I had three children, none of them geographically close to me or to each other."

"Not as I had hoped," he sighed. "I grew up with several siblings, and we were inseparable until death, children, work, all those things, separated us. But we had many good years together."

The two of us gazed off, a bit wistful, thinking about good times, missed opportunities.

"I had two daughters, and lucky I was to have them," I began. "My parents, my husband, and I lived in a compound of farmhouses in the country in Minnesota. There was no hospital nearby, but both deliveries worked out fine with the support of my mother and a neighbor woman who boiled water and put down clean sheets, serving more or less as a midwife."

We grew reflective again, the waves crashing, the sun high, and still, we sat.

Now we would say it.

"My marriage was disappointing, my spouse, contemptuous, dismissive," he whispered.

"My marriage too was disappointing, my spouse contemptuous, dismissive," I said a little louder, a little bolder.

"'Painting is a waste of time,' my husband had said to me. 'Put your effort into something that will earn money. What are you going to do with all those pictures?'"

"My wife called me a silly man. 'Painting is not a pastime for strong men,' she said. 'Take out a canoe or build a tree house for your son.'"

His face so pensive, I wondered, was he remorseful, angry, bitter? What exactly was he thinking?

Likely he was trying to imagine me as a young pregnant woman in a farmhouse surrounded by cows, frightened at the ordeal of giving birth in an unknown place. But there was no doubt how I thought of him - trying to paint his soul with a harridan wife chiding him for the paint on his hands, his canvases littering her premises, getting in the way of her broom and thinking his pictures just so much nonsense.

Artists, like writers, seek quiet spaces, I thought. *Their creative work is most often done in isolation. But how pleasant it is to be here together in our now-beloved park, facing this sometimes serene, sometimes wild body of water.* And Justin thought, *Our children are grown, our difficult spouses gone. And nothing in the world to do but paint at our leisure with this dear person, who possesses and understands a similar passion.*

The next day dazzled. Justin moved his easel next to mine but not without asking.

"Do you mind?" he asked. "Would I disturb your concentration?"

We laughed. "Of course not," I answered, though we both knew he most certainly *would* disturb me and that I would most certainly disturb him. And I knew he knew it. And he knew I knew it. And it was delicious.

So this is how we became involved in each other's work and lives.

I might ask Justin, "What made you put that purple-green over there?" a nod with my brush to the left corner of his canvas. And he might ask, "How did you place that shadow beyond the rocks like that?" Happily becoming both critics and admirers of each other's work.

We were now together every day, painting, lunching, talking, visiting museums, attending concerts.

And then one day, I made Justin dinner at my house, a cottage, really, just five snug rooms. And in the back, an English garden where a dozen flowering plants in soft colors such as mauve, sage, and pale gold were flourishing together. Justin chopped garlic while I readied the clams for *spaghetti alle vongole*. My paintings of the water, the cove, hung on the walls, as well as a few photographs of my little town in Puglia. In the dining room, propped on a table was a mysterious portrait of the back of an unknown man whose form resembled Justin's.

"Tell me more stories about your little village," he asked.

After dinner, we leaned back into the soft cushions of ample chairs upholstered in violets and held hands while Maria Callas sang the thrilling aria from Tosca, *Vissi d'arte*: "I lived for art, I lived for love."

Justin then cooked dinner for me in his house, a long walk from mine. It was a neat structure in the arts and crafts style, filled with spare but authentic mission furniture. It was a man's house - mini-

mal, leather, straight-lined but happily slightly disheveled with paintings stacked against the walls.

He put on a long apron, wrapped the cords twice around his
waist.

"My domestic smock," Justin called it, laughing and sipping
wine as he deftly prepared his favorite fish dish from the lake outside his childhood home - pan-fried trout with lemon and butter.
"Sit," he had insisted, handing me a glass of white wine. "Just watch."
He looked like an Italian chef, I told him, with his apron, the fiery
enthusiasm in his eyes, the whole presented with panache and a few
bars from Verdi ("Verdi, just for you," he said) ringing from his lips
as he squeezed the lemon over the fish.

"*Deliziosa!*" I applauded when we finished. He smiled at my
pleasure. "*Grazie, mia cara,*" he responded. And I blushed to hear
him say, "My darling."

And so ours was a gentle conjoining with a precious freedom we
had never known except as children.

Moving freely between our own houses, canvases were propped
everywhere - on floors, on counters. Often, we gave one to the other
on a whim or as a gift, a thank-you.

"Here, this is for you because I was thinking of you when I
painted it," he once said. It was a small abstract oil of tempestuous
grays and blues with one dot of bright red off-center that he then set
on my bedroom windowsill. "Where you'll see it first thing in the
morning."

Justin and I.

He loved the way my Italian accented my English, often asking
for specific words just to hear me say them - *absolutely, fantastic,
come hug me.* I loved the way he cleaned his hands after his work,
fastidiously, without wiping them on his jeans. He loved my old
smock with the hundreds of paint swipes. And the way I asked for his
advice, "Justin, that yellow over in that corner. What do you think?"

And I loved when he said, "Rosa, how did you paint those ripples on the water? When I watch you watch your subject, I long to be your eyes."

Every day, we piled into his car, stashed our supplies, and set off on a new adventure, painting on hilltops, in meadows, alongside gardens. *From where did this blessing come?* I wondered. And at our age, our visions so closely aligned? But then, breaking into my speculations, Justin would gasp and point, "Look there! The dappling through the trees, and those wildflowers," and I would abandon my notions and turn gratefully toward him.

But it would be untruthful to say that I felt no fear of our future together. At our ages, death was not far off. Most of the time that thought was a mere philosophical musing, and I was able to toss it off. Until the day I could no longer do so.

On that day, I knew which of us was to die first.

It was the middle of summer. Justin and I were sitting arm in arm in the gazebo of our initial meeting. The air was warm but without the discomfort of intense heat. Sailboats skimmed back and forth.

"Justin," I said.

"Yes, my lovely girl."

My mouth was dry. I couldn't swallow the fig Newton. *Say it, Rosa.*

"I'm feeling a bit tired, a bit sick, my darling."

"Sick? Let me take you home. Some tea with honey? A brief nap?" he asked. Solicitous, ready to provide care.

"Justin. It's not that kind of sick."

"What can it be, my love? Your cheeks are rosy. Your eyes are sparkling."

"It's only the beginning. Nothing has changed yet. They won't be rosy and sparkling for long. I'm so sorry."

It pained me to speak. He saw and did not press further, but he slipped his arm around my back, and in the silence of despair, we watched the seagulls diving into the waves.

During the next few months, changes did indeed begin to appear. My cheeks grew pale and gaunt. My eyes dimmed with sadness. Doctors gave me pills that made me weak and nauseated. Although I moved about cautiously, we still sketched together. Justin's charcoal pencil moved slowly over his sketch pad, a deliberate effort to show me he was still working. But he filled page after page with sketches of me. Every so often, he would hold them up and say, "Did you ever see a more beautiful model?" I knew he was doing this to remember me in all sorts of ways - gazing out to sea, fixing my hair, snipping flowers from the garden. *Dear Justin, knowing nothing about gardening. Still, you spent two mornings a week out there under my direction, doing your best.* Occasionally, he moved to my side and held me gently while we glided silently on a swing he had bought for my front porch.

Never did we speak directly of death but only of required medicines and procedures. We stayed home now or made a simple trip to a nearby cove where Justin opened my chair and sat me down with a blanket over my lap, placing my pad and charcoal in my hand. It was on one of those days that I knew I had to make a plan. For love of Justin, it must be so. What way would best enable him to carry on?

Suddenly, it all came clear what I *must* do, with the help of my friend, Matt.

When Justin was out for an afternoon of errands, I asked Matt to keep me company. The two of us made phone calls, arranged details.

This dear man would settle me into an inn by the sea, owned by kindly innkeepers and old friends, Claire and George. They agreed to care for me until the end. As soon as I moved in with them, Matt would see to it that my house was immediately emptied. All this, Matt and I figured out precisely to the very hour.

When Justin returned from his errands, I asked him for a favor, to visit various galleries upstate and inquire if any might be interested in exhibiting my paintings. Quickly, he rallied and stowed a half dozen canvases in the car. He also made a presentation notebook of many others, meticulously photographed.

"Matt, keep an eye on my special lady," he ordered.

"And you, my love, I won't be long. Wait right here for me!" he said, kissing my nose, my forehead, my palm.

As Matt later told me, it happened just as we had planned. After three days, Justin jumped from his car and raced toward the house. "Darling, I'm home! I have great news about possible shows! Wait till you hear!" only to find the rooms empty and Matt waiting for him on the porch glider. All that remained was this - a large painting on the barren floor, set against a wall. My portrait of him. My best work. His dark eyes direct, fervent, an artist's focused eye.

"Matt! My Rosa! What is this? Where is she?"

Leaning against the edge of the portrait was my note. He scooped it up then fell to his knees.

"My darling Justin," it began, "this is the only way. I will not die in your arms. Do I want you to bear such pain? That would be crueler than my departure now. Rather, remember me when we first met, that very same moment I knew I loved you.

"You are my memory, and I am yours. May God keep you strong. Your Rosa."

And as I knew he would, as Matt told me he did, Justin crumpled in tears.

The Family Zirofsky

In this small village in the Pale of Settlement in Russia, the Zirofsky family - seven children, a mother, a father, and a grandmother - were so poor they only had two chickens for ten people for the Sabbath meal. Now and then their compassionate neighbors, the Beyneshes, who had fewer children to feed, generously gave over their own meager carrots and onions to thicken the Zirofsky's soup.

The Zirofskys were Jewish, and they never forgot - how could they? - that the Cossacks, those elite Russian military warriors who waited somewhere in the surrounding hills, were their mortal enemy. With the least provocation, these fighters stood ready to swoop down and destroy the Jews in a frenzy of swift, violent carnage. Galloping hooves, war cries, men in uniforms riding high in the saddle, sabers cutting the air. So the Zirofskys tried to live a quiet life. The children played only with each other and were clever at inventing games with their hands and eyes and a small red ball.

The grandmother had a sister in Warsaw named Pesha. Although the two women wrote each other long letters every month, they had not seen each other for many years. Pesha lived in luxury with her daughter, Chava, who had married a wealthy businessman named Shimon. She was careful not to write about her pleasant situation considering her sister's sad letters bemoaning the insecurity of their daily lives, the heartache, and worry. Bad times in the mother country were all her unfortunate sister knew, waiting fearfully for anything that went wrong with the ruling classes, the political leaders, the bourgeoisie, for then surely the Jews would be blamed. And then there would be a program, the Cossacks storming down from the hills. Would they appear at her door, throwing the two daughters, Shifra and Raysel, across their saddles and ride off or force the boys to join the army and kill their own people?

The Shimon Rosistskys lived on the fanciest street in Warsaw. A childless couple, their lives were comfortable and prosperous but without children, threaded with sorrow. Pesha saw the sadness in her daughter's eyes and had an idea. Settled in the small salon after dinner, she read aloud her sister's most recent letter - the children at school, at play - then concluded with descriptions of the destitute and frightening circumstances in the village.

"A pity, really. Some folks have so much, others so little," Pesha said, patting the opulent sofa on which she sat.

Chava listened and said to her mother, "Family. They are family. We are obligated to help. I wonder what we can do."

With a nudge and a whisper and a few minutes of earnest talk from her mother, Chava Rosistsky made a life-altering decision.

"Shimon," she said to her husband, "since God never blessed us with a child, let's take one of these children. Why not? We can raise it as our own and give it special privileges that the child would otherwise never know."

"A fine idea, Chava," Shimon said.

So Chava wrote a letter to her aunt in the poor village in the Pale of Settlement.

"You choose, my dear aunt. Send me one of your children and I will give that child a fine education and all the special benefits at my disposal."

"Why ask for only one?" the mother wailed to the father. "Why not two? In a wealthy household with maids and cooks, what is two if you have one?"

"Just one," Chava had written, nervous enough at this good deed for which she felt obligated but was not at all sure would work out. Nor did she know if she would have the taste for being a mother. Or being responsible for a child not her own.

But this she knew. If she was not to be shamed before her family, could she do otherwise? All of them knowing what terrible conditions existed in the Pale of Settlement and what bounty existed in Warsaw. Besides, how would she face her God on Yom Kippur?

The mother and father Zirofsky huddled over a waning fire in their small hut, the children long asleep, piled here and there on blankets tossed over a rug, a pallet.

Tormented, they sat.

"Am I Solomon?" the mother asked. "Am I someone who can pick a favorite child?"

And the weary father, head in his knees, had no words of comfort, no advice. "May as well spin me around blindfolded and the first one I catch will be the one," he said.

"Maybe we should not do this thing," the mother said. "The children will mourn the one who is missing."

"You mean refuse this offer?" the father asked.

"I don't know what I mean. My heart is ripped apart," she answered, pacing four steps to the fire, back to the table, back to the fire, worn hands rending her apron.

"But how can we do this?" the mother cried.

"My dear wife," the father said, "how can we not?"

They went through the names of their children, oldest to youngest.

Yaakov was the clever one. Shmuel was the fixer of anything broken. Raysel had the beautiful voice. Shifra was mama's best helper, never a word of complaint. Mendel was the student, always reading. Levi was fun-loving and mischievous. Noam, the youngest, was adventurous and bold.

Deeply troubled, they tried to sleep. In the dark of night, each could hear the other praying, beseeching God for wisdom, knowing that in making this choice, there was not enough wisdom for them on this earth, in this poor village, in the Pale of Settlement.

When they rose from their bed, the sheets twisted and damp with tears, they said together, "Mendel. Of course, Mendel.

"Mendel because he always wants to learn and will best benefit from such favor."

Although they wondered, maybe Shifra, so pretty, no trouble at all, always pleasant. Perhaps she could make a match with someone who could earn a good living, not be a poor laborer like her father.

Or perhaps Levi, such a lively companion that after a few months, Chava might be prompted to request a second child.

But for now, at the last, it was ten-year-old Mendel.

Mendel, tall for his age, and skinny, often forgetting to eat so intent was he on his book. And a curious one, forever asking questions. Why this, why that? Why God this, why God that. His quick shining eyes were restless as the others sat at the table watching him, wondering, *What is he thinking?*

Yes, Mendel. He will know how to gain an advantage from this extraordinary privilege.

His parents took him aside. "Mendel, you are to going to live in Warsaw with Aunt Chava and Uncle Shimon."

"Really?" he asked. Astonished. "And Bubbe Pesha too? What about the others? Why me? Noam and Raysel and Yaakov, they all deserve to go."

But even as his heart was heavy at parting, Mendel was already imagining what it would be like to live in a city with paved streets and tall buildings. Did Uncle Shimon have a carriage? he wondered.

There were tears and hugs that bleak damp morning as the train huffed its way into the tiny station. Mendel's brothers and sisters filled his pockets with whatever tokens of love they could gather - Shmuel, five chestnuts from under a dying tree; Shifra's crude drawing of the family; Yaakov, a poem that was also a riddle, *Don't forget me* scrawled at the bottom. The mother and father's last words reminding him to study Torah every day.

The sooty engine snorted and belched, like the Cossacks' horses, pawing the ground, impatient to run. At the final whistle, Mendel climbed aboard, his child's face dazed and bewildered, dragging his few belongings in an old sack bound with string, his mother crying into his father's rough jacket. The train gave a final blast, started its engines, and disappeared down the tracks into the fog.

Mendel wrote letters.

In the beginning, he spoke with wonder of the abundant food served by a maid in a black dress and white apron and the extravagant bed he had all to himself with a comforter filled with real duck feathers.

"My own bathroom, a miracle. A toilet and shower, miracles, miracles. I'm learning new words like *toilet* and *shower* for things I never dreamed existed. Mama, Papa, you cannot believe it. Not an outhouse like at home that we shared with the Beyneshes. I don't deserve this when all of you remain in the village."

But soon, the letters arrived less often. A ten-year-old boy, after all, was not inclined to sit with a pen and paper no matter how much he missed his family. It was left to Pesha to send them news of how Mendel was faring.

"Mendel is such a good boy," she wrote. "At first, he ran around looking at everything, asking so many questions, examined every corner of the house as if it were a palace. It's a big, lovely house, true, but a palace it's not, believe me. Little by little, he grew used to things, as children do when they are facing a world out of their own storybook. And soon enough, he settled in. The boy is curious and eager but comfortable.

"Language isn't the problem we thought it might be," she added. "Many in Warsaw speak English, as we do, but Mendel is receiving private tutoring, and he's picking it up fast."

Shimon was a kindly man, always striving to put the boy at ease. He took long breakfasts, waiting for Mendel to finish his early morning Torah studies. Then the two of them climbed into his carriage and were whisked off to his factory. Staring out the window, Mendel was captivated by the streets - paved streets, not mud - and the houses, not huts, made out of stone, some three stories high. There were busy shops and people freely walking about in fine clothes. No one seemed in a hurry. No one seemed to be hiding from the Cossacks.

Mendel was soon fifteen and starting to grow a beard. With the respect accorded the owner's nephew, the factory workers greeted him with "Good morning, Mr. Mendel," "How are you today, Mr. Mendel?" and "So good to see you, young man." In Shimon's own office, Mendel learned the ways of business, the purchasing, the costs, and inventories; and before he knew it, another year had passed, and his beard had grown a full two inches.

One evening after dinner, Shimon said to his wife, straight out, no preamble, not even a clearing of his throat, "Chava, what do you think of this idea? To send young Mendel here, along with my manager Saul, to open up a branch of our factory in America? With some capital and both their brains and a bit of *sechel*, common sense, I think we can manage a small beginning in New York City that can grow into something."

Mendel bolted up in his chair. America? His first thought was for sailing ships and vast oceans and a country where all prospects were possibilities. His second, instantly taken up with some remorse, was of his family and the Cossacks waiting in the hills.

Chava trembled. Why hadn't Shimon first discussed this with her? *Probably because he knew I would raise a fuss in front of the whole family*, she decided.

But her tears caught Chava by surprise. She loved Mendel with all her heart. How could she part from him?

She had assumed he would stay in Warsaw forever, work side by side with Shimon and someday take over the factory. Have a family. Grandchildren. Maybe even live here, in this big house.

Knowing Shimon, Chava was sure he had thought this through before making such a public suggestion. She knew there was no hope he would change his mind.

"Shimon," she said, "I'm not happy, but if you think it's for the best…"

She consoled herself. Mendel was far better off than so many others younger than he who had traveled to America by themselves in that abominable steerage with rats and little food. Mendel, a man now, at sixteen. And he would not be alone. With his fine capture of English and Saul by his side with a wallet of Russian rubles, her mind would be eased somewhat. And look at his face. Her boy was eager.

Shimon arranged letters of introduction, sent off notices to banks, arranged ship's passage for two, and began telling Mendel stories of this great land. America.

Two months before their departure, Mendel and Shimon were riding in the carriage, the horses jaunty and lively, when a wayward dog ran across their path. Such a fuss those horses kicked up! Snorting and spitting, legs in the air, fear in their eyeballs. The driver lost his reins, his hat. And when the screaming and disorder had died down, a fine young man lay crumpled in the street, his wife and two small children hovering over his still body, shouting, "*Tati, Tati! Papa! Papa!*"

Shocked by the scene, Mendel clung to the window, thinking this, that not a minute before, arms linked, the family was headed to the tearoom for afternoon pastries. And in the next instant, a completely random act, and four lives had been completely altered by a common street incident.

In a startling moment of discovery, of clarity, Mendel put his hand over his heart. *I don't want to work in Shimon's factory*, he suddenly realized.

My Torah studies have guided me for years, and this is what I have learned, to make the world a better place and serve others. That will now be my mission.

Chava sat quietly while Shimon and Mendel argued.

"I'm sorry to disappoint you, Uncle Shimon. You have been so good to me, and I'll be grateful to you for the rest of my life."

"You know, Mendel, that Jews are not accepted into medical schools in Warsaw," Shimon answered, not angry, but still, his voice a bit gruff. "There is not even the most remote possibility," he told Mendel.

"Then I will go to America," Mendel asserted, "if you will help, dear uncle. Do you know if a Jew can go to medical school in America?"

"Not many," Shimon answered, but already he could tell that his argument wasn't persuasive. Mendel may be a dutiful, grateful child, but once he made up his mind, that was it. This Shimon could see quite clearly.

Again, Shimon sent letters. This time, with each request, he added a substantial donation, with promises of more to come. Not with the first and not with the second but with the third, he indeed secured a place for Mendel in a New York City medical school with the caveat that he change his name. Only two other Jews on staff, you understand, the letter implied, and those both American born or, as it said precisely, "Might we make a suggestion? Perhaps Mendel would be more comfortable living in America with a modern name." Hence, Mendel Zirofsky became Michael Zirof. Would Mendel mind that? Shimon asked. Becoming "Americanized" in this manner? Would he regret abandoning the name Zirofsky?

Mendel didn't care what his name was. He only thought, America, a doctor, no matter what. But he remembered with almost a quaint longing the village and family he was leaving behind. It was likely he would never see them again. Would they be shamed by his acquiescence in this naming issue? The image arose of his mother at the train sobbing into his father's shoulder. "Be a good Jew, Mendel. Study Torah," she whispered as he turned to go.

Mendel knew this kind of separation between generations had occurred repeatedly throughout the centuries. In his own life, first, it was his own mother. This time, it was Chava, another mother weeping on her husband's wool suit. And it was his fault. But they all realized that when your child was granted a promising opportunity, it often carried with it mountains of grief and despair such as separation, all that a mother could bear.

For this passage, there was no dirty train bellowing and burping. Only a huge ship. Mendel's pockets were fuller this time. Now there were more than a few chestnuts and a poem. Now there was candy and money, sandwiches and a new suitcase, new clothes, and a tearful letter from Pesha tucked in his pocket as he hugged her goodbye.

And there was Chava, crying bitterly into Shimon's shoulder.

In America, Michael's letters were brief. He was doing well but so busy studying night and day he made the personal acquaintance of a mere few of his fellow students.

During the many years he spent working to become a doctor, the kind and generous Shimon had started to send over each of the Zirofsky children to join him. One every year except for the last three coming together. It was urgent that they leave their village. There were rumblings of unrest. Pogroms in the countryside. Even in Warsaw, a few threw stones at Shimon's carriage. His factory produced essential metals used in war and peace, but from one day to the next, a government official could walk through the door and confiscate the business. Shimon's household was at risk. Despite Chava's pleadings – "Bring me Shmuel or Shifra, or any one of them into the house"

- Shimon paid little attention. How could he put even one child in danger? Leave they must. America was good. America was safe.

So Shimon booked passage and sent them over in order of age, oldest first. And he gave them new names.

Yaakov became Jake. Shmuel was Samuel. Raysel was Rachel. Shifra became Shana. Levi stayed Levi - the boy put up a ruckus - and Noam became Noah.

The children were learned in Torah, but only Mendel had a secular education. Only Mendel could speak English. But fortunately, on the Lower East Side, all the Jewish immigrants spoke Yiddish. And with the help of night school classes that taught English to immigrants, the Zirofskys were soon comfortable with the language of their newly adopted country. Stories of their difficult voyages, bittersweet departures and sweet arrivals were not so different, one from the other. It was the changes that happened to Mendel that mattered most.

That was the real story, the real sorrow.

Jake became a street peddler, a vendor with a fruit and vegetable cart. After a long struggle, he opened a small produce shop next to a ladies' dress store.

Samuel, nimble of hand, worked in a blacksmith shop fixing harnesses and wagons. Eventually, the blacksmith made him a partner in the meager but steady business.

And the girls, Rachel and Shana, married almost immediately and lived in the same tenement building raising six children between them. They were not as poor as in their old village but were hardly flourishing. Both their husbands were tailors, and they themselves worked long hours in a shirt factory under slavish circumstances.

Levi never made it to the big-time such as playing fancy gigs in the Catskills, but he was good at telling jokes, leading the dancing at local weddings and bar-mitzvahs. And oh, how they loved his Yiddish jokes!

And then Noah, who one day packed his bag and took a train to Omaha, where he connected with the Jewish community that set him up with a modest dry goods store. Their preference was to buy supplies from a Jewish shopkeeper. Besides, he would order certain kosher products especially for them.

All the siblings were determined that their children become assimilated into the American culture so they could become doctors and accountants.

It was to Mendel they kept referring: "See? Our own brother from the village back home. Work hard and you can be like Mendel."

Mendel watched these various unfoldings of his siblings and their families as he himself became successful and acquired his own family. At the hospital, his fees were lower than the gentile doctors, and although his doctoring was respected; there would be no promotion for a Jew on the hospital staff. He overlooked this slight, as long as he was able to care for his patients and make a living. Above all, Mendel was a humble man.

Still, Mendel was unhappy. In fact, he was inconsolable.

My siblings will never know anything but the poorest of livings, he thought time and again, helpless to remedy. *No education, no higher learning, and me with all the advantages. And for no reason other than I studied the hardest when I was a boy. But I am certainly not the best among us, for sure*, he thought. *The noble Shifra, the hardworking Samuel. But what can I do? Where would I* begin *to help?* Although not a single sibling had requested aid of any sort, he knew that their needs were endless, relentless. But on his salary, with substantial alimony going to Deborah in the divorce and school tuition for Amir and Rebecca, not a cent remained.

When Mendel was middle-aged, he met a psychiatrist friend for lunch. They sat on the terrace of the hospital cafeteria eating their salmon in the warmth of an early spring. After the man watched

Mendel drop his fork three times and then thrust the tongs fiercely into the wood surface, he gently laid his hand on Mendel's arm.

"Come to my office, my friend. Let's talk," he suggested.

So Mendel sat on the couch, his heart burdened, facing his friend Jacob. And he spilled out the stories of his life from its very beginning. The poverty, the fear, yet the family all together, seven children playing with a red ball.

His productive and loving years with the Zirofsky family.

But then the recent past. A people's insurrection, the government intervening with clubs and guns. His childhood village, his beloved father too sick to leave, his dear mother loath to leave him. The Cossacks torching houses and stores as his parents huddled together in the burning hovel. Shimon's factory was confiscated, his house ransacked, and Mendel was unable to learn of their whereabouts. Were Chava and Shimon murdered? Imprisoned? Surely Bubbe Pesha had died years ago. But mainly, there were many words, so many, about the extravagance with which he spent his formative years and his guilt at his siblings' deprivation of prospects as if it were his fault.

"Embedded in their faces were deep lines, years before their proper time," Shimon said, weeping.

"How they must resent me," he said. "All these years here in New York City when I hardly visited them because it pained me to see them so poor. 'Must see a patient,' I would tell them when refusing to attend a bar mitzvah or a seder. And then on the phone, I would hear the parents murmuring to their children, 'Your Uncle Mendel is a busy man, a very important doctor.'

"I was given every opportunity. They were given nothing."

His psychiatrist friend Jacob replied, "How do you know they are envious or resentful? Maybe they are proud. You just said you heard the parents say to their children that very thing: 'Your Uncle Mendel is a very important doctor!'"

For two long years, Mendel lay on the couch and faced his friend, but he was a stubborn patient. He would let no words, however soothing and wise, lessen his despair. How dearly he loved his brothers and sisters and how proud he was of them! Each one, brave and strong, each making his or her way from unspeakably poor beginnings. And they all had families, while he rarely saw his own son and daughter who lived across the city with Deborah.

All these years, Mendel had kept Shifra's drawing and Yaakov's poem tucked in his desk. Even the remains of Shmuel's chestnuts, now almost like grains of sand, were carefully preserved in a tiny black velvet drawstring bag.

Three weeks before his fiftieth birthday, Mendel was desolate and alone after his last girlfriend, Marion, departed a few days before with a huffy "Michael, you better learn how to deal with your dark moods or no woman will ever want you, doctor or no doctor."

But then a distraction. He received a mysterious invitation in the mail: "Dr. Michael Zirof's presence is requested on the twenty-third of March at the Century Hall Ballroom in Brooklyn."

Mendel almost tossed it in the trash. Another hospital function? But the invitation *did* have his name specially imprinted.

I must go, he thought.

On the designated evening, he put on his best suit and made his way up the subway stairs, walking the few blocks to the sprawling brick building.

Ballroom 4A - yes, this was the place. The doors were closed. He listened. No sounds. As he tentatively pulled the handle toward him, it was yanked full open, and there they were - his family, dozens of them, all dressed up. There were Yaakov and Shmuel and Raysel and Shifra and Levi and Noam with husbands, wives, and hordes of children he did not recognize. Even a few babies were there, the grandchildren now starting to come.

"Happy birthday!" they shouted. "Siman Tov u'Mazal Tov!" banging tambourines, snapping photos, Levi's daughter pounding away at the piano, and the children dancing.

"What?" What is this?" poor Mendel sputtered.

"What do you mean, what is this?" they all chorused. "We're here to celebrate *you*, our beloved brother on his birthday!"

Beloved? Mendel heard. *Beloved?*

"Sit, sit," Shifra said, leading him to a special chair on a small stage at the far end of the room.

"Just sit and listen. And watch," she said happily, the children jumping underfoot, adults clapping hands and laughing.

One by one, his siblings stood up. Each in turn read a few words they had written, oldest to youngest. Yaakov led off.

Yaakov said, "Mendel, you saved my life, all our lives. You are the dearest brother anyone could have. I love you."

And Shmuel said, "Mendel, you were just a boy, and all alone. What courage. I am honored you are my brother."

And Raysel added, "Mendel, my dearest brother. I never thought Deborah was good enough for you."

Shifra was next. "Mendel, Raysel's right. Deborah didn't deserve you. You can do better."

Then Levi said, "Mendel, it isn't only your family that loves you, but look at the sick people, so many through the years, you have cared for, who also owe you their lives and gratitude."

And at last, Noam stated, "It took two days on two trains to get here, but here I am. How could I miss this chance to tell my brother I love him? How much I owe him. How much this entire family owes him. If it weren't for you in that big house in Warsaw, if Shimon didn't love you like a son, where would we be today?"

And now, while Mendel sat stunned, they settled in a circle around him and continued to tell stories.

How much they had missed him when he left. How happy they were for his good luck. How they had waited eagerly for his letters and for those colorful ones from Bubbe Pesha. How they never had a thought for comforters and toilets and showers since those were things they could not even imagine. But how proud they were that he was learning Torah and being a good boy because of those things they *could* imagine.

How it was only through his shining spirit in Shimon's house that they were also given the gift of coming to America. "And look," they all said, "now our sons too can become doctors. But none of our lives would have turned out this way without your making the first journey. If not for you…God forbid, we would have been killed by the Cossacks."

They were *grateful* to him. They *owed him their lives and well-being*. Sure, they were poor, they continued. "It's a hard life, but it will be easier for our children living in this great America."

As Mendel wiped his face, tears wetting his cheeks, his beard, the grandchildren placed a wreath of flowers they had made on his head, chanting, "*We love Mendel. We love Mendel.*"

When the party was over, the toasts finished, and the children needed their beds, Mendel was finally allowed to depart. Although he was by himself, he was no longer alone. He stepped out of the building and looked at the full moon, letting the tears come. So much excitement in that room tonight. So much dancing and schnapps. And those speeches. *Taking it all in won't happen overnight*, he thought.

I will get to know the children of my brothers and sisters and hold their grandchildren. And I will tell them stories of the hard life in the Pale of Settlement and of their dear grandparents and how their own mothers and fathers played games together as children, games with a red ball. And how in the old days, Chava, Shimon, and Bubbe Pesha lived in a big house, when the streets of Warsaw were paved with gold.

Ghost Stories

Abby, the social worker, stood in the doorway of the library watching the four old ladies in their wheelchairs grouped around the fireplace. It was a fake fireplace, but still, perhaps their arthritic hands felt an imaginary warmth. Today was day one of her experiment. Three weeks ago, she had an idea for a new project, and after the activities director gave her the green light, she made her choices. These four women were as good as she could hope for to participate in the initial *Gabbing with Abby* program. Of all the patients on floors 4 and 5, they were most cognitively alert, still in command of carrying the thread of a conversation. Their minds didn't trail off into make believe. True, they often spoke haltingly. True, they often took a minute to search their brains for the right word, but eventually, they found what they were looking for. And they found it well enough for laughter, for tears, and hopefully, today, for sharing. All four had the same mental time-lapse problem, to be expected when you were in your eighties and nineties. She hoped that the ladies would be patient with each other.

They were gathered to talk about their own lives.

That's what Abby had told them. No staff member had ever asked them to talk about themselves before. The one thing they knew for sure, a week after being admitted into this place, was that no one cared a hoot about their pasts. The staff was taken up with the patients' medical needs, occasionally calling the doctor in for a look if an unusual ache or pain presented beyond their scope. Well, it seemed Abby *was* interested in their stories. And being excused from Wednesday afternoon bingo would afford a welcome reprieve.

Adelina - they called her Lina - was pointing her finger, leaning forward precariously in her wheelchair. Abby was concerned - would she be a bit too presumptuous for this group, talking over the others? Lina had been a famous opera singer who well knew how to control her voice, and it still carried a ring of confidence. Abby watched as Lina continued to wag her finger.

However, Lina and Abby both knew, as did the others, being of this esteemed age, that whatever one remembers is merely conditional, or partial, truth. Often, our hearts power the mind to repress emotional distress, embellish the glories, tolerate the pain. And lordy, they all had plenty of that. So people lie, intentionally or not, not only when memory begins to lose its clarity but all through our lives. And we repeat these particulars until we believe them. The four, plus Abby, were thinking that this meeting was going to be an interesting experience.

But the question was if truth does not exist as one complete, irrefutable entity, does the search for truth matter? Is the only issue of consequence what we believe to be true however we fashion the story?

After all, we only have *our* opinion. Others have theirs. And who is to judge?

The group was enthusiastic about this opportunity, but with caveats. They had promised themselves to speak as honestly as they could. Yet Abby worried. Every individual present worried. Would they be able to sustain an hour or so of serious talk? Would Harriet fall asleep? Would Edith ring for the aide to take her to the bathroom? Would Blanche complain that the heat was too hot or that the air-conditioning was blowing on her bursitis? Would Lina's hearing aid be adjusted properly? One or another of them was often querulous Many small details required Abby's attention in order to make them all comfortable. Busying herself with adjusting lap throws, sweaters on, sweaters off, she was curious at what these four ladies would discuss, their day otherwise filled with injections and enemas and weariness from moving their bodies from place to place.

Adelina (Lina), Harriet, Edith, Blanche.

In preparation, Abby had gone round to their rooms, issuing invitations. She had asked each of the women, "Wednesday afternoons in the library. Would you like to share stories about your life with a few other gals?"

Their responses were similar.

"Talk about my life? In an afternoon chat?" Smiling at Abby, they said, "At our age, we have so many stories, too many stories. There's not enough time to listen."

"We don't expect your *whole* life," Abby reassured them, "just whatever parts you want to share. Try it. If it's not to your liking, you don't have to participate a second time."

The four were willing to try anything once. Did they have something better to do on Wednesday afternoons other than play bingo in the multipurpose room?

And now here they were, all together. Not so much shy as hesitant. The fragments of so many years had carved lines into their faces, the hollows of their eyes. Four women with short, straight white hair worn like a cap, all with glasses, all wearing shawls they had made in knitting class. They hardly knew each other, mostly offered a nod in passing as they wheeled themselves into the dining room looking for their assigned tables.

Abby stood.

"Welcome, everyone," she started.

Just like an Alcoholics Anonymous meeting, Blanche thought nostalgically, ironically.

"Tell us your name, going around the circle."

"I'm Harriet."

"I'm Blanche."

"Edith here."

For sure like AA, Blanche concluded - only first names.

"And I'm Lina."

And so they began.

"Adelina, sorry, Lina," Abby said, "tell us something about yourself. You can start anywhere you like."

Anywhere? Where does one begin? Lina thought. *Just anywhere? With my earliest childhood memory? With the endless parade of humans who changed something in me, every spark or whisper either adding or taking away? Should I begin with my birth in an Italian ghetto in the Bronx, my Italian father a bus driver who sang Italian arias around the house? Or when I was taunted by other kids for thinking me weird, listening to opera even as young as seven, or this? The day twenty years later when Roberto left me, taking my precious little Anthony with him, accusing me of being away from home all the time, traveling the world singing, even after he had told me to "Go, go, go, I'll be here when you return. Your voice belongs to the world."*

Her head ached. It had been so many years since she had raised these questions, buried purposely so that she could manage her life.

She adjusted her seat, her sweater. Cleared her throat.

"I made a life-altering decision early on," Lina began. "My German voice teacher Mrs. Kuntz insisted I had 'an undeniable gift.' I was fifteen, singing in her living room, doilies on the chairs, doilies under the plants, and she in a caftan of shabby lace.

"My father had a beautiful tenor voice. Music in all forms defined my waking hours. We were poor in our pocket but not in our art. I couldn't be content with skipping rope and riding bikes. But I paid a price," Lina sighed. I always wondered if my traveling career was worth the fateful loss of my son's presence. At one time, I'd say yes. But sadly, reluctantly, now maybe not. Anthony grew up to be a thriving, prosperous man with a family. He owns a company that makes musical instruments. So that is good."

Lina's voice cracked. *Now*, she thought, *I must say it*. "But I haven't seen him since he was a young man." She started to cry and reached for the tissue that Blanche handed her. "He knows I'm alive, but he was very angry at me. His father remarried a long time ago… so it was to his stepmother that he has always turned."

She finished. She had done it. Shared as honestly as she could.

Pleased, Abby stood and smiled at Lina. "Thank you, Lina, for your special sharing. All of us are very grateful for your honesty in telling your story. Aren't we, ladies?" The three gray heads nodded. Yes, yes. And Blanche thought, *Yup*. AA. "I know sometimes it's difficult to open up with painful memories."

Edith said, "I think you were right to do your singing. Roberto was a cad."

Harriet said, "Thank you, Lisa."

Blanche thought again of her favorite slogan of AA: "Lina, honey, you lived life on life's terms."

Abby bought in a tray with glasses of cranberry juice. The first session of "*Gabbing with Abby*" was over.

As the ladies entered the dining room for supper, they greeted each other with a wave and found their places. Nothing more than that. Each was still unsure how these gatherings would unfold, though Lina had been so courageous to start them off. Lina wasn't shy. She was candid, plain-speaking. Could they be the same?

The following Wednesday, Blanche was jittery. She thought her story was ugly yet heroic in its redemption. But would her old feelings of unworthiness resurface again? She reminded herself, as she had learned, that excessive drinking was not a personal moral failing but an illness. Oh, she had confessed it a thousand times, "Hello, I'm Blanche, and I'm an alcoholic." Everyone's story was different, though all present had the same inability to control one's drinking. She had been a patient in this facility for ten years and thus deprived of AA meetings. Perhaps Abby's invitation and Lina's opening had been fortuitous? If by some divine gift, these women before her came to understand her emotional journey, it might provide the final resolution to her dying in peace.

So Blanche began.

"My real life started when I was forty. I decided then that I would finally take responsibility for my own actions. I couldn't change the past. I couldn't foresee the future. But I *did* have the power over my own attitude at any moment. I was in AA for a year when I learned this, and it was the hardest lesson of my life." Blanche kept her head down. Even now, her fingers quivered just thinking about a shot of vodka. AA members told her such images would stay with her forever. It was the support at meetings that would help her manage those inclinations and temptations.

Her listeners sat quietly. With sympathetic faces, they waited to hear what she would say next. No one seemed surprised. No one shifted around or called an aide or fell asleep.

"My father was abusive, hitting me, raping my mother." *There, I said it*, Blanche thought. "From when I was a little girl until I was sixteen when he died. Drunk, he fell overboard in a fishing accident. I didn't shed a single tear. But my little brother Colin was with him. He was ten. He didn't deserve that death."

Blanche stopped, looked away, looked back, took a chance.

"My father had just started going after him too."

"I drank to get away from it all."

Blanche's tears flowed quietly. She had never before put together so many words at one time. *No matter the years separating sad episodes in life, each time you relive a particular sorrow, you feel the pain almost as bad as the first time*, she thought. She lifted her small white head. The room was still. Perhaps her story was not a surprise to anyone. Perhaps one of them, or a friend or family member, had also had a similar experience.

"So that's where I started my life, ladies. Reborn at age forty. Would I have been able to survive my two failed marriages and the death of my little girl Sophie without the support of AA? Never. Surely I would have drunk myself to death. So I especially appreciate our group today, thanks to Abby."

What a brave woman! the ladies thought. In the background, the women could hear Ms. Cara down the hall calling out the numbers for bingo. They could hear the cage rattling as it spun around with the numbered discs inside. They could hear a voice call out triumphantly, "Bingo!" They expected Blanche to continue her story, but suddenly, Abby was standing before them with the tray of juices, apple and orange this time.

"How the hour has disappeared!" Edith cried.

"Thank you, Blanche," they chorused.

"Yes," said Abby. "You're a courageous woman, Blanche. You too, Lina. This is turning out to be a very special group."

Edith added, "Till next week, Blanche. We're looking forward to hearing the rest."

The next week, Blanche picked right up in the middle of her story.

"Does anyone know the twelve steps of AA that lead to sobriety?" she asked.

No one answered. Well, perhaps they *hadn't* confronted this ordeal.

"For me, the second step was the most difficult. *You must turn your life over to a Higher Power,* whatever that is - God or nature or some other spiritual entity. But believe me, when you knew only hurt from your own father, there isn't an ounce of trust in you to turn anything over. I needed a lot of guidance and support from others. And then there were eleven other exhausting steps. Grinding through them thoroughly is the work of a lifetime.

"But those twelve steps finally did away with the notion that everyone owes me special favors because of my terrible childhood. It was a humbling experience, but it kept me sober. Isn't that what you do on Yom Kippur, Edith? You're Jewish, aren't you? Look at your behavior, then make an apology or a remedy to those you've hurt? To this day, I keep the big blue book of AA on my bedside table.

"I've liked saying out loud how I feel," Blanche ended. "It feels good to share."

What she did *not* say now, and what the others likely did not know, was that despite her long abstinence from alcohol, substance abuse can move slowly into terminal disease at any age. And right now, Blanche was developing damage that could not be reversed: swollen legs, bruises on her shins, reddening of her palms. Loss of appetite, increasing bouts of nausea - a relentless, frightening, ongoing assault.

Abby was pleased. Her new program was a success.

At their next meeting, Lina told Abby that the four women had decided they wanted to continue their meetings but without Abby's presence. They were quite fond of her, but Abby was only thirty-four, and what did she know about being eighty-five? She didn't have a husband or a child. They felt freer to talk about aging and mistakes and regrets just among themselves. But still, Lina told Abby, "We are grateful that you rounded us up and started us off. We wouldn't have done it on our own."

Abby cautiously agreed, though every week, like a shadow, she entered the room and made herself busy on the fringes with placing flowers or tidying up. But their talk was only murmuring until she padded on out.

They also made another arrangement. Lina asked the head nurse if their seating at meals could be rearranged. Could the four eat together from now on?

Mealtimes were now lively occasions. Others watched enviously as the chatty foursome exchanged tasting portions of their own particular meal and even occasionally shared forks!

Edith was next.

She too was determined to speak honestly. This was the moment. If not, she feared going to her grave with concealed emotions she had harbored all her life. So after she folded her hands in her lap and wiped her glasses, she was ready.

"Compared to the stories of Lina and Blanche, I feel my life was boring, uneventful. Even my worst moments seem rather ordinary, so *unglamorous*. I have never traveled more than two hundred miles from my hometown. The folks I knew in my childhood I have known my whole life.

She paused, looked around. The ladies sat quietly at attention, so she pulled herself together and found her voice.

"At twenty-four, I married Henry, a master carpenter. Over the years, he developed a building empire. A good man, as skilled with architectural plans as he was with a saw and hammer. It seemed everyone in our part of the state had his house built by Andrew Brothers Contracting. Henry's brother, Hal, handled the business part.

"'Whatever you want, just ask,' Henry would say to me. He gave me a little boy, then a little girl. He built me a lovely house on a lake surrounded by beautiful forests that I filled with furniture and pictures. Yes, Henry was a generous man."

Edith broke off. The women all sensed that a *but* was coming next. They recognized that pause when one decides what and how much to say next.

"But all my life, I hankered after Hal," Edith confessed. "My very brother-in-law, who had a family of his own."

And there it was at last.

The room was so still you could hear Harriet's feathery breaths.

"The brothers worked and played together," Edith continued. "Not for a single day could I escape Hal's mischievous spark, his lanky shape, loping along with that slight hitch of his right hip. Oh, and he had such beautiful hands, like a woman's, unmarked by manual labor like Henry's, which were rough and chapped. So tall I had to look way up into his sparkling blue eyes, as sunny as the lake in summer. His hair was a thick tangle, unlike Henry's meager strands who was, by the way, three inches shorter than his brother. Henry always wore a baseball cap to make himself look taller or maybe to hide his encroaching baldness - which one, I couldn't say."

Edith closed her eyes. Was she remembering, or was she just tired? "Ladies, do you mind if I continue next week?" she asked.

"Of course not," they all replied.

They could hardly wait. Here was a story of unfolding drama, and they would have to remain in suspense for a whole week! As they wheeled themselves to their rooms for their afternoon nap, they tittered like teenagers at the prospect of salacious details forthcoming.

On Wednesday, the four arrived straight from the usual mid-week lunch of meat loaf and mashed potatoes. All agreed it was the chef's best dish, and it always put them in a good mood for their afternoon chat. But today they were grouchy. The kitchen had run out of coffee cake, replacing it with stewed prunes.

They fussed about, settling themselves. When Edith set the brake on her chair and adjusted her feet on the pedals, the women immediately forgot about the prunes and remembered Hal.

Lina urged, "Go on, Edith, finish your story."

"For my entire marriage, there was the awareness that I had made the wrong choice, like I was *in* the marriage but *apart* from it. You know what I mean?" she asked, glancing around. "Fancying Hal, shortchanging my husband.

"Well, a few days before our twenty-fifth anniversary, Henry had a heart attack. Sitting by his bedside, realizing he could die, I also realized something awful about myself. I had been badly remiss, never truly grateful for my blessings. Oh, I always said thank you. But inside, I can tell you that feeling entitled to more than what you've got is a mean and selfish trait.

"My dreaming about a relationship with Hal was so intense that it seemed like an actual deception, the same as having a real affair. All that useless imagining of what if Hal and I lived in this house, what if Hal and I walked in the woods, what if it was Hal who slept in my bed? And all through the years, Henry, loyal and generous, supported me as I had never done for him."

Blanche blurted out, "Did Henry have any sense of all this?"

"I'm coming to that," Edith replied, as the women strained forward and Lina turned up her hearing aid.

"A dozen times over the years, Henry asked, 'Is something wrong?' I always said, 'No, nothing,' so he went his separate way and hoped the issue would somehow resolve. Of course, it never did, and over time, we drew increasingly apart."

What happened next?

"Shortly after his heart attack, it was June because I was in the garden the day before, my sister-in-law Lois staggered onto the porch, sobbing, her shirt misbuttoned, her hair uncombed. My sister-in-law never left the house unless her hair was in perfect order.

"Edith, Edith, my Hal, my Hal. I found some notes from him to the bookkeeper, Sally. Would you believe that he has been sleeping with her for ten years? Dumpy, frumpy Sally, for God's sake!"

Edith thought she heard Blanche mutter "The bastard" and Lina take a deep breath and Harriet put her handkerchief to her eyes, but she couldn't stop now.

"My first thought was Lois was so pretty and Sally was plump. But you want to know something, ladies? The whole time, as Lois was crying and I was handing her tissues and rubbing her back, I thought that I would have given my life to be in Sally's shoes. It was only days later, when I had time to think about it, that I realized, Oh, that bastard Hal. Good thing I didn't get involved with him. Who knew if there were others?"

"Still, it didn't kill my desire. In an odd way, he was now even more attractive.

"So here I am, ladies, a ninety-one-year-old fool who wasted her life in hollow dreams, who let goodness slip away by taking it for granted. My two kids, Betsy and Hal, grew up and moved a thousand miles from home. And not long after his first attack, Henry died from a second one while carving a $2,000 coffee table from a hunk of pine."

Lina and Blanche sat up, about to lecture their friend. "Yes, you *are* a fool," they wanted to say. "How many of us have had a reliable, loving force at our back?" But they refrained, for they also thought, *How many of us have dreamed of a lost love? How many of us longed for an unattainable soul mate or, like Edith and Henry, spent years with someone who didn't understand our true selves?*

Each lady held out her wrinkled, understanding hand to the one sitting closest until they were connected like a wreath of flowers long desiccated but yet still left hanging on the front door.

It was Halloween.

The facility was abuzz with witches dispensing pills, ghosts making beds. Patients in the auditorium were putting finishing touches on funny pointed hats sprinkled with orange and black sequins. Staff was handing out plastic pumpkins filled with chocolates and marshmallows.

The group paid no attention.

"Let's pass," said Blanche. "It's Wednesday. Today is Harriet's turn."

"Yes, let's pass," joined in the others.

As the gray-haired ladies, shawls in place, positioned themselves around the fireplace, they realized what a lucky bunch they were. Who would guess that at this age - they with such wildly dissimilar lives, a beautiful diversity that left them breathless in its ability to nevertheless connect - would discover a new kind of love, based on compassion and trust and the ability to look back? See how we opened our hearts so others could peek in? they marveled.

This lovely, miraculous affection slowed their descent into the loneliness of old age, the futility of battling infirmity and disability. For now, their being together did all that.

Harriet lifted her eyes. *Their stories are so much more terrible and shocking than mine*, she thought. *I'm embarrassed at its lack of spectacle.*

"I never got married," she began. "I'm over ninety years old, and not even once."

The women gasped. *Everyone* got married in their generation at least once. Was there something wrong with her? She *looked* just like them.

"I had several prospects. Even, you know, ladies, a fling here or there. But none worked out. Once or twice, the man seemed promising. But when we were apart, I never thought about him. Well, I ask you, is that an auspicious sign? And too soon, a couple of dozen years passed. By then, I was on photography shoots all over the world, more interested in lions and mountains than any traditional relationship. Besides, men were a nuisance. They all wanted to be taken care of."

Mildly agitated, the women were yet curious. Who didn't get married in the old days? Even if you had to "settle." Their minds leaped from one possibility to the next. Each of them had been tethered to a practical world, abounding in obstacles, conflicts, struggles. Surely Harriet had faced her own battles, but her challenges in foreign places seemed exotic, dazzling. And she appeared able to control her choices.

And no children? Imagine that! Of course, the young folks today make that choice all the time, but not then. Certainly not in their generation.

Had they selected the mundane over the exalted? Had they missed the magic?

"Friends told me it was my moral duty to continue lifelines, to procreate, but I didn't feel capable of shaping another's life. The responsibility, the lifelong worry. And a child would have moored me, a very unattractive proposition."

Just as she was finishing her story, a group of children in Halloween costumes rushed into the room, handing out Hershey's Kisses and singing, "Ding dong, the wicked witch is dead," causing Lina to lower her hearing aid.

"We'll meet next week," Lina called out.

As they parted, they all shook their heads. "Yes!"

Something unforeseen happened at their next gathering. A shyness unexpectedly set in. Each one had now given up their lifelong ghosts. Each now felt vulnerable, uplifted but exposed by the intimacy of their sharing. After those pivotal dramas, all else seemed trivial. What next? They turned to discussing the lunch of meat loaf and mashed potatoes and how pleased they were that this week there was coffee cake, not prunes. Oh, and that night, there was to be a movie, an old Cary Grant film they had all seen sixty years ago.

Blanche was unusually quiet. Lina noticed that the sclera of her eyes had turned from white to pale yellow. She also observed that the bruises covering her sadly thin shins had spread to her ankles. Suddenly, Blanche said, "I don't feel so well," and bent her head low over her lap. An aide was summoned, swooping in and whisking her away.

Upon inquiring, the women were told Blanche was resting in bed.

The following Wednesday, the nurse entered the room and stood before them. She looked at each one individually, waited a moment, then said, "She's in the hospital, ladies. I'm so sorry. She's very sick. It's doubtful she'll return."

And if she did, they murmured, they knew she would be transferred to another part of the facility, the one where patients lay waiting to die. Dazed, their weak hearts jumped and ran. Lina asked the nurse to take her blood pressure. Harriet requested a pillow behind her head. Edith reached in her pocket for a nitroglycerin.

Indeed, Blanche died that evening.

Through their stories, they had become young once again. For a brief moment, they had felt indomitable. But now, they had to face it. Blanche's fate would inevitably be their own.

The women grew silent at meals. They picked at their food, sent back half-eaten trays. Though they continued to meet on Wednesday afternoons, they were now just three old women - forlorn, aged, unsure what to say. Circumstances had bestowed upon them a surprising but abiding intimacy - four together, they had virtue, significance. Broken up, they were incomplete. Mortal.

But silence was not a condition they could sustain. The women were reluctant to return to their former ways. They had come to depend on giving of themselves in the most personal ways. The need to maintain their close friendship was more urgent than this isolated existence.

Lina spoke first.

"I want to talk," she said.

Edith and Harriet adjusted their sweaters, patted their hair.

"Did we ever expect at our age that this group would go on forever just as it was when we started? We weren't sure if it would work out at all. But look how grand our Wednesday afternoons have been. We look forward to them. Why throw up our hands and be depressed? I say, let's do better. Let's talk."

Edith raised her hand.

"I'm afraid of dying," she said meekly. "Or just as bad, getting sick and being in pain. And like Blanche, *knowing* you're going to die."

"There's death and illness in this place all the time," said Edith. "But when we are in our group, no one thinks of it. Let's get back to where we were and enjoy whatever days we have rather than mope around, thinking of dying all the time."

"I like that," Harriet said. "Shoot, I've been alone all my life and never feared anyone or anything. I could have died a hundred times in all the dangerous situations I've been in. I agree, ladies. Hell, let's perk up."

Edith added, "When Hal died years ago, I died. Maybe now is the time for me to start living!" Laughing, they all agreed, giving Edith a thumbs up!

Harriet suggested, "I say, let's talk about Blanche. Let's talk about her terrific spirit and the great courage it took for her to triumph over a terrible addiction. The more we talk about her, the more she'll remain in the circle *with* us. What do you say, ladies?"

"I say yes!" Lina answered. "Even a single day of being close to anyone at this time of our lives should be a cause for gratitude. Look how many lovely days we've had already! For my part, I feel blessed," she managed, tears in her eyes. "And I want *more* of us."

Now the group once again anticipated their Wednesday afternoon get-togethers. They told stories about Blanche. Their talk was lively at mealtimes. And they finished everything on their trays except for the damn brussels sprouts that they all hated.

It was only two months after they were given the terrible news about Blanche that Edith did not come to group. Harriet and Lina waited. Concerned, apprehensive. Edith was always punctual. They summoned the nurse, who soon arrived in the library, pulled up a chair.

"Ladies," she started, and Lina burst into tears, "I'm so sorry, but our beloved Edith died peacefully in her sleep last night. Her aide was tucking in her covers when she gasped and said, 'My dear friends…,' her last words. Again, I'm so sorry. I know how important you gals are to each other. Can I get you anything? Some juice? Cookies?"

Lina and Harriet reached for each other's hands, their bony fingers still strong enough for a squeeze. Yet they remained silent for almost the entire group time. What could they say about Edith's death? They had no words.

The following Wednesday, Lina started.

"Please, Harriet, let's talk about Edith. Poor thing with that whole Hal mess. What do you suppose it was like for her pretending to love her husband? Edith always thought she was a timid person, but staying with him required so much inner strength. It's sad. But I think she was a very good mother."

"Do you think she ever got used to the fact that he had an affair with Sally?" Harriet asked.

"No, I don't think so," Lina answered. "Didn't she say she still pined after him even when she found out?"

Edith and Lina talked together. Upstairs, they ate together, sharing their food. At last, they summoned the dietician and told her never again to serve them brussels sprouts.

Almost a year later, on a winter day close to Christmas, Harriet wheeled herself into the library and braked in front of the window to watch thousands of snowflakes drifting peacefully over the landscape.

So much beauty and so quiet. Noiseless, really. *Snow always makes me feel I can begin anew*, she thought. *I like to think of my body as one of these snowflakes, gently and eternally falling and no two alike, as lovely a blanket God could ever devise.* Harriet looked toward the clock. Lina was late. She grew anxious, eager to share her thoughts about the calming comfort of the snow.

She turned to ready herself for her dear friend just as Lorraine, the floor nurse, appeared in the doorway, her face drawn and sad. Harriet could see the deep breaths of her chest move in and out.

Watching her approach, Harriet unclasped her hands and reached for her handkerchief.

Giulia

Recalling his high school Latin, Oliver thought for the hundredth time, *Roma caput mundi.* Rome is the center of the world. He waited eagerly in line at the seventeenth-century Galleria Borghese in Rome, the elegant villa, now museum, of Cardinal Scipione Borghese, patron of the great sculptor, Gian Lorenzo Bernini. His heart was afire anticipating the moment when he would be surrounded by his beloved Bernini masterworks. A painter of local renown back home, he understood the artist's struggle with creating original work, never mind producing a legion of masterpieces out of a hunk of marble.

Visions of Isabelle and Jeremy, his pre-teen children in New Hampshire, popped up. They were old enough now to appreciate the works in this museum. After all, he had given them their own brushes and paints as soon as they could hold a spoon. "I'll bring them next time," he sighed. Oliver had received the highly regarded grant at the American Academy in Rome for a year. Its bestowal demanded that he work day and night, without distraction. And besides, his wife, Lolly, wouldn't be taken with the idea of a stay in Rome. She was seriously involved with her social work in the city's slums, not having much interest in any endeavor other than those dealing with poverty and deprivation. In fact, though she never said it, he always had the sense that she considered painting an indulgence, extraneous to the real world.

Would Lolly even notice I'm gone?

Suddenly, there was a light tap on his shoulder. When he turned, he noticed right away that the woman's eyes were the deep blue of a night sky full of stars, smatterings of gold dust in their centers. Then he saw she was beautiful.

"*Scusa*," she said. "*Sei Americano*? An American?"

He swooned a bit, as he always did when an Italian or French woman spoke his language, the two accents mingling, oozing charm.

"Yes," he answered. "May I help you?"

Oliver's thoughts tripped over each other. Grateful was he that there was another twenty minutes until the doors opened, grateful to God the earth and the sun that he decided to wait inside rather than in the exquisite outdoor gardens, surely missing those dark eyes dotted with those extraordinary bits of sparkle. Then an additional prayer of thanks if she, please dear Lord, spoke English.

"Have you ever seen the Bernini works before?" she asked. Oliver nearly wept. English!

"Do you know if *The Ecstasy of St. Teresa* is here, in this museum?"

"Yes, I've been here before," he murmured. "Often. And no, *St. Teresa* is not here. She's in the Chiesa di Santa Maria della Vittoria, a rather distant walk, but I'd be pleased to show it to you after your visit upstairs."

A radiant smile broke across her face.

"*Molto bello grazie*. Very nice, thank you," she said. As she spoke, he noticed that her eyes turned a lighter blue when she looked toward the light like the precious gem lapis with its gradations of hues that he saw last month at an exhibition of jewelry - either at the Barberini Palace or the Palazzo di Venezia. He couldn't remember the specific site, but he recalled a small sign that stated lapis was prized for its intense color. And that the Sumerians believed the spirit of their gods lived within the stone. He could believe it. He also knew that the measure of this woman's eyes would be impossible for an artist to capture.

"My name is Oliver," he said.

"And mine is Giulia," she replied.

Strolling through the galleries, they were thrilled by the procession of astonishing masterpieces. The works throbbed with organic life, their sense of movement, expression, and animation of character so acutely rendered in marble it was as if the figures were alive, holding their breath in complex positions. So different from classical architecture with its portrayal of universality that created an ethereal and eternal distance. In front of Bernini's *Apollo and Daphne*, they were mute. Words would have diminished the genius before them. On the walls were painted masterpieces by Caravaggio and Rubens. Titian's *Sacred and Profane*. Oliver noticed that depictions of war and adversity were mostly absent. Both the paintings and sculptures were largely romantic in nature, casting an intimate net over Oliver and Giulia as they circled the great room. The massive windows brought in sunlight that dappled the floors, framing the garden's cypress trees and beyond.

And here they were.

As he promised, they walked together to the church that displayed Bernini's *St. Teresa*, stopping at a trattoria for lunch. Surrounded by pots of pale pink begonias threaded with strands of lemongrass, Oliver marveled yet again at how the Italians brought their breathtaking hand to everything they touched. Like Giulia's face. Calm, new, mysterious. He wanted to know everything about her. This Giulia - did she live in an *appartamento* with begonias like these on her windowsills?

"Where do you live?" he asked.

"I'm from Bracciano," she began, "a small town thirty kilometers outside of Rome. Perhaps you have heard of Lake Bracciano? It's a lake of volcanic origin, a crystal-clear reservoir that provides drinking water for the city of Rome. When I am able, I come into Rome on my day off. You see," she said shyly, looking down, playing with her fork. "I work in the office that maintains the quality of the lake. *Ah, bellissimo lago.* The land is quite beautiful, but in my heart, I always wanted to paint. I fear that my few attempts were not fit to be seen. So I come to see the great paintings of others here in the city."

Oliver suddenly longed for his brushes. He would have Giulia paint something on this very tablecloth, perhaps the begonias, and see to it that the result would please her.

"But where are you from?" she asked.

"I'm from New Hampshire in northern New England, a dramatic land of forests and freezing cold," he offered. "Such cold that you Italians from the south do not know. But we also have many lovely lakes. I live and work in a small university town, teaching art in a studio that has very tall windows facing the woods, and a river running through them."

He mentioned his grant from the Academy but did not mention his family. Nor did she mention hers. They were just two people having lunch together, everything fresh, everything unknown. *What is this?* Oliver wondered. *I'm a practical man with a home, a position in the community. I have a family. I've never had a casual extramarital affair.* And yet, for all that, here and now was his only reality. The other seemed a dream. Was it those deep pools of her eyes? The sensual way she tilted her head, lifted her arms, rested her hand on her cheek? The swaying of her hips as she moved her body over cracks in the cobblestones so as not to catch her heel? *There is an incandescence about her*, Oliver marveled.

This morning, I waited in line to enter a museum. And now, at midday, nothing outside of this table, this Giulia, exists.

When they rose again, Oliver slowly took her hand, small and soft. His own felt clumsy, like a peasant's, rough and chapped from turpentine and paint, from a thousand winters. Yet she didn't pull away. Oliver's almost middle-aged heart was quivering, thinking himself long past such foolishness as this flirtation.

"I live with my parents," Giulia said. "They are elderly and need my caregiving."

"I have two children, but my students are also my children," he said.

"How old are your children?" she asked. She didn't ask about a wife.

"Ten and twelve. But tell me, is there no one to help with your parents? A brother or sister? Aunts, uncles?"

"No, no one," she answered sadly. "There is only my brother, Piero, and he went north to learn a trade. He returns only occasionally for brief visits."

Just outside the intricately wrought-iron gate of a splendid palazzo, an old man on a stool was playing Elgar's haunting Violin Sonata in E Minor, its beauty available to any passerby. A few yards on, Giulia paused to look into the soul of a coral-colored peony on a flower cart. The young vendor plucked it from the bouquet, bowed ever so slightly, and offered it to her.

"*Grazie*," she whispered, her nose to its petals.

Wandering farther, they casually shared more fragments of their lives until, turning the corner of Via Venti Settembre, they stood before the five-hundred-year-old Chiesa di Santa Maria della Victoria. Softly, they climbed its steps to the great front doors. Inside, their eyes watered from the bright Italian sun. Oliver reached for his handkerchief, asking, "May I?" and gently dabbed her cheeks.

They whispered and gaped, as did most visitors, stepping carefully among the tombs and burial vaults, sanctuaries, and altars sublimely and ornately rendered. At last, along the left transept, they found the Cornaro Family's funerary chapel. A small sign was posted.

L'Ecstasy of St. Teresa by Gian Lorenzo Bernini,
commissioned by the Cornaro Family.

Oliver fumbled for coins to insert in the pay-for light box, a token gratuity in most churches which are not permanently well-lit for viewing great art. As they waited reverently, suddenly, out of the murky air, there was an eruption of shocking brilliance, like fire-works, startling Giulia, who gave a little jump and reached for Oliver. And there before them was Bernini's angel and *St. Teresa*.

The two figures were surrounded by an ornate entablature and pediment of gilded bronze, marble, stucco, paint, the whole sup-ported by magnificent blue marble columns. The reclining nun's face portrayed a sublime, illuminated rapture. Her heavy-lidded eyes were partly closed, her lips loosely apart. She rested at the border between sacred mystery and indecency, surely in the throes of apparent ecstasy. But were they viewing the mystical levitation of a saint or a woman in orgasmic convulsion?

"It would have been heretical at the time," Oliver commented, catching his breath, his eyes misty, the same reaction every time he sees this statue, "to depict such a direct sexual expression on a woman of God."

Yet here Bernini had exquisitely mated sensuality with a spir-itual closeness to God. His mastery conveyed the alliance between earth and heaven, matter and spirit, directly drawing the viewer into the scene with all its apparent emotions. Oliver and Giulia stood rooted by greatness, and as their fingers found each other, they were sure of their destiny.

At last, they turned away, silently making their way to Oliver's studio in the American Academy on the Janiculum Hill, high above the old section of Trastevere, astonishing views of the sprawling city with its gilded domes following them as they climbed higher and higher.

Oliver didn't expect to fall in love. It could have been a tempo-rary dalliance in which one indulges when alone in a grand, romantic city.

But he thought, *No, I am in love with this woman.*

Propped on his side, his heart thudded with fear and awe as he watched Giulia sleep, her lips parted like St. Teresa's. She would soon awaken and open those dazzling eyes, reaching for him. He knew that whatever little he grasped about this woman was enough. Never had he felt this connection with his wife. Not even in the beginning, not even before the children. Right then, his body had wings, but he knew they would eventually fail. How could this end well? As he lay back, about to relive this day, he decided, no. He would not dissect this fragile gift. For now, he would set aside his alarm and dwell in wonder.

Oliver and Giulia continued to live their usual lives, she at her office, he at his easel, each consumed with thoughts of the other. How long until they will be together? Only a few days, but those moments were full of longing. And when they met, they came together with the fervor of lovers long parted.

He wanted to paint her, but he could not bear the separation of their bodies, even the eight feet from his easel to her chair. Not even when fetching cheese and focaccia for their weekend breakfasts. Or when they strolled Rome's streets, both seeing the familiar glories as if for the first time. Even then, they were attached to each other.

On a day when Rome was readying for Christmas with municipal workers stringing decorations and lights across every surface in the city, Oliver said, "Giulia, I must fly home for Christmas. My children expect me. Only ten days, my darling."

She did not pout or cry or stamp her feet. But her eyes were wet as she stood on her toes to kiss his nose, his forehead, his lips.

In his absence, Giulia began to wonder about Oliver's family.

On his return, they covered each other with kisses and promises never to be separated again. And now, the next day, Giulia sat on a bench, her lap laden with coral and white peonies from the flower vendor. They were comfortable in this spot along the Tiber River opposite Castel Sant'Angelo, the personal mausoleum of the Roman Emperor Hadrian. The tomb loomed ominously against the sky while Ponte Sant'Angelo, or Bridge of Angels, spanned the river leading directly to the site. Ten splendid marble angels stood majestically atop its balustrades, each carrying an instrument of Christ's Passion.

"Pope Clement IX commissioned Bernini to create all ten," Oliver said. "But the pope decided to keep the first two for his personal pleasure. The remaining eight were finished by others according to Bernini's vision. Next weekend, I can show them to you. They're on display at the Chiesa di Sant'Andrea delle Fratte. Would you like that?"

"Oliver, tell me about your family," she answered.

Carefully, in the simplest way, he would tell her the truth. It was only fair now that she had asked. Hordes of tourists were crossing the bridge, taking photos. Long lines waited for admission to Hadrian's burial place. On the river, an eight-person shell manned by young students from the university glided by.

"I've mentioned the two children, Isabelle, ten, and Jeremy, twelve. They're wonderful kids," he began. "We spend a lot of time together. Hiking, camping, but also painting, doing crafts. You should see how they painted our front porch - pine forests on the walls, a moose sticking his nose through a tree, a deer and a bear on the floor."

Darn, he thought, *far too many words. Painting the porch is not keeping it simple. And how stupid to say, "You should see..."* Sei un idiota. *You're an idiot, Oliver.* Angry at himself, he fell silent.

Giulia folded her hands in her lap, struggling for control. Once again, she was taken over with the familiar pain of loss, the hurt of having missed out, the empty space that children fill. The week before, when her parents were asleep, she had read about the life of St. Teresa, finding an affinity that was consoling. She struggled to remember the very written words of the saint. Something like "*I saw in his hand a long spear of gold, and at the iron's tip there seemed to be a little fire. He appeared to...thrust it...into my heart. When he drew it out...he left me all on fire with a great love of God... Sometimes love,* like an arrow, is thrust into the deepest part of the heart, and the soul doesn't know what has happened or what it wants, except all it wants is God."

Yes, she thought, *that is how I feel. Both of us, Teresa and me, the same. An arrow thrust into the heart. But when the arrow is drawn out, I don't see God anywhere. I see Oliver. Teresa saw God.*

What is she thinking? Oliver wondered. He dared not ask.

"Lolly is my wife," Oliver continued, more mindful now.

"Her real name is Lillian, but everyone calls her Lolly, a name that of course reminds me of sweet candy. But every time I say it or think it, the image is one of something that ruins your teeth."

Giulia smiled. Oliver waited. Even mentioning his wife's name in her company seemed profane.

Still, she sat expectantly, so he went on.

"She's a social worker and spends all her time with people in the slums, redeeming the children. Of course, it's noble work but frustrating with only infrequent rewards. Her only diversion is her garden, in which she labors incessantly. We're not close as husband and wife. If it weren't for the children…"

Giulia wanted more, of course she did, and not objective facts. Did they ever hold hands? Did they share glances, touches? How did he feel when she opened the door to him after an absence? What did she look like? What was it like between them in the beginning? Giulia shuddered. Never would she ask Oliver these questions, plunked down ever after into the love between them.

She reached into her bag for their breakfast leftovers, bits of *cornettos* filled with jam. She tossed them to the pigeons who swooped down like a great wind. Oliver thought, *Not now. No questions. I'll wait until she makes the choice to speak about herself.*

They had no more words at the moment. Eventually, they stood, and arms around each other, they walked along the Tiber's stony embankments, the sun casting threads of light on the water that rippled like hammered gold.

After a walk, they entered the Chiesa delle Fratte and stood before Bernini's two angels - the *Angel with the Crown of Thorns* and the *Angel with the Superscription*. The first figure was agitated, tormented, folds of marble swaying with distress. The latter was a womanly form of supple grace.

Giulia burst into tears. These statues were two halves of her own soul - *Serenity*, the one who received Oliver's love with joy, and *Tormented*, the one who knew Oliver would never be hers.

Gently, he led her to a pew in a far corner. The church was vast and dim. Hardly any parishioners were nearby.

"My darling," he started.

She wept again. The wrong words. Too kind.

After her hiccups stopped and the gasps subsided, she spoke.

"I had an early love," Giulia began.

"His name was Carlos. He was Spanish, here to study antique methods of carving. But after his apprenticeship, he had to go home.

"He left me," Giulia managed. "Just as you will."

"Never," Oliver murmured, "never will I leave you."

In his arms, Giulia calmed down; her body ceased trembling. Oliver whispered words of comfort, of fealty, but when she looked off to the *Angel with the Crown of Thorns*, she was reluctant to believe them.

It was in the Roman streets that they spoke most easily and intimately. The city itself provided visual distractions to explore or discuss should there be an awkward moment. And so their connective seeds grew and flourished. Luxuriating in the monumental layers of history through which they strolled, they were linked to Ancient Rome, the Etruscans, the Roman Empire. Then Medieval Rome, the Papal States, followed by Byzantine Rome, then Renaissance Rome. Taking it all in was a dazzling feat of fortitude and willingness.

Much of the architecture and art remained intact or was authentically restored. Oliver and Giulia were reminded of this one day when they almost fell over an obstruction in the path and realized it was a collection of rock boulders from Medieval Rome. Modern commerce had simply left them in place and built around them, as noted by a tiny brass plaque posted nearby.

Their deepest concerns fell from their lips.

"If I sometimes resent my parents, am I a bad girl?" Giulia asked.

"If I love only you and not my wife, will God strike me down?" Oliver asked.

"If I live forever, will you be with me?" Oliver asked.

"If I want a child with you, what would you say?" he asked.

"Yes," she said. "I would say yes."

Oliver made the arrangements for a life of deception. Leaving his wife would have meant abandoning his children, so never would that be a consideration. He secured a teaching position through the Academy and told Lolly he would split his time between Rome and New Hampshire for a few years. Generously remunerative, she had no objections. His kids made a few faces, then said, "Bye, Dad," throwing kisses, running out to meet their friends. Would they miss him?

And so it was decided.

Oliver now had two children in New Hampshire, and soon enough, a son, Matteo, in Rome.

And a small apartment in Trastevere for himself, Giulia, and Matteo, Giulia's brother now married and back home, taking his widowed mother to live with him.

Initially, the arrangement turned out to be more difficult for Oliver than he had anticipated. Living two disparate lives in different cultures forced him to be attentive to the appropriate emotions and issues belonging to each. He was not normally a secretive man. Living in a guarded manner was tedious, and he remained circumspect as a hawk, circling, watchful. Once he had made a mistake, calling Jeremy *Matteo*. But no one noticed.

After some months, thankfully, as most life's dilemmas slowly resolve over time, his emotional sparring diminished. He fell into easy patterns and habits, and his ardor for Giulia only increased.

So he did not expect to face a surprising revelation when he and Giulia were sitting at a café, having a cappuccino. A few young friends called out her name, hurried over to their table with effusive greetings and constant chatter in Italian. An assistant museum curator now, Giulia was taken up by a wide world of fresh experiences through work and Matteo's school - folks she had met apart from him. While Oliver remained in place with the same job, the same friends, his children no longer at home, Giulia had expanded her circumstances.

And Lolly? He hadn't really noticed what Lolly was doing for a very long time.

It was the spring of Matteo's fifth birthday. Oliver stepped off the plane laden with tubes of paints, a child's smock, and an easel. He thought Matteo was now ready for this adventure. The little boy's fingers were agile, he noticed, his eye quick, observant.

Seeing his father, Matteo shrieked with delight - "Papà, Papà!" - then got right down to squeezing small bits of paint on the palette as Oliver directed. Very soon, he filled the paper with orange and red circles. "Oranges! Tomatoes! Papà," he said, pointing to the basket on the table. "My first *immagine*!" Holding up his finished work, he added, "*Immagine* means 'picture,' Papà."

After dinner, when the paint tubes were sealed, the dishes put away, and Matteo was in bed, Oliver and Giulia sat at the table with their cups of coffee. Church bells tolled nine o'clock all over Rome. It was a moment of peace, of camaraderie.

Until Giulia looked at Oliver and said softly, "Oliver, I'm getting married."

Nervous, she talked quickly.

"Matteo is getting older. He needs a full-time father. A man from the museum proposed, and I've accepted."

She took his hand across the table.

"Oliver, you will always be the love of my life. But I have to think of my future now, of Matteo's future, and you're married. Please understand."

Her words were platitudes, rubbish, yet he couldn't blame her. Yes, Matteo *did* need a full-time father. But Oliver knew that he would eventually be forgotten by his young son, lost as a lovely dream. He would be put away along with the tubes of paints, the smock, the easel, on a shelf in the closet.

Oliver pushed himself up from the table. No words would change her mind. In despair but resigned, he found his jacket and pulled Giulia toward him. For a brief moment, he held her close. And then he let her go and walked out the door.

As Oliver wandered the streets, the piazzas bright with gaiety, everything he had loved about Rome now angered him. He felt imprisoned by its beauty - there was too much of it. Everything was so dense, so significant. Every stone and bowl had a history, a specific meaning. Living here took effort - no viewer could simply appreciate this city without placing it in its spectacular historical context every moment. Its glorious sights always competed for his eye, his mind. It was a place where he fought to empty his head, to allow in other visions. It was easy to fall in love with Rome, but staying in love required his full devotion and effort.

Unlike the New Hampshire that he also adored, where love was easy, with its expansive spaces of lakes and forests, and towns that were quaint and quiet, embracing without making demands. He had always loved that simplicity where he could paint with a freedom Rome never allowed.

Oh, the anguish of life without Giulia., without Matteo, and without his difficult, beloved Rome.

Sitting on the edge of a fountain, the spray wet his hair, his shirt. He wished he could fall into its waters and emerge totally cleansed of deceit, a new self with a new name. But no, he would board a plane, fly over the ocean, and unpack his suitcase in the room overlooking the grove of sugar maples unless he made another choice - to leave Lolly and appeal to Giulia, "Let your husband be me. I will stay."

The ancient dark buildings around him spoke of centuries past, and he now felt as aged as they. Giulia had passed him by. Was this to be his fate - God's punishment for the cheating he had perpetrated on so many people for so many years?

Where *was* home now? *Who* was home?

How would he *exist*?

Once, Twice...Thrice

He had come to paint our house.

He was just a painter, wearing a clean white T-shirt and bleached white coveralls.

We had only spoken on the phone, so when he showed up, I wasn't prepared for his clear blue eyes that shone like ice splintered into tiny facets, blinking points of light going on, off, on, off.

Hell, I was immediately smitten. Only twice in my life had I seriously fallen for a guy, and both had eyes that gleamed the same way, hinting at imminent mischief - not prankish, annoying behavior but intelligent, clever roguishness. Daniel was my first real love, though his eyes were brown; and the second was my husband Josh, whose eyes were gray and who was sleeping upstairs at the very moment I opened my front door to the painter.

Darn my heart, jumping and popping like a firecracker. *Pray, Diana girl, that your face is not flushed or he'll know right away. You'll be forty-five in a week*, I reminded myself. *Yes, still slender and fair, even after three children, with wavy blond hair not yet in need of a hairdresser. But married, don't forget, for twenty-two years. And your grown children are coming home this weekend to celebrate your birthday.* This painter with the dancing eyes, I would guess, probably celebrated his fiftieth about two years ago.

"I'm Earl," he said, smiling, his pupils like sparks.

"Of course you are," I answered, starting to flirt. "You told me on the phone. How many painters named Earl are there who show up at my house at seven on a Saturday morning?"

He laughed. Now I was entirely enchanted. Standing aside, he introduced me to his assistant Tommy, skinny as a scarecrow, slouching against the porch post with his eyes closed, a goofy grin on his face. Perhaps too much pot last night?

"My man here needs a strong cup of coffee," Earl explained as Tommy dangled a thermos from his finger, managing a weak twirl.

"Let's see the property," Earl suggested.

We left Tommy sitting on the grass, trying to pour coffee into a cup, his head between his knees. How could he climb ladders today? My homeowner's policy flashed through my brain. As Earl and I strolled around, our talk was flavored with an immediate, playful intimacy. And yet I would soon be employing him.

"Do you do small repairs as well as paint?" I asked, pointing to a few loose garden tiles.

"Sure. I do it all. I'm especially good with household repairs. My wife calls me *her honeydew*, as in 'Earl, honey, do this. Earl, honey, do that.'"

"My husband can't put together a child's dollhouse without banging his fingers," I answered, grinning, holding up my two thumbs.

Earl smiled with surprising sweetness. His eyes like glowing flares, he suddenly looked away and murmured, "I'll start with the garage," tossing his thick gray hair back from his face. As he arranged his supplies and we continued to banter, I glanced up at our bedroom window. The curtains were still drawn.

"Great idea, the garage, yes, of course," I answered, reassured our voices hadn't carried into the house.

When he propped the ladder against the wall and started climbing, tools hitched onto his belt and pockets, I watched his ascent from behind the dining room shutters. He had the aura of a man who would capably take on any task. As he stepped ever higher, there was no fumbling or hesitation, just a careful mounting, back straight while looking up, hands holding sure, silver hair shining in the sun.

And I thought, *This Earl, this painter, is the sexiest man I've seen in a dozen years.*

Suddenly gripped by a surge of lust, my head pounding and pulse racing, I ran upstairs, threw back the covers on our bed, and rolled onto Josh. The poor man rose to the task but then immediately fell asleep while I lay next to him, listening to his breathing, a man whom I loved dearly. Yet thinking of Earl right outside my window in his crisp white pants, whose eyes, clear as glass, sparkled with notions of naughty shenanigans.

So It Shall Ever Be

For a nineteen-year-old boy, Simon sat surprisingly still as the plane flew over the Atlantic Ocean. His unruly dark hair had been trimmed and tamed. His new jeans from Clark's Mercantile were a bit stiff, and he was annoyed he hadn't broken them in a couple of weeks ago. He chose a red sweater, something different and happy from the somber colors he usually wore in the difficult Maine weather. His earnest gray eyes, curious and eager, were impatient with longing and a bit of uncertainty, though perhaps more concerned than anything else.

His head lost to fancies for so long and were now about to come true.

The small package on his lap was wrapped in gold paper with purple ribbons. He would not let it go even for a moment, this small ivory notebook with lines printed in gold, waiting for her pen.

Because, you see, Simon was in love. His girl had big dreams that needed to be written down, and this small offering was his gift to her.

It began when Simon was fourteen.

By chance.

Something he stumbled upon on an idle Saturday when it was raining and he couldn't play ball with his friends. He was watching *Batman* reruns on TV and casually picked up one of his mom's ladies' magazines sprawled over the coffee table. He flipped to the back section where there were ads for all kinds of things: the sale of a used motorcycle, the rental of a house in Aruba, a half-dozen kittens needing a home.

And then he noticed this.

Middle-schooler pen pal wanted. Lonely in the countryside with a head full of stories I want to share. Anyone out there with stories to tell?

What is this? he wondered.

Then he thought of how just this term in school he had loved his creative writing elective more than his math class.

That's all it said. An address in England. In middle school, just like him.

He tore out the page and put it in his pocket, ate his lunch, watched the Discovery Channel, played video games, called his friend Jeff. After dinner, he pulled the sheet from his jeans and smoothed it out on his desk.

What an adventure this could be, he thought. *A secret of my own. Why not? Nothing else is my own in this house. My grandparents come for long stays, taking my room and forcing me to move in with my annoying younger brothers. There's frantic activity in every corner night and day.* He put his fingers on the computer keyboard.

"Hi, my name is Simon. I have lots of stories in my head. Most of the time, people aren't interested in listening. Are you?"

"Hi back, my name is Lydia. Tell me a story. I'm interested."

And so it began.

At first, they each described where they lived, basic information.

Lydia's stories about life in England in a small Cotswold town, just a few shops on a short street surrounded by meadows of gorse and heather that began almost at your back porch. An enchanting Palladian library of intricate stonework with tall windows in the back facing the river was tucked between the wine and cheese shops. No one ever moved in; no one ever moved out.

Simon's stories about living in a white colonial house with dark-green shutters and a weather vane on the roof. A coastal fishing village set on a peninsula in Maine, in northern New England. The fishermen dropped their traps right on the pier, where the waiting vendors boiled up those lobsters straightaway. Folks sit outside waiting at picnic tables with the sea smells right in their noses, and wolf them down as soon as they are plated and handed over. A shoreline of endless coves and inlets, the most beautiful scenery anywhere. And lighthouses on rocky ledges. Everyone knows everyone, and here, too, no one moves in, no one moves out.

And then, those particulars given, they began to talk about themselves.

"Do you eat lobster in England?" Simon asked.

"No, I never ate lobster, but I would like to. But mostly I would love to see the lobstermen bringing in their boats and unloading their catch on the wharves. I draw a little and would love to capture that on paper."

"Did you ever eat bangers and mash?" Lydia asked. "Or toad-in-the-hole?"

"Surely, you're joking. Such odd names for food! Not very enticing for taking a taste! Although, if I can manage eating almost raw mussels and oysters, I'm sure a toad wouldn't scare me off!"

It was to the precious and the picturesque that they were attracted. Their imaginations were afire from heather and lobsters, those worlds forging an enduring connection. Both Olivia and Simon were writers in their sensibilities. And at their tender age, fully taken up with the romance of words and ideas. How quickly their emotional leashes loosened up! Imagine - another with a soul similar to yours, eager to share.

"Does it ever get freezing cold in England? So cold and so bright at night from the moon's reflections on the water that you can see the trout and bass jumping high up toward the sky? Do you ever feel as if you are the last person on earth? I sometimes walk out alone while everyone is warm inside and pretend that I am strong enough to withstand any force I meet. It's so cold that I can't feel my own face. I wonder, if I shouted into the wind, would anyone hear?"

"No, Simon, England gets chilly and damp but not cold like Maine. However, in spring, when the poppy fields are blazing red and the purple lavender smothers the hills, filling the air with sweet scents, you could die from pleasure. It is then that I have a similar feeling to your walks in the moonlight. That I am strong enough to withstand any difficult things that come my way."

"Do you believe in God?" Simon asked.

He fell asleep dreaming of Lydia, just as she awoke thinking of him. One weekend, he worked long hours at the dock just to earn money for his own personal printer. He accumulated page after page of her work and stored them neatly in a blue wood box decorated with whales that his mother had bought him for his last birthday.

"Lydia, I've been thinking of this. The name *New England* refers to an 'empty' land starting fresh that may be shaped in England's image but with a whole new vision unhampered by the rules of the old country - your country. I love that I live in a place that reminds me of us. A starting over fresh, wherever and however that may be, keeping the best from our old lives and making something new together."

"Oh, Simon. Yes, that's just how I feel. We are making something special, aren't we? Your wonderful sense of the sea. My love of flowers and the countryside. Together, we span God's earth. What should we make of that?"

And so, five years passed. Five years of teenage longing and dreaming. They grew from children to young adults. Their bonds grew tight like thick fishermen's ropes that seemed invincible, strength itself, able to tow cargoes of inestimable weight. Their young love had a ferocity of devotion that only occurs in those early years. The first taking up of their lives. The first intimacies awakened. Emotional magnets that would be remembered sixty years hence. Each to the other.

"Simon, do they have fireflies in Maine? Here, in summer, they light up the dark over the meadows as if a thousand stars have fallen to earth. I want to gather them up in my apron and spread them over your life."

"Yes! We have fireflies. In summer. If I could, I too would collect them for you to thread through your hair."

And now, a hundred stories later, but a mere five years after their first meeting, Simon was flying over to meet Lydia on this jet now hurtling through the sky. His father was unexpectedly sent abroad on a company mission, and Simon was grateful for a discounted fare. This was his first plane trip, leaving from Boston, a city he had never visited - Portland was as far west as he had ever traveled. With its abundance of colleges and museums, ethnic cafés, pretty girls, Boston was a glamorous destination. How his pals envied him! Yet he passed it by as if he were going through a tunnel. So too with London.

"Dearest Simon, I wish you could see the sun right away when you open your eyes. But as you've told me, most Maine mornings start out misty and gray. So let my words be your sun. My dog Rupert wakes me long before I'm ready to dress. But it is nice being awakened by a lick on the nose from someone who loves you. You should see his confusion when he tries to catch those fireflies!"

"Lydia, yes, we have two dogs, Tom and Tillie, brother and sister. However, I have two brothers, Mason and Jeff. And they think we should each have our own dogs. So that means one more. My mother says to count ourselves lucky. Even two is one too many. They are huge collies, friendly as pups - I think they like chunks of lobster better than they do our noses! When you finally taste that much-discussed crustacean, I want to be the one who puts on your bib, wipes your lips."

Simon looked out the window yet again at the endless sky, the endless water. Four hours of flight time were gone; two remained. What would she be doing this minute? Wandering the house distracted, forgetting to put the milk back in the fridge? Trying on dress after dress, finding none pretty enough to wear for their meeting? Surely she was pleased that the yellow gorse and purple heather were flowering. "In full bloom," she had promised.

"Oh, Simon, gorgeous, blinding colors blanket the fields, mile after mile. And fragrances that will make you swoon. Such a sight!"

The real beginning of his life, as if reborn.

The second hand on his watch hardly moved. Would there be a disaster? Would the plane's motor be compromised? A wing on fire?

Think of Lydia, he told himself. *Think of her.*

His mind burned with wild musings. Thoughts scampered from one to another as he wrung his hands and flexed his fingers, praying the other passengers couldn't hear the raging beats of his heart. He would scoop her up and bring her back to his little town in Maine. Or if she wished, he would stay by her side in England.

But then he was seized by this terrible consideration. What if Lydia is dismissive when she sees me for the first time? Or a pout crosses her forehead before she can wipe it away? I would see. I would know.

Looking down the aisle, he watched the stewardess calmly pushing her cart, serving drinks, smiling, nodding. His father was reading the *Daily Telegraph*, business section. No one suspected that his eyes and ears were full of her name.

Finally, London's Heathrow Airport. I said goodbye to my father and found the bus that would carry me on this final piece of my journey. The driver tipped his cap. "Welcome aboard, mate," and whisked me off into the countryside.

Yes, this England, her England, just as she described, Simon thought, nose to the window. There was an English spring, so lovely he could cry for its beauty. And the allure of the village names - Burford, Chipping Camden, Dursley. Cricklade, Stow-on-the-Wold - right out of an English child's playbook! He had memorized all that were within a stone's throw of Lydia's address.

The bus rambled on into a small village with a few cozy shops along cobblestone streets; exuberant window boxes lush with flowers like a tiny and perfect toy village; and snug, petite houses of lime-stone, some with thatched roofs of straw, sedge, and reeds, others of slate. Many were hidden behind immaculately trimmed hedgerows, others whose facades were covered with climbing vines. A tidy stone church sat on a hill. At the end of the street, keeping a watchful eye, a grand manor house rose, sprawling and imperial, of ancient but beautiful yellow stone, a fiefdom unto itself. Moving quickly through and out again, the village disappeared in less than a minute.

Back onto the narrow, winding roads, the low foothills, a lift into the landscape, then the return of the heather. Another town, its houses with gables and dormers, this one along a river with low arched bridges, then through and out again into the surrounding greenery. Soon enough, another village, and here, on the main street, an attached row of dwellings, timeless, idyllic, and out again, until finally, the driver called out, "Hey, mate, we're here. By the way, these are the Cotswolds, you know. Very famous. Very pretty," in that lilting accent Simon had heard only in movies and now quickly embraced, beside which the broad flat sounds of southern Maine sounded decidedly uncouth.

Suddenly he smiled, realizing that Lydia too would sound like this driver and not like his mother or his friends at school. That she too would speak with these charming intonations and inflections. Like the queen. He thought if she told one of her stories in this delicate voice, he would sit at her feet with his eyes closed, listening for all eternity.

A middle-aged man with flashing eyes, his ruddy face creased from the sun, wearing a suede cap and smoking a pipe, leaned against the bumper of an open jeep. Eagerly, he came forward with a hearty, "Good day, young fellow. You must be Simon. I'm Lydia's father, William. Welcome to England!"

"Thank you, sir," Simon replied, thinking William a cheery chap, straight out of an English novel with the earthy vigor from living the country life, his tweed jacket with leather elbow patches.

Stowing his gear, he scrambled aboard.

"Ready to go, young Simon?" William asked, giving the jeep a start.

"Yes sir, all ready," he answered, immediately at ease with this amiable fellow.

At the end of the outrageously charming street, gigantic old trees framed the massive iron gates. *Odd,* Simon thought, *that the one main street in town led directly into these gates.* A stranger driving this road would find it dead-ended right at this private estate and would have to turn around and find his way back. The jeep lurched into the enclosed compound surrounded by low walls of that ancient yellow stone seen in the various towns, then stopped short with a thrust and a bounce. We parked before a small replica of the splendid manor house just beyond the courtyard. A dozen outbuildings - stables, dairy, granary, barns, guest houses, were scattered about, folks going in and out, busy with their tasks. There was an air of abiding, enduring serenity over the entire scene as if imbued with a noble entitlement. Whatever his eye rested on was older and more enchanting than anything he could have imagined.

"Sir, these walls are so fine, and I've seen many small buildings in the towns I just passed through made of this same material."

"My boy, oh yes," William began in his melodic voice. "Cotswold stone is a yellow limestone rich in fossils, particularly sea urchins. When it weathers, it becomes a honey, golden color. Pulled right from the quarries in these hills around us. And I'm the fortunate fellow who oversees this marvelous property. Owned by Lord Devonshire, you know," he said with a nod to the great house.

Oh, the seduction of it all! Would Lydia think his New England docks and harbors and mountains equally fetching? Would she smile or run at a deer digging up her favorite petunias, her ripe tomatoes? What if a moose casually walked across the road as she was getting out of her car?

Lydia's father reached for Simon's luggage, beckoned him inside.

Simon's heart was thrumming; his legs wobbled. *Wait, wait, I need a minute*, he thought, gasping, frantic with apprehension. *This is my Lydia. My Lydia. Please let me enter in some dignified manner for our first meeting.*

Her father called, "Lydia, he's here!"

Dare he enter? At this ultimate moment of exposure, he had no idea what lay beyond the threshold. Would he love her unreservedly? Or would he find fault after years of holding her soul in his palm? Could he now yet turn and run away to the ends of the earth? Simon's brain tripped over itself with prospects and consequences. *Stop*, he told himself. *Be an adult. Having courage is what it means to be an adult. I'm still a kid!* he wanted to cry.

But his heart said, *You're an adult. You've long been an adult.*

"Come in, come in," her father urged.

And so he stepped inside.

Lydia was seated, facing me as I crossed over the threshold.

A soft English light warmed the ancient mellow floorboards. The heavy scent of unfamiliar flowers drifted through an open window. A new and wonderful scent.

My first thought was ordinary, one most fellas would think of first. She's so pretty - light-brown hair to her shoulders, straight but full; a pale-blue dress, modest, with a white collar and some white trim on the sleeves; and a beautiful, gentle smile. She had soft green eyes. Green! Maybe an Irish ancestor? There was something different, something serene, about her. Was her aura of graceful refinement a particularly English quality? How patiently she sits and waits.

My Lydia put out her arms.

All this at the first glance.

And just then, the sun's rays bounced off the metal frame of her wheelchair.

God help me. God help Lydia. God help us. Simon's soul cried out.

Did his face reveal alarm, dread, dismay? Misgiving? Horror?

Slowly, he walked over to her, fell on his knees, and put his head in her lap. "Forgive me," he said silently.

Lydia's gentle hands comforted as she tenderly stroked his head.

And this is how the two stayed, until Simon's heart returned to its regular rhythm, his throat cleared of fright. Then he looked up.

And there she was, his Lydia.

And he knew then, telling himself with a soul that wept, *This is* our *story, not one we have constructed.*

How would they manage? *Please*, he pleaded to himself, *please, let someone else write the ending to this story.*

But by the time this man/boy's heart took another dozen beats, he was perfectly sure of what would happen next. He held close her small hand and recalled her lovely outpourings stored far across the ocean in his precious blue box. He reached for one particular exchange as if it were a pearl he would place in that tender, childlike palm - the story he told her years ago of his walking out under the brilliant moon on a freezing-cold Maine night, feeling he could conquer any force which stood in his way.

And he remembered her reply, so apt that it seemed a sacred blessing had been bestowed on them at this moment. Her response when she witnessed the glorious red poppies and purple lavender wrapping the English hills in spring, that she felt exactly the same as he, that she was strong enough to vanquish any misfortune.

Oh, Simon, wait till you see.

My Mother, My Ben

My mother's friend and attorney, Joel, knew first that she had died. He had been visiting when her monitor's rhythm quivered, gasped, and quit. From the phone on the wall of the hospital corridor, he dialed my number.

"Sharon, come now," he said, "your mother has just died."

There was a cloudless blue sky that farewell noon. Gentle twitterings from above caused me to look up. A dozen scarlet tanagers were settling in the leaves of a spreading maple tree. A bright sky, dazzling birds, both too beautiful, I thought, to be at the scene of a funeral. A cloudy day, a few raindrops, seemed more appropriate for the mourners below seated on flimsy metal folding chairs.

At her grave in this remote, agreeably pastoral cemetery, my elegant husband, Ben, talked to his mother-in-law. The guests sat propped, wooden. *What are we doing in this place so far from my family burial plots, the graves of aunts, uncles, grandparents?* I wondered. But then again, this was no ordinary funeral, if any ever are.

Ben stood before us, so fine-looking, so at ease in his gray suit, hand in one pocket - dignified, composed. He was the successful psychiatrist, not uncomfortable with death's presence.

"Adele," Ben said, looking down at the open grave waiting to receive my ninety-two-year-old mother. "Julia Roberts just won the best actress Oscar at the Academy Awards. I know you would have wanted to hear that," he said, smiling at us.

Smiling back, we knew Ben had said just the right thing.

"El Maleh, Rachamim," we murmured, the Jewish prayer said absent the ten men necessary to recite the Kaddish.

Anecdotes followed as folks stood up to pay tribute to her long life, an uncomplicated, straightforward recounting despite her children's recently acquired unease in Joel's office and despite the fact that the reason for our being here was preposterous.

"Her work with Jewish charities," cousin Jonathan said. "She ran a lot of fundraisers, those afternoon card games, teas, club events. Sent a lot of checks over to Hadassah Hospital in Israel."

My sister Barbara reminded us of her many golf trophies. "And Mom's bridge tournaments, even once when she was up for a state championship, coming in fifth."

Then her canasta partner, Lois, spoke, "Adele never forgot Jimmy Menuchi, her favorite second-grade student, almost sixty years ago now. The stories she told of Jimmy's endless mischief!"

No one mentioned the simmering sibling rivalries between her, two brothers, and a sister that led to painful alienation and recrimination. My grandmother Sadie might have been partly to blame, Mom always feeling she was the least favored. And given what I myself saw, my grandmother granting her siblings special indulgences, she was probably right - the cashmere sweater, the silk ties, and often something bigger (a Burberry raincoat) that Sadie had given to one of my uncles without even asking permission. Taken right off the shelves of my father's store! My mother didn't speak to either my grandmother or my uncles for two months after each of those incidents.

No one addressed the grievous toppling she endured because of two employees who had robbed the business. Nor did anyone mention Adele's noble but surprising selflessness when she took a job in a local stationery store to add to the family bank account.

So swiftly had she fallen, from grande dame in a Los Angeles suburb to commoner in a village in wine country. And then after Napa, another dramatic move to Vermont. "Why Vermont?" we asked her. The weather! But my father had died in Napa, where she had never felt at home. She would never return to Los Angeles, and she had two old friends who urged her to come and live near them in Vermont.

However, after she settled into that austere little village, the truth was that no one there cared one whit about her previous life as a community leader someplace in California. She enjoyed chatting about her troubles, but everyone she met had their own stories to tell, and they wanted *her* to be *their* listener.

The flashing scarlet tanagers were beating their wings, making soft chirruping sounds. There was a comforting rhythm coming from all that energy that lulled me into reflection. And so I lingered over the mysterious notions of my mother's past - never adequately explained, never appropriately confronted. Many were surely tied to the news Joel had given us yesterday. Now seemed the proper time to make some sense of this whole business.

Why was she unmarried until age thirty-three? In her generation, marrying that late was rare. She was pretty, smart, and educated, but when we three sisters asked why the late date, her answer was always the same. "You get married when you get married."

And something else, something she said when I married - "Hopefully, love will grow with the years. But, if not, you can still have a strong marriage." Were these appropriate words from a mother to a young bride? It was a disturbing comment. In their own time, my sisters received similarly cryptic remarks. On Barbara's marriage, she said, "Sharing intimate concerns is not always the best thing." On Laurie's marriage, she remarked, "Whatever you want, just hope for the best."

And this, the biggest mystery of all, an annual occurrence that had always bothered my sisters and me. Now, in light of recent revelations, we found it essential to solving the conundrum of why we were all gathered in this particular spot.

The situation was summed up in this manner. A question we all asked our mother every couple of years: "Mom, those long gaps, a few weeks now and then, mostly in summer, when we kids spent eight weeks at camp. I know you went to a spa in the country, but without Daddy, what did you do there so long?"

"Oh, not much," she answered. "Rested. Ate healthy meals. Took long walks."

Being away from your husband for several weeks was not something I, as a young girl full of romantic fancies, could comfortably accept.

It had been a small gathering of mourners. Three or four cousins, two elderly friends. Her generation, my uncles and aunts, were all gone but for Aunt Ruth, who had dementia and lived in a Florida nursing home. There were no fractious, sagging contortions of grief, the ones that tore your heart out. Here, despair remained stiff, sedate. A mere dab or two of tears from her friends Lois and Simone. We sisters were full of sorrow but not taken with tears, too stunned by the news imparted to us yesterday in Joel's office.

We pretended this was an inevitable, acceptable life occurrence, the burial of a matriarch. But it was certainly not that. Rather, it was the beginning of a journey none of us could have imagined - the quest for an answer to the question of who exactly *was* Adele Kroner.

We rose from our chairs, hugged one then the other. Pledged to stay in touch. Then everyone dispersed, toodling off to their cars and planes.

Honoring her wishes, we left her there, buried next to a stranger.

The day before the funeral, her children and their spouses sat in front of her lawyer's austere desk. The reading of the will immediately after the death, before the burial, was a bit unusual. But Joel had insisted.

None of us harbored the usual expectations other families might have. No windfall of cash or a stash of found treasures. Our mother had already made her wishes known. Months ago, she had clasped her gold watch around my daughter's wrist, handed over her "lucky" putter to my son. Childhood photos from her camera were already installed in my sister Laurie's house along with directions about how they were to be displayed. The rented apartment would be returned to the landlord and offered to the next name on his list. She had mentioned the proceeds from my father's life insurance policy on which she had lived for the last few years. Divided among three daughters and five grandchildren, the remaining funds were nothing to argue over.

So we weren't intimidated by the solemnity of the room or the hasty summons to this meeting. But we *were* curious. Over Joel's shoulder, the stern painting of his father, the judge, kept a sharp eye. Linenfold paneling in dark walnut covered the walls. Red velvet draperies further darkened the room. *A painting of lilacs would have been welcome*, I thought. *Or a pot of green ivy in the corner.* My mother's papers, bright white, sat in a neat pile on the dark mahogany desk. Otherwise, the surface was bare.

Joel stood to greet us. He sorted out the chairs, expressed condolences. Cleared his throat, shuffled his papers. Then he removed the cover from his pen and lifted the corner of the first page.

Stolid as a banker addressing his staff, he slowly began to read. "I, Adele Kroner, hereby declare…"

Routine legal terms. We looked at each other. Why had he called us to this emergency gathering? And then, a recently added codicil.

It was her written desire not to be buried next to her husband - our father - in the communal plot marked off for our family dozens of years earlier, the grave next to his specially reserved for her. Rather, her wish was to lie beside a man named Burton Schekman in the village of Cranston, New York, upstate.

Keeping an even tone, his eyes down, Joel continued, "I arranged it all three months ago, according to her wishes."

Stunned and bewildered, we dared not speak.

Secrets - she had secrets. The papers drooped; the curtains wilted. Her long summer visits to a spa. Our father, shunned.

So this was why the lawyer wanted to see us before we made funeral arrangements. This was why after the meeting, we had all trooped up to the town of Cranston, in upstate New York.

After the funeral, my sisters Barbara and Laurie, and two friends from her complex, Lois and Simone, made the long drive back across the New York border to our mother's apartment in Vermont. There, the family was to observe the ritual of shiva for a week, the seven days of Jewish mourning.

As we took off our coats, Laurie said, "Closing her apartment won't be too difficult. Just three rooms, and then the assisted living facility will take it back and repaint."

"Yes," Barbara said. "Easy. Unlike her previous houses, and thank goodness she gave up her antique collecting! At last, here she chose to keep things simple. No rugs to trip over. No fancy furniture to detract from the view. She kept the antique mahogany desk and the blue Chinese bowl with the red dragons, but otherwise, a plain tweed sofa, a few chairs."

"She was lucky to find this place," I added, "and especially this particular unit. I love these huge windows facing the woods, so beautiful in the snow, and the cozy patio in the spring."

Laurie remarked, "Remember what Mom always said when she looked out that window? Sure, it's pretty in winter, but it's too cold to go out. For months, I stay in. When I see the first daffodils, then I go. But I should have moved to Florida."

But when any of us suggested we could help her make that happen, she ignored us.

Without her presence, we felt like interlopers. As if someone would catch us opening drawers or examining closets. But perhaps these feelings arose from the discomfort of discussing her life and she absent, unable to explain or defend herself.

As we sat shiva, friends from the complex paid their respects. They took tea from her kettle, pastries from the counter. Sat a few minutes, then left.

We three sisters sat patiently, but underneath, we were simmering, longing to shout, who was Burton Schekman? Our mother was a woman of gaps, of an emotional retreat we had always felt but had believed was due to a moody character flaw. Or a personal reckoning from the loss of her community stature. Perhaps a feeling of dislocation from the physical moves she had been forced to make. But who could imagine such a catastrophic reality as this unknown man lying upstate in his grave buried next to our mother?

On the seventh day, we got up from our low chairs. Each of us chose an object as a remembrance. Barbara tapped the Chinese bowl with red dragons. "It's really not my thing, but if Mom chose it as one of her favorite items, I'll take it." Laurie, the magazine editor, found mother's daily logs in the walnut desk and snatched them up. A quick glance revealed only shopping lists, household notes, but "maybe I can find something of interest," she said. "I'll let you guys know. Boy, I forgot that she had such beautiful handwriting." I took her tea kettle with purple violets on white ceramic because when she was too weak to cook a meal, she could always boil water for a cup of tea.

Then we settled in for a long chat to talk about what was really on our minds.

Laurie started, "What gives? Let's go over this."

Then Barbara said, "First off, do you think Mom had other children? Maybe before she married Daddy?"

I replied, "Whoa. Are you kidding?"

Laurie asked, "Did she love this man her entire adult life? Or was it a romantic, short-lived affair? What do you think?"

I said, "Remember, those long summer absences lasted over many years while we were at camp. And later too when we spent our college summers away from home. I would guess it was over a lifetime. Or at least over a long time."

Barbara added, "Do you think she committed a sin of some sort against Judaism with this act? You know, like suicides can't be buried in Catholic cemeteries?"

I commented, "Poor Daddy."

Laurie asked, "Do you think Dad knew? He loved her enough not to see. You know how naïve he could be. That whole embezzlement thing and all."

I said, "We don't know anything. Let's ask some folks if they have any thoughts. Maybe talk to her housekeeper June. Then we'll meet up at my house on Thanksgiving. That gives us six months to do some sleuthing. How about that?"

We packed all her things, the entire three rooms except for her mattress, and shipped them off to the oldest grandchild, Eva, in San Antonio. She had just married with a new job and a new apartment and was the only one among us in need of furniture, pots and pans, towels. Then we all hugged, walked out the door, and went back to our lives.

Without any warning, Ben died suddenly.

He died only a few months after he stood by my mother's coffin, looking so handsome, saying things that made us all smile. He died not from stress at the hospital or from eating rich meals. Not an accident. Nothing dramatic. Rather, the most stupid way imaginable to die - a heart attack while talking to a patient. Just sitting at his desk one minute, then slumped over and gone the next.

No therapy or turning to God or speaking to friends or being good to myself could begin to touch the pit of my despair. Alone, I mourned. Alone, I lived in hopeless grief. My children tried to mend the breach, but alas, they bore their own sorrow.

It is wrong to do so, I know, but I can't help compare Ben to my mother, their deaths occurring so close together, as if some special meaning was to be therefore inferred. Ben was the opposite of my mother - a pure soul. There was not a dissembling cell in his body. Full disclosure of mind and spirit, my Ben, an authentic man. We had made a pact for candor from the start. And we kept our bargain, soldiering successfully through some difficult sharings. I knew more about his heart and dreams from one long dinner together than I ever knew about my mother after dozens of years in the same house.

Desperate to get away, I would go to London. The city was foreign, yet the language was English. Staying close to where Ben was physically centered, dropped me into a wretched melancholy devoid of any comfort.

So it was in London's Bloomsbury district where I unpacked my suitcases and set out photographs of Ben and me, Ben and the children, Ben and his colleagues. Here I could think about my sisters and myself, ignorant pretenders living in each other's lives for almost half a century, surrounded by my mother's mystery. And I could dwell on Ben without seeing the faces of my heartbroken children.

Hunkering down at a tea shop under the arch of the great St. Paul's Cathedral, I shuffled around my cheese toast and apple tea. Made friends with James, the waiter. The tolling of church bells, an ancient, eternal sound, touched my sadness. And there, I dug in and talked to myself, wondering where I definitively fit into our family scheme. All kinds of doubts erupt when your mother dies and wants to be buried next to a stranger. *Was I even my father's daughter?* I had Daddy's round nose and his stocky hands, but what did Mr. Scheckman's nose and hands look like?

I had examined microfilm in the library at home and found a small obituary notice in a New York newspaper dated three years ago. Mr. Scheckman was a widower with no children. He was a rep for adult clothing, selling the goods of several companies to retail stores. Likely he met my mother through my father, who was a clothier. Yes, that was possible. If it were true, he might have known my mother for dozens of years. Other than the fact that he lived near Cranston,

New York, and had two brothers who predeceased him, that was all the article said. There was no photo.

The information revealed nothing of the elements that drove my relentless curiosity. What kind of man *was* Burton Schekman? Was he moody or congenial? Stubborn or generous? I longed for a picture of this man, Burton Scheckman, to examine his face, his smile, seeking similar features to any of us girls. Would his personality show in a photo? I wondered. Did the affair last until his death? He died three years ago. I remember a weekend four years ago when Ben and I had visited my parents. I remember it particularly well because it had been postponed once due to my having a bad case of flu. We four had a pleasant enough time, taking long walks, lounging about. Now I wonder if all that time my mother had been longing to be with Mr. Schekman rather than in that house, at that meal, on that walk.

I assumed my parents loved each other. But did they? From time to time, Daddy put a hand on my mother's shoulder or her waist, but she shrugged it off, walked away. Witnessing other folks make the same gestures, I never gave it a thought. After all, people show their love in different ways. Not everyone is a hugger like me, like my father.

The only person alive to offer information was Aunt Ruth, but her dementia led us nowhere. She didn't even recognize Barbara and Laurie when they stopped in for a visit. They had hoped for an opening up of her clouded mind, just long enough for them to walk through. But no. And when they questioned June, the housekeeper, and even Fred, the longtime gardener, they too offered nothing useful and had no suspicions, no guesses.

My mother left no clues. How had she managed the strain of handling her secret for so long? Surely there were arrangements to be made, cancellations and changes to deal with, an ongoing host of logistical issues.

After weeks of unending pots of apple tea, my mind was a useless, exhausted vessel. Constant examination of my mother's life made no sense. She had made her choices. If I didn't want to be distracted forever, I would have to leave her story without an explanation. It was time for a change in my attitude, an acceptance that there would never be conclusive answers, only speculation.

So I chose to be more open of myself, grateful to share my troubles and joys with my sisters so that after I die, my life won't be a mystery that they must unravel. So those closest to me would say, with all her flaws, they knew me well.

And my Ben?

The reality of his nonexistence was unacceptable. I continued to tell him news of the children and me, but I felt like an old lady babbling to herself. And my conversations with him hardly appeased my enduring anguish. But I was patient. I could wait.

I continued to sit in front of St. Paul's Cathedral, at this tea shop where the waiter James now knew me so well that he set down my tea and pastry without taking my order. Although I remained like a ghost, he knew when I wanted to chat and when I did not. He was a sweet man, and there was worry in his eyes when he served me. But a bit of hovering and attention was what I needed right now, and I was grateful for his ongoing consideration.

And here I shall sit until one day, I will rise and walk over to the river Thames to see for myself if it is indeed as beautiful as people say it is.

It's Love, It's Milan

After my divorce from that bastard Doug, I was ready to learn all kinds of things, though I knew I wasn't going to learn anything new hanging around the old places. In twenty-five years of marriage, except for the kids, I had learned mostly bad things. I didn't know *what* good there was out there. Like me, everyone has secrets, everyone puts on a false face. Who tells the truth?

And so wounded and confused, in the middle of an unseasonably warm April day, I left Chicago and flew to Milan, Italy.

Websites abundant, the easiest part was booking a room. More difficult tasks followed - customs, currency and, the most challenging, language. Doug had always taken care of those details. Imagine me, a middle-aged gal, a bitter wife in her mid-forties, making arrangements to run away from home! Well, teenagers trek all over the world with just a knapsack on their back, so surely I could handle this. Fortunately, I had a passport from an anniversary trip planned to Paris three years ago. But as usual, a week before, Doug had canceled. It mattered at the time what excuse he gave but not so much now, knowing what I do.

I locked the house, had a word with my neighbor about the plants, then made my way to the airport. Everyone was helpful, no problem, and some hours after I had boarded my Alitalia flight, I landed at Milan's Malpensa Airport. It was easy. Why do my friends make such a fuss about the logistics of travel? Doug always acted like it was a big deal, getting worked up as he did. Maybe to show off.

Although the seats in economy were cramped, the crew was attentive. Tiny pizzettes, chicken on shredded carrots, and Italian cookies were fine meals; but what did anything matter? I was flying away from my life. A kind porter in baggage claim even placed me in a cab, giving the driver my destination address. Off we went, he jabbering in Italian, I in English, both of us laughing at such silliness all the way to the door of my building - rather, *palazzo*. Yes, *palazzo*! Eighteenth-century.

Beautiful frescoes covered the walls of my bedroom: gondolas, waterways, ancient buildings, the faded paint worn away here and there. The elegant armoire was as old as the Renaissance with cherubs and garlands deeply carved in the wood. Stacking my jeans and shirts inside stoked my abject sorrow at not hanging long gowns with lace and beads in such a noble piece of furniture. Surprisingly glamorous, the bathroom was finished in black marble. Next to the toilet, a bidet. I hadn't seen one of those for ten years, not since Doug's parents treated us to an anniversary weekend at a lakeside hotel run by Europeans - bidet, croissants, cappuccino. Good thing I had the booking receipt for this place, confirming a reasonable rate. Likely, I slid in on the cusp of their slow season, the tourists about to pounce in another month.

I slept for ten hours, awakened by tolling bells. My senses were shooting off sparks of anticipation. Looking around again at my walls in this ancient palazzo, once home to a papal nuncio, I marveled at my audacity. I had hardly ever left Chicago, and now, on a whim, here I was in Italy! A whim and a credit card, that's all it took.

A few steps outside of the palazzo gates, I was forced into a nearby doorway to escape the splendid ruckus unfolding before me. A parade, I liked to think, welcoming me to Milan! Along the boulevard, hanging from street lamps shaped like lanterns, banners and flags fluttered between the ancient buildings. Striped in brilliant green, red and white, Milan's colors, they were stamped with images of the city's patron saints wearing monk's robes, the second-century Christian martyrs Gervasius and Protasius. Ten-foot-high statues of the two saints wobbled down the avenue on floats festooned with swags of red and white tulips, making their way toward the great basilica to celebrate their martyrdom. Milan's colors were apparent as well in the clothing of tradespeople, parade participants, onlookers. Red or green shirts, red or green skirts, white hats. Sumptuous baskets of red begonias and white petunias elegantly cascaded down iron posts as children clenched balloons in red, green, or white.

A pageantry of color, sound, and motion.

Soon enough, I would discover that even the smallest gesture, mood, happening, relationship in this country was composed of a similar theatricality. Looking around, words like *flourish, pomp, flamboyance* came to mind. Grandmothers or *nonnes*, as I heard, called out greetings and strutted with panache in silver or gold heels, skirts flaring around their ankles. Toddlers in their best going-to-church outfits dodged and ducked around their parents' legs. Young couples bright with vigor shook sprays of voluptuous lilies, shouting, "Fantastico, fantastico!" while tradesmen in their long aprons watched from the doorways of their shops. Old men waved toy flags as they sat along the route on cheap white plastic chairs woven with red and green streamers. The surging procession took care to detour around their wrinkled feet as joyful children tossed sweets to the crowd.

Observing this spectacle while leaning against the entrance to a sixteenth-century chapel, I reflected, *Was it only yesterday that I had been in Chicago - rainy, crowded, and noisy?* Smiling faces passed by. I smiled back. Like a party going on, or a local holiday in a small village. Nothing was out of control or veering toward bedlam unlike the mobs back in Chicago, the whole state with its wild, drunken pandemonium every time there was a Chicago Bears or Chicago Cubs win. Here the excitement and celebration were neighborly and congenial.

My world had moved because of me.

From out of the throng, a man about my age in a green bowtie, and a much younger woman with red cheeks and red lips, popped up, pulling me into the festive crowd.

"*Vieni a ballare.* Come dance," they cried. "Come celebrate!" Ah, they knew by my clothes, sandals and denim skirt that I was American. Or perhaps it was by the incredulous look on my face.

"*Tu come ti chiami*? What is your name?" the man shouted.

"Anna," I shouted back.

"Ah, Anna, *vieni a ballare.*"

As quickly as that, my loneliness lifted like a cloak from my slumping shoulders. Two strangers, unknown even to each other, swept me generously into the heart of their joy. Doug's face went poof, into thin air. Here was a woman with a broad smile wearing a gauzy white dress that twirled as she turned, and on her dark hair, a homemade tiara of red and white roses. Here was a good-looking man with a short beard, inky black eyes, and thick silver hair, a red kerchief tied around his neck, and white pants with a green stripe down the side like a matador, only long cuffs falling to his ankles. Here was *another* man. I had thought Doug was the dominant male on earth - his hubris, his bluster dominating our family domain.

Now simply by accepting the hand of another, I no longer felt like an abandoned wife defined by the missteps of her husband, a serial philanderer. Instead, seen afresh by new eyes, I had hope for shifting into a fuller life.

Shopkeepers cheered, "*Bravi, bravi!*"

"Bravo, bravo," I quietly repeated, adding *amen* and a prayer to make becoming part of these vibrant people possible - an American speaking no Italian, grateful to be freely invited in.

Every day brought a similar flood of zestful living.

Street musicians - violinist, accordionist, flutist - played tunes from Napoli while everyone danced, an old man with a little girl, four little boys, a young girl alone, spinning. Families picnicked on the edge of fountains, at the base of statues. A cloth was pulled from a basket; hunks of *parmigiano romano*, shiny black olives, and crusty ciabatta bread were brought forth. And of course, glasses of Valpolicella Classico were uncorked. Lovers kissed often and fervently, leaning into grand arched doorways built by the House of Sforza, 1450.

The street activity never ceased. Nor did its exuberance. Once, I possessed a similar zest, but it was snuffed out by Douglas years ago.

Children ran freely over the uneven cobblestones or fiercely pedaled their scooters. None wore helmets as they wove in and out of the crowd, fearlessly flapping their arms and tooting their horns. No parent uttered warnings. My own instincts to console or heal were rarely required.

For the Italians, this was their due, their birthright. For me? It was my awakening.

During Chicago's windy falls and dark winters, children were wrapped and swaddled. Each figure layered thickly, the natural inclination for gaiety was shuttered. When spring suddenly arrived, it seemed the adults had forgotten how to retrieve the sensation of freedom. Overheard were parental rebukes - in the park, on the playgrounds. "Hush, behave yourself, or there will be no television, no iPad." One child or another was always crying or wailing for its mother, its nanny.

As I thought of issues around raising our children, it brought me back to Doug, who hovered over my appointments and controlled my life while he cavorted freely in his, ignoring our family. This unsavory man had shattered my backbone and stolen my grit. Abruptly, I pulled out from the crowd and stumbled to a bench, panting, my hair wet with sweat. I wanted to call for a doctor. Heal me. Mend my heart.

The new man bent toward me.

"*Che si stia divertendo*, Anna. Are you enjoying yourself?" he inquired.

It was a simple question I couldn't remember Doug ever asking me.

Catching my breath, I stood to find my balance. Rejoining the parade once again, I vowed to share in this Italian *entusiasmo*, this gusto.

I stayed out late. Watching, listening, walking until the stars begin to fade. A lone guitar twanged plaintively from a café. Couples strolled in the dark along the canals. It was only just before dawn broke that I rested, the Italians not fond of rising early, the piazzas quiet at that early hour. Only a few *nonnes* with their string bags over their arms were about, gossiping and waiting for their favorite vendors to open so they could pick through the produce, planning for their *pranzo*, the family's long lunch.

Everyone gathered in the piazzas. Tables fronting cafés overflowed with warmth and good cheer. Beautiful young adults laughed in small groups, greeted each other with kisses on both cheeks, holding a goblet of wine in one hand, a cigarette in the other. Here, a woman with her apricot *pasticcino* and *caffè* read a book. Time seemed not to matter. A waiter took me to a table where soon I was sipping Frascati and nibbling warm *sfogliatella* filled with divine pistachio custard. I closed my eyes and savored the lavish kindness from the hand of the pastry chef.

I allowed myself to go back in my mind to Chicago. With this comforting ambience, the waiter tending to my wine, my pastry, asking nothing in return. Perhaps it will afford me reflection filled with insight, less anger. Swaddled like the children in Chicago but longing to be free, like those laughing around me.

And so I recalled the day.

An ordinary Thursday afternoon some years ago. There it was, on the second page. Just as I was turning to the film section. A picture of my husband at a charity event. He was standing next to a woman I had never seen. The caption said her name was Maureen.

There were three others in the photo on their right, but I somehow sensed that those first two were together. In fact, I absolutely *knew* they were together. Suddenly, it all came clear - unforeseen meetings, aborted family trips, half-muted phone calls, the low moments that had been my life.

I felt it all again anew, with the same vigor. Anger and sadness both at once, rising from my gut as I sat with my pastry in this Milanese piazza.

And I let my outrage come.

I remember crumbling the newspaper in my fist, cursing, throwing pillows, and shouting to the walls, "Doug, for a smart man, you can be awfully dumb. So common. So obvious."

But I had misjudged how devious Doug was. The man had his plan ready. It was clever yet uncomplicated. He simply started false rumors. A mere hint, a word, an insinuation, and the falsehoods traveled fast as one tongue could reach another. He made subtle complaints to his colleagues and to our friends about me, the faithful, dutiful wife of twenty-five years.

"I wasn't attentive enough," he told others.

"Not home when I'm available," he said.

"She was tired when I felt like having sex," he confided.

"She didn't love me," he added.

So what was he to do? he asked his friends, his colleagues. His attentions to other women were justified and reasonable, weren't they? Suddenly, Maureen reigned, and I became the *other* woman. For the shame of it, I rarely went out, and only at odd times for ordinary errands.

Speculation and gossip among our acquaintances ran amok like a tiger released from its cage.

"Maybe she shouldn't have taken those classes that kept her out three evenings a week," Annie, my yoga buddy, said to Denise.

"Maybe she should give up her painting so she could go on business trips with him," Denise, with whom we shared theatre tickets, said to Annie.

"Maybe she should have turned the other cheek," Glenda offered as she, Annie, and Denise were having their nails done. "That way, she could have stayed in the house."

So many opportunities for conjecture as the ladies met for long lunches. Folks I knew well no longer called. Others I barely knew joined in with the malicious hucksters. When there is trouble in a marriage, everyone takes sides - friends, colleagues, children. And all sided with Doug.

But what else could I have expected?

Doug was rich, so Doug was admired. A man to whom women pandered, submitted.

Doug was a lawyer. Doug collected secrets. Wouldn't those involved in confidences with him be compelled, even wise, to take his side, knowing what he knew?

My wineglass was empty. I paid the bill, hoisted my bag over my shoulder, and started walking.

Eventually, I saw a dab of red, the flash of a Cardinal's cape. In the Milanese world of gray and ocher stone, the red spot drew me like my eye to the North Star. As I walked closer, I thought of the red of a ripe tomato from the farms of Bergamo Alta; the red of Santa's suit; the red of Doug's eyes after a drinking party with his girlfriend, Maureen, the current one, the bitch.

I found the red.

Two towering stone urns, almost as tall as me, decorated with frolicking nymphs, regally standing at the base of a looming staircase. Carved by a master's hand. Both burst with blossoms the size of two fists together, bright-red geraniums rising from shiny green leaves.

The flowers beckoned.

First, a regal staircase took me upward to the princely entrance. Then another staircase of elegant stone, so far-reaching I could hardly make out where it ended. Niches along the sides were filled with statuary of Milan's renowned statesmen. And finally, I was on the ancient building's *piano nobile*, the floor above ground level containing the principal rooms. As I took the last step onto the landing, the rooms before me exploded with dazzling opulence like the inside of a castle, glitter on every surface; gilt, marble, and mirror, sterling; damasks and velvets. There were choices of rooms, a sharp left or a sharp right, a diagonal left or a diagonal right - all ablaze with splendor.

I was uncertain, so I walked straight ahead. On the ceiling, a seemingly infinite expanse was painted with magnificent frescoes in the style of Leonardo, perhaps by his dear friend Bernarino Luini, portraying the history of Milan, its conquerors, princes, wealthy merchants. Although the figures and objects depicted were far above me, the paintings were clear and complete, shaded and brilliantly colored. I stared as if the bodies were alive, and I was watching their adventures occur at the moment.

Being a painter, I knew that many pigments are named after Italian cities, and for some reason, that pleased me as I tried to analyze what I was seeing. *Later, I must read about this ceiling*, I reminded myself, although everything I saw in this city required study - Pompeian red, a rich, gorgeous hue, the color of frescoes in the wealthy villas; Naples yellow, slightly grayed, earthy, found on early Sicilian glazed pottery; and sienna, reddish-brown, the town of Siena famous for its medieval brick buildings. Each was symbolic of that particular city's mood and personality.

Three massive windows twenty feet high looked out on the spectacular view. I saw the dome of the noble basilica, the final landing place for the remarkable parade that had "welcomed" me to Milan. I turned my head and faced the walls, adorned with massive canvases of early and late Renaissance masters Caravaggio, Botticelli.

I could not look away.

Slowly, my body lost control and I sank down, huddling in despair on the mellow Parquet de Versailles floor, hundreds of years old. I put my head down and wept, unleashing all the tears I had kept inside my soul all my adult life.

In the quiet of this splendid ballroom, I remained on the floor for a long time, listening to the echo of my own tears. No one entered. When I felt more composed, I glanced once more at the ceiling. Suddenly, I had a moment of self-realization. I gasped, taking it in. Some would call this stirring insight an epiphany or a vision. I called it a sign that would alter my life's journey. Just from the act of looking up at such an expansive span of time, all rendered in paint, I was humbled by the genius, emboldened by its bravado.

And I decided that I was actually quite sufficient and content by myself. I didn't need Doug or any other man to complete my life. Death, deprivation, or separation and divorce can be a deep trough of pain, not mere adjustments of a complicated life - and I had fallen into that dark ditch of sorrow. But I would peel off my troubles, shed the hurtful detritus of those twenty-five years. Doug will have no power over me. I will give this place, this room, this country, the power to gratify me.

Yes, I was in love with Milan, with the Italian people.

Goethe's words came to me at this perfect moment: "Whatever you can do, or dream you can, begin it. Boldness has genius, magic, and power in it. Begin it now."

A uniformed guard appeared. He and I were alone in this great room. An old man, He shuffled over with a slight limp. Silently, he handed me his immaculately pressed handkerchief as naturally as if everyone who entered here wept on the floor. He didn't offer to help me up, sensing I was not quite ready, but turned, walked quietly back to his post.

A decision was made. I wanted to take for granted the freedom to sit on an ancient floor without a printed sign that warned "Keep off." I wanted to cry in public, if I must, and be in a place where a complete stranger offered me his personal handkerchief.

Get up, Anna, I said to myself. *Let Italy seduce you. Put away your tears, though they surely will come again. Be daring and unafraid, not angry. Embrace possibility. And worry not, your children will find you here, stronger, gutsy, resilient.*

As I turned the corner into my courtyard, the man with the red kerchief around his neck was sitting on a bench opposite the entrance. Only now he was wearing jeans and a striped T-shirt. I hardly recognized him. He must have remembered this very doorway from which I emerged the day of the parade.

"Anna, my name is Tomas," the man said, as a carillon of church bells, one after the other, called the faithful to worship, rolling in from a hundred churches throughout the city. Far off, I also heard the voice of the muezzin intoning the Islamic call to prayer. The church and mosque spoke to each other, rhapsodic sounds thousands of years old. They went on and on, as if dozens of bell ringers started up all at once, then left for their afternoon *riposo* or siesta, forgetting to shut down the chimes.

Be bold, I thought. *Begin it. Begin the life you never imagined.*

"Tomas, do you know," I asked, shyly pronouncing his name. He pounced on the *m* and stressed the *s* with the dramatic flair of an operatic *divo*.

"Do you know where I might rent an *appartamento?*"

He smiled. "*Signora, certamente!*"

We sat back down on the bench. I pulled out my guidebook and looked up descriptions of various neighborhoods. *Does he understand English?* I wondered. I read out loud. I marked the pages.

"Look here!" I said, my enthusiasm out of control.

"Tortona, so many *chiese*, churches! Or Isola Bella, an island, with ferries, but how wonderful to paint in such a place! Or Porta Ticinese with their medieval gates? Perhaps the old harbor of

Darsena." I kept turning, folding down corners. "Or possibly some-thing on one of the Navigli canals with their historic bridges. An area of artists' studios and romantic cafés. Flea markets and concerts in summer. It's all so marvelous. How will I ever choose?"

"Ah, Anna, we'll look together, but there's no hurry. In Milan, we do things slowly. We take our time for ordinary tasks. First, let me show you a *trattoria* in a little corner of Porta Ticinese where the *cassata* is superb," Tomas, the man of the red kerchief, said, speaking excellent English, offering me his arm.

Sweeping the Floor

The tired broom, bristles bent, some missing, others with curled edges, were all I had. Not even a bed, just a few rages piled on top of a worn pallet. Looking around at the vast space of the abandoned building, I uttered a sigh, the air leaving my chest in sorrowful gasps. *There is no way I can make these old floors clean*, I thought. *No way to gather the leavings of shattered lives. All is lost, gone. The task is hopeless.*

But here is where, for now, I live, though if there is a God, not forever. I will sweep and sweep until the floor glows. Then if in this life a final redemption is granted, I will put away my broken broom and leave.

I tried not to think of her very often, especially not the way her blond curls tangled in knots as she jumped rope. Nor her blue eyes, a purple glint in their center as she coyly begged for extra ice cream. If my mind wandered there, my hand would falter, my sweeping cease. Nor would I bring back my little boy's joy when he raced his cars and engines down the garden path. If my rhythms were lost, I was lost.

Please. Let me have a brief return.

Just one sweet thought of my little girl, I pleaded with myself, my dark side fighting for control. *Those blond curls, her blue eyes. And my sweet son, flashing eyes always looking for mischief. And Susie, my dearest wife, may God strike me dead from the pain of hearing her beloved voice.*

Let me lay down to rest on the pile of rags on top of this worn pallet and think of my family, though my mind commands, "Do not go back there. Not even for a moment. Danger awaits."

Please. One moment. That's all.

"I won't lose control, I promise," I said aloud.

And so I succumbed once more.

"Such a handsome young man," everyone said. "That wavy hair and deep brown eyes that are like looking into a stormy lake. Oh, what beautiful children he will have someday. But look what a wonderful son he is right now," the neighbors added. "Would that all our sons were so accommodating," they whispered enviously. "Fetches groceries for his mother, vacuums the house, even helps her put in the summer squash, the two of them laughing while they turn over the soil. Never heard him raise his voice or slam a door."

Well, why not? Why shouldn't I be a good son? I thought, overhearing their talk. I had a wonderful mother. With all on her mind, working in the hospital all day, paying the bills, still she took care of us at home with kindness and patience. It was not an easy task with three rambunctious little kids running around. She did the work of two parents so we wouldn't miss our dad after he died way too early ten years ago, and he not even forty-five. I was just a teenager and sure missed him, but I guess sometimes accidents happen no matter how careful you are. And Mom, ever after thinking of me, ruffling my hair as I sat in a chair, draping a sweater over my shoulder. Always with a sweet, low voice, not shrill and bossy like some mothers of my friends.

And besides, two years in the army taught me that each life is precious, that I hadn't wasted my time crouching in those filthy trenches, making sure one's buddies were still alive.

Of course, I would be good to her. That is the Lord's teachings. "Honor your father and mother."

And the best thing - the absolute best - was that she showed me what a good woman is. She was my perfect example. Year after year, I watched her closely, how she handled the rough stuff yet celebrated the good. The best was when the family gathered in the kitchen after dinner and played games and told silly stories. Nothing fancy but all together.

That pretty much put me on the good and proper path right from the beginning. When I saw my Susie, I knew she was the one for me. She was like my mom.

Well, Susie married me. Yes, she did.

We did the whole thing the old-fashioned way. Took our vows after passing through a double line of sabers arched high, held straight up by my army buddies in dress uniform. Susie's and my little cousins tossed rose petals into the crowd, surprising us both that they weren't a bit shy or frightened. Rather, they showed off with cute smiles and curtsies in their pretty white lace dresses with flowers woven into their braids.

Such a great day. Everyone was happy for us without any envy or pouting. Anyone with an old grievance left it outside the church. My only sadness was my dad's absence. "Pop, look, a woman just like Mom," I would have told him as he gave me a thumb's up, one arm resting gently on Mom's shoulder, the other on my new wife's.

Susie sure looked beautiful that day, but still, even at that moment, not as beautiful as the day I got off the train from Fort Campbell when she was on the platform waiting for me - calling my name, "Danny, Danny," as she started to run, to cry, to hold onto her hat, a bouquet of summer lilies in her arms. Waiting for me. Waiting to marry me.

Right away when we moved into our little house with the fresh white paint and sky-blue shutters, hardly a mile down the road from my mom, Susie planted a garden. First, green peas and summer corn. Then lettuce, onions, peppers. Mom would come over with my sister and brother, Kim and Pete, to help with the planting when the garden kept expanding. We hung out on the porch just laughing at crazy jokes, tossing balls, and drinking ginger beer. Those were good times; and it was mighty terrific to see my two favorite women side by side in their summer dresses, pretty and lively as if they had known each other all their lives. The good stuff - friendship, support, concern.

Every night, when I walked in the front door at the end of my time at Bill's Contracting - he made me his foreman; "A wonder with machinery and fixing things," he said - she came running down the stairs, her eyes bright, her throat catching as she called my name, "Danny, Danny." Boy, I loved hearing the excited way she said my name.

One day, work had been especially exhausting. Three tractors in the shop at the same time, two with their engine's cylinder blocks messed up, another with ignition points burnout. And the roof at the Walters house was going too slow to please Sam Walter. Not our fault the shingles had come two weeks late.

I walked into the house as weary as I've ever been.

A perfect dinner was laid out on the special tablecloth our friend Ginny Barnes crocheted for our wedding present. My favorite biscuits too and hot stew, potato salad, and corn. Even an apple pie on the counter. The table was right out of a magazine, and Susie in her red gingham jumper with a yellow blouse looked just like that character in the book *Heidi*.

Something fluttered in her glowing eyes. I didn't know what surprise she had waiting for me, but it looked like something special for sure. So I played along. Washed up, changed out of my work clothes.

She couldn't wait. After only my second bite of that biscuit…

"A baby," she cried. "Danny, a baby. Our baby!"

Surely the whooping and hollering could be heard all the way down to my mom's house.

"Wow," I said. "Wow."

We looked at each other, the radiance in her eyes reflected in mine.

I heaped a large portion of stew onto her plate. "Gotta eat extra for now," I said as we picked up our forks with our right hands, holding tightly to each other with our left ones, almost like saying a prayer around the table. And that's how we ate all the way through to dessert, holding tight.

And sure enough, little Amy showed up right on time without giving her mother too much trouble.

When I saw her sleeping on her mother's chest in her little pink cap, I was filled with such happiness I couldn't speak.

"Pretty terrific, isn't it?" Susie said, and I nodded, yes, yes. "Pretty terrific," I managed, "more than terrific. Amazing, the best thing in the world." And then I put my head down on her shoulder and cried like our new baby.

Amy's eyes turned out to be like her mom's, that crystal-like, aquamarine blue that was so clear you could almost see through them. This I could tell after three weeks when her eyelids fully opened and her tiny hand grabbed my finger.

As a toddler, she always wanted to help in the garden. For her birthday, I bought her a child's apron imprinted with apples, tiny pockets sized for a child's tools. Susie marked the spots, and Amy dug the holes, dropping in seeds one by one. "Mommy, can we do the pumpkins now?"

When I walked in the door, Amy came running, teetering, shouting, "Daddy, Daddy!" her mother right behind, both of them running, Susie calling "Danny, Danny, you're home" in the way I loved, saying *Danny* so softly yet with a need I craved in my gut. From the moment I was home, Amy was mine - mine to run with in the fields, mine to gather wildflowers for her mom, mine to bathe, and mine to put to bed with stories and cuddles.

And so our family began, precious Andy following soon after Amy. Watching him sleep at Susie's breast wearing a tiny blue cap, his eyes brown and shining like mine; I almost stopped breathing for joy.

And what a mischief-maker he turned out to be! Andy didn't have much patience for the garden. He was fonder of pulling up the carrots than putting them in, so we kept his tractors and cars in a toy box on the porch, hoping he would play there. But no, he was always racing a car between the rows of vegetables.

Mom walked over whenever she had the time. Each show of our kids' growth made her smile. Right from the beginning, two babies putting on a show - how they laughed and made sounds, looking at her, at us. They'd grasp a toy then fling it in the air, pointing to where it landed with a chubby finger – "I want *that*." And we'd all scramble to fetch and return. My mom sure knew what to do when Amy or Andy had colic or didn't feel like a nap. If we had the need, she was there. And the kids always calling for her. "Where's Gramma?"

So I will relive my favorite Amy/Gramma story.

You see, Amy's curls were impossible to comb, but no way would she let her mom take a pair of scissors to them. One day, she got some gum stuck in those curls and agreed to a haircut at "a real beauty parlor like Mommy's, but only if Gramma takes me." Once her curls fell to the floor, she turned to her grandmother and said, "Gramma, let's be twins!" so Mom took the chair and acquired a short bob while Amy gave the hairdresser directions.

One particular Saturday was to be a special family day.

After I finished some paperwork at the shop, we were all going to Lookout Park for a day of boating, games, a picnic. A barbecue. Our supplies were already stored in the car. Spring was especially beautiful that year, with the bright sun of late May and the sky a cornflower blue. Masses of yellow daffodils were popping up all over the meadows and fields. Towering magnolia trees, dropping those pretty pink and white petals the kids loved to gather in their baskets.

Amy was five. Andy was three.

Mom was coming with us.

Though my mom must have been lonely, she never had a lonely face. After all, she was still young, and very pretty. Only fifty-five years old, she had never dated anyone after my father died. My sister

Kim and brother Peter had been long gone from the house into their own adult lives. And though they weren't far away, even frequent visits didn't fill the gaps of the need to talk together, man and wife, his deep voice calling, "Hey, honey, I'm home."

A working nurse all these years did not alter Mom's slim frame, nor take the luster out of her dark hair. Her straight posture remained despite the hard work, although it was her playful eyes that held yours, she always willing to take on a bit of sport or fun.

So after signing off on the tractors at Bob's, ready for Lookout Park, I eagerly walked up the front path.

And right away, I saw the wreckage.

The clay pots of our beautiful red tomato plants by the front door were shattered. Dirt was everywhere, and the ripe beauties were strewn across the porch like shiny marbles.

Did someone accidentally knock over the pots? Was Susie right now inside preparing to clean them up? Or a game of some kind? Would the kids jump out and yell, "Daddy, surprise! We're here! Ready to go as soon as Mom fixes the pots!" They loved to fool me as I put my hand over my heart and collapsed in feigned surprise at their silly hijinks.

But no one ran to me shouting, "Daddy, we've been ready to go for *ages*!"

There were no whispers or giggles from hiding places.

Nothing.

I ran through the kitchen, the living room, then up to the bedrooms, into the bathrooms, even pulling back the shower curtains. I called out, "Susie? Susie? Hey, guys, where are you?" Outside, I continued my search, running behind the shed, the garage.

But no one. Nowhere.

Suddenly the clutch of terror. Where? What? Susie's car was still parked. Mom's car next to hers.

I banged on a neighbor's door, shouting, "Did you see them?" No answer.

Then to the house across the street. "Hello? Hello?" No answer.

Back to our house. Again, I walked through our rooms, more slowly this time, looking for anything out of place.

A kitchen chair was overturned. Amy's beloved doll, Soft Baby, the one from which she was never separated, lay on the floor. Andy's football, the one he was to take to the park, had rolled into a corner of the living room.

Nothing was violent like slashed furniture or smashed dishes, but a familiar situation was now suddenly horribly unfamiliar and disorienting. Mom's purse was thrown onto the counter, the clasp undone.

Loving objects were askew. And the worst, no one home. And there was deadly silence.

A kidnapping, it had to be. Where were they?

I called the police. They came immediately, sirens wailing.

Half a dozen cars appeared, headlights bright, the police chief in his captain's hat. And such noise - megaphones, walkie-talkies, cell phones. Men with papers and questions to answer. Men in big boots who traipsed through the house looking, searching.

A couple of hours later, the slew of cars revved up and backed out. They were so sorry. They would keep in close touch. They would avidly pursue this case.

Then silence once again.

Of course, this theft of my family was on the news all over the country. Signs were posted. Rewards were offered. The FBI showed up.

All I could do was sit in our kitchen and hold Andy's football, Amy's doll. Neighbors came in and out, leaving food that dried up. They kept saying how sorry they were. Kind words. But words that only deepened my grief made me more desperate.

No request came for ransom. Money from me? Who would think I had money working for Bob's Contracting? But there were no calls. No notes.

So I sat.

I was waiting, you see.

Waiting for my family to come home. All four of them. Susie and the kids, my mom holding Amy's hand, singing, "Old Macdonald had a farm…" Amy skipping along, Andy just behind in his Superman outfit.

Occasionally, I heard a rake and hoe in the garden. Thoughtful neighbors kept up the radishes, the okra, leaving them outside the door. I never brought them in, and a week later, they were rotten. Slowly, the days grew shorter, the air cooler. Trees lost their leaves. The garden was done. And the neighbors stopped coming.

And still, I sat.

Susie's car in the driveway, Mom's next to it.

Were they alive?

The police were baffled.

Finally, the day came when I would shut the door of that white house with the pretty blue shutters and walk away. Quiet as a crypt, it felt as if I had been buried in a cave.

It had to happen, that I started to wander.

Into little Andy's backpack, I stuffed an extra shirt and pair of pants, a toothbrush, Amy's "soft baby," Andy's football. I cleaned up the tomato plants. Placed the leftovers in a container just in case Susie returned and wanted to replant.

I left everything, including my car, and wrote Susie and Mom a note telling them I would send an address when I had one. And then I walked for miles and months until I found an empty warehouse in the middle of a field. Maybe it had once served as a barn. It was sturdy enough. The boards were tight. The roof didn't leak. The enormous interior was empty but for an old broom and a few rags on a torn pallet.

So tired, I lay down on the mat for a long sleep.

When I finally awoke, I started to sweep out the place. I had to make it clean for Susie because you see, she would say, "Danny, honey, the corner over there, it needs some of your magic touch with a broom."

When I was alone in this deserted place, I had no choice but to do some thinking. No way could I run away from myself and from my memories.

So I talked to God.

And cried and cried to Him. Praying, begging Him to take pity on me, to wipe out images of their possible suffering, to erase the thought that they were calling out for me to save them.

I looked for comfort in years of Pastor John's homilies but found none. Oh, lots of talk about mercy and goodness and doing right, but it sure seemed my innocent family got short-changed somewhere along the way.

Sweep, sweep. Sleep. I went outside for some berries. Then I hiked to a café a half mile away whose bins offered up remnants of bread and cheese. One day, I found an abandoned blanket. Another day, a coat too big but warm. Back to sweep, to sleep. Nightmares, sweats. Relentless, terrifying fears - every night, charging through my brain, recollections of broken flower pots. Ruined tomatoes scattered about, rotting in the sun.

Two cars side by side in the driveway.

If you cannot fill it well, time can do terrible things to your head.

It can be a thief. One day, time bestows a gift; and the next, it snatches it away.

It deceives. Good things pass by in a flash, though in real life, they occur over pleasurable spans of time. Like a picnic, gone with the snap of a finger, when in real time it would last a whole long day.

Same with a wedding.

But bad times - like an accident, a loss, a disaster - felt incalculable, like the longest distance without end. All I knew was that the leaves had fallen off the trees twice already. So there must have been two springs, but I didn't notice spring, only the leaves falling.

Lying on that pallet, I brought back my life with Susie and the kids.

It was important that I remembered. I was the only one alive who had the memories.

Of Susie on the red sofa showing the kids a book of ABCs. Of my children playing ball or making trouble in the garden. Of our many friends and relatives, the many birthdays and holidays, what their faces looked like when they were sad or happy. Sometimes, the details blurred, so much going by so fast in life, like an old movie reel, the months and years getting mixed up. I hoped I had been a good friend to all and a good worker at Bob's. He must have missed me, Bob. I didn't tell him I was leaving, but I don't think he was surprised. Nor did I tell our friends. They would ask questions that had no answers. With every encounter, I would have to confront those maddening looks of sympathy, repeat the story once again. Maybe sometime far in the future, we could talk, but not yet.

Thoughts of my soldier buddies came back to me. Jake, who died in my arms. A crazy bomb in the road got him. He was twenty-two, never had a chance at any of life's good stuff, and we weren't even fighting a war. Just some routine reconnaissance of a small village.

And Brendan. *Where he is now?* I wondered. We were tight at one time. Brendan, in an unhappy marriage, had gone to the army to get away from the wife who had betrayed him. Was he now living a pleasant life, or was he bitter, taking drugs as he did now and then after lights out and some townie had smuggled them in? You just friggin' never knew which way your life would go.

And Mom? How I loved to talk with her about Dad - their Saturdays spent down by the river just being lazy, watching for beavers or field mice; their nights at the drive-in with the three babies asleep in the back seat, giving them five minutes of alone time; and her saying she could never remember the movie for all the kissing that went on. And then he died. A bad accident cutting down that tree.

But what hit me the worst about that terrible day was Mom probably running to my kids and wrapping them in her skirts, trying to hide them or save them or comfort them, whatever she could do in the five seconds she had.

The leaves were falling again. They were always falling through the door, the cracks, and when they did, I once again picked up my broom. Susie would take one look and say, "Danny, honey, it's so clean, we can have our picnic right on the floor!"

I must have swept this floor a hundred times. A thousand. This floor is proof of two things: my devotion, in some manner, to our life, our family, to God.

And also the other proof in which I now believed that in some way of blessing, it was possible to put down the broom.

Winter was done. Finally, I was leaving tomorrow, when the sun rose.

I knew a lot more now than before when the world was all love and I thought I knew everything.

And this is what I knew.

Fighting with God has not worked for me. I had to hold some sliver of faith or the world would make no sense. Just a sliver or I would surely lose my mind. And I knew Mom and Susie would be disappointed if I lost my faith on their account. "Maybe we'll come back if you believe hard enough" - I could hear them. That seemed a foolish notion for sure, but in the end, I would reluctantly accept that God had reasons which I would never understand.

I reminded myself every day that the evil that walked into my white house with the blue shutters had nothing to do with us.

It wasn't my fault that I had to finish up the paperwork at Bob's. Old Tom Bevins needed his tractor that morning.

"And, Lord," I begged, "please, this at least: keep my mind from dwelling on their possible endings. Let me stay with all the beauty and love we knew together for that full part of our lives.

"Let me remember Mom and gain strength thereby from her, she who had her own early loss of love and, despite that, was so brave in her life and still had so much love to give."

The Letter

It's the same old problem on airplanes. Too much time to think. Powerless, trapped in a steel bubble hurtling through space, one is constantly disturbed by wailing babies and flight attendants passing drinks. The only solution is to huddle inward, close your eyes, and try to avoid the emotional assault of a total stranger rubbing your elbow.

As I hunker down, my mind returns to lost possibilities and old regrets as I pull your letter from my purse to reread once more; how many times now? Such an old love, Lucas, and we so young, way before our various marriages and children. And yet you now write to me and my heart races as if it were yesterday.

And I wonder yet again, what really went on then?

Write it out, you taught me, when there is doubt or confusion to find clarity and dispel uncertainty. When you later read your notes, things will come clear.

So I pull down the tiny tray table before me, place my paper, and take out my pen and begin my imaginary letter to you.

My dear Lucas,

We are an hour out of New York. I imagine somewhere over Altoona, Pennsylvania, about now. My college roommate was from Altoona. I can't remember if we three ever visited together. Did you know her? Barbara, we called her Binky.

I have just finished writing out a few words to my daughter, to be delivered at a small celebratory gathering. Pity you never met her, Lucas. I will surely end up weeping my way through the tributes to my medical school graduate. A doctor now - who would have thought it when at age ten, she blanched at a spot of blood? Poor thing, crying without mercy as the doctor swabbed and stitched. And now she is the one who swabs and stitches.

The book I am about to read rests urgently in my lap, a fictional memoir by the Irish author John Banville, *The Sea*. Do you know it, I wonder, you who have so beautifully tamed the written word? Dear old Lucas, see? I have read your books.

All of them.

You write nonfiction, and that is good since it enables me to follow your adventures. Lucas, you have become your dream - an explorer, a discoverer of people and places. Oh, the unimaginable sights those shimmering blue eyes of yours must have seen. Alas, our love was cut short before I learned to read them clearly. But I see you climbed your mountain somewhere over in Nepal and tamed that wild elephant in Nairobi and those intriguing experiments with space telescopes! But there's no sequel about your space adventures, or not yet. Were they successful, I wonder? Knowing your abhorrence of failure, perhaps they were not. But bravo! You learned to make a decent shepherd's pie for a fellow Brit! I notice that you carefully avoided mention of

wives, friends, emotions, intimacies. Only that
which kept your inner self hidden did you share.

But getting back to my need for writing,
that useful means to formulate, to illuminate.

Sorry for wandering off!

How many young people today relish the joy of losing oneself
in good writing - at its best when it abandons the rational self to
imagination? Very few, I'm sorry to say. These days, their time is
taken up with mechanical devices, plucking the synopses of stories
from a screen one taps and swipes (deferring to another's opinion)
rather than a book we mark up, a real book in the hand culled from
trees and grass whose corners we fold down on a line or passage to
which we desire return and without which our lives seem, somehow,
bereft, even desolate. Of course, the professors have some part to play
in this debacle.

I pray my beautiful young doctor does not abandon her love of
books for the necessity of tablets just when she will need them most,
to hold her steady when confronting relentless medical challenges.

It does seem as if we have lost so much in our modern commerce. I think of the leaf-blowers here whose machines serve up pandemonium for hours on end. If it is not one house, it is another close
by, beginning at breakfast and going on the entire day, an incessant
racket that brings on tinnitus of the ears. As if the gardeners over
there in England would ever allow such a thing. One cannot imagine
them using anything but a bamboo rake to tidy the yards. Anything
but their fingers to sort out the debris rooting around your spectacular English hollyhocks.

Ay, an infant is crying. The new mother three rows behind me
has no idea how to quiet her child. She is bouncing him relentlessly,
furthering his agitation. Should I take him from her? Read him a passage from Banville - prose thrumming with poetry, those Irish - that

describes the sun shimmering over a field of sunflowers? Its cadence is a sure lullaby for a fussy baby.

I see that my handwriting is a bit shaky now. Never mind the cross-outs, clearly visible, showing my intent, my original thought, before my second notion. The one that changed or hid the original. All very interesting, I think. Remember the old days when receiving a personal letter was an event with its own dramas and rituals and when such an ordinary occurrence as the daily mail held unknown promise?

No young person I have asked owns notepaper.

"Are you kidding?" they say. "What for?"

Will I ever forget the day?

The day our mailman, Bob Henderson, trekked up the path, his sack, as usual, overburdened. They used to be called the postman once upon a time. Nothing seemed out of the ordinary that day. Nothing was expected but a bill or an advertisement for the symphony. I was on my way to a lecture on Delacroix at the museum when he rang the bell - not his usual sliding the papers through the slot - and handed me your letter, saying, "Looks like something special today, something from overseas."

You wrote my address in elegant cursive, the result of our generation writing uppercase and lowercase letters between the black lines of our school notebooks. As if we were constructing musical notes - staves, flats, and sharps, precisely slotted. The envelope was dark gray like smoke and heavy. My own notepaper is pale blue, or ivory, and was purchased years ago in a quaint stationery shop that sold only writing goods and Parker pens with ink in a bottle. Imagine anyone today trying to earn a living these days selling only writing goods!

Slowly, I turn the envelope over while anticipation sends my mind quivering. You see, I recognized the return address, and only by your return address do I know it is from you. I do not even know what your handwriting looks like. This is the first time you have ever written. In any case, don't you think our handwriting wobbles terribly as we age?

Holding it carefully, as if it were broken glass and not paper, it reminds me that with a letter executed at a desk in a quiet room, there is time to deliberate, to make decisions. There need be no indication of hesitation, error, no change of mind. Nothing erased or marked over, nothing underlined, not like my messy markings scribbled now on the plane. However, as well, alas, nothing that aids in the detection and unmasking of purpose or impulse or mood.

My heart thrums and runs as I wonder why you are writing at this time, in our later years. Did you know Gordon has died? Someone mentioned something at a faculty gathering discussing famous writers. Your name came up. There was some chatter that your wife had died. And then someone else said, "Oh no, the poor woman ran off." Well, if it was the former, I hope it was not a terrible, painful death like Gordon's. And if it was the latter, I'm not sad if you're not. If you are, I'm so very sorry. In any case, we are now a widow and a widower unless, of course, you've remarried.

As I began to read, the first sentence was immediately disappointing and brought this instant thud to my heart, like an anvil crushing my chest. Why? These many, many dozens of years later? You begin with an apology, and such an opening is not a favorable way to begin a letter.

The beginning is not the story for which I had longed.

You wrote that a long-planned trip during which you hoped to find me is canceled. You said that you have an unexpected commitment that takes priority. You told me we will meet sometime in the future. How long a future does one have when one has reached seventy?

Could this letter, I wonder, be written by the part of you I know well that perhaps remained constant - the often unreliable, whimsical part which acts on impulse? The consequences for another's emotions are hardly considered.

So why write at all merely to explain why an act that might occur is not going to happen after all? For some unexplained reason, you must have felt it important to send this now. After forty years!

You mention a more pressing obligation. What would that be?

The stewardess sets down a lovely glass of Chardonnay. A few sips and my heart beats evenly once again. For the moment, I will put aside my writings on this flimsy airplane tray. Instead, I will recline my seat and close my eyes, and in my head, I will compose my own story. A story I would not need to do, Lucas, if you had written a different letter on your dark-gray notepaper. A story that I had dreamed of and which would have been our reality if things had been different.

"My dearest Olivia," it would have begun.

The forecast was for a sunny morning this late fall day, a last fling of Indian summer before the crusty edges of December set in. But instead, there is dampness, a foggy mist, and you pull on your sweater as you walk toward me.

As I waited for you on my rock, I could guess what you were thinking earlier, sitting at your dressing table, brushing your hair. Though he swims well, he does not surf, you are thinking. He is a writer yet twinned with a surfer's adventurous spirit, adrift on land, adrift at sea.

When we first met, you told me you could not imagine that I lived in a house. How we laughed at that romantic notion. You said surely I was a sea creature come aground with a pen in my hand, residing among the waving seagrasses and wild roses.

I liked that, the way you thought of me, my dear, sweet, poetic Olivia.

Well, I have written a poem about you. You said you wanted me to read it aloud where the land meets the sea.

You are almost here.

"Olivia, hello," I say.

And then, "My dear Livy."

And so I begin.

"Fingers cannot reach across the interstice between those who love and those who want to."

Startled, you lift your head.

Pleased you are, I think. Was it more than you had hoped for?

"Though the night speaks a thousand words…"

Had my wish been granted, this is what you would have written on your smoky-gray paper.

But it was not to be.

I remember when I was fifteen, I thought she was old, the girl behind the counter in the dress department, but she was only thirty. When I was twenty-five, I thought *she* was old, the nurse in the emergency room, but she was only forty. And when I was forty, and I could not fancy being sixty; the woman who cut my hair was divorced and sad and having a fifty-ninth birthday, and I knew there would be no youthful return, no redemption for me when I reached her age.

But lo! Here it is now, this envelope delivered from across the ocean. Could there be a second chance with my first love? A retrieval after all, at a later age?

Even though I am no longer beautiful?

Even though you might still be overtaken by that reckless, irresponsible streak of yours? The one which, unfortunately, was part of your allure?

All this I remember, as the plane takes a series of dips and lurches on the long plane ride to my daughter.

So now, dear Lucas, I am home again, still holding your letter. The graduation was lovely and my beautiful daughter, memorable.

Shall I answer your note? Sit down at my desk and tell you about my whimsical musings on the plane?

And then add this, that youthful love goes and is not the same later but can still be *something* later and something good.

How can I tell *you* this? Wouldn't you know it on your own?

Alas, what does it matter? It is too late.

You canceled.

Why then did you write the letter, Lucas?

Some wild, irrational need for connection? A tumultuous, frantic memory from the past? Did you have immediate regrets upon posting?

More likely, it was a manifestation of your carefree, careless attitude. Act as whim dictates. Perhaps you were sitting in your garden thinking, *Oh, I wonder how Olivia is getting on these days.* Cruel, really, your letter showing up this way.

Unless this time, you have true need. Perhaps illness or remorse. Something?

Shall I tuck it away in a drawer? Pretend it doesn't exist?

And yet the mailman rang the bell.

"Here is your letter."

Anka

Anka stared out at the now-barren fields of her father's farm in southern Massachusetts. Smiling, she thought that the oval-shaped tobacco leaves now hanging in the barn looked like giant versions of those on the elm tree shading her front yard. She must tell that to her father, now finishing up tending to those leaves suspended from high horizontal posts, one after the other like a series of seats on a train. She would go into the barn every few days to check on the curing process before those leaves were bought by vendors making them into various products, mainly cigarettes. Ten-year-old Anka thought on this as she considered her family's hard work these past months and marveled that she hadn't collapsed from exhaustion, this her first full-time season in the fields.

In preparation, there were weeks of sowing seeds in wooden frames then covering them with thin cotton fabric. Next was the tedium of transplanting the small shoots into the fields. Finally, after a long summer, when the plants were lush with leaves and growth, the stalks would be cut off at the ground and speared onto sticks, four to six leaves each, then at last hung up on the poles to dry.

Anka rested on the porch stoop, drinking a glass of milk. A poor farmer's daughter, no member of her Polish family was exempt from work. In the adjacent field, she observed that her neighbors, the Kowalcyzks, had also finished bringing in their crop. She sighed, leaning against a post to rest her weary back. The notion of farming tobacco for a lifetime was a terrible thought. Nothing but hard work and a thousand worries - too much rain, not enough sun, bugs chewing the leaves, feral cats or raccoons. And the best a farmer could hope for was a decent crop and a fair price with which to buy food and pay the mortgage.

Staring at row after row of the neatly organized leaves, Anka was suddenly reminded of bats; that time she saw a dozen of them under the eaves in the barn. Who could forget their fluttering wings, their pointy ears and short snouts, large ears like a rat? Ugh, their fur-covered torsos, hanging upside down, just like the leaves.

Anka told herself then, *Why should I run from scary things?* Most of the time, when you find out about something, it's not as scary as you thought anyway. So she had asked her teacher for a book about bats and learned they weren't at all what she expected. In fact, the bats were smart, even friendly, the only mammals that truly fly, not just glide.

This Anka considered as she rubbed her sore feet. Even when she was very tired, her mind was thinking of other worlds.

Anka's part in the harvest was over. School would begin soon. She could hardly wait to return to the library and check out more books about the special habits of bats. She only liked to read about real things. Could any pretend story about bats be more exciting than knowing the truth about the world's largest bat colony, the Bracken Bat Cave outside San Antonio, Texas? Every March to October, she had learned, female bats flew from Mexico to this particular cave in order to give birth and rear their babies. But why, Anka wondered, that particular cave? Over twenty million bats lived there at one time and ate two hundred tons of flying insects a day. How did they measure that? And where did so many insects come from? The article said that a government agency gives public tours of the Bracken Cave. She looked up how far Texas was from Massachusetts and wondered if she would ever be able to take that tour and see for herself.

Her only regret at the opening of school was leaving Zofia, an old lady who lived alone two doors down from her own overcrowded farmhouse. Zofia loved Anka and welcomed her anytime she sought an escape from her boisterous household of three brothers and two parents and who knew how many cats and dogs. Perhaps ninety years old, Zofia's kind face was now wrinkled like those apple dolls on a stick sold at carnivals, real apples that had dried out.

Anka sat at Zofia's feet while the old woman reminisced about the old country. Mostly tales of the Polish People's Republic, the revolts in Poland against the Communist regime.

"Terrible times," Zofia said. "Thousands were slaughtered. Many more thousands left. That's how your parents and all our neighbors ended up right here in this town."

Zofia occasionally laid her hand over her heart. Sometimes she sighed and even cried. But then she would perk up and smile sadly, her thoughts dreamy, far in the past. "The farms were so green, but our village, you wouldn't believe how poor it was. Everyone worked hard. But we were like one big family. Like Southfield, like here," she said as she held out her arms to take in their world.

In Zofia's tiny kitchen, the cracked but spotless linoleum curled in the corners. A rocking chair waited near the stove, a cat asleep on its cushion. Zofia had told Anka many stories about Szymon, her husband, and Anka loved when she talked about him.

"When I was a young bride, maybe seventy years ago, I painted these kitchen cupboards with daisies and ivy. Now the color is almost worn away. My Szymon, so tall and handsome he was. A really hard worker, my Szymon. And strong. Who would have thought that such a man could have been killed by a copperhead rattlesnake while he was cutting tobacco? Right out there in the field. He didn't see it coming." Anka stopped breathing, held by Zofia's wide eyes and silent tears.

Anka tried to picture it, but she couldn't. Had the snake bitten him on the hand? Found its way into his shoe? She was afraid to ask.

It was a strange thing - the room so orderly, so peaceful, yet with Zofia's sad stories, the space also felt tight and melancholy.

As she spoke, Zozia's gnarled, arthritic hands would open a skein of wool and place it around Anka's short fingers, like holding a cat's cradle. Then she took the end string and wound it over and over, turning and turning until she had a neat ball and Anka's hands were empty.

"So the yarns won't tangle while I knit," Zofia explained.

Entranced, Anka watched while Zofia's knitting needles clicked and tapped. She waited eagerly for something to appear, never knowing what Zofia was making until a few lines of a scarf or the curve of a hat would emerge and begin to grow, little by little.

For many months, it never occurred to either of them that Anka could have her own needles. Until one day, Zofia raised her eyes to see the child staring at the bright red scarf with tiny snowflakes beginning to take shape. She immediately set aside her work, rummaged around in her supplies, and found a smaller pair of needles, pale silvery green like the underside of a young tobacco leaf. She placed them gently in Anka's hands. Slowly, Anka turned the needles over and around, looking, holding, touching them in wonder. Her family was so poor the four youngsters had no toys except those they made themselves out of discarded scraps - a piece of burlap, a box, some wood. Even leftover seeds. *And now Zofia was giving me a gift*, she thought. Her heart ached with gratitude. If she worked hard, maybe she could also create something pretty and useful. Zofia then pulled out a roll of bright blue wool and fitted it around her own hands.

"Now you," she told Anka, pointing to the dangling thread so Anka could start winding her own ball of yarn.

After Zofia showed her how to cast on and knit the basic knit 1, purl 1, they sat quietly together, each intent on her own work. Anka's little fingers flew across the yarn, and in no time - it seemed like only days -she moved on to the garter stitch, the rib, the seed, the moss, the slip-stitch. Then Zofia showed her how to bind off and finish the edges. Almost every few days, she learned something new. Anka lived for those moments after school when she walked up Zofia's splintered steps, took her place on the worn, tired floor, her back warming against the stove, and picked up her needles.

Trying things out, she played with various stitches for scarves until she had completed two for her parents. Next up were winter hats for her brothers made with Zofia's circular needles that produced the stockinette stitch. As Zofia watched her student, focused and determined, she thought, *Ah, the young. How quickly they master something new!* While Anka knitted at a fierce pace, Zofia knitted leisurely, humming tunes from the old country, occasionally commenting, "My dear child. Knitting is an easygoing pleasure. Why are you rushing?"

But all winter, when her brothers wore her warm hats low over their ears and her wool scarves were wrapped tightly around the necks of her mother and father, nothing pleased Anka more, thrilled as she was to give them something she herself had made.

Who would have thought the town library stocked knitting manuals on its shelves? Here were *The Knitter, Knit Now,* half a dozen other knitting magazines within whose pages were astonishing pattern collections. Look what wonderful things could be made from two needles! And oh! The female models themselves were so beautiful. Anka had never seen any woman who looked like them. Sighing, she turned from this diversion and bent to the task of absorbing complex explanations of advanced knitting. Often, she checked out a magazine or two and spread it out on Zofia's floor, following pattern directions under the guidance of her teacher.

As they sat together, the only sounds in the little kitchen were the *clickety-clack* of their needles, the groan of a plow far off, and Zofia's random instruction to correct or clarify. The chirping of robins perched on the windowsills.

This day, the path to Zofia's porch was muddy from rain. Anka would always remember that and how her socks got splashed with dirt. Inside, she shook herself off and warmed up by the fire. Zofia sat quietly, hiding her impatience, hands clasped in her lap. After Anka was settled, she stood slowly, hunched over, reaching for her cane.

Smiling mischievously, she said, "So, my Anka, today I have something special for you. Are you ready to knit a winter skirt?" Anka gasped. Surely this charge was beyond her capabilities. As Zofia pulled out several skeins of luscious green wool, Anka burst into tears. She knew every scrap in Zofia's bag, and these were not included. For this soft, elegant yarn, the old woman had to stumble down the road to the country store and hand over a couple of precious dollars she could hardly spare. Anka prayed Andrezj, the storekeeper, had given Zofia a break on the cost.

Andrezj was a good man, Anka knew. In the winter months, when she was not needed in the fields, she would put in a few hours after church to do small chores for him, a way of paying for her small purchases, always the cheapest yarns, the leftovers, the damaged goods.

Anka jumped up, fiercely hugging the old lady.

"Enough of that." Zofia beamed. "Let's get started."

At twelve years old, nothing much had changed for Anka in her daily life except that she now wore her beautiful new skirt to church on Sundays. Skinny and undeveloped, she still had the traits of a farm girl - innocent, unworldly, dressed in clothes sewn by her mother, saddle shoes her brother Bartek had outgrown. It was the same routine - working in the fields in summer, knitting with Zofia, and reading in the library if she had any spare time. When a knitting magazine arrived, Ms. Kowalski, the librarian, put it aside and offered it to her before she put it on the shelves.

On a blustery cold day in winter, together in her warm kitchen, Zofia started to giggle. She put her fingers to her lips as if others were in the room.

"Anka, I'll tell you a secret. I'm wearing knitted underwear! Oh, over my plain cotton underpants, of course, but you'd be surprised

how warm it keeps me in this freezing weather!" Anka smiled, thinking it a bit silly, trying to imagine what that looked like. She had
never seen directions for underwear in any of the knitting magazines!
But then she thought it a wonderful idea. Something new and different. Maybe a welcome addition under the farmers' overalls for those
working in their icy barns all winter? Would her father wear a pair if
she surprised him with such a thing?

Anka began to study the long history of wool, beginning in
the eleventh and twelfth centuries among the British and Flemish.
How different sheep from different countries produced an astonishing variety of fibers. Staring at pictures of sheep in need of shearing,
laden down with such enormously thick coats, she wondered how
they managed to walk and was relieved to know that the shearing
process didn't hurt them. The yarns Anka worked with came from
sheep, but there were others - mohair from goats, angora from rabbits. She must ask Andrezj if he could order some mohair. Perhaps
she would make a collar for her mother's best Sunday dress.

Before Anka learned about the actual process of dying natural
wool, she had assumed it was a complex process. But no! It was a
simple recipe, like any recipe, not much different from her mother's
preparation of *karpatka*.

> Roll out pastry of potato flour. Mix salt,
> butter, vanilla cream. Add the eggs last. Sprinkle
> with powdered sugar.

> As well, there was a simple recipe for dying
> wool, just as in baking a cake.

> Put 1-5 teaspoons of dye for every pound of
> wool in a big pot. Add 3-9 teaspoons of salt. Heat
> together before adding two-thirds cup of vinegar.

Simmer ten minutes. *Karpatka* or a pink dye for
a sweater in about the same time!

"Zofia! Can I try this in one of your old pots?" Anka asked.

"Of course," Zofia replied, pleased that Anka had learned this
on her own, something she herself did not know. As the days passed
and her knowledge and skill increased, Anka felt sure of one thing.
Somehow, in some way, her destiny would be tied to the craft of
knitting.

Christmas was a month off. The people of Southfield pulled
out boxes stored in attics and began to decorate their houses with
colored lights and candles. Spruce trees cut from the fields appeared
in front windows, draped with tiny sparkling red and green lights.
More strings of lighting edged doors, rooftops. Some placed a lighted
plastic nativity scene on the front lawn. Blinking lights on trees and
bushes transformed each humble dwelling into a magical fantasy.
Oh, the wonder of strolling after dark along the few short streets of
this little town, Anka's family bundled into her hats and scarves, calling to the neighbors, "Good health! Merry Christmas! May the New
Year bring us all a good crop!"

The town hall was planning its annual celebration. Folks from
surrounding communities would show up for square dancing and
a community supper. Farmer Jakub was tuning his fiddle and the
boy Mikolaj testing his tambourine. The women mended their best
frocks. Volunteers polished the pews and gathered evergreen boughs
for the altar, readying the church for midnight mass.

Suddenly, in the midst of this excitement, an astonishing
thought popped up in Anka's mind. Could she do it? *Why not try?* she
asked herself. She started to plan, telling no one, ferociously knitting
away, pleading with Zofia for a few extra dollars in return for doing
her marketing and cleaning her little house.

On the day of the holiday party, women streamed into the hall, carrying platters of pickled beets and rolled herring. Cabbage rolls and *kolaczki* (cream cheese) cookies. Piles of fresh *paczki* (doughnuts). While the women were busy, Anka silently moved along the walls, looking for an unused table. Yes, good, there was one. Rickety but no matter. She covered the front with a few pine branches. Then she made two signs out of white cardboard, lettering in red and a Christmas tree drawn in green. She hid them under the table until the last minute. When Jakub and Mikolaj took their places, she brought out her knitted items from a paper bag - fleecy hats in green, blue, and red and two scarves in red and white, the national colors of Poland, knitted horizontally as they were on the flag. And her prize pieces, two cable-knit sweaters, one in gray, one yellow. She waited for a few more heartbeats until Jakub began to take up a tune and everyone readied themselves for a spin. Then she whipped out her two signs and taped them on opposite ends of the table – "Handmade Garments by Anka" and "Special Orders Taken."

Anka sold everything and took four orders for custom items besides. After the hall cleared out and she could sit for a moment, she considered an exciting but unfamiliar feeling. Indeed, an emotion that became an extraordinary notion. She was too young to define or understand it, but if a good friend were watching her face while she was musing, the friend might have said Anka seemed flush with confidence. Perhaps it was the power of possibility that was not present in the little girl when the bazaar started. Perhaps it was the idea that she now had a way to manage her life, beholden to no one for permission or approval. An idea that flowed over Anka's heart and awakened her mind. At the age of twelve, she hadn't thought further ahead than the next school term, but suddenly, Anka sensed that her future would not lie in the tobacco fields. No sir, not the fields, where farmers and their families labored from sunup to sundown, praying to the Lord for good weather.

It was her own ambition that now settled itself into her thoughts.

Anka knew this town, and its neighbors were not a continuing market for her goods, being struggling farmers and all. She had no specific idea how this new sensation would unfold, but she didn't worry about it. Off she went to Zofia's little house, quietly slipping $2 into Zofia's bag of supplies. Taking her place on the floor, her back to the stove, she started to knit.

Anka would soon be sixteen but no longer was she thin and undeveloped. In fact, a few of the older ladies whispered, "She's becoming a beauty, that one." Still, life followed its old routines. Summer in the fields, knitting at Zofia's, reading in the library, and in addition, mending the family's clothes, having taken over that task from her mother. Zofia was now very old, her hands crippled with arthritis. But no matter. She had already taught Anka everything she knew. Mainly, she dozed in her chair while Anka, constantly inventive, turned out item after item - mittens with a little mouse knitted into the palm, a hat with the Polish flag across the back. Plastic bobbins holding different yarn colors hung from her needles as she deftly wove first one, then another, into her work to make a specific design. Nothing she knitted now was simple. If you didn't know what she was doing, it looked like magic. Anka thought it was like weaving on a loom.

Soon, she would graduate from high school. Her parents expected her to marry another farmer. *No*, she thought. *Never.*

There was no talk in Anka's family about college. The Poles in her neighborhood married each other and spent their lives in the fields, and that was that. Besides downright economic necessity, it was a way of preserving the ways of the old country, of their parents and grandparents. However, Anka had always had the feeling of a different kind of life. Her mother was not yet forty-five, but on her face, Anka could already see the beginning of facial puckering, like Zofia's.

Four miles and two towns away, Holmes College loomed like a sophisticated bastion of glamour. She saw pictures of the school in the library. It looked like nothing she had ever seen, but how would she have? Her eyes saw only flat farmland and a tiny town center with a white church and a community hall that looked like the church. She had never ventured farther. In the Holmes catalog were beautiful young men and women dressed in fashionable clothes, holding books and entering buildings that looked as grand as those in Boston or Philadelphia.

"I will go to Holmes," she decided.

Cards requesting pamphlets and applications were tucked inside its pages. These did not interest her. She had her own plan and prayed that somewhere there would be another receptive venue, another table on which she could prop signs for her knitting.

Aha, here's something, she thought. "Christmas Crafts Sale. Interested applicants fill out the form below." Anka tore out the sheet, stuffed it in her book bag, and completed it on Zofia's table using Zofia's return address.

When the packet arrived, she clutched it close and ran inside. As usual, Zofia was dozing in her chair, but Anka was comforted merely by being in her presence. This kitchen was as familiar and soothing to her as anyplace she had ever known. The old woman had been responsible for her knitting achievements, and Anka never for a moment forgot how much she owed her. Zofia had given her far more than her first pair of needles and years of knitting instruction. She had given her a way out of the farm life.

Zofia was snoring, her headscarf askew, but it was important for Anka to be near her when she slid out the pamphlets. Quickly, she skipped the descriptive information about admissions and courses, facilities, and degrees and went straight to activities - soccer tournaments, debate competitions, semesters abroad. Then yes, there - holiday bazaar in three months' time!

"Staff and other interested parties are invited to sell their goods to the extended Holmes community." *Am I an "interested party"?* Anka wondered. "By appointment only, applicants are invited to show their products for approval to Ms. Bateson of the Fine Arts Department."

Anka made her appointment. Then she began to knit with purpose, willing herself not to think of the audacious step she had taken. Often, she awoke in the middle of the night, crept out of bed, and spent an occasional hour or so knitting by a small corner light until she crawled back to sleep, wearied, worn out.

On the morning of the appointed Saturday afternoon with Ms. Bateson, Anka put on her best dress and carefully folded her knitted work into an old tote Zofia used to store her cat's toys. Then she began the four-mile walk to Holmes.

Enthralled, Anka took her first steps onto a college campus. Electrifying, even shocking in its visual presentation, it was far more beautiful than the photos; there were sounds, people, moving images, great architectural beauty. Skipping beats, her heart sputtered and ran. *Stop*, she told herself, *you are here on a mission. This is business. Keep your head down.* Determined not to get distracted or, worse, intimidated, she found her way to Ms. Bateson's office.

Anka was immediately relieved. The woman was not at all frightening. Rather, Ms. Bateson took her hand and welcomed her warmly. But despite her kindness, Anka's own hands perspired as she realized she was in a personal office with hundreds of books, all of them belonging to this congenial woman. *Keep your head down*, she reminded herself. *This is business.*

"Welcome, my dear. I'm so happy to meet you. Anka, correct? Are you a student here at Holmes?"

"No, no," sputtered Anka. "I'm not old enough for Holmes yet. I live on a farm a few miles down the road."

She immediately bit her tongue, ashamed to reveal her humble roots. Did Ms. Bateson wonder what this poor homespun teenager could possibly offer Holmes? *Answer direct questions in the fewest words possible!* she scolded herself.

Like a happy young schoolgirl, Ms. Bateson clapped her hands.

"A farm? Really? I too grew up on a farm. But it was far away, in Minnesota. A dairy farm, and we had fifty cows to tend. Plus, chickens and other small animals. It was a hard life for a young girl, I can tell you that!"

This graceful woman sitting before her, awards of distinction crowding her shelves, all those books, and she was raised as humbly as herself?

"Come, let's see what you want to show at the holiday bazaar," Ms. Bateson urged gently, moving aside the papers on her desk.

Anka carefully laid out a gold sweater the color of corn under a hot sun, its buttons covered in a darker hue. Two pairs of gloves, a manly one in dark green using a rough cast-over stitch, the color of tobacco leaves ripe for harvest, the woman's in sapphire blue with tiny diamonds, the color of the sky just before night fell. And her finest piece, of which she was immensely proud, a gorgeous coat in the brown of a mink's fur with wide cuffs and deep collar.

"Oh my!" Ms. Bateson cried. "These are exquisite! Do you mind if I try on this wonderful coat? My favorite shade, that lovely rich color of the earth when it's ready to accept the farmer's seeds, isn't that right, Anka?" she said, laughing. "My dear, how old are you? How is it possible for a young girl to possess such astonishing skills? Not only your knitting ability but also the clever designs you've created!"

Anka sat very still. Silently, she said a prayer in Polish to the god of her family, her country, and her Zofia.

"It's a perfect fit! I must purchase this right now. And that astonishing gold sweater as well. What were you thinking to choose that particular shade? Do you have prices on these?"

Anka, in her surprise and confusion, mumbled a number that covered the cost of her materials plus a few extra dollars. She hadn't expected to sell anything here today.

"Impossible!" answered the woman. "That isn't nearly enough for such a gorgeous hand-made garment. You couldn't buy this in New York for twice that price. I'll double your price and a little extra besides. Is that agreeable with you?"

Anka eventually stumbled out of that splendid room of books and tributes, the coat and sweater remaining behind with their new owner. Both pairs of gloves as well, purchased as a gift for Ms. Bateson's parents. The vision of this graceful woman swirling around her office wearing something that she, Anka, had made, would remain embedded in her mind forever. The stunned teenager left Ms. Bateson cooing over her new purchases, promising to alert her friends to Anka's table at the Christmas bazaar. Her heart singing, her eyes teary with relief and blessings, Anka buttoned her coat and began the four-mile trek home.

After she finished the supper dishes and fed the dogs, she fell into bed, exhausted. From under the covers, she watched the moon cast a sliver of light on the red columbine she had gathered on her way home. With a heart full of hope, she whispered to herself, *I did it. I took the hardest step. Now, surely, I can handle whatever comes next.*

The Holmes gymnasium was aglitter with seasonal sparkle and spangles. Silver and gold streamers hung from basketball nets, from the scoreboard. Pine wreaths were tacked to green velvet fabric draped across paneled walls. As Anka entered this enormous room, Ms. Bateson saw her first. With a wave and a smile, she walked over wearing Anka's gold sweater, gave the girl a hug, and led her to her table. It was a long, ample rectangle, of sufficient size for Anka to show her stock without the need for stacking. A large sign said, "Handmade Garments by Anka," just as she had marked on the acceptance forms. The words were written on a stiff easel board done by a professional calligrapher, not in her own childish hand on a piece of throwaway cardboard. As she unpacked, staff members came fluttering around, eager to see her work. Ms. Bateson had surely spoken to them.

Amid the shrieks and squeals over her garments, the group plum cleared her out. Just snatched each item as she laid it on the table. In fifteen minutes, it was all over. With the disappearance into the throng of each item, Anka grew increasingly nervous. *What will I do when the event opens?* she asked herself, quickly tallying the bills and making notes. She walked over to three women, who were even now ogling their purchases. Ms. Otero from Spanish; Ms. Jamison, chemistry; Mrs. Hunter, tennis - they had told her their names, made her write them down on the list for the next bazaar. Anka asked to borrow back a few of the items to display for an hour or so. Then she made two additional signs in her own writing: "Sold" and next to it "Special Orders Taken." Dazed, she sat on a metal chair and watched in amazement as the dramatic scene unfolded and the orders piled up.

And now?

In Zofia's kitchen, Anka sat down on the floor beside the old woman she loved. She laid her head on the old woman's knees and began to jabber away, trying to arrange fleeting schemes and ideas into a logical scheme, working through one, then another. What would Zofia think about this - or that? she wondered, lifting her head, looking up. Zofia's eyes were closed, but occasionally, she reached out a hand and lovingly touched Anka's hair. Yes! Zofia had heard! She approved!

In the library, Anka spread out newspapers of the surrounding areas, up to a hundred miles in any direction. She then copied down names and addresses. When she was finished, she pulled out her stationery and wrote to crafts shows requesting participation, to yarn shops seeking employment. While she waited for replies, she thought seriously about how she would tell her parents. She was sick with worry that she might hurt them, but she was determined that no child of hers would plant tobacco.

Had she been so nervous or fearful about expecting any positive responses that she was astonished, dumbfounded, really, when she opened a letter saying that Anka's letter was an answer to a woman's prayer? The owner of Ye Olde Yarn Shoppe - "Call me Fannie" - had just broken her leg and needed help. She couldn't get out of her chair. Who would reach the goods on the shelves and take payment besides? Never mind the restocking and the hundreds of other details requiring attention. Could she come right away? Anka looked at the address. An hour's distance by bus, the same bus that came routinely through Southfield. She could come home whenever she wanted. Maybe frequent visits would lessen her parents' disapproval.

With the whole family seated for supper, she began, "Mama, Papa, and you all too." She gestured toward her brothers. Looking around the table, she paused, waiting for her fast heartbeat to settle down. And then, "I want to see if I can make something of myself with my knitting skills," she blurted out. "I'm going away but not too far."

Shocked, they remained quiet. Then her brothers began teasing her, "Hey, Anka, can we go too?" Both parents cried. Anka was surprised when her mother said, "You know? There are better things out there than farming. You're a special girl with special talents. Yes, see where they take you. We'll be here." Her father blew his nose, patted her back, said he had to tend to something in the barn.

And so Anka, at age sixteen, found herself boarding the bus in front of the community hall that would take her into her future.

Fannie's shop was small but charming. Fannie herself was middle-aged. Feisty, generous, and bossy. She put Anka right to work, and in giving her directions, over time, she taught Anka the skills of salesmanship, purchasing, inventory, managing a shop. And Anka was thrilled to receive this information but, even more, to be surrounded with knitting supplies from counter to ceiling. Not just wool but mohair and angora. She lived in a room above the shop and had ample time in the evenings to knit, taking only partial salary in return for free yarn.

Within a year, Anka was a confident young lady. She even taught Fannie a thing or two such as how to arrange a more alluring window. And how to stock more efficiently, the yarns by type rather than color. Anka also started a knitting class and was allowed to keep the fees as long as the students bought their supplies from the store stock. When Fannie's leg finally healed, she said to Anka, "I'm going to recommend you to a much bigger shop a few miles away. You've outgrown me here." Anka was fond of Fannie and grateful but relieved. She *was* ready to move on.

After six months in the new shop, similar to Fannie's in management but larger, the buyer for a national crafts company came in to take his semi-annual orders. Luckily for Anka, she was the one to greet him. The rep took one long look at her robust beauty and innocent demeanor and was breathless for one long minute. But then, as they talked business, he was unexpectedly impressed with her accomplished head for numbers and stock, the whole business. He decided right then to steal her away. Immediately, he placed her in the knitting department of his company as a buyer, and after only three months, she was promoted to head buyer for the organization's two dozen outlets in twenty-four states.

Before she was twenty-five, the entire industry was talking about this talented gal named Anka. She knew this buzz was going around and made her calculations accordingly. And she decided to make the leap. Her proposal seemed timely and appropriate. So she called a small meeting of three company executives who had personally witnessed her astonishing rise and presented them with her bold business plans in a neatly managed unveiling.

"Gentlemen, I am asking you to subsidize me in my own business. Its name will be *Handmade Yarns and Garments by Anka*. I hope to go national immediately."

The executives were at least twice her age and had been in their respective positions for years. None of them was known for being particularly daring or inventive. She kept telling herself. *Remember Holmes College. Remember Ms. Bateson.*

She could almost hear them mulling it over in their heads as the room hovered in stillness. They looked at her, doodled on their pads, calculated numbers, glanced at each other. And then, "Of course! Yes, you can do it. We're in," they chorused.

Anka had already scouted venues and negotiated prices, so she quickly rented office space and hired a few women reps; her hires had to be knitters with business experience. It was essential that those going out on the road be familiar with the use of her product. Alas, no men fit that requirement for this position, but she did add two as an accountant, a lawyer. On the day of the lease signing, she brought in platters of Polish desserts, *karpatka, kolaczki,* and her favorite, the rich *paczki* filled with custard, and numerous bottles of Tyskie beer and *krupnik,* the honey vodka of Poland. She celebrated with her new staff as well as with the grown daughters of a Polish family from Southfield she had convinced to open a bakery around the corner. The next day, she hired away two of her former company's best ad men to start promoting her products at department stores across the country.

Was it any surprise that when her secretary buzzed him into her office, she would succumb to the charms of Ted Masters? Especially after he added that he knew one of her brothers and was to deliver a personal message for Anka? True, Anka was a canny entrepreneur in the business world, but emotionally, she was the same unsophisticated young woman who had sat in Zofia's kitchen with her first pair of knitting needles.

As Anka rose to meet handsome Ted Masters, it was his swagger she noticed first, then his eyes - clear, colorless, like glass. His irresistible smile had already seduced her secretary.

"You know one of my brothers?" Anka asked.

"Well, not exactly," Ted answered easily.

"May I sit? I wanted to meet you and heard you had a family with three brothers in Southfield. So I decided to take a small liberty to get my foot in your door. Forgive me?" he asked with an apologetic grin, knowing no woman had ever turned him down with that smile and deferential manner.

It was right at that moment that Anka should have sent him away. She knew it.

But she didn't. "Yes, you may sit," she answered.

And that was the beginning of the next phase of her life.

On their first date, he took her to a candlelight dinner at an old inn whose walls and arches were made of hundred-year-old stone and through whose open spans were views of a dark, mysterious lake.

Next, he took her to see the most romantic film of all time, *Casablanca* with Ingrid Bergman and Humphrey Bogart, where she soaked his handkerchief with her tears and vowed to forevermore try to be as noble a person as Ms. Bergman.

On their third date, he packed a picnic lunch which they opened at a table aside a pond with ducks and swans swimming among the water lilies. Gardens of white hydrangeas and pink hibiscus, low mountains tinged with a purple haze rising dramatically beyond.

On the fourth date, sipping white wine at a Mozart concert under the stars at which Ted rested his arm on the back of her chair, he proposed that he become her business partner. Not an equal one, of course, but if he proved himself, at least a significant one. He would be the idea man, her adviser, offering ways to expand the company. He would go out in the field, not as a seller of yarns but as the one to make arrangements for craft shows, to convince various venues to offer competitive knitting contests, that kind of thing. Entrepreneurial start-ups.

She thought a moment. Ted was offering an entirely new approach, an expansive, canny one for the business. And he had the charm to woo any potential client.

But did she trust him enough? This was only their fourth date. She needed a few days to think it over. But they were sitting under the stars, and he had just poured her second glass of wine.

"Yes, Ted, that might work out quite well," Anka replied.

Ted traveled throughout the States, courting rather than merely soliciting possible customers. Flirting with pretty secretaries, he was wildly successful in acquiring contracts for Handmade's goods. Agreements from senior centers, adult education departments, church groups, all kinds of sources, agreed to start up knitting circles with products purchased from Anka's company. A discount was promised and given after Ted first quietly raised the list prices 10 percent.

During this time, Anka was becoming well-known, even famous. She had steadfast fans who bought whatever merchandise she discussed on television talk shows, becoming a national phenomenon in the art of being creative at home. "The Martha Stewart of the knitting world," they called her.

It was not an uncommon story.

Wooing, seduction, then a slow but clever manipulation of the information going on the books, Ted had privately cajoled the head accountant into being his accomplice - Larry Jarvis, a man with three young children, always in need of extra cash. Every couple of weeks, Ted returned to home base and to Anka. He reported enthusiastically on his successes and picked up his commissions then met privately with Larry to adjust the company's numbers. Larry bought a new car; Ted was more discreet. He and Anka would resume what she considered a courtship. *Let's face it*, she told herself, *I'm mad about this guy.*

Six months after they first met, Ted took Anka for dinner at the same candlelight inn by the lake as he had on their first date. They dined on the terrace and watched minnows flashing by in the shimmering water beneath their feet.

When the waiter delivered their strawberry shortcake, Ted pointed to something on the wall behind Anka. As she turned to look, he whipped out a small box and set it next to her plate.

"Ted, oh no! What is this?" she cried, looking back, her hand to her heart, her eyes filled and shiny.

"My dearest Anka," he said, "open it, slip it on, and say yes!"

It was Anka's wish to have the wedding back in Southfield, in the community hall, the entire town invited. Her brothers had increased the family acreage, but now, infants slept in baskets and toddlers crawled underfoot. Jakub still played his fiddle, Mikolaj his tambourine, and they would provide the music. Ted ordered champagne, not beer or vodka, not the honey liqueur *krupnik* they were used to. He brought in a feast of French food catered by a high-end restaurant in a city fifty miles away. The provisions arrived in a white van with a serving crew of four. The town was aghast. Usually, all weddings were a community effort, and no one remembered a time when the townspeople did not have to cook potluck themselves for every special affair. The women talked about it all night and for weeks afterward. Behind the makeshift dais, Ted hung a huge sign, "Ted and Anka, Knit Together on This Spot."

A month after the wedding, munching on chicken sandwiches by the pond with the ducks and swans, Ted offered this proposal. "It makes good business sense, my dear, to amend our documents. Much easier for tax purposes, even some financial benefit there, to have all our holdings in both our names, held jointly. There's always a delay every time we have to sign papers or have things notarized."

"Of course, Ted darling, you're absolutely right. Thank you for suggesting it. You're always thinking of ways to make my life easier, to make our financial dealings run smoother."

A month after that, Larry, her chief accountant, gave notice. Anka was surprised, thinking him quite happy with his position. Someone in purchasing said it was sudden and thought he was moving to Florida, or was it Texas?

The next week, when Ted didn't return her phone call from - was he in Chicago? - Anka grew worried. She had left several messages. *Perhaps he's seeing a client and doesn't want to disturb me calling afterward at such a late hour, those inconvenient differences in time zones. Ted is always mindful of small considerations*, Anka thought warmly. So she went to bed mildly concerned but not with a heavy heart.

At nine the next morning, Larry's assistant, Jim, waited outside Anka's office, stiffly perched on the rim of a chair. Anka's secretary, Judith, thought he looked worried. Usually, he was chatty, eager to engage in office banter; but on this day, he sat like a stone. Even more alarming, when Judith asked if he wanted coffee, he looked straight ahead as if he hadn't heard her.

Jim was recalling the many stories about his much-admired boss, her beloved mentor, Zofia; the farming community in which she grew up; and her lack of education compensated by the grit and determination that powered her success. Anka had a certainty that acquiring a skill and believing in yourself would drive you forward. She had never been shy speaking about these issues, sharing her stories on television interviews, in newspaper articles, at annual Handmade meetings. It was with these sentiments that she mentored many others.

Now he remained silent, overcome with remorse, with guilt. He blamed himself for this imminent debacle. But why? Nothing had aroused his suspicion. The figures Jim was handed always computed accurately. Larry had simply done too neat a job of embezzling funds.

"Morning, Judith, your new hairdo makes you look as young as your daughter!" Anka remarked with her usual generous flourish as she stepped off the elevator. "Why, Jim, how good to see you," Anka added, noticing him waiting. "We up here on the fifth floor never see enough of you down on three. Come in, come in. You look well. Coffee?"

Anka bustled about for a moment, taking off her coat, patting her hair, glancing at her personal phone number - no calls yet from Tom - then became concerned as she looked at Jim's stricken face.

"What is it?" she asked, now a bit tremulous herself.

Rather than speak, feeling his own voice unreliable, he spread out various papers before her. She looked down to see bank statements showing numerous withdrawals within the last two weeks - and no deposits. Then twenty-four hours ago, two of her business accounts had been closed.

She looked at Jim. "I don't understand. What's happening here?"

Her questions made Jim feel he had failed this wonderful woman, though what should he have said? "Anka, your husband is a cad, a thief"? Jim had always thought Ted a self-serving braggart, marrying Anka for a sweet deal, but it certainly didn't mean he was skimming money from the business. There was no evidence that any financial funny business was going on. Larry always signed the final tallies, and Jim had trusted Larry.

How could this crackerjack businesswoman have fallen for such a slick and unsavory guy? Couldn't she see?

There was more. Other accounts. Numbers that didn't add up or were missing.

Stunned, Anka went very still. She couldn't take this in. Her Ted? Always attentive, reliable Ted? Always offering suggestions to do things a better way, innovative in expanding and financing the business? Yes, apparently, her Ted.

She would not cry. That bastard was not worth her tears. No challenge was more formidable than a sixteen-year-old farm girl walking four miles to keep an appointment with an important person on a college campus that she thought existed only in the movies.

As she slumped forward, Jim jumped up to console her. But there was no consolation to be had. The figures were in front of her.

"Excuse me for a moment, would you, Jim?"

And she raced past Judith, out the door of her own building, into her car and home. Running in the door, she grabbed trash bags from the kitchen and stripped the bedroom first. Into the bags, she threw Ted's beautiful clothes, his golf outfits, shoes, toiletries, gold-edged bedside clock, and anything that belonged to him. She lugged the bags down the stairs and left them in piles outside the back door. In she went again, this time with bags for the downstairs. For the library, especially the library with his personal journals and photos. Then the kitchen, his silver martini shaker, crystal decanter. In an hour, the house was totally purged of Tom Masters's belongings.

But not of the man.

Anka sat on the stairs, sobbing. The deceit! She had been swindled by a master manipulator. First, she blamed herself. *Maybe I had it coming. I ignored my initial gut warnings. I had hardly dated before Ted. I had no experience with men.* Then she cursed and called him names. *Bastard. Lowlife. Liar. Thief. How dare he?* Then she asked questions. *How could I have known?* There had been no hints, no sense of this occurring. *Were all his loving behaviors, his endearments, a fraud? Did he ever love me?* Then more blame. *Where did I fail him?*

She called her office.

"Judith, I'm taking a few days off."

She called Jim. "I'll be out of the office for a week. Keep things under wraps until I get back."

Then she walked out the door and got on the bus to Southfield.

As the bus swung into town, she saw the church spire in the distance, farmland stretching out all around. It wasn't simply nostalgia she felt but also an ease, a thankfulness that she had been able to make something meaningful of her life. As the small houses came into view, one of the first she saw was Zofia's, still empty and now somewhat dilapidated since her death two years earlier. Zofia had left the house to her, but who would ever move into Southfield and buy it?

She suddenly knew who would live there. *My baby brother Lukasz*, she decided. *He has been watching over it for me all this time, and soon he is to be married.* The plan was for him to live with his wife's family, but hers was a crowded house. *I'll restore it and give it to him as a wedding gift. Yes, I'll repair it and give it to Lukasz.*

Then she remembered she had no money. And who knew if debt was incurred? Yet Anka's familiar feistiness rose up. *Never mind, I'll manage it somehow*, she told herself.

The bus stopped in front of the community hall where she was married, and she started walking home. It was late summer. She knew everyone was finishing up the day in the fields. She waited on the front step of her childhood dwelling as she did when she was ten years old, dreaming of an unknown destiny. And there she sat until the sun set and the figures in the distance wearily began their trek home. Her mother moved a little ahead, impatient to start supper. Then together, her father and the boys.

"Anka!" they shouted, running now, and soon the boys were whistling a polka and dancing her around the kitchen, her mother crying as she sliced the potatoes. "Anka, you look wonderful, my precious daughter." She pulled out tissues from her apron pocket. Her father threw his hat on the wall peg and took his turn lifting her off the floor and swinging her around as if she were still a child.

After dinner, Anka told them the entire story. "Damn," the boys said. "Hush, no cursing," the mother said. "I'll break every bone in his body," the father said.

During the day, Anka went to church. Then she visited Zofia's house and traced with her fingers what was left of the daisies painted on the cupboards. She strolled over to the hall where at Christmas she had sold her first scarf and hat. And two sweaters too as she recalled. She noticed that the country store was shuttered. The shopkeeper, Andrezj, must have passed away. She wondered how her folks managed now that there was no place nearby to buy milk, butter, eggs. She must remember to ask her mother about that.

But mostly she strolled up and down the little road that ran alongside the open fields, resting now and then on a large, flat boulder marking the edge of the Kowalcyzks's property. She chatted briefly - they all had work to do, end of harvest! - with the townspeople, and met a few of the newest babies. In her pocket, she still had her key to Zofia's house. Letting herself in, she carried Zofia's rocker out to the porch where she sat and watched the busyness of the farmer's life unfold. Oddly, Ted was not her first thought. He was not nearly as keen an emotion as those her heart turned to on returning to Southfield. But mostly, rocking and rocking, she let her mind drift.

After a few days of family meals, everyone trying to make her laugh, Bartek with his silly jokes, she was ready to go back. She had shed enough tears. When she watched these noble folks of hers - honest, decent, working to the bone for every penny, rarely complaining - her heart hardened against Ted. Did she even know the truth of his background? He said he was from Ohio, that he was an only child, orphaned now. But she had never checked. No, he did not belong in her world. He was an imposter, not only endangering her and her business but everyone who worked for her - Judith, Jim, dozens of others, and their families.

Everyone hugged and kissed and cried. Her mother stuffed her pockets with *kolaczki* wrapped in a cloth, and Bartek's two-year-old Alicja handed her a piece of paper with "xoxoxox" scribbled all over it. In the distance, Anka heard the rumblings of the bus, saw trails of smoke emerge from its exhaust. When it braked with a belch and a thump, the doors gave a mighty whoosh, and she stepped inside. Leaning against the window, Anka waved to her family as the children threw kisses, and her father stood solemnly with his hat over his heart, and her mother wiped her eyes, and the boys did handstands and somersaults until the bus turned a corner and drove out of sight.

On Monday morning, Anka stepped off the elevator on the fifth floor of her building. Judith waited at her desk for her boss with hot coffee and slices of *placek*, the Polish sweet bread studded with dried fruit, Anka's favorite.

"Good morning, Judith," Anka sang. "I love that blue scarf. Makes your eyes look as blue as that sky outside. Any calls on my personal line?"

"Sorry, no, none," Judith replied, handing her the coffee.

"Please have Jim and his assistant, Ben from accounting, come up right away and hold all other calls."

When the two men were facing her, she began.

"Fellas, I have a plan. This is what I'm going to do. Call the top people at our three banks. Notify the company attorney - have him bring his paralegal. Also our stockbroker and financial adviser. See if you can arrange this for tomorrow at eleven o'clock. Any questions?"

"Oh, and worry not about all this. Handmade by Anka will rise again."

And Anka thought, *I must restructure the accounting department. No single person will ever be solely in charge again.*

Jim looked down, cleared his throat, checked out the ceiling. "Um, er, uh…"

"No Jim, I'm not going to call the police," Anka said. "I won't criminally prosecute Ted, though Lord knows he should be in jail. I don't want this issue all over the newspapers. Nor do I want it hanging over all of us here at the company. After we have our meeting tomorrow, I'm going to have that private detective whom we keep on retainer come over. We'll see if he can track Ted down, even if he has to go to the Cayman Islands or beyond. Maybe he can threaten him with criminal charges to get back some of that money he stole. That's as far as I'll go."

The two accountants stood, dipped their heads, and backed out the door, scanning their notes.

Anka stood at the window behind her desk, looking down at the lovely courtyard with the massive pots of overblown yellow dahlias and ivory roses encircling the fountain. The flowers were having their final burst of bloom before fall. She couldn't quite see it clearly, but she knew for sure that just beyond the streets with the tall buildings, just as the city edged into the country, there were endless acres of apple orchards that she had heard belonged to a group of four women, all mothers. She reminded herself to look into that. Every spring, the endless rows of trees were completely covered with white and pink blossoms, just before their branches bore delicious fruit that nurtured the world and supported four families, and whose glorious sweet scent drifted over town and field for a few precious days.

Then she turned and sat at her desk, pressed a button, and said into the intercom, "Judith, will you please come in with your pad? We have work to do."

About the Author

Formerly an interior designer and painter, Pamela Hull wrote her first book, *Where's My Bride?* at age sixty. This venture was to be a one-time effort, a tribute to a remarkable man and marriage. However, as the endeavor unfurled, she unearthed a keen love for writing narrative.

Her second book, *SAY YES! Flying Solo After Sixty*, explores how neither age nor being single is an impediment to living a rich life - a subject relevant to all ages and genders.

Moments that Mattered followed *SAY YES!* and explored how ordinary, everyday experiences can prove to be life-altering.

And now, for the first time, a work of fiction. *What Love Looks Like* is a complex, often bittersweet collection of unforgettable short stories involving very disparate relationships.

Ms. Hull's essays and poetry have been widely published in select journals such as the *Bellevue Literary Review, Ars Medica, Lumina* and *North Dakota Quarterly*.

Her two children were born on the East Coast and raised on the West. Despite bicoastal lures, the author has chosen to reside in Manhattan for the grand adventure of flying solo in a great city.